New York Times bestselling auth[...] had over thirty novels published [...] fans with her seductive Dark Carpath[...] tales. She [...] received numerous honours throughout her career, including being a nominee for the Romance Writers of America RITA and receiving a Career Achievement Award from *R[...]antic Times*, and has been published in multiple langua[...].

Visit Christine Feehan online:

www.christinefeehan.com
www.facebook.com/christinefeehanauthor
@AuthorCFeehan

Praise for Christine Feehan:

'[...]r Bram Stoker, Anne Rice and Joss Whedon,
[...] Feehan is the person most credited with
popularizing the neck gripper'
Time magazine

'The queen of paranormal romance'
USA Today

'Fee[...] has a knack for bringing vampiric Carpathians
to vivid, virile life in her Dark Carpathian novels'
Publishers Weekly

'The amazingly prolific author's ability to create
captivating and adrenaline-raising worlds is unsurpassed'
Romantic Times

CHRISTINE
FEEHAN
ANNIHILATION
ROAD

PIATKUS

PIATKUS

First published in the US in 2021 by Jove, Berkley,
An imprint of Penguin Random House LLC
First published in Great Britain in 2021 by Piatkus

1 3 5 7 9 10 8 6 4 2

Copyright © 2021 by Christine Feehan
Excerpt from *Savage Road* copyright © 2021 by Christine Feehan

The moral right of the author has been asserted.

A CIP catalogue record for this book
is available from the British Library.

ISBN: 978-0-349-42838-3

Printed and bound in Great Britain by Clays Ltd, Elcograf S.p.A.

Papers used by Piatkus are from well-managed forests
and other responsible sources.

MIX
Paper from
responsible sources
FSC® C104740

Piatkus
An imprint of
Little, Brown Book Group
Carmelite House
50 Victoria Embankment
London EC4Y 0DZ

An Hachette UK Company
www.hachette.co.uk

www.littlebrown.co.uk

For all the readers who wrote to me
and asked me for his story so many times.
For the ones who took the time
to answer my questions
on my wall in my community.
You said he needed a happy ending.
You were right,
and it took more than one book to do it!

FOR MY READERS

Be sure to go to christinefeehan.com/members to sign up for my private book announcement list and download the free ebook of *Dark Desserts*. It's a collection of yummy desserts that we all certainly could use right now. Join my community and get firsthand news, enter the book discussions, ask your questions and chat with me. Please feel free to email me at Christine@christinefeehan.com. I would love to hear from you.

ACKNOWLEDGMENTS

As in any book, there are so many people to thank. Brian for competing with me during power hours. Leslee for encouraging me over and over when I didn't think I could do it. Domini for always editing, no matter how many times I ask her to go over the same book before we send it for additional editing. I really couldn't have done this book without you. You were amazing hanging in there with me for this one and talking out every problem. Denise for staying up nights and letting me write while she did the brunt of the business I never want to do. I can't thank you enough.

TORPEDO INK MEMBERS

Viktor Prakenskii aka *Czar*—President

Lyov Russak aka *Steele*—Vice President

Savva Pajari aka *Reaper*—Sergeant at Arms

Savin Pajari aka *Savage*—Sergeant at Arms

Isaak Koval aka *Ice*—Secretary

Dmitry Koval aka *Storm*

Alena Koval aka *Torch*

Luca Litvin aka *Code*—Hacker

Maksimos Korsak aka *Ink*

Kasimir Popov aka *Preacher*

Lana Popov aka *Widow*

Nikolaos Bolotan aka *Mechanic*

Pytor Bolotan aka *Transporter*

Andrii Federoff aka *Maestro*

Gedeon Lazaroff aka *Player*

Kir Vasiliev aka *Master*—Treasurer

Lazar Alexeev aka *Keys*

Aleksei Solokov aka *Absinthe*

Rurik Volkov aka *Razrushitel/Destroyer*

NEWER PATCHED MEMBERS

Gavriil Prakenskii

Casimir Prakenskii

Fatei Molchalin

PROSPECTS

Glitch

Hyde

SIBLINGS WITHIN THE GROUP

Viktor (Czar), Gavriil and Casimir

Reaper and Savage

Mechanic and Transporter

Ice, Storm and Alena (Torch)

Preacher and Lana (Widow)

TEAMS

Czar heads Team One

> *Reaper, Savage, Ice, Storm, Transporter, Alena, Absinthe, Mechanic, Destroyer*

Steele heads Team Two

> *Keys, Master, Player, Maestro, Lana, Preacher, Ink, Code*

OLD LADIES

Blythe, Lissa, Lexi, Anya, Breezy, Soleil, Scarlet, Zyah

ONE

Today was the day Savin "Savage" Pajari was going to die. And it was okay. If it hadn't been for the boy, a part of him would be rejoicing. He was a monster, and monsters weren't for this world. But there was the boy, and that meant he had to try no matter what. Not give up.

He wasn't going to make it. He'd been too slow. The truck was too fast. The mother screamed seconds too late to draw his attention. He'd laid his bike down to get to the kid as time tunneled. Slowed down. He scooped the boy up, right out of the middle of the street, and ran like hell.

He sprinted to get the kid out of harm's way, but he knew his effort was futile. He was just a step too late. All he could do was try to protect the child. He wrapped him up in his arms, tight against his chest, hoping when the truck crushed him, his body would keep the boy alive. He was a big man, heavy on the muscle, so maybe the kid had a chance. He kept running, but it was over, probably for both of them.

As if from a distance, he heard the scream of the brakes

as the driver slammed them on, the skid, the smell of burning rubber and brakes, the desperate cries of those on the sidewalk watching the drama unfold. Then the vehicle was there, much bigger as it bore down on them. He kept running, that next step, heart pounding, because there had never been a time in his life that he could give up—and he had that little boy, who deserved to live. Something hit him hard in the back, coming at him from the side, throwing him forward, giving him that last momentum, the speed he needed. That one extra step.

He found himself rolling on the ground, the kid tucked in to his body to prevent him from hitting the asphalt. The roaring in his ears was loud, but not as loud as the distinct and sickening *thunk* he heard. He knew immediately it was the sound of metal hitting a real flesh-and-blood body. He turned his head to see a woman rolling across the road. Other sounds erupted around him: screams, the driver's door slamming. He swore, forcing his body to move, getting his legs under him, standing, the boy still protected in his arms.

The kid's mother rushed to Savage, tears streaming down her face, thanking him as she took the child. He thrust her aside and sprinted to the fallen woman. She was small, a broken doll lying on her belly. The denim she wore hadn't protected her leg. The material was shredded along with her skin. The wounds looked ugly, vicious even, going from the top of her ankle to the top of her thigh. He couldn't tell if her leg was broken. The rest of her clothes were shredded on that side as well, her narrow rib cage bloody, the side of her breast and her arm.

Savage crouched down beside her. She groaned, letting him know she was conscious at least. She had hair, a lot of it, a rich honey color. He gathered it into one hand and pulled it away from the blood on her arm. "You're alive, baby, but don't move until the paramedics get here. Tell me where you're hurt."

She made little sounds of distress in the back of her

throat, and then turned her face toward him. Her eyelashes fluttered. They were exceptionally long, and there were diamond-like drops on them. She opened her eyes, and he found himself looking into the bluest eyes he'd ever seen. That got him straight in his scarred, uncooperative cock. She was lying there broken and bruised on his account, and his fuckin' body suddenly decided to come to life all on its own. He was shocked. More than shocked. He didn't let it show, but that had never happened that he could remember.

She would have bruises and lacerations on her otherwise flawless skin. Her bone structure was perfect. Savage noted every detail, the way he did everything. Her mouth was . . . *Bog*. Her mouth. Deliberately, he looked away from her face and once more looked at her body, trying not to notice that her ass, cupped in those tight jeans, was just as perfect as her tits.

"I'm going to run my hands over you, looking for broken bones. I'm not taking advantage." He knew he looked rough. He *was* rough. He was wearing his colors, so it wasn't difficult to tell he was a biker. He was tattooed, and he kept his head shaved. He was intimidating, because he was the kind of man that beat the fuck out of someone if they crossed him. "That all right with you?"

She tried to move her arm and groaned. He put his hand over it to stop her. "Tell me your name."

Her eyelashes fluttered. A tear rolled down her face, and he had an uncharacteristic urge to lick it off her cheek. He hadn't done that in a long, long time. Now that she'd woken that beast, it roared hungrily, eyeing her ravenously. He shoved his cravings away.

"Come on, baby, I can hear the sirens. Medics are coming." When she moved slightly, he saw the bump on her head. It was pretty impressive. "Tell me your name."

Her tongue touched her lip, drawing his attention to her mouth again. He didn't want to look there. The moment he did, his fuckin' cock jerked. There was no precedent for that. None. He was always in control of his body, and here this woman—who had most likely saved his life—was lying on the ground injured and he was having some kind of a perverted reaction to her.

Her lashes drifted down, and his heart jumped. For a man always in control of his body, he was losing it. "Babe. Tell me your fucking name right now." He wasn't going to lose her, so he poured command into his voice.

A few of the bystanders gasped, and one started to protest, but when Savage turned ice-cold eyes on him, the protester thought better of it.

"Seychelle." She whispered it. "Seychelle Dubois."

The ambulance arrived, and when the paramedics hurried to them, he gave them a cold stare as he shifted to one side. "Thank fuck. She's trying to drift away."

The two men moved their hands over her body, and something twisted in his gut. He stepped back. The deputy sheriff had arrived, and he didn't want any part of that.

"He saved my boy." Savage heard the woman distinctly, and he began to make his way through the crowd toward his bike. Shit. It was still on the ground where he'd laid it down to run for the kid. That was what he got for interfering. And now this woman. Seychelle Dubois. What the fuck kind of name was that? He'd killed three people in France. He knew the language, and she pronounced it with a French accent.

"Savage."

He crouched down beside his bike to inspect it for damage, not looking around. He knew the voice. Jackson Deveau. They'd met on several occasions. Technically, they hadn't exactly exchanged names and pleasantries—Savage left that to others in the club—but they knew each other. A shadow fell across him, and as he rose to pick up the Harley, Jackson helped. Ordinarily, Savage would have decked anyone touching his bike, but the man was helping, and he wore a badge. So maybe not the best idea.

"Any damage?"

"A few scratches. I got lucky."

"From the sound of it, very lucky. They're taking Seychelle Dubois to the hospital in Fort Bragg. Do you know her?"

Savage was tempted to tell him he did, but he had no idea why, so he shook his head and kept going over his bike.

"You saved the kid."

"Technically, she saved the kid. She shoved me out of the way and took the hit. I don't know how she angled it, but at least she wasn't killed." He glanced across the street to the mother who was rocking the little boy, more to comfort herself than the child. "The kid all right?"

"Yeah. I'll need your statement."

Savage leveled his gaze at the man. "Just gave it to you."

Jackson shook his head. "You've destroyed your hard-ass image, Savage. You've got all these people looking at you like you're some kind of hero."

"Shut the fuck up," Savage snapped. He swung his leg over his bike and settled on the familiar leather. His Harley felt like part of him. Home. If he had one, it was on this bike. It was a Night Rod Special, all matte black with dull gunmetal-gray trim and blacked-out chrome and his one concession—the image of a dripping gray skull. He loved his bike, and it was a fuckin' road rocket, sheer speed thanks to Harley-Davidson and a little help from Transporter and Mechanic.

"You headed back to the club?"

"You my mother now?"

Jackson grinned at him, not taking offense. He never did. He wasn't a man to pull a power play just because he wore a badge, and that told Savage he was someone to contend with. Jackson was confident, which meant he didn't need an ego for a reason.

"Don't forget to wear your helmet," Jackson said.

Savage flipped him off as he fitted the ridiculous half dome to his head and then waited for the deputy to step back. He got the hell out of there, thankful his bike had minimum damage, all cosmetic, and that the kid lived through the entire thing. With the wind in his face, he let the sea air unravel the knots in his gut he always got when he was around too many people. Usually, he could dismiss everything when he rode and just feel complete freedom when he was on his motorcycle, riding along the coastal highway.

Yeah, he was going to the clubhouse. He told himself that a million times as he neared the turnoff to Caspar, but he didn't make the turn. Swearing, he continued to ride the highway, cursing himself for being all kinds of a fool. He knew better. He didn't give a shit about a woman. He didn't need or want one. He knew what he was and what he would do to one—what he needed from a woman. He got those things from women he paid or the patch chasers who would do anything at all for a chance at a man in a club. When he was particularly bad, he went to the underground clubs for satisfaction. No woman would want him or ever stay with him. She sure as hell would never love him.

He swore as he turned off the highway onto the road leading to the farm. Six families owned the farm jointly, and each had their own five acres. The rest of the acreage was dedicated to the very thriving farm. The ornate gates were open, and he drove through, knowing better—telling himself to turn around and mind his own fucking business.

He knew the way to the president of Torpedo Ink's home. They all did. Half the time the entire club ate there. He rode in slowly and parked his bike in the designated area. He was thankful there were no other bikes present to indicate anyone from his club was there. He didn't need any witnesses when he made a fool of himself.

The front door burst open, and Emily and Zoe waved enthusiastically from the doorway. The two girls had been adopted by Blythe and Czar along with their sister, Darby; a boy, Kenny; and the newest boy, Jimmy. The new kid was only six and still scared, but Savage was certain Emily and Zoe would help him adjust. They were sweet kids.

"Uncle Savage." Emily jumped up and down. Zoe just smiled.

Savage picked up Emily and hugged Zoe. "Hey, you two, is your mom home?"

"In here," Blythe called from the great room. "Having a cup of tea. Your favorite." There was laughter in her voice. She knew he despised the stuff.

He put Emily down and watched as the two girls skipped off, and then he shut the door and stood there awkwardly, leaning against it. He wasn't a talker. He left conversations to others. He was the man who took out their enemies, and he lived mostly in the shadows. Blythe was . . . sacred. To him. To all of them. The last thing he wanted to do was upset her in any way.

"Is everything okay, Savage?"

It wasn't curiosity. That was the thing about Blythe. She really was compassionate. She cared about each of them as individuals. Czar had brought the club members to her when he'd returned to his wife. Seventeen members, all trained assassins, and every one of them royally fucked up. She didn't flinch. She took them on right along with her husband.

He hesitated. If he told her, she'd share what he said with Czar. They were like that. What one knew, the other did. "Need to give this to you, but . . ."

"I'll tell Czar it's confidential."

That was Blythe. Quick to understand. She was difficult not to love. He glanced toward the stairway and then the kitchen, not wanting the kids to overhear.

Blythe read his concern easily. "They're in the den watching television. They only have an hour, so they'll hang there. The girls heard the bike and thought it was Czar coming home."

He decided to quit stalling. If he was going to do something stupid, he might as well just fucking do it. "There was a thing. Happened in Fort Bragg. Little boy ran into the street. Truck coming fast. I laid the bike down, scooped the kid up and ran for it. Knew I wasn't going to make it." He talked fast, clipped. Abrupt. Feeling like an idiot.

Blythe put down her teacup, genuine concern on her face. "Oh, Savage."

"This chick hit me from behind, shoved me and the kid to safety but took the hit for us. At first I thought she got away with maybe a broken leg, maybe just hurt, you know, but then she turned her head and she had this bump the size of an ostrich egg. Definite concussion, but I don't know how bad. Asked her name, she told me, but kept drifting off."

"You're certain you weren't hurt?"

He shook his head. "Kid's fine too."

"I'm so sorry this woman was injured, but grateful to her at the same time."

Savage shrugged, doing his best to look as if it didn't matter one way or the other. "You still friends with that nurse? You talked about her a lot. She's head of the emergency room or something like that. She's a big deal."

"Tammy O'Neil? Yes, of course."

"Think you could ask her how this woman is doing and whether they're keeping her there or if she was sent home?"

Blythe studied his face for a moment too long. He didn't like that she saw things she wasn't supposed to see. At least not in him. He wanted her to think he was naturally worried about a woman who had saved his life. He told himself that was the reason he was asking a favor, but it was so far out of character, he knew she thought there was more to it. He didn't know what to think, so he kept his expressionless mask and forced himself to look straight at her.

"Yes, of course I can do that for you. What's her name?"

"Seychelle Dubois."

She stood up. "Give me a minute."

"If they've kept her, can you get her room number?" Shit. He hated to ask that. "Should probably thank her."

Blythe studied him again and then slowly nodded. "I agree. She's definitely owed at least that much. I'm extremely grateful that you're still with us."

Savage wasn't certain why. He had the opposite point of

view to Blythe's every time. She never seemed to take offense, and she didn't start yelling to make her point. He appreciated that trait in her. She'd gotten under his skin. It was the children. She genuinely loved them. The club had rescued Darby and Zoe from human traffickers. They'd had no family other than Emily. Blythe had lied her ass off, bringing forged papers with her to claim the children. Darby had backed up her claim, and Czar and Blythe eventually adopted the three girls.

The club had found Kenny in the basement of a mansion in Occidental. Needless to say, the teen had nowhere to go. No one knew what to do with him, so they'd brought him home to Blythe. She had taken him in, and the adoption was in process. They'd be signing the papers to make the boy theirs in a couple of weeks. Kenny was pretending it didn't matter, but everyone knew he was happy.

The latest family member, a six-year-old boy named Jimmy, they'd stumbled across on the internet. There was an auction for him, and they'd ended up in Vegas to free him. He had no family, so naturally, Blythe and Czar took him in. He hadn't been with the couple long, but Savage knew it was only a matter of time before he came around. He seemed to like the survival classes Torpedo Ink gave to the children every other week. That was Blythe, taking the children in and then allowing them to do whatever it took to find their way to sanity.

Even Savage could see that Blythe was special. Every single member of the club would give their life for her. She was that kind of woman—the kind for pedestals. He hadn't believed a woman like her existed, although Czar had told them she was the best. Now they all knew it and guarded her like the treasure she was.

He stayed close to the door, looking the way he always did: calm, expressionless, menacing. He didn't move a muscle, going still so that he seemed to fade into whatever background he stood in front of. Shadows were what he was most familiar and comfortable with. He didn't feel calm inside, and that was something he wasn't familiar with.

He didn't like anything that he couldn't explain. Whatever the weird reaction he had to Seychelle—and God help him if he was that big of a monster that his body reacted because she was hurt or crying—he had to see her. He shut down that way of thinking.

He knew he needed violence. The rage would begin to build in his gut first, churning there like some terrible storm he couldn't control. It would spread through his body like a cancer, and when it finally hit his brain, he would go to San Francisco and participate in the underground fight clubs there. His brothers went with him to pull him off his opponents before he killed them. He needed violence. He needed to feel his fists hitting flesh. He needed the blood . . .

"Savage, she's got a concussion and there's some damage to her leg. She didn't call anyone, nor did she put down anyone as an emergency number. She was just admitted. This is her room number." Blythe pushed a folded piece of paper into his hand.

He closed his fist around it. "Thanks, Blythe. I appreciate it."

"Please tell her thank you from me as well. If you think she needs anything, let me know. I don't like to think she's alone in the world and needs help after saving one of ours."

He hesitated, but he wasn't the type of man to hug or kiss. He didn't like to be touched. Reaper, his birth brother, was the same way.

Savage stuffed the paper into his jeans pocket and gave a casual shrug. "Not certain when I'll have the chance to follow up, but I'm going to try."

That performance should win him a fuckin' Oscar. Not because Blythe believed him, but because he was trying to believe it. He told himself it was the truth and he wasn't going anywhere near Seychelle Dubois—that if he did go, it would be to thank her. Or just check on her like any decent man would. He knew he was lying to himself and Blythe.

He turned abruptly and stalked out, heading for his bike,

the only real thing in his world. His club. The bike. They were wrapped up together, and ever since Reaper had found Anya, and Savage knew he was happy, he had been slowly separating himself from his brothers. He took more and more trips alone. He spent time away from the others. He talked less and less. There wasn't a place for a man like him in the new world Czar was creating for the club. There wasn't a place in the world for him, period.

He wasn't a man to pretend. His brothers were fucked up. Hell. Alena and Lana, his sisters, were fucked up. Reaper was a mess. But not one of them was a monster. They might think they were. They were dangerous, and they didn't hesitate to kill, but they weren't like he was.

There was no cure for a man like him. He knew because he'd looked that shit up. A person could find that information on the internet, and he'd logged over a hundred hours looking. He wasn't the only one. Absinthe, the brainiac of their club, and his wife, Scarlet, put in even more hours referencing journals in order to try to find a way to make him different. That hadn't happened, and he'd finally accepted the fact that he was what he was. He had a code he lived by, and he kept to it. That had to be good enough.

He took his time heading to Caspar. He even looked at the sign as he went on past. Shit. There was no hope for him whatsoever. He kept going though. Even knowing he was acting like a moron, he kept going. He drove straight to the hospital and parked his bike, sliding off to stand in front of the doors for a few minutes, pretending to himself that he was debating about whether or not to go in.

He wished he smoked so he could stand outside longer, but he hunted men, and it was easy enough to find them if they smoked. The scent carried, and sooner or later, anyone addicted to cigarettes or weed had to light up. The moment they did, he had them. Easy enough to slide up behind them and slit their throat—or arrange an accident—and he was stalling. He knew he was going in, so he just had to get it over with.

He stalked inside, putting on his most intimidating face. It wasn't hard to do. He pretty much just had to look at anyone and they pissed their pants. He went straight up to the desk, pulled out the paper Blythe had given him and told the woman sitting at the desk the room number.

The woman was older, and it said right on her little power badge that she was a volunteer. She didn't like him. She pursed her lips. "I can't just let you into the hospital."

"Actually, you can. Seychelle is my fiancée." He was pretty damn certain, since Seychelle hadn't given anyone's name as an emergency contact, he was safe. "I want to see her now. Visiting hours aren't over, so point me in the right fuckin' direction."

The woman, Ms. Pruit, gave him her prune face of absolute disapproval. He wanted to growl, but he'd probably give the bitch a heart attack. She told him how to get to the room, and he didn't waste any time stalking past her to the door. She took her time hitting the button to unlock the door, but he didn't deign to so much as turn around. He was used to the bullshit. He was tatted, bald and wearing his Torpedo Ink colors and looked what he was—a killer.

He just needed to see Seychelle look at him with that same bullshit, judgmental, dismissive look he got everywhere he went, and he could walk out of the hospital and never look back.

He pushed open the door to her room. The curtains were drawn to darken the space and she didn't have a roommate, which he thought was good, or maybe it wasn't. He went straight to the bed. Her gaze jumped to his face immediately. *Bog.* Those fuckin' blue eyes of hers. Long lashes. She didn't give him the prune face. She gave him a faint smile instead. *Bog.* That fuckin' mouth of hers.

There were bruises and scrapes on her face. One cheek was swollen. The bump on her head, just above her eye, was enormous. Her arm was bandaged in places, and from what he could see of her leg, it was as well. He couldn't help himself: he touched one of the scrape marks near the giant goose egg. "Looks like it hurts."

Her smile widened just a bit, and he caught the faint hint of a dimple on her left side. His heart contracted. "A little. They gave me something for it. I remember your face. You tried to help me."

"You saved me and the kid. Thought I'd thank you, but Ms. Prune at the front desk thought your virginity had to be protected, so to get in, I told her I was your fiancé. I was going to add that it was too late for your virginity to be protected but thought she might have me arrested just for sayin' the word."

He figured she'd order him out. He was deliberately crude and thought the claim on her would frighten her, but she did the unexpected. She laughed. Little golden notes flickered in the air above her head and surrounded him, taking his breath. It had been a long time since he'd seen notes like that floating just from a voice. The sound played over him like some kind of song, and once again, just to piss him off and show him it wasn't a fluke, his body responded.

He became aware of every nerve ending coming to life. His blood surged hotly and rushed through his body to pool like hot magma in his groin. His cock was scarred, and filling with life all on its own was impossible—and yet she'd managed to make it do just that. Not to mention he had learned, almost before he knew what a cock was, to control that shit. The shock was almost too much for him to comprehend.

"Thanks for the laugh. I'm not fond of hospitals." She turned her face away from him.

He parked himself alongside her on the bed, crowding her a little. He heard the note in her voice that told him there was a reason—a sad one—that she really didn't like hospitals.

"I could break you out of here," he offered. "I brought my bike, so it might be rough going, 'specially with you in that gown, but it's doable."

She laughed a second time just like he'd hoped, and the golden notes scattered in the air around him like confetti. He fuckin' loved that sound and ignored the strange phenomenon. He could only deal with so much. She turned her face back to him.

If he was any kind of decent man, he'd wince at the damage, but instead he touched the scrape marks gently with the pad of his finger. They were badges of courage. She'd done what no one else had. She'd risked her life to save him—to save the kid. Those raw scrapes and that hellacious egg were suffered to save him. She'd made that choice. He couldn't help but think those lacerations, bruises and bumps said quite a lot about her.

"Are you going to tell me your name?" Seychelle asked, her blue eyes drifting over his face, touching on the scars there, on his jaw and the light growth of beard and mustache.

Was he? Hell. "Yeah, baby, I can do that. My brothers call me Savage. Probably for a reason you don't really want to hear."

That little dimple flashed again, and his cock jerked. His reaction to her was genuine. Real. Maybe it was because she had risked her life and wasn't a vain, haughty, judgmental bitch, or someone who chased after him not because they knew the first thing about him or cared but because they wanted something from him. Seychelle hadn't wanted a thing except to save him and the kid. More likely it was because of the lacerations and bruises that belonged to him.

"Savage." She repeated the name softly. Her voice was melodic. A whisper of sound that played down his spine like the touch of fingers. Three golden notes floated into the air.

He liked the way she said his name, a little too much. He shook his head. If he had any kind of sense at all, he'd leave. Right the hell now. Just get up and walk away. He was there to thank her, and he'd done that. He'd wanted to know she was all right, and he'd done that too. Instead of thinking with his brain, he was thinking with his dick. He looked around the bare room. "How long you in for?"

That smile came out again, tying his gut into tight little knots. The dimple was a turn-on any way he looked at it, when nothing turned him on. Her mouth? Those lips? She was lying there bruised and scraped and his body was re-acting all on its own, proving he was an even bigger mon-ster than he'd thought. But damn, it felt good. He hadn't known he was capable of getting it up without commanding it first in his brain. His brain wasn't even engaged. He had proof of that, because he was still sitting on her bed.

"It is kind of a prison, isn't it?" She looked around the room as well. "Although I've never actually been to prison, have you?" She looked up at him.

His gaze met hers. Those damn eyes. So blue. Seeing too much. One eye was very bruised. She was going to have a hell of a shiner. It was already coming up, dark purple and swollen.

"Grew up in a prison. Been there a time or two since." Both times he'd been there to assassinate a prisoner. Why the hell had the truth come out of his fuckin' mouth?

He never talked. He kept his mouth shut. He didn't like people or their reactions. He didn't understand them, and he didn't want to. Most of the time, he was contemplating killing them. He was disciplined and had been since he was a child, yet he couldn't stop himself from telling her the truth because he hadn't thought before he answered. Star-ing into those blue eyes, he drowned. Went under and acted like a fuckin' pussy-whipped asshole. He had to get out of there before he ran his mouth and had to take her out. He had too many secrets to just sit there and cough them up because his dick was hard.

"Harsh. But you survived. Good for you." Her voice

sounded drowsy. Sexy. It was that tone she had. Musical. Low. Soft. It played over his entire body as if she was stroking him with caresses—or licking him with her tongue.

Her lashes lowered, those long, thick, feathery lashes that he knew he was never going to get out of his mind. At the same time, she touched him. A brush of her fingers against the back of his hand. On his bare skin. His body went still. That small brush got under his skin and rippled outward, spreading slow, flickering flames that kept growing hotter and hotter. It was as if she'd branded him inside his body and that stream of heat turned into a smoldering fire that began to consume him from the inside out.

He had to get out of there. She was tying them together in some undefined way he didn't understand, but whatever magic she wielded, it was dangerous to both of them. She was . . . nice. She was beautiful. She was normal. He couldn't be in her life, and she sure as fuck couldn't be in his. He didn't want a woman. He didn't need a woman. Not full-time. Not when he knew if she belonged to him, he'd become an even bigger monster than he already was.

He picked up bitches all the time. Always, always, he was in charge. He did his thing, they blew him and some of the time it brought relief. Not most of the time, but some of the time. Once in a very long while, he snagged a woman who let him use her roughly, completely on his terms, and when she blew him, the relief lasted more than a few hours. The results were days, weeks and once in a while a month or two where the monster in him settled.

"You goin' to sleep on me?" He hoped she was. He didn't want her to. He'd never sat with a woman in the dark and just talked quietly. Maybe he just needed to hear the sound of her voice.

"No. I don't like places like this. They walk in and out and think they aren't disturbing you, so you have to be nice. They're helping you. But if I fall asleep, when I jerk awake because they're in my room, my heart goes wild and I don't like the way it makes me feel."

Her lashes fluttered. The dimple appeared. He found himself looking into the deep blue of her eyes. His heart contracted. She was so fucking beautiful he had no right to even look at her. He'd heard the fairy tale—*Beauty and the Beast*. Sitting on her bed, looking at her face, that body that was created just for him . . . that story could have been theirs.

"Savage, why are you looking so sad? Everything ended the best way it could. The little boy lived. You lived."

Once again, she touched him. This time on his face. That same brush of her fingers, featherlight, but she created that same strange, shimmering fire that sank under his skin and spread through his body like living flames. He should have knocked her hand away—that would have been the sensible thing to do—but already those flames had made their way into his bloodstream and were growing, spreading fast, picking up speed as the firestorm rushed through his body and then settled in his groin, robbing him of breath.

He wondered what she'd do if he took out his cock and jerked off. Could he do that without ordering his dick to actually work? Coat her skin with him? With his seed? Brand her his? Fuck. Write his name on her from breasts to pussy. His alone. His property.

"Savage? You look tired."

She scooted over, wincing when she did. Her leg? She had it completely out of the sheet now. He ran his hand over it very lightly, feeling the swelling, feeling the scrapes, most of all aware of her body giving a little shudder as he inspected the damage. It obviously hurt her to be touched, but she didn't pull away. She seemed to know he needed to see what she'd suffered on his behalf. What she didn't know was that she was putting even more steel in his cock. So much so that he dropped his hand over the front of his jeans and rubbed in an effort to try to ease the ache. The burning. The rabid hunger that was beginning to consume him.

"That hurts, doesn't it?" he whispered, stroking caresses over the scrapes. He could feel each individual laceration where the asphalt had chewed up her skin. He was the devil, courting disaster for both of them.

"Yes," she admitted. "Not as bad as my head, but it hurts."

He shifted his weight until both legs were on the bed and he could ease some of the strain on his groin. "Did you cry?"

"Yes." She whispered the confession in that velvet voice that wrapped him up in sin and temptation.

He leaned back, and when he did, she lifted her head, took one of the pillows and pushed it behind his neck. When she moved, a soft, hastily cut-off groan escaped. He touched her face and found it wet with a few more tears leaking out. His cock reacted, leaking his own pearly drops as he leaned in to her to sip at the ones on her face. He closed his eyes to savor the taste of her teardrops.

"You need to stop moving around, Seychelle. Just lie still." He made it a command. When he told others what to do, they tended to obey him. Her gaze moved over his face almost as if she found his tone amusing, but she didn't attempt to move again.

His hand slid over her injured thigh and found more scrapes there. A very small shudder slid over her body when, featherlight, the pads of his fingers found the lacerations and stroked small caresses over them.

He kept his gaze on her face. It was easy to read her every expression. He moved his hand up higher, still gentle, still that light touch, stroking along her rib cage. "Are you hurt here? Bruised?"

"A small scrape. The road chewed me up more than the truck did. It was already stopping and caught me at an angle."

He pushed her hospital gown aside, easy enough to do when it was simply tied around her neck. He leaned down to examine the laceration along her ribs. The scrape went up her side, shaving skin off, pitted where they'd clearly dug out some gravel. "Fuck, baby, this looks angry."

He ran his finger up her side until he was touching the underside of her breast. "Did they put any antibiotic cream on this? Not certain I was worth all these scrapes and that goose egg."

She started to move, but his gaze pinned her to the bed. She went very still again. "You were worth it, Savage. I honestly didn't see the child at the angle I was coming from." She winced when his finger slid back down the scrape and then over the side of her breast, where the full curve was scraped. The sensitive skin clearly hurt, because she shuddered when he ran the pads of his fingers over the marks, but she didn't pull away.

"You need more ointment on this. Where is it?" His heart had nearly stopped when she admitted she'd flung herself in front of the truck for him. To keep him alive. To keep him safe.

"They never leave anything in here."

"Would you do it again, knowing you would have to endure this all over?" He kept his voice low. His heart accelerated while he waited for her answer. Hot blood rushed through his veins and pounded through his cock. He dropped one hand over the front of his jeans and rubbed through the material. It was sick. It was perverted. She should have screamed for the nurses.

Her lashes lifted all the way and he found himself staring into her clear blue eyes. "I told you, it isn't that bad. You're worth this and much more."

"With my fuckin' hand on my cock in your hospital room. I'm worth it." Savage wanted to sneer. He wanted to rip down his zipper and pull the monster from his jeans and jack off. He wanted his brand on her. Everywhere. Dirty.

His way. His voice, damn him, stayed soft, and the question was genuine. He was angry at her. Terrified for her. For him. For both of them.

"Of course you are. Everyone masturbates. If a nurse comes in, you're going to shock her panties off." There was that hint of laughter in her voice, and he caught the glimpse of her dimple. "That would be the most entertaining thing I'd see my entire stay, but she'd have you arrested, so not worth it."

He couldn't help rubbing his finger back and forth over the scrapes on her ribs and the side of her breast. Each pass sent more blood pounding through his cock, but that only made him feel as if he was really alive when he'd been dead for so fucking long.

Savage closed his eyes against the sight of her bruised, swollen face. Her tears. She wept, but silently. He wasn't positive she knew her tears were there, but he did—and that was so dangerous when she was with a man with cravings and addictions like his.

He shook his head. "You do know that something's wrong with you. Why aren't you screamin' for help?"

"You're my fiancé, right? You're my very first fiancé. I've never had one before."

The laughter in her voice stunned him. She was hurting. He read it on her face easily. He could feel the fine tremors racing through her body as it shuddered in pain. Still, she had that sense of humor. A little sick like his. He was trying to scare her so she'd throw him out. He didn't belong in the same room with her. Not now. Not ever. He was trying to let her know what a sick bastard he was, but so far, he hadn't succeeded. She was making it impossible to save her. To save both of them.

He stroked caresses over her cheeks, those high cheekbones. Her soft mouth. Both eyes. He lingered over the dark-colored bruises and then swept the pads of his fingers very lightly over the knot on her head.

"This hurts bad, doesn't it?" His breath was a whisper of warm air blown softly over the swelling. He brushed his lips lightly over it as if he could kiss her better. He kissed both eyes lightly and then followed the trail of her tears, licking and sipping until he was certain he'd collected every last one of them and there were none left.

"Yes," she whispered again.

"I can make it all better. I can turn your pain into something else." His voice, his touch, was mesmerizing. He knew because he had been raised to be compelling. He knew every expression to use, the tone of his voice, the octave that appealed. He just hadn't bothered for years, because he hadn't wanted to keep anyone.

Savage pulled back abruptly. What the fuck was he thinking? Tying her to him? That wasn't happening. Not now. Not ever. He sat up and rubbed his head. He kept it shaved, although he had thick hair. He liked the look and he knew it added to the intimidation factor. He was Savage and he always would be. He didn't keep women. Certainly not *a* woman, not one like this woman, not one for himself. He slid off the bed.

"Gotta go, Seychelle. Hit the call button after I leave and tell them to up your meds. There's no reason for you to suffer like this." For him. She was suffering for him.

He turned back to her, because he couldn't stop himself from making what he knew was a huge mistake. "I'm fuckin' going to kiss you, Seychelle. Just this once. Gotta leave with the taste of you in my mouth. If you object, now's the time to say it. Don't know if it's goin' to matter to me, but I'll take any objection you might have into consideration."

He wasn't joking, but that dimple of hers came out again, making his cock leak like a sieve and his heart stutter in his chest. She didn't voice an objection. Her blue eyes drifted over him as if she was claiming him. He felt the touch of those blue flames licking his skin, burning him so deep he knew he wasn't getting her out of him anytime soon. It didn't matter. He would never see her again. It wasn't safe for either of them.

His mouth settled on hers. Her lips were full, soft and paradise just to feel. He was risking everything just to kiss her, and the moment he did, the moment his mouth was on hers, she gave herself to him. Fire. Flames. Passion. They poured into him. She tasted like heaven. Something he'd never experienced. An angel sent to save him, and all she got for her trouble was bruised and scraped flesh.

It didn't matter. Nothing mattered but kissing her. Taking her taste into his mind, then his body. Setting up an addiction. He was a fucking fool for kissing this woman. He'd known he'd be lost, and he was. Thunder roared in his ears. His blood thickened into molten lava. Electrical sparks seemed to dance over his skin. She tasted like innocence. She tasted like sin. Passion welled up, hot and undeniable. Real. Every single nerve ending that had been dead since he'd been ten years old flared into fiery, hungry predatory need.

Abruptly, he lifted his head. He caught her jaw in his hand, thumb pressing deep. "Look at me, Seychelle." He waited until those eyes of hers looked straight into his. "Your life is worth far more than a fucking bastard like me. You don't ever trade it for anyone's again. You got that? You deserve it all. The white picket fence. The dream. All of it. Don't throw it away on someone like me. Do you understand?"

She was looking right into his eyes. She had to understand. She had to see him. Right down to his rotted soul. He was a killer, and she couldn't fail to see that. He wanted her to see him, to see inside, where he never let anyone see. He wanted her to know what she'd saved today. How close she'd come to death for a man who was trained to kill and had been doing so since he was a young child. A man whose first thought was to kill when anyone crossed him. She saved that. Worse, he was a monster. The real deal. She saw that. And still she didn't flinch. He wanted to shake her.

Instead, Savage's hold on her face gentled and he touched his lips almost tenderly to hers. He wasn't going to see her again—not ever. That would be a disaster. He knew her now, knew how soft she was inside. Knew her compassion and her need to save others. He had to stay as far from her as possible. He wasn't a man who saved lives—he took them, but he would make an exception this one time, even though she saw the monster he never let anyone see unless they were going to die.

Seychelle took a deep breath and stared at the door. The moment she had put her hands on the man and pushed him to move him out of the way of the truck, she had felt an overwhelming darkness in him. Her heart beat too fast. She couldn't look away from the door. She didn't react to men. She just didn't. Women either. There was something terribly wrong with her. Until him. Until she saw him in motion, running across the street directly in the path of that oncoming truck. She didn't know why, only that such a beautiful man couldn't die.

Touching him wasn't a good idea. Having him lie on the bed in a dark room with her wasn't a good idea. Kissing him was probably the worst idea of all. He'd moved his hands over her lacerations as if he claimed them—claimed her. It hurt, yet she couldn't make herself pull away. In some way she wanted him to do it, because she felt even more connected to him. The way he looked at her, touched her, was more intense than she'd ever experienced in her life. For the first time in her life, despite the fact that she was hurting like hell, when he touched her like that, even before he kissed her, she felt herself go damp with arousal.

It was a damn good thing she was never going to see him again.

TWO

Maestro glanced at his watch. "If we're going to ride to Willits tonight, we've got to wrap this up now. Sorry, Czar, but I'm fairly certain the others are going to lose it when they hear her sing, so I don't want to take the chance of missing out. We've got to move."

For the first time in a very long time, Maestro was enthusiastic about a singer for their band. Keys, Player, Master and Maestro were outstanding with instruments, any kind of instrument. They had incredible gifts and spent time together jamming. They played at the bar Torpedo Ink owned and occasionally at the parties the club threw. They'd been looking for a singer for some time, and Maestro didn't want to lose the opportunity with this one, which meant she had to be good.

"You need me on the ride?" Savage asked. "Thinkin' about heading to San Francisco tonight." Which meant he was going to beat the holy fuck out of someone—most likely a lot of someones. If he didn't do something soon, he was going to lose his mind.

Czar looked him over. "Yeah, go with them, Savage. Diamondbacks sometimes show up at that bar. I don't want a war, but we don't take shit from anyone. You in control?"

Savage shrugged. Hell no, he wasn't in control. His brain was looping like mad, demanding action while the monster in him demanded blood. So no, he wasn't all right. "Just fine, Czar," he lied. He'd been lying so long about how he was doing, he couldn't remember the last time he'd told the truth.

Absinthe flicked him a glance. Shit. No one fooled Absinthe. He was a human lie detector, and just by the look on his face, he knew Savage was talking bullshit. Savage turned abruptly and stalked out. He didn't need to hear or see any more. He was hopefully going to beat the crap out of a Diamondback. Once he did, the entire Diamondback club would be out for blood—his blood. Just the thought made him feel better.

He swung his leg over his bike and jerked on his gloves. Willits was only thirty-three miles away, but the road was so filled with curves that it took most cars about an hour to drive it. He'd straightened the road out more than once and made it in record time. He wouldn't be able to do that this time. He was going to have to listen to his mind totally losing it while he made the run to the bar to hear some bitch sing while drunks tried to pick each other up with the same tired lines.

His brothers fired up their bikes, and, pipes roaring, they set off for the bar in Willits. He didn't give a damn about a singer, although if it was important to Maestro and the others, it was important to him. He just didn't give a flying fuck who she was. There was only one woman he was interested in. She crept into his thoughts night and day.

He swore under his breath. She was already there. He could taste her in his mouth. On his tongue. Her tears. They were golden, the finest wine, champagne. Hell. Four weeks and she hadn't gone away. He shouldn't have kissed her. He'd known when he did it that it was a bad idea.

The wind helped for a few minutes, and then she was back, winding herself around his insides. His gut had been in knots since he walked out of her hospital room. He could have found her. Code was the best on a computer. He could track anyone down. He knew he had no choice but to ask Code to do a search, because he was going to be a first-class pussy and find her. He had to, because he was going out of his fuckin' mind. First, he had to make sure it was safe for her, and that meant a trip to the fight club and maybe a visit to one of the hard-core underground kink clubs after that.

"Shit." He shouted it to the world, let his protest rise to the tops of the redwood trees. He'd set up some kind of addiction just with kissing her, and now he couldn't resist her. He shouted it again, because the thought of touching another woman was abhorrent to him, and that was a very bad sign for both of them.

He took the curves on autopilot, never a good thing when on a motorcycle. His body and his bike moved together, man and machine, wind in his face, but it wasn't strong enough to blow him clean. Nothing was. Nothing would ever be. He loathed his needs. He loathed himself. Most of his brothers were damaged. They were even broken. They just weren't damaged, broken and programmed to be monsters.

Absinthe was riding behind him and suddenly moved his bike up to ride beside him. Absinthe took the next curve with him, side by side, coming near a drop-off, dangerously close, riding in perfect sync with him. That brought Savage up short. He wasn't about to take one of his brothers with him because he was being deliberately careless. All this over a woman. Absinthe had a wife. A good woman. Savage liked Scarlet. Respected her, and he respected few people. Torpedo Ink was his family, and Scarlet fell into that category. He took that very seriously. Nothing could happen to Absinthe on his watch.

He glanced at Absinthe and nodded, letting him know

he was paying attention again. He knew he was going to ask Code to find Seychelle. Code could break into the hospital computer records and get her address easily. It would be a piece of cake for him. Savage would hate that his brother would know Savage wasn't strong enough to stay away from her. Hell. He dreamt about her every fuckin' night. She not only invaded his thoughts during the day, but he found himself fantasizing about her all the time. She wouldn't let him go.

It was possible, even probable, that if he saw her again, she wouldn't have the same effect on him. A month had passed, and she wasn't lying in a hospital bed, hurt. She probably wasn't that woman. She most likely was really completely different than he remembered. His dreams and fantasies had colored his memories. He hoped like hell that was the case.

Frustrated that she'd crept into his thoughts again, he clenched his teeth and focused completely on the open road. He'd been doing that a lot, just allowing his thoughts to turn to Seychelle and not letting himself enjoy the moment. His bike had been saving him more and more. That and the fight clubs in San Francisco.

They parked their bikes in front of the bar. They'd been there half a dozen times but didn't come often. Torpedo Ink owned their own bar, and they kept to themselves for the most part. The others went in. Maestro was eager to have the band hear the singer. Savage didn't give a fuck about the singer, or whether or not she was good. He did give a fuck about his club, and he was responsible for their safety. He needed action to drain off the pent-up fury that kept building and building until he thought he might explode. That wasn't what was best for his brothers, so he had to keep his shit tight. In check.

Rage was white-hot, smoldering inside him, so deep no one looking at him would ever know it was there. He looked cool on the outside. He carried himself with complete confidence and wore an expressionless mask. Still, he gave off dangerous energy, and most people avoided him, which was a good thing when the devil was riding him so hard.

He took his time pulling off his gloves while he straddled his bike. He was giving himself time to look around the parking lot, noting every vehicle there. Savage was able to map out areas in his head, like grids on charts, placing each car, truck or bike exactly where it had been, even months later. He rarely forgot even the smallest detail, and he practiced every single day. That was automatic, to map out territory, not to miss even a hint that something was off. He memorized faces. Names. He could recognize a bike he'd seen once and know who rode it.

He walked around the outside of the building, noting escape routes, windows, exits for employees. At the moment, none of the Diamondbacks were at the bar. That wasn't unusual either. They didn't tend to frequent this one. He skirted back around to the front entrance and made his way inside.

It was crowded far more than it had ever been the few times he'd been there. Several women turned and looked at him, two smiling an invitation, swaying to the music the band was playing. Worst band ever. The drummer was actually behind the guitarist on the beat, and the keyboard player lagged completely. He didn't understand how Maestro and the others could take the shit music. All four had incredible ears, and anything not in tune just about drove them insane. He had a good ear and it was killing him.

He looked the two smiling women over. They wore tight jeans and tanks, boots and heavy makeup. He knew the type. They were looking for a rough ride, a biker they could take home so they had bragging rights. Neither knew what rough was, but the blonde might do. He ignored them both and walked toward the stage. His brothers had a small table set to the right side of it, mostly hidden in the shadows.

Then the singer's voice cut in, and he stopped dead in

the middle of the room with people pressing close all around him. His heart clenched hard in his chest. He refused to rub the spot, refused to give in to the need. He would recognize that perfect pitch anywhere. She was singing, not speaking, but it was that same melodious voice that haunted his dreams. Seychelle Dubois.

He stayed still, not wanting to be seen, allowing the other patrons to move around him. The bar was dark, and many couples or groups of women were dancing. He slipped behind the row of tables and leaned against the wall, his gaze fixed on the woman who had all but ruined him this last month. Savage studied her. She was under the lights and he could see that her skin looked soft and invited touch. Her mouth was generous. Made for sucking cock— his cock. She was shorter than he remembered, but he'd only seen her on the ground and in a bed. She had curves. Real curves. The kind of figure a man could hang on to.

It was hell. It was heaven. He felt as if he was actually a real man, not a walking killer with no emotions. She was in a short little burgundy cocktail dress that hugged her hips and emphasized her small waist. An intriguing glimpse of skin showed between the halter top and the tight skirt. The top clung to her tits. And she had them, full and round.

That damn top was open down the middle, showing enough skin, showing the lacerations that ran up the side of her body—the ones that belonged to him. The dress was short enough to show the deep wounds crawling up her leg unashamedly, all of which belonged to him. Those tits, that dress: he'd like to say they were what made the blood pound through his cock so hot he was afraid he'd burn up. He wasn't the only one either. Damn her. If she were his, there would be hell to pay.

He hadn't believed his body would react to her on its own, not once she was on her feet and not crying on the asphalt, but he was hard. Steel. Titanium. He wanted to take his dick out and jerk off, just watching her. It wasn't normal for him to react like that to a woman, but he knew it was those lacerations, the ones she'd suffered on his behalf. The ones that were his.

His parents had been murdered. He'd been taken, along with his brother and two older sisters, to a brutal training school in Russia. Those schools were supposedly to turn young boys and girls into assets for their country. The school he was taken to was run by criminals, pedophiles, allowed to do whatever they wanted to the children. In reality, no one was supposed to survive.

Two hundred and eighty-seven children were taken to the school over the years. Only nineteen survived. He was one of those nineteen. They had been taught, above all else, to have complete control over their bodies. The experiments conducted had been designed to stamp out the natural libido in all of them. It had worked, until now. Until Seychelle.

He watched her, his heart doing some wild hammering and his stomach tying itself into tight knots. It was crazy how his body reacted to her. The feeling was addictive. A rush. Hot blood rushed through his veins, and little whips of lightning flicked his groin until he was full and hard and so uncomfortable, he was afraid he would embarrass himself. Sparks of electricity seemed to be flashing over his skin. He was alive when he'd been dead for so long. Inside. Outside. She crawled over him. Into him. Found a home.

That voice of hers didn't belong with men who couldn't play their instruments, men who were jacked up on drugs. Leaning against the wall, eyes half-closed, he could still see the golden notes scattering across the ceiling and sliding down the walls, building a net over the room. She spun magic. The crowd couldn't see it, but they inhaled it. They drank it in and they reacted to it. It was as if the more they breathed in those golden notes, the more they needed.

He wanted his reaction to her to be because of her voice, but he knew it wasn't. He knew it was her. He'd tasted her tears. She'd given him pieces of her soul when she took the fall for him. She'd let him kiss her. That had been a mistake. Tasting her at all had been a mistake, but he still didn't have to make this one. He could walk out now, but he knew he wasn't going to. He knew it was too late.

There was no way to save her. He didn't even want to anymore. Not when he could feel like this just looking at her. She was better than any alcohol he'd tried to drown himself in. Better than any drug. She was real. That face. That mouth. That body. Those fuckin' eyes and her voice, whispering to him. Tempting him.

He stayed still, never taking his gaze from her. He watched her body sway and then undulate to the music. She was sultry. Sexy. She was a sinful temptation. The light played over her, one moment spotlighting her and the next bathing her in shadows, nearly mesmerizing him when he caught a glimpse of those lacerations up her leg and thigh and then along her breast.

It took a few minutes before he realized he was so caught up in her voice, in the woman, in the brief glimpses of the damage on her skin that belonged to him, that he wasn't doing his job. He was Torpedo Ink, first and foremost. His club came first. His brothers. He should be making certain he had his pulse on the room. He should know which clubs had members in the bar. Who was likely to cause trouble. Who the problem drunks were going to be. Which of the patrons considered themselves badasses and which really were. He should have been scanning the bar, the dance floor, the tables, noting who was the drug dealer and who was always stepping outside with someone.

He forced his gaze away from Seychelle and deliberately scanned the room, noting each person at or near the bar. One man on the end, a tall, dark-haired man wearing a denim vest and motorcycle boots but no colors, sat watching Seychelle, drumming his fingers on the bar top. Three members of a local rider's club sat drinking, watching Seychelle as well. Most of the others in the bar were regulars, or they were locals, coming to dance.

Maestro leaned up against the wall next to him. "I think we're too late. Some asshole pretend scout is looking to sign her. Her band knows he's here and they're pissed as hell."

"They can't play worth shit," Savage observed.

"True, they're amateurs thinking they're cool, but the only thing they have going for them is the singer."

"Seychelle. Seychelle Dubois," Savage offered, without looking at Maestro or Seychelle.

There was a small silence. "You know her?" Maestro proceeded with caution.

"Yeah. I know her."

"If you have any influence, tell her the scout is as full of shit as her guitarist. He's trash, looking for easy money, looking to ride on her coattails. He may have a couple of second-rate contacts in the music industry, but men like him are cons. He'll talk her into believing he can offer her a glamorous world, but he'll just take everything she has and then dump her when he's used her up. I saw the bastard buy drugs from the dealer."

"Dealer has lots of spiked hair and a strange orange jacket?" Savage already had the dealer pegged.

"Is that the color? I thought it looked like vomit. Yeah, he's the dealer. He's doing a brisk business."

"She'll listen to you," Savage said. "She isn't the type to be snowed." He knew, from the brief time with her, that he was right. She made her own decisions; she wasn't going to be pushed into anything. But she could be influenced . . . "Give your pitch and then let me talk to her. See if I can do a little persuading."

Just the thought of sparring back and forth with her again sent the blood rushing through his body in anticipation. He found himself looking forward to just talking to her. That was so far out of character that he couldn't let himself examine the why of it. Frankly, he didn't give a shit. He just wanted to be close, to talk to her, to breathe her in.

"She one of your crazy bitches?" Maestro studied the singer.

"No." Savage didn't offer any more information, although he read the curiosity in Maestro. Of course he'd be curious. Savage never talked about women or what he did with them. If they wanted to talk, that was on them. "You have Code look into her?" He asked the question of Maestro deliberately without inflection, as if the answer wouldn't mean a damn thing to him.

"Yeah. The one thing I do have going for us is that she lives in Sea Haven. She owns a little cottage there, so she's very close to Caspar. Maybe she can work in the bar when we're not playing. She has experience as both a bartender and a waitress. I think she'll draw a crowd."

"You already draw crowds," Savage pointed out, watching the supposed scout at the bar. "Who the fuck is he?"

"Name's Joseph Arnold. Came here from San Francisco. And Code couldn't find much on Seychelle other than her parents were French. Both of them deceased. Father came over from France, met her mother and fireworks went off. Seems like life with her parents wasn't everything it should be."

Savage's gut tightened. He didn't know why, other than he just plain didn't like the fact that Maestro was going to make him ask. Testing him to see what Seychelle was to him. He remained silent, letting her voice carry him away from the sounds of screaming. Of blood. Of eyes begging him to save them when he couldn't even save himself. Silence stretched out for nearly an entire song, but in the end, it won him the information.

"She took care of both of them. Father had heart disease and mother had a rare type of blood cancer. Mother went first, and her father died about two years ago. From everything Code found on the parents, they were decent people, just sickly. She stuck it out with them, though. Fortunately, the father made a great deal of money from home. Like Code, he was good on a computer. He came up with some kind of software that made them a fortune. She doesn't need money."

Savage didn't acknowledge the additional information. He simply filed it away like he did everything. He wasn't a man to forget details. He'd learned that details saved lives, and he'd learned the hard way.

The music faded, and the lead guitar player stepped forward and all but yanked the microphone from Seychelle. Savage didn't like the way he did it, grabbing it out of her hand and nearly pushing her aside with his body. She stepped back, avoiding contact, and then walked off the stage on the opposite side of where Savage had draped himself on the wall. She hadn't seen him, or at least if she had, she didn't acknowledge him. Maybe she'd been too ill to remember him. She'd definitely had a concussion.

He began to thread his way through the crowd, lagging just a little behind Maestro and Keys. Both men followed her while Master and Player blocked Joseph Arnold and refused to move so he could get around them. They did it easily, naturally, a move they'd perfected years earlier. Backs to their target but mirroring his every move so he couldn't do anything but get frustrated.

Maestro was imposing, and when he moved through a crowd, others got out of his way. Savage hung back just a little farther, staying to the shadows so he couldn't be seen. He didn't want Seychelle to know he was there. He definitely wanted to hear what Joseph Arnold had to say to her.

She kept walking until she neared the end of the alley, her back to them, and lit a cigarette. That pissed Savage off. First, she'd separated herself from safety and didn't even check behind her when she went off alone. Then there was the fact that he detested cigarettes and no woman of his was going to smoke. He'd had enough cigars and cigarettes and other hot objects put out on his body. He had the scars to prove it, and just the smell could trigger him to episodes of extreme violence.

What the fuck was he thinking? She wasn't his. She couldn't be his. He was like some whack job, stalking her. He was becoming the very thing his club went after. Still, he didn't move from the shadows, where he knew Seychelle Dubois would be safe from everyone but him.

"Seychelle?" Maestro spoke softly, hoping he didn't startle her.

She swung around fast, gasping, smoke drifting through the alley. "Yes?"

Savage had to give her credit. She covered up her shock fast. She even managed a faint smile directed vaguely toward Maestro.

"My club, Torpedo Ink, owns a bar in Caspar. Caspar's a small town right off Highway 1."

"I'm aware of it. Hank does all the booking." She gave him another smile and started to turn away.

"We don't want to book your band," Maestro said. "Can you give us a few minutes of your time? This is Keys." He indicated Keys, who tried not to look intimidating. "I'm Maestro. We have our own band, and we play mostly our bar, but take a few gigs other places, so not a lot of travel, but it tends to be very lucrative. We'd like you to come to our place next Thursday night and listen. If you like what you hear, we'd like you to sing for us. If it works out, we want to hire you to sing in our band."

"You don't have a contract with this group, do you?" Keys gestured toward the door of the club.

She shook her head. "Hank was adamant he didn't want a contract with me because he said I didn't have any experience, no fans, and he wanted to be able to dump me when he could." There was no bitterness in her voice. If anything, there was amusement.

"You have perfect pitch," Maestro said. "Perfect. You have to be aware that Hank can barely tune his guitar."

She gave him a much more genuine smile. "Only he seems unaware of that fact."

"Oh, he's aware," Keys said. "He's so aware he's trying to make you think you need them. You don't. We've been looking for a singer for some time and held out for the right one. We think you're that singer."

Maestro handed her a card with their number and the address of the bar. "Please come on any Thursday. The other two members of our band, Master and Player, are holding back some idiot scout who is high on coke and wants you to listen to his proposal. Before you take his offer, give us at least another opportunity to persuade you."

She inclined her head and watched them as they left. She had that little enigmatic smile on her face that told Savage nothing. She looked beautiful, even there in the shadows as she watched Joseph Arnold approach. He looked puffed up with his own importance. He didn't walk, he swaggered. Seychelle's eyebrow went up and the smile was instantly gone.

"Mr. Arnold. I thought we'd settled this already. I see you've tracked me down again."

Savage had been leaning against the wall, but something in her voice made him come to full attention. Evidently, she'd met the man before and she didn't like him. He watched as she carefully put the cigarette out under her foot but kept her eyes on Arnold the entire time, almost as if she expected an attack.

"Don't be such a fool, Seychelle. You're not going to make two dollars with this group, not unless you whore yourself out."

"You have such a pleasant personality. I'd like you to leave."

Joseph Arnold stepped forward, right into her personal space, forcing her back against the wall of the building. "You think you're so high and mighty, always superior. I'm not putting up with it. You'll work for me or you're going to be very sorry. No one in the industry will touch you. You'll spend your life with going-nowhere bands."

"Better than spending my life with a grubby little man who tries to force himself on women. First you try to ask me out a million times, and now you're suddenly a music scout. It's a crock of shit. Get away from me."

"You little cunt. You're nothing without me."

"You're drunk and high, just like you were the last time you made your pathetic little pitch. Get away from me now."

He grabbed her around the throat and started to shake her, squeezing hard with his big fingers. Savage was already on the move, exploding out of the shadows with blurring speed. "Get the fuck off her," he snapped, grabbing the scout by his hair and wrenching him back away from Seychelle.

Joseph hung on grimly to her, roaring with rage that someone dared interfere. He pulled Seychelle with him over backward so the two nearly fell to the asphalt. At the last moment, to try to save himself, Joseph let go of her and threw out his arms to prevent his face from hitting the hard surface.

The moment Joseph let go of Seychelle, Savage was on him, punching his ribs, his chin, back to his ribs and then pummeling his face. The nose squelched with blood, was sickening when it broke, and then Savage smashed a fist to his face again.

Seychelle caught his arm when Savage pulled back for another punch. He whirled around, nearly knocking her over.

"He's had enough, Savage," she said. "He's the type to call the cops and then sue you."

"I don't think so." Savage took pictures of her neck and then crouched down beside Joseph. "You call the cops, I'll make certain you go to jail for attempted murder. If you go near her again, this is nothing compared to what I'll do to you, you piece of shit."

He straightened slowly and turned to Seychelle. She was attempting to light another cigarette with shaky hands. He pulled it out of her hand, crumpled it up and tossed it right onto Joseph's bloody face, and then, catching her by the arm, walked her to the far entrance, away from the groaning, writhing man.

Savage pushed her up against the wall, back into the shadows where he was most comfortable. "You're not smoking anymore. I don't like it."

Seychelle raised her eyebrow and edged back a little from him. "I don't think that's your business, Savage. I pretty much do whatever I want."

"You can kiss that good-bye."

She gave him that faint smile, a flash of the dimple that might someday really manage to drive him insane. He seemed to be able to read everyone but her. That mysterious little smile intrigued him and yet made him want to do all sorts of sinful things to her that he would get off on, but she might not like so much—at first.

"Nice to know what you're really like. You do realize I might not want to smoke but I'm addicted, so I can't stop."

"That's pure bullshit. Everyone is addicted to something, Seychelle. You're strong. If you want to quit, then you will. I say you will. I don't want to see you with these again." He snapped his fingers. "Give me the pack."

She stood there for a few long moments, studying the hard line of his jaw. His expressionless mask. Those blue eyes of hers drifted over his face, and for a few moments his heart stuttered as if she were touching him. He couldn't let her mesmerize him.

"Baby, you don't hand them over, I'll just take them."

She shook her head, her chin going up defiantly. Savage was all instinct. He didn't do well with defiance from his woman. In any case, he had to test the waters. So far, she'd reacted exactly the way he needed her to. He caught her hips, spun her around so she was facing the wall, yanked that fuckin' little sexy dress right up over her hot little ass encased in the prettiest, sexiest, mint green lace panties he'd ever seen. He smacked her ass hard. Three hard strikes on each cheek and then whipped her dress down before turning her back around.

"Give me the fuckin' pack of cigarettes, Seychelle. I'm not playin' games here."

Tears spilled over, but she hadn't made a sound when he'd spanked her. "That hurt."

"You weren't supposed to enjoy it, angel." It took effort not to take her tears right off her face with his tongue. He wasn't going to be able to resist for long. He waited for condemnation. A screaming, deserved temper tantrum.

"You do realize you're being a first-class dick?"

"I realize I'm saving your life and you aren't thanking me. As I recall, I went out of my way to thank you. In fact, I risked going to hell and jail for lying when I told Ms. Prune I was your fiancé."

She hadn't screamed for help. She hadn't run away. She wasn't condemning him. She just regarded him with those liquid sea-blue eyes. She was beyond anyone he'd ever imagined.

Seychelle shook her head and then those fantasy lips curved into a smile and his heart clenched hard in his chest. He wanted to be closer to her. He couldn't help stroking his fingers down the marks Joseph had put on her neck. No one put marks on her skin but him. No one. He wanted to kick the shit out of the little dick.

"Hand the pack over, Seychelle." He didn't give in for one minute. He couldn't. If she belonged to him, she had to know what she was getting into. What the hell was he thinking? But he couldn't stop himself.

She heaved an exaggerated sigh. "I suppose since you went to the trouble of announcing you were my fiancé, I should give you a pass."

"*And* I'm saving your life." He held her gaze captive, refusing to look away.

Another exaggerated sigh. Another flash of that little

heart-stopping dimple. "Fine. You're probably saving my life as well. I've been wanting to quit, but I'm so addicted."

"Addiction is meant to be overcome."

He took the pack from her and crushed the remaining cigarettes.

"Even you?" she demanded. "Are you addicted to something as well? Or are you above the rest of us?"

"Even me." He looked her in the eye. "You have any more?"

She shook her head. "What are you addicted to?"

"You." He put it out there, uncaring if it freaked her out. "You should run while you have the chance. It won't do you any good, but you can at least try."

"Maestro and Keys just asked me to join their band. That's what started this." She gestured toward Joseph on the ground, where two members of her band crouched to make certain the scout was still able to get to his feet. "There's no doubt you can track me down."

"Hell, man, you nearly killed him," Hank, the lead guitarist, accused.

Savage ignored him, unconcerned if Joseph was alive or dead. He'd made certain to take a photograph of Seychelle's neck and the finger marks there. The asshole tried to strangle her right there in the alley. Savage probably wouldn't let that shit go. More than likely he'd slip into the man's hotel room and break his fuckin' neck.

He took Seychelle by the arm and walked her back down the alley, away from the others and toward the bar. "No doubt I will track you down." He snapped his fingers. "Address."

She lifted her chin. "Do you think I'm crazy? You're so far out of my league I can't even consider encouraging you." Her gaze once more drifted over him from head to toe, once again giving him that strange feeling that she was physically touching him. "You're dangerous to women. I'm not the type to live dangerously, Savage. A man like you never sticks around. You don't, do you?"

He might not be her type, but she was definitely his. She was exactly what he was looking for, she just didn't know it. He liked that she knew he was dangerous. He liked the way she was sure of herself. He liked the way she sacrificed herself for others. Her parents. Him. The little kid. "Nope. Don't fuck them either. Just their mouths. Don't buy them meals or take them out. We don't converse either."

"Sounds so wonderfully tempting."

Her sarcasm stroked his cock like fingers whispering over him. He grinned at her. "I don't kiss them or get all cozy in bed with them. And I don't spank their asses when they don't hand over cigarettes in order to save their lives."

"You are *such* a catch." That damn dimple of hers was going to keep him up all night.

His grin was suddenly genuine, shocking him. He hadn't known he could actually feel amusement, let alone smile. "I guess you're forgetting I kissed you, conversed and got all cozy in your bed as well as spanked your ass to save it."

Her smile lit up the shadowy alley. "I guess you did."

"That deserves something."

Hank stood up and nudged the drummer, who had come out with him looking for his singer, worried now that he knew a scout was after her. "Is he bothering you, Seychelle?"

"No, Hank, we know each other. We go way back."

"I'm her fiancé," Savage announced.

Seychelle tried to muffle her laugh against his shoulder. He wrapped his other arm around her waist and pulled her in close to him.

"The hell you are," Hank snapped. "Who is he?"

Savage turned his head slowly and met Hank's eyes. He didn't mind Hank seeing the killer in him. He let his stare go cold and flat. Hank and the drummer both backed up and nearly tripped over Joseph, who had staggered up and nearly fell over again.

"I'm Torpedo Ink," Savage announced. "And Seychelle's fiancé. You have anything to say to her in that fuckin' tone of voice, you say it to me first."

Hank swallowed visibly and cast around for something to say that wouldn't make him look like a pussy but wouldn't get him into trouble. "We've got a show to put on."

"She'll be right in," Savage said. "A few more minutes."

Seychelle waited until Hank and the drummer got Joseph between them and helped the scout back into the bar. Savage knew Maestro, Keys, Player and Master were right there in the shadows. Absinthe was somewhere, probably inside, keeping a pulse on the bar.

"Seriously, Savage? You'd better stop saying things like that. Torpedo Ink is news to a lot of people now. You're going to find that little rumor sweeping through the clubs."

"I could give a fuck what other people say. I don't live my life by gossip, and neither do you. Am I right?"

She gave him that smile again, and his lungs burned for air.

"No, I don't pay much attention to gossip, although when everyone warns a woman about a man, she had better listen."

"Someone warned you about me?"

"Not me specifically, but I hear rumors and you're considered hot and sexy, so yeah, you get mentioned. They say you don't stick around. At. All."

"And I don't fuckin' kiss them, converse or cozy up with them in a bed."

She laughed again, just like he knew she would. That sound was shockingly beautiful, the golden notes scattering like tiny little crystals around them.

"Since you're no longer smoking, there's no reason for you to frequent alleys and get your sexy little ass in trouble. I mean it, Seychelle. Don't go where it isn't safe. That man who is supposed to be a scout sounded like a stalker."

"How would you know what a stalker sounds like?"

"I'm stalking you, aren't I?"

She shrugged, amusement climbing to her eyes, lighting them. "I suppose so. Since you're such an expert, I'll follow your advice. I really do have to go back in."

He stood there blocking her path, knowing it would be a mistake to kiss her again, but the craving was there. She just waited, not in the least concerned that she was seemingly alone with Savage, a Torpedo Ink sergeant at arms. He leaned in to her deliberately, wrapped his palm around the nape of her neck and put his lips against her ear.

"You aren't nearly as safe as you think."

Her blue eyes stared directly into his, and there was a hint of laughter that sent his cock into a frenzy of urgent need. She wrapped her hand around his upper arm, or tried to, but her hand barely made it halfway around his biceps. That didn't deter her. She put her lips against his ear, going on her toes to do it.

"You're so full of shit." She pulled back immediately. "I have work to do, my darling fake fiancé. Step aside."

He'd never wanted to kiss a woman more. Okay, he'd never wanted to fuck a woman more. He stepped back from the temptation. She was pure sin and he needed her. He wasn't comfortable needing anyone, let alone a woman. She had a smart mouth on her. He loved that about her. She also wasn't afraid of him when everyone else was. He didn't know how to take that. She even appeared to think he was amusing when he was seriously warning her. She didn't believe he was attracted to her. That much was clear. He found himself wanting to smile again.

He let her go around him. She didn't look back when she went inside. His brothers immediately came out of the shadows.

"What the hell was that, Savage?" Maestro demanded.

"I told you I know her," he said.

"Yeah, you know her. You said she wasn't one of your weird fucks. I want that woman singing in our band."

Master nodded. "Shocked the hell out of me, but she's damned good."

"You can't fuck this up for us because she's got a nice ass," Player said.

Keys just looked at Savage and then shook his head. "You might as well pack it in, brothers, he's gone on this chick."

Savage didn't deny it. He just gave them the death stare. What was there to say? It was true, but he wasn't sure what he was going to do about it. He wished she were one of his weird fucks. It would make life so much easier for both of them. She was far more than that. She'd never be just another one of his weird fucks.

"She'll sing for you. Preacher needs another bartender. You said so yourself, Maestro. She can fill in when you're not singing. She lives in Sea Haven, so that's a plus."

"It won't be a plus when you kick her to the curb," Maestro said. "Do you have any idea how difficult it is to find a real singer? One like her? It's nearly impossible."

"She isn't kick-to-the-curb material, is she, Savage?" Keys asked.

Savage didn't answer him. He had no idea what he was going to do with Seychelle.

"If she joins the band," Player said, "we have an obligation to her. She'd be under our protection."

Savage turned cold eyes on him. Inside, all the unfamiliar amusement, all the fun he'd had sparring with Seychelle, faded away to be replaced by that ice-cold rage. "No one interferes with her. She's under *my* protection. What happens between the two of us is ours alone. You're my brothers, but she belongs to me and I expect you to respect that and have my back."

There was absolute silence. It wasn't as if he could blame them, and worse, deep inside, he had no idea what the hell he was doing. He had no business claiming a woman. He knew it. They knew it. Half the time he couldn't be in anyone's company. Violence rode hard on his shoulders when the devil was on him. The death in his eyes was real. He was barely civilized, and most of the time he hung on to sanity by a thread.

It wasn't as if Seychelle was a biker bitch who knew the rules of the game. She was no patch chaser, wanting the protection of the club and some man to take care of her. She didn't even appear all that interested in him or the club. If anything, she was more amused by him than attracted to him. He pulled back, thinking about that kiss they'd shared. The one he still tasted in his mouth. Now he wasn't going to get her out of his mind. Not that he'd been able to before.

"Savage," Maestro said, caution in his voice. "This woman. I don't know that much about her, just the little that Code gave me before we came here, but she seems to be someone we ordinarily would consider off-limits."

Savage shook his head. "She's going to say yes to singing with you, but you just remember what I said. Seychelle belongs to me. That's the bottom line." He turned on his heel and stalked back into the bar. Already she was interfering with their club. That was the kind of woman she was. Shit.

He faded back into the dark, where he could watch Joseph Arnold drink and glower at Seychelle from a chair close to a wall. Joseph should have gone home. He was beat all to hell. His face practically caved in. His nose was swollen and one eye was closed. His ribs had to be bruised, but he was staying, his eyes on the singer, his cell phone out, recording or taking photos.

By midnight the place was so packed the dancers could only hold on to one another and sway. Word had gotten out that the singer of the band was damn good, and the locals—and bikers—had dropped by to see if it was true and stayed. The bar was still packed at closing time.

Seychelle caught up her jacket from behind the bar, waved toward the bartender and left before the band had

broken down the stage. She didn't stay to help, which indicated to Savage she wasn't happy with the way Hank
treated her and she wanted to avoid Joseph. He followed her
at a distance, needing to make certain she got home safely.
The road was very dangerous and took an hour for her to
drive even without fog. He hung back, but he followed all
the way to her cottage and waited until she was safely inside before heading back to Caspar.

She knew better than to allow Savage anywhere near here.
Seychelle still felt every single smack of his hand on her
bottom. There had been heat spreading through her body.
Fire. Her sex had clenched and throbbed. Every nerve ending in her body had leapt to life, just the way it did when he
came near her.

She should have reacted completely differently when
Savage pushed her up against the wall and smacked her on
the butt. No one had ever hit her in her life. He could say it
was a punishment if he wanted to, but she felt the sexual
intent behind it. Or maybe everything about Savage was
just sexual. To her, he was the epitome of sexual. She'd
never been able to respond to anyone or anything the way
she did to him. He scared her. Terrified her. She scared
herself, because she had no idea her body would respond so
completely to him.

A part of her was elated that she even could respond. A
part of her was appalled at herself. Just thinking about him
and what he'd done to her made her sex throb and burn. She
found herself wanting to cry but not really knowing why.

THREE

Savage sat up in bed, scrubbing a hand down his face, wiping the sweat away. Another fucking nightmare. He couldn't close his eyes. He hadn't for a long while and he needed sleep. Desperately. If he didn't get sleep soon, he was going to explode, and anything in his path would be annihilated. He glanced at the clock. Fifteen minutes. That was how much sleep he'd managed before the nightmare woke him—again.

He threw back the sheet, the only thing draped over him, because sometimes he'd get twisted up in his nightmare world and come up fighting. That was never good, considering he slept with weapons close to his hand at all times—except he wasn't sleeping.

It took only a few minutes to take his third shower that night. The first two had been in hopes the hot water would get him to sleep. The third was for her. Seychelle. He'd held out for nearly a week. He had this itch he couldn't get rid of. He wished it were in his cock, but it wasn't. He rubbed his chest.

He didn't want to give in. She was coming to their bar on Thursday . . . that was the damn problem. He wasn't certain she would come, and he was probably the reason she wouldn't. She knew if she did, he wasn't going to let her go. It didn't matter, because he was going to her. He didn't want to. His seeking her out would let her know she had the upper hand. She was the one woman in the world who could actually make him feel like a real man and not the walking dead.

He pulled on his jeans, boots and a tee, stretching it across the heavy muscles of his chest. His vest was next. Then he was gone. The sound of his bike was loud, rivaling the boom of the ocean as the waves hit the cliff and sea stacks to throw white, foaming spray high into the air. The fresh air held salty mist, hitting his face and clearing his head. Being on his bike and riding the ribbon of coastal highway always helped rid him of the worst of his ever-present pent-up rage—at least for a little while, until something triggered it again.

It only took a few minutes to get from Caspar to Sea Haven. He drove through the narrow streets until he came to the small cottage at the end of a dead-end road. The headlands stretched out on the other side of the street, forming the cliffs directly above the ocean. From the vantage point of the cottage, she had an excellent view of the stormy waves.

Savage backed his bike into her drive, right up to the small garage. He sat for a moment, listening to the pounding sea. It was angry tonight, matching his mood. He scanned the neighborhood. The little house was a distance from any other homes, with a field stretching between her cottage and the closest neighbor. No dogs barked. No one was moving.

He prowled around her house. Easy break-in. The front door had a shit lock. The back door was unlocked. He looked up at the heavens for a moment, wondering what the hell he was going to do to her for forgetting to lock that door. There was no alarm and the windows had no locks. One was open. Peering in, he could see the bed with Seychelle curled up in it, facing away from him. He sighed. Anyone could break in. A kid could do it.

He caught the window ledge and slid into the room easily. He was a big man, but it was a good-sized window with no covering. He wanted to shake her. Instead, he sank down on the edge of the bed and leaned down to take off his boots. He heard a gasp, and she sat up, throwing a punch at his head. He ducked it easily.

"Knock it off. You deserve to have the crap scared out of you. This place is an invitation to perverts and serial killers."

Seychelle scooted to the headboard, pulling the sheet up to her chin. "Which are you?"

He glanced over his shoulder at her. She looked outraged. She also looked as if she might burst out laughing at any moment. Her damn dimple was very much in evidence. He concentrated on taking off his remaining boot. "I'm a pervert, of course." He thought about it. "I might be considered a serial killer by some people. I don't know. No one's put that label on me yet."

He shrugged out of his colors and folded them neatly, putting them on the end table. She had little girly things on it, none expensive. Nothing in the house really was, with the exception of an amazing blown-glass sculpture of two roses intertwined together. Both red, the stems dark green, winding their way lazily up toward the layers of soft petals, the entire sculpture nearly sparkling brightly with color from within. The two flowers were permanently set in a crystal blown-glass vase that sat on a small round base of moving colors. It was beautiful. Stunning even.

Two intertwining hand-blown crystal roses? Who had given her that? Some other lover? He didn't like the idea, but he was careful not to knock it off the edge when he pulled his T-shirt off with one hand and put it on top of his colors. The damn sculpture was the centerpiece of the room, and clearly it was the one thing she treasured.

She didn't protest when he folded his shirt. Why the hell didn't she stop him when he took it off? He'd been counting on that.

"You know I could have shot you." She sounded very solemn.

He stretched out on her bed, close to her, pulling one of her pillows out from behind her so he could jam it under his head. "You don't have a gun, Seychelle. It's impossible to shoot me if you don't even have a fucking gun."

"The point is, I could have had a gun, and then you'd be dead right now."

"If you had a gun, I would have taken it away from you."

"You can't take my gun away from me. I'd shoot you first." Now she sounded indignant. "That's the point I'm making. You can't just break into my house . . . How did you get in? I locked the front door." She frowned. "I'm not certain I locked the back door. Did I?"

"No, you didn't lock the back door. And you didn't lock the windows. That one is wide open." He pointed to the bedroom window. "I just came right in." He turned his head to narrow his gaze and give her his killer stare. Maybe he should have really frightened her, so she'd learn a lesson.

"No one really locks their doors around here, Savage."

"I'm changing the locks and you're going to use the new ones. You made an enemy of that scout, and he's the vindictive type. You haven't seen the last of him unless I do something about it. I haven't decided yet what to do about him."

Her hand dropped to his head. He'd shaved it the night before, and she rubbed gently. It felt soothing. He never liked to be touched, but she felt different and he didn't knock her hand away. Her touch was like her voice, a kind of magic.

"What would you do to make him stay away?"

"That's where the serial killer part comes into play." He stared up at the ceiling. She had a fan. It had wide paddles on it, and the light fixture was ornate. "Lie down." He patted the bed beside him. "It isn't like we haven't done this before."

"That's true. You broke into my hospital room by lying to the nurses."

"Just one old biddy that didn't want me anywhere near you."

"She was very wise." Seychelle slid down the bed until she was lying beside him, but under the covers.

Savage lay on top of the comforter. Still, he could feel her next to him. Her heat. Every breath he drew brought her scent into his lungs. That circulated through his body, sending her everywhere until she seemed to be flowing through his veins like a drug.

"She was afraid I'd teach you all sorts of dirty, sinful things." Dirty, sinful things were beginning to insert themselves into his mind. Once there, there was no pushing them out.

Seychelle was silent for a moment. When he looked at her, she had that little smile, the one that made his cock come to attention when he thought about it, along with those lacerations that were all his. He didn't fight it. He wanted to feel alive. She wasn't afraid of him. She had a smart mouth, sassy as hell, but no sense of self-preservation at all. He was going to have to change that. He reached under the covers to pull her left leg out so he could stroke the pads of his fingers along those indentations in her skin. She didn't resist or try to pull away.

"Do you know all sorts of dirty, sinful things?" There was real curiosity in her voice.

His entire body tightened. His cock was beginning to go past a pleasant ache to an actual pain. "What kind of fuckin' question is that? Look at me, woman. Of course I know all sorts of dirty, sinful things."

"Cool." There was a teasing note in her voice.

He turned his head and glared at her. "Are you just trying to piss me off? I want to shake you right now."

"I'm so sorry I damaged your fragile ego, Savage." She laughed softly, and the sound sent musical notes floating through the room, touching his skin until little electrical sparks danced over him, this time in various shades of gold. He hadn't expected the show, but there it was, another thing she gave him that he wasn't going to just be able to walk away from.

She didn't sound in the least remorseful or even like she

had an inkling of why he was angry with her. Clearly, she didn't believe he was any kind of a threat to her. He'd been a threat since he was a little kid, and anyone seeing him knew it. Not her. Not Seychelle.

Her laughter made him want to smile. The sound found its way inside him, just like the stroke of her fingers on his head seemed to push out demons one by one. His body relaxed, the tension draining out of it slowly. That swirling pool of rage deep inside of him where the monster dwelled subsided as well, just calmed as if her fingers were magic.

He put his arms over his shoulders and tucked his hands behind his head, not wanting to make the mistake of touching her again. Smelling her fresh, clean scent was bad enough. She was everywhere in that room. It was very small, but it suited her. She was short. And curvy. He liked curves. Her curves. And her skin. Like a canvas. A fresh canvas just waiting for him. Her hair was like a waterfall of honey gold, with sun-kissed platinum streaks spilling across her pillow, all silky soft and brushing his shoulders. Shit. He wasn't a fucking poet.

"Lay the fuck still." He snapped it. If she moved and all that hair slid over his skin, he was going to do something both of them were going to regret.

"This is actually my bed, which you were not invited into, so don't tell me what to do in it. And while we're on the subject, what are you doing here?"

"You have a good mattress."

She scooted back up to the headboard again, but he was lying on top of the blankets and she couldn't pull them with her. He turned his head to look at her. She wasn't wearing much. It was some little top that barely covered her tummy. Little shorts clung to her thighs, and if he wanted, he could have run his hand right up inside, where she was warm. Damp. Waiting for him. And there was her leg and her rib cage. That side of her breast. The side of her face. That little laceration over her eye. All his.

"Wait a minute. You knew my mattress was good, so

you came here tonight? That's the answer? How did you know that? Have you been here before? Because if you have, that's just plain creepy and you need help."

"I'm the one who needs help? It's creepy that I came here tonight. I crawled through your open window and climbed in bed with you. You don't think *that's* creepy. Woman, you are very disturbed. And no, I haven't been here before. I was just commenting you have a good mattress."

"It's important to have a good mattress."

She said it like it was gospel. He wanted to laugh. They kept having the strangest, most ludicrous conversations, and the more she talked, the more he wanted to strangle her—or kiss her until neither of them could breathe.

She'd gone silent again. He found himself looking at her bare left leg. Mesmerized by it. The one that had been scraped along the ground so he could live. Those scars that weren't healed all the way were red and raised, marring her perfect skin. Those scars were his. They belonged to him. He touched them with the pads of his fingers. Gently. Running his fingers from her ankle to the top of her thigh right over the evidence of the scrapes and lacerations.

"You still haven't answered me, Savage. What are you really doing here? We both know we aren't going to have a thing. I'm not a one-night-stand kind of girl. You don't even give a girl an entire night."

His hand slid up her thigh and circled it. "You want me. You think I can't tell when a woman is attracted to me? We have chemistry, baby, and it's off the charts."

She didn't remove his hand. She should have. Most women would have. Most women wouldn't have let him crawl through their window and lie on the bed next to them. Those incredible blue eyes of hers moved over his face and then his body. She took her time, looking at the tattoos. Looking at his scars. The burns that were the most disturbing of all. He had a lot of them. He didn't cover them up. He let her look her fill, and she did. She didn't ask why he had the words *Whip Master* burned into his chest, but her gaze took it all in.

She gave a little sigh. Regret? Maybe.

"You're hot as hell. And you just admitted to knowing dirty, sinful things. What girl wouldn't be tempted? You're scary dangerous-looking. Tatts. Muscles. A history of scary scars. Those eyes of yours. You look at a woman and she's going to get hot. The thing is, honey, I know myself very well. You would eat me up and spit me out. I can't take that kind of hurt, and I wouldn't be able to separate my emotions from the wild, clearly awesome sex we'd have together."

She was so fucking honest she tore his heart out. He hadn't met too many women who just put it out there. Every word she said felt like a brand sinking through his flesh right into bone. Her brand. Her name. His addiction, his craving for her wasn't going to get better. They were both in trouble. He wrote his name on her thigh with his finger.

"I didn't come here for sex, Seychelle. I can pick up any bitch in a bar and get what I want. I came here because . . ." He trailed off.

His hand went back to the long, pitted lacerations in her leg. The ones that were raised. So many. He felt his heart shift. His stomach did a slow roll. She stayed silent.

"I couldn't sleep. I haven't slept in days. If I do, I get nightmares. They're bad," he confessed. "I wake up fighting. It can be . . . dangerous." What kind of pussy was he to tell her the truth when he wouldn't even tell his brothers? He let go of her leg and lay back, staring at the fan on the ceiling.

Her hand went to his head again. Her fingers drifted over his scalp. He counted his heartbeats there in the darkness. Felt the magic in her touch as her fingers began a deeper massage.

"You came to me because you couldn't sleep? I'm not certain how to take that. It could mean I'm the most boring woman you know."

"Take it as a compliment. I'm not the kind of man to

throw that shit out there very often. You're restful. You chase the demons away."

Seychelle looked down at Savage as he closed his eyes. She didn't know whether to laugh or cry. She did neither. He was the most beautiful—and damaged—man she'd ever met. He was absolutely gorgeous. He had the kind of physique a sculptor would go crazy over. Every line in his body was purely masculine. He had more muscles than she'd thought possible in a man, and she was so attracted to him it was a sin. But she knew better.

He was everything she shouldn't get near. Everything she was attracted to. Those scars. Those burns. Those terrible words someone had burned into his flesh permanently. *Whip Master.* He needed violence. He craved it in the way others might a drug. His world revolved around it. Worse, he had a darkness in him that she couldn't even fathom, but she knew it was real and he was capable of things she couldn't conceive of. She was drawn to that darkness like a moth to a flame, and she would burn up in his fire. She would. She had no protections against a man like Savage. She felt his loathing of himself and the demons that plagued him and she wanted to be the woman to bring him peace.

Savage was the type of man she wouldn't resist, and if she got too close, he would eventually take all of her. She knew she would want to sacrifice herself for him. Give him everything she was, and he would swallow her whole. Men like him couldn't help themselves, they didn't look after someone like her. They took and took until there was nothing left.

Savage . . . She sighed and scooted closer to him, so she could use both hands to massage his head. She'd learned to do a scalp massage when she was ten years old from a professional masseuse, so she could massage her father's head when he was in pain.

"Baby, you don't have to do that," Savage said without opening his eyes. "Just lying next to you makes it better."

Her heart lurched. That was bad. Really, really bad. He

wasn't there because he thought she was beautiful. Or because he was so attracted, he just had to have her. He could lie in bed next to her and not reach for her, which really was an insult because Savage was the most sexual man she'd ever encountered. He radiated sex, and not just sex, but carnal, sinful, wicked sex, the way he radiated pain and rage. His kind of sex was something she'd dreamt of, fantasized about, was scared of and knew was not for her. She was too . . . tame. He was too wild.

He wanted to be with her for purely platonic reasons—she brought him peace. That was her gift and her curse. She had hoped he wouldn't feel it—that what worked for some, didn't work on him. It wasn't like she didn't have men flirting outrageously all the time. She sang in bars. That would naturally follow. Aside from the fact that she was maybe—okay, very—curvy, she was good-looking if she wasn't being critical of herself. She just didn't react to men the way she should. She craved . . . something she couldn't name. She needed something darker. Something someone like Savage might offer, just not quite so intense.

"You've gone quiet on me, Seychelle. I'm not sure what to think about that."

Looking down at him, she could see those ultra-long lashes. No man who looked as scary as he did should have his lashes. "I'm thinking."

He sighed and started to turn his head upward, so he could see her. She held his head still. "Don't move. Just lay there. You're disturbing my sleep, so I should get to do whatever I want with you."

His mouth curved into a smile, but she couldn't see his eyes, so she couldn't tell if it was real. She doubted it. Savage wasn't a man given to smiles.

"I crawl through your window, take off most of my clothes, get in bed with you and all you want to do is rub my head?"

"You are bald. It's possible I could get three wishes to come true."

"That would only work if I were really bald. I shave my head. There's a difference."

"Receding hairline?" Deliberately, she pushed sympathy into her voice, when she wanted to laugh.

He moved so fast she barely had time to blink when he caught both her arms and yanked her down over the top of him. She landed across his lap, face buried in the mattress. His hand smacked her bottom hard and then he pushed her back into a sitting position over his head. Clearly, he was much stronger even than she had imagined.

"Ow." Seychelle rubbed her bottom and glared at him, not that he was looking at her. "Sheesh. Will you stop doing that? It's not like I'm wearing much padding. I guess I should qualify that statement—I meant in the way of clothing."

"You deserved that. And don't remind me of your lack of clothing."

"I take *great* exception to your reasoning. Receding hairline is the number one reason for men shaving their heads. I'm sure I read that statistic on the internet."

He reached over his head, found her hand and put it on his head. "Get to work, woman, and stop trying to defend a completely indefensible position."

"You told me I didn't have to massage your scalp."

"I changed my mind. Fuck, woman, you have a mouth on you. Why aren't you afraid of me like everyone else?"

She could tell him the truth. But if she did, if she told him she could "see" inside him, he would probably take out one of his many weapons and shoot her. Or he'd leave, and she'd never see him again. Because she wasn't going to go to the Torpedo Ink bar and audition with their band. She didn't dare be around Savage more than she absolutely had to. He wouldn't want her to know his secrets, and he had so many it was frightening. She could see straight into him where no one else could, where he had gifts he didn't want anyone—especially the men and women of Torpedo Ink he loved—to know about. She saw into him and knew he was a good man, when he didn't know it and would never believe it even if she told him.

"If you crawled into my bedroom to hurt me, you already would have done it."

"Not if I wanted a killer scalp massage first."

She heard the trace of amusement in his voice, and it slid inside her like a gift. Instinctively, she knew Savage didn't do with anyone else what he was doing with her—sparring verbally and enjoying himself. It was a little exhilarating.

"I see. You plan to kill me *after* the massage."

"Maybe, so you'd better make it a long one."

She gave an exaggerated sigh. "Turn over, then. I'll massage your shoulders and back. You carry a lot of tension in your shoulders."

There was the briefest of hesitations. If she wasn't so tuned to him, she wouldn't have noticed, but she saw everything about him. Inwardly she cursed herself for gravitating toward the wounded and the dark. She couldn't go near him after this night. She vowed to herself she wouldn't.

Her life had been about taking care of others, watching herself, being disciplined when she had to, so she could take this night, for however long he stayed, and enjoy herself. He'd made it clear he wasn't after sex, so she didn't have to worry that she would have a wild night with him and then stalk him evermore.

He rolled over, a show of muscle, and the light spilling through the window spotlighted his back and the tattoo he had there. She'd seen the Torpedo Ink insignia on their vests. But this one was very detailed. The light also highlighted the terrible burns on his back. Like on his chest, someone had burned letters into his flesh. *Master of Pain*. The letters were distinct in spite of the fact that the skulls buried in the roots of the trees had been inked over them. She hadn't known one could ink over burns, especially burns so severe they went layers deep.

She reached for a bottle of lotion she kept on the night-

stand, shifted position and straddled his thighs, reaching up
to run her hand over the exquisite ink work. "Who did this?
It's beautiful." It was. She wasn't going to comment on the
Master of Pain and what that meant because she was afraid
she already knew. She'd seen the other burn, the one in
front proclaiming him the *Whip Master*.

"Usually don't let bitches touch my tatt." His voice was
gruff. Muffled by the blankets. He turned his head and looked
at her with cold blue eyes. So cold. Flat. Almost dead.

"Well, since I'm not a bitch most of the time, and I'm
massaging your shoulders and back, I guess it's sort of man-
datory that I touch it." She didn't. She waited for his permission, because it meant something big to him. Huge. The
tattoo was not just on his skin. It was a part of him and it had
great meaning.

She actually felt him at war with himself. He didn't
show it outwardly, other than in the tension running
through his body, but instinctively she knew this was another first. No one really touched his tattoo—or those
burns neither of them were going to talk about.

Seychelle counted her breaths while she waited. She didn't
know whether she wanted him to give her permission or not.
It would tie another thread between them, and she knew she
couldn't afford too many more. Being close to a man like
Savage was dangerous. Trying to soothe him, trying to help
him with the horrible monstrous demon that was eating him
up inside, was a two-edged sword. She wanted to just take it
all away for him, tell him she'd do whatever was necessary,
be whatever he needed, but she already knew she wasn't that
woman. He was so damaged, and she was terrified for him
and terrified for herself.

"Get to it, woman."

She closed her eyes briefly, not certain if she was drowning in those dark waters already. Taking a breath, she
poured the lotion into her palms and started with his shoulders. He was much taller than her and she had to lean over

his body in order to work on his shoulders, but she didn't want to sit on his butt, or just above it, where part of the tattoo was. It was very large, spreading across his back and down to the very edge of his buttocks. Thankfully, he'd kept his jeans on, but she could see the roots and skulls crawling below the low-slung material.

"Seychelle."

"Yes?" She tried to calm her accelerating heart at his tone. He always sounded so dictatorial. So in charge.

"Slide up higher. You're going to get tired trying to massage my shoulders like that."

He had eyes in the back of his head. That was the only explanation. "You just said no one should touch your tattoo. I don't want to sit on it."

His body jerked, and for a moment she thought he might be laughing. She couldn't imagine it, but one never knew. "You don't want to sit on my tattoo?" he echoed. "Why? Do you think it would be disrespectful for your sweet little pussy or your prizewinning ass to rub around on my tattoo? Get serious, babe."

"Don't talk about my ass or my . . . er . . . pussy. You don't know me that well." She forced indignation into her voice and then scooted up, settling herself comfortably before her fingers dug into his shoulders extra hard. He didn't so much as flinch. He had scars everywhere. Everywhere. And burn marks. Really awful burns aside from the letters. She didn't ask him a single question about them.

"I talk about anything I damn well want to when it's mine. I claimed you, remember? I'm your fucking fiancé. I wouldn't forget that if I were you."

She burst out laughing. Who knew that Savage would actually have a sense of humor? "Fine, but if I'm your fiancée, I should know a few things about you."

"Before you get all nosy, it goes both ways."

She put more pressure on his muscles, determined to loosen them. "I'm agreeable to that. It's not like I have tons to hide."

"Anything we say doesn't affect the relationship. You can't get weird because you don't like an answer I give you, or a question I ask."

That gave her pause. She moved over him to work the muscles she could feel were knotted and giving him trouble. Maybe it wasn't such a good idea to enter into this strange game with him. It was the middle of the night, and she was draining herself by letting him take pieces of her. Still, she didn't stop. She couldn't. She could only try to save herself.

"I thought you were going to sleep."

"You're not a coward, Seychelle. Ask a question."

"What does the tree represent?"

"It's not a what, it's a who. The trunk of the tree represents Czar—he's president of Torpedo Ink. There are seventeen branches. That's the rest of us. The crows are those that never made it out. The skulls are the ones we did in to escape, or for our country."

She closed her eyes against the wave of rage rising in him. It swirled hot and fast, threatening to engulf her. As it was, the waves crashed over her like a tsunami, drowning her in his terrible need. He didn't even know what he was doing to her. He'd lived with that feeling for so long he didn't acknowledge it to himself. She saw how it stayed inside of him, waiting to flare, building slowly, waiting for a moment to erupt. Savage was a very scary man. She tried to remind herself he wasn't a pet. He was more of a feral tiger, raging in a cage, waiting to rip anyone apart to escape.

He was telling her the truth. Whatever he had been through with the rest of his club had been horrific. There was a reason for that rage, and she didn't want to know what it was. He was pulling her down with him, and on some level, he knew what he was doing. Unlike with the rage he couldn't rid himself of, which he mostly ignored until it was too late, he knew that by lying on the bed with her, he was leaking his nightmares right into her.

Never made it out of what? Of where? He'd been somewhere terrible. She caught glimpses. Images. Blood pouring down his back. Stripes on flesh. Children screaming. Moaning. Crying. Chains. She smelled burning flesh. She snapped her head back and forced herself to breathe, not to go there. Not to let herself see anything but the beautiful ink work on his back, and his muscles knotted and needing her touch.

She changed the massage to soothe him, her fingers not digging so deep but moving over the tree and branches with reverence. She worked the skin over the crows with a gentle touch. The skulls rolling through the roots were given a much harsher treatment. So many of them. Some old, some newer. She didn't want to continue their game.

"How many men have you let screw you?"

The breath rushed out of her in an angry gush. "Oh my God. Are you kidding me? You can't ask a question like that. What if I asked you that question?"

"I'd have to answer honestly, that's the rule we set up. I'm not a coward. You ask, I tell. You want out of the game, you have to acknowledge you're afraid."

"You're being *such* a jerk."

"Babe, you knew the first fuckin' time you saw me that I was a jerk. Are you going to answer, or are you going to renege?"

She wasn't a quitter, and her answer would only seal the deal between them. She couldn't *ever* fall for this man. Not ever. He would eat her alive.

"None." She said it fast and kept working on his back, but she could feel the color sweeping up her skin.

"Fuck. Are you lying to me?" He half turned over to try to get a glimpse of her face.

She pushed him back down on the mattress, not wanting him to look at her. "What possible reason would I have to lie? It's my turn. How many women have you had?"

"Too many to count. Hundreds. Could be more. Probably in the thousands."

She closed her eyes and shook her head. She always, always had to remember that answer. This man was not for her, and he never would be. He was so far out of her league. She'd be better off with perverted Joseph the parasite than him.

"Okay, then."

She had worked her way down to the band of his jeans. "Are you feeling better?" She moved off of him to her side of the bed.

"Why haven't you been with a man?" Savage rolled over and once more reached out to the leg that was pitted and scarred, running his hand from her calf to the top of her thigh, rubbing gently as if he could remove the marks.

"My parents were both ill. My father had a heart condition and my mother had cancer. I was around eight or nine when my father's condition was discovered. I took care of both of them. They homeschooled me. They were wonderful, and my childhood was happy. I never felt deprived. I started working outside the home when I was a teenager to help bring in money, but I always went home as soon as I could. That didn't leave me a lot of time to find someone."

She wasn't going to tell him about the many dates she'd been on. The kisses that left her feeling ice-cold. Empty. She felt safer sitting up, keeping her back to the headboard. "Have you ever been married or had a child?"

"Technically, that's two questions, but I'll answer because you're being so honest. Never been married and never had a kid. You ever fantasize about bondage?"

"Bondage?" she echoed faintly. Her heart began pounding in her throat. Could he read her mind? What did he know about her? "Why are all your questions sexual?"

"You can't ask me that until you answer my question." There was amusement in his voice.

"Yes, but it scares me. It would definitely have to be with a partner I trusted."

"Doesn't the fear heighten the sexual intensity?"

"I wouldn't know, since I've never tried it, and won't with someone I don't trust. Maybe I'll never try it. How many women have you played this game with?" She wasn't going to let him win. Damn him, anyway. She would answer every question as honestly as she could, and she wouldn't be embarrassed if she ever saw him again.

"None. You're the first and the only, and there won't be another."

"Why?"

He turned his head to look up at her, his fingers around her leg. "Because you're the first woman I've ever met who is so fuckin' honest you turn me inside out, and I want to know everything about you."

That wasn't the answer she was expecting. Looking into his blue eyes, she felt her heart stutter. His eyes were like blue flames. Intense. Burning through her. It was difficult not to see the honesty there or hear it in his voice. It was a compliment. A genuine one, and coming from him, when he clearly didn't give them out easily, it meant too much to her.

"My turn."

He grinned at her and she knew she was in trouble. "Are you certain you don't want to just go to sleep?"

"No. I want to keep you talking. But you could go back to rubbing my head."

"You're so needy." But her hand dropped to the top of his skull and she began a slow, gentle massage.

"Were you going to audition with the band Thursday night?"

Her stomach knotted. This could be trouble. "No."

"Because you wanted to avoid me?" He turned his head again to look up at her.

She couldn't look away. "Yes."

"Because you're attracted to me."

"That's one of many reasons to avoid you, yes."

He gave her a slow grin, and this time, it lit his eyes. The smile didn't last long, but she'd seen it and she was happy she'd answered honestly.

"You do realize how bizarre this game is, don't you, Savage?"

"Yes. Are you going to go on Thursday night now that we've gotten to know one another better?"

"It's my turn to ask a question." She glared at him indignantly.

"You asked me if I knew how bizarre this game was and I answered you. You have to answer my question. Pay attention, babe."

"No. Absolutely not."

"You know if you don't come, I'm going to be here every single night until you do."

Her fingers stopped. "That's blackmail."

"And you know I'll do it."

He sounded all too happy to annoy her.

She took a deep breath. He wanted honesty. "Savage, you know it isn't a good idea that we spend a lot of time together. We aren't . . ." She didn't know what to say. "Compatible, for lack of a better word."

"Baby, don't fight the inevitable. I learned a long time ago not to do that. When you can't change things, you go with the flow. We're better friends than most people are. We might come from different worlds, but it doesn't matter."

"You aren't going to get hurt. I will."

There was a part of her that wanted him to deny that, but he didn't. He fell silent for a long time, so long she thought about abandoning her bed and leaving him to it. She could sit in a chair for the rest of the night.

Savage suddenly turned over onto his belly, his arm sliding around her hips, pulling her down so he could rest his head on her stomach, as if seeking comfort. She couldn't help but massage his neck. His arm was slung around her and he actually held her tight.

"Would that be worth it? You ran in front of a fucking truck to save my life. Are you saying you won't take the chance of being my friend because somewhere down the line you might get hurt?"

"I *would* get hurt," she corrected. He didn't go without women, and it would hurt every single time she saw him with another woman, just to use her sexually.

"Our friendship wouldn't be worth it to you?" he persisted.

There was an ache in his voice that tore at her heart, but she couldn't just respond without really thinking it over. Would it? Savage didn't have friends outside of Torpedo Ink. She instinctively knew that. She hadn't called the cops the way she should have when he crept through her window, which was creepy any way you looked at it, yet she didn't think of him as a creepy stalker.

Maybe the accident had tied them together in some way. But she knew it was far more than that. It was her personality, the way she was so drawn to him. She managed to give him whatever it was he needed. She drained off the rage and the need for violence swirling in him. More, she saw the good in him when not even he did. This wasn't about her personally; this was about what her presence did for him. It was also what he gave her. She needed to be needed. She was desperate to give herself to someone who really needed her. That was so ingrained in her, she didn't know how to live on a daily basis without some direction.

"You're thinking too much," he said, and turned his head to kiss her bare belly.

His lips just whispered over her, but it was a brand. A hot brand. She froze. "Savage. You can't do that. I mean it. If we're friends, you have to behave."

"I don't even know what that fuckin' word means." He turned his head, rubbing his face against that little strip of skin showing between her tank and her shorts, as if nuzzling her stomach.

She could feel the scrape of the shadow along his jaw. "Go to sleep. I mean it. I don't want to talk to you anymore."

"Two things and then I promise I'll be quiet."

She sighed and closed her eyes, her palm cupping the back of his head as he lay on her. "Just tell me. You're not going to shut up until you get your way."

"First, you're coming on Thursday to audition with the band. I don't want you to let them down on my account. Second, they'll offer you the gig, because you sing like a fuckin' angel. No one in their right mind would let you go. The money will be right and it's close to home. If you want to earn more, they'll offer you a bartending job."

"How would you know if I can bartend?"

"The members of the band found out as much as they could about you. You were a waitress and then a bartender. Sometimes both. You don't want to work the bar, then you could waitress for Alena. She's got her restaurant opened and it's always packed. So, plenty of work if you want the money."

"Savage, you're backing me into a corner."

"I know. I'm good at that shit."

His hand had slid down her thigh again, massaging the scars there. The sensation of his warm palm sent little darts of fire through her body. At the same time a shiver of awareness crept down her spine and fingers of desire danced their way up her thigh.

Did he know what he was doing? She doubted it. How could he know her reaction to just his light touch? He was rubbing her leg the way she massaged his head. Being sweet. But . . . he wasn't sweet. Savage wasn't the kind of man to do anything without purpose. He was very, very experienced in all things sexual. He knew she was physically attracted to him.

Narrowing her eyes, she glared at him and nearly shoved him off the bed, but then she realized he had gone to sleep. Just like that. Silently. He didn't snore. He didn't make a single sound. He just fell asleep, his breath coming and going from his lungs evenly.

Seychelle lay staring at the wall, her hand on his head, her heart pounding nearly as loud as the waves booming as they hit the cliffs.

FOUR

Seychelle pulled her Mini Cooper into the space allotted for parking in what was supposed to pass for the entrance to the garage at Doris Fendris's little home. Doris lived on one of the well-kept back streets of Sea Haven. The Victorian-styled houses had small but beautifully manicured yards surrounded by little fences overgrown with flowering hedges. Seychelle was very grateful for her choice of car and her ability to maneuver into small areas. For some unexplained reason, even the garage and space in front of the garage were tiny.

Of all the people she tended to visit on a regular basis, Doris was probably her favorite, because she was always upbeat. Her house smelled like fresh-baked cookies and it was always clean. The atmosphere was warm and welcoming. The porch was badly in need of repair, especially the front stairs. Seychelle carried her tools in the trunk of her car all the time. She wasn't the handiest with them yet, but she was learning. She'd discovered she could find tutorials on just about anything on YouTube, and she visited the website regularly.

She'd purchased nails and a few other items she thought she'd need, but really, Doris needed the wood on her entire front porch replaced. Seychelle wasn't quite up to replacing a porch yet. She'd bought the proper lengths of already cut wood necessary for the stairs, and then stained and sealed them herself. She thought she could pull up the old stairs and replace the boards with the new ones. She really hoped whatever the top boards sat on wasn't rotted as she feared it might be.

She needed to keep herself busy. The moment she stopped, her mind went straight to Savage, which wasn't a good thing. She thought about him far too much. She thought about the way his body felt next to hers and the way his hand felt crashing down on her nearly bare bottom. Long walks didn't wear her out, and she didn't sleep most nights. She hadn't gone to the club Thursday night because she knew Savage would be there and she'd be too tempted to take the job just to stay connected to him.

Instead, she'd driven to El Matador Beach and stayed in a bed-and-breakfast she'd found after her parents had passed away. It was her go-to place when she was upset. She spent a week there, taking a picnic basket and book and going to various hidden coves she'd discovered. She did her best to try to forget all about Savage. She rented a bicycle and spent time exploring places she'd never been before, and then walked for hours in order to rid herself of the restless energy she found she had—or the dark fantasy thoughts she shouldn't have.

Her phone rang the second day she was there. She saw it was a call from Savage and her heart went wild. It took every ounce of discipline she possessed not to answer it. He called on and off all that day and into the night.

Text messages began coming in. One after another. **You all right?** She didn't answer. A day later: **Getting worried, woman.** The temptation to answer almost overcame her good sense, but she didn't want to engage with him. The third day he had clearly lost his good mood. **What the fuck, Seychelle? Getting pissed here. I'm worried.**

Okay, that wasn't fair on her part. She didn't want to worry him. She just didn't want to get her heart broken. She thought a lot about what to say back. **I'm fine, just thinking about things. Tell the band thanks, I really appreciate that they liked my voice, but it would be better if they got someone else.**

Apparently, Savage was more adept at texting than she was. His reply took seconds. **You're going to get yourself in deep shit with this nonsense. And you damn well better not be smoking.**

She hadn't been, but the moment he sent that little order, she instantly felt like finding a pack of cigarettes. She didn't, because she had really wanted to quit. She started after her parents had died, when strangers around her seemed to be sucking the life out of her and she couldn't find a way to make them stop. She didn't know how to protect herself from the bombardment of their illnesses for the longest time, so she kept to herself as much as possible.

She'd been so exhausted she hadn't been able to move. Not just for a few days or weeks; it had taken months to recover after her father died. Even now, sometimes a long walk could make her lungs burn for air and leave her body exhausted.

"Are you going to sit in your car daydreaming, Seychelle?" Doris demanded, startling her. "Come out of there and have some tea and cookies."

Seychelle heard her phone play "Wrong Side of Heaven" by Five Finger Death Punch and knew Savage was texting her. He had stopped after their exchange eight days earlier. It had gone on for too long, and she'd let it, engaging with him because she couldn't help herself. That was the trouble. She just couldn't stop herself where he was concerned.

Ignoring her phone, she waved at Doris and hopped out of the car. "I was contemplating whether to start on the stairs right away or drink tea. I'm not the best carpenter, and if I mess up your stairs, it will be terrible. I won't have time to fix them before tomorrow."

"I have a back door in the kitchen, Seychelle, that leads to the outside," Doris said. "I can always use that if I have to. Let's have tea and sit on the front porch in the rocking chairs. It's ready now. It will get bitter and cold if we wait."

Seychelle couldn't help but admire the woman. She was just so pragmatic about everything. Her porch had needed repairs for a long while. The stairs were so bad that she had to avoid one of them to keep from falling through, and the railing around the porch was rickety, yet she was all smiles and welcoming. Her favorite thing was to sit with visitors on her porch in the rocking chairs and just talk.

"Sounds like a plan. You get the tea and I'll get the tools. I can get set up out here while you're getting everything together."

Five Finger Death Punch played again, warning her that Savage was getting restless with her lack of replying. It made her want to smile. She was certain if she texted him first, he would take his sweet time answering, but she never did. She wouldn't. She was lonely and she knew it. She didn't have friends her own age. She couldn't. She didn't know how to protect herself. It was easier just to stay in the little world she'd created for herself. When she needed to, she would find people like Hank and his really bad band, sing with them for a short while and then, when it got too much, she'd quit and walk away.

Doris waved at her, turned to open her screen and disappeared inside her house. Seychelle pulled her phone out of her back pocket and looked down at the message. **You aren't home.**

Her heart jumped and then accelerated. He was somewhere very close. She was almost afraid to inhale, afraid if she did, she'd take him into her lungs. She immediately texted back: **Visiting an old friend.** She thought that was very clever. She wasn't even lying.

Better be a female friend.

Sheesh, the man could text fast. Where had he learned to do that? Smiling, she sent a few laughing faces his way that told him nothing at all. He sent her back a series of hands smacking bare butt cheeks, which made her burst out laughing and grow warm at the same time. Truth be told, her panties went a little damp. Where did one even get emojis like that?

She pocketed her phone and carried the wood and then her pink toolbox up to the porch, feeling inexplicably happy. She loved sparring with Savage. It was insane and a little bit like poking a tiger, but it was thrilling and made her feel alive when most of her days were spent alone on long rambles, hiking to the waterfalls or walking the headlands.

Doris poured tea from her blue polka-dotted teapot into two mismatched polka-dotted cups. The saucers were different colors as well. It was Seychelle's favorite set out of all the tea sets Doris had—and she'd collected quite a few over the years. The little sugar pot was very cute, with hot pink polka dots, and the creamer holding milk had red dots.

Doris had a plate of oatmeal raisin cookies as well as chocolate chip cookies because she never wanted to be caught without something for her guests. The little table had plates and napkins because Doris believed in making her visitors feel special.

"You really don't have to fix my stairs, Seychelle," she said as she rocked gently and looked out over her small garden of roses. "You know I just love your company."

"I've really had fun learning all about it," Seychelle admitted, pouring genuine enthusiasm into her voice. "I don't think I'm ever going to be a master carpenter, but I like learning new things. This has been a challenge. I just hope I don't find dry rot or whatever they call it when I take off the top boards. The man at the mill told me I should have checked."

The tea was excellent as usual, a black currant, one Seychelle had never had before and probably wouldn't have thought of trying. She had learned Doris was very adventurous with her tea choices. When she'd asked her about it, Doris had laughed and said she had few ways left at her age to be adventurous.

"Well then, dear, I suppose I'll find my old pair of overalls and help you, although once I get down on my knees, you might need to call the fire department to get me back up again." Doris burst out laughing.

Seychelle laughed with her, feeling lighter than she had in a long while. Doris was genuine in her moments of sheer joy. "I don't think I'll need help. You can sit in the rocking chair and advise me."

"But there might be some cute single firemen," Doris objected. "I'll sacrifice the knees to find you a man."

As if on cue, Seychelle heard the unmistakable rumble of a Harley as it approached. She took a sip of the black current tea, her pulse kicking into high speed. Immediately, every nerve ending in her body went on alert. Her gaze jumped to the street. He was there on the bike, looking every inch the dangerous biker. He didn't so much as glance up to check if she was on the porch; he just drove right up as if he owned the place and was there every day, parked his Harley behind her Mini Cooper and got off with that hot fluid grace that took her breath every time.

"Oh my," Doris said, fanning herself. "It looks like we have company. I wore my watch with the heart monitor, and it's a good thing. That man would give any woman a heart attack."

"I agree one hundred percent, but let's not tell him. He's already arrogant enough," Seychelle whispered, taking a bite out of an oatmeal cookie and trying not to wish it was Savage.

She watched him stalk up the walkway like some jungle cat, setting her heart pounding. Muscles rippled visibly beneath the tight black tee he wore under his open vest with his Torpedo Ink colors. He didn't stop coming, taking the steps, his weight making them sag and creak, blocking out the view until he was the only thing she saw. His large frame. That broad chest. The intimidating muscles that went on forever. Eyes so blue they could be a glacier but burning so intense they were like a flame moving over her. Lines carved deep in his face. Strong jaw.

"Scared the crap out of me, woman. Don't fuckin' disappear on me like that again. Next time, I'll have the cops lookin' for you, and you know how I feel about them."

He bent and brushed a kiss on top of her head. Just that gesture, coupled with the intensity in his blue eyes, set her heart pounding.

"Would you care to introduce me to your friend, Seychelle?" Doris said, her voice a little faint. She fanned herself with her hand. "I can get a chair from the kitchen so he can join us."

"I'm Savage, ma'am."

He introduced himself because Seychelle couldn't find her voice. She pressed her fingers to her lips and stared at him, shocked that he could do that to her, just short-circuit her brain with that look on his face.

"Doris Fendris."

Savage threaded his fingers through Seychelle's left hand. "I'm her fiancé." There was a trace of amusement in his voice, although his expression didn't change. He looked as scary as ever. "Been missing her, and she forgot to check in with me again, so I came looking."

Doris's gaze dropped to Seychelle's bare finger. One eyebrow arched.

Seychelle tugged at her hand, finally managing to find her voice. "He's full of it. He's my *fake* fiancé."

"She says that because Ice hasn't finished the ring yet." The pad of his thumb slid over her ring finger once. "Looks like you're working on repairing the stairs?" He made it a question. "Have you checked the supports under them, baby?" He was already reaching for the toolbox. He drew his hand back and turned slowly to level his glacier-cold eyes on Seychelle. "What is this supposed to be?"

She did her best to glare. It was difficult when Doris giggled like a schoolgirl and fanned herself again. Savage's hand did look ludicrous hovering above her pink toolbox. Nevertheless, she refused to smile, sticking her chin in the air. "I presume you are speaking of my toolbox in that derogatory tone."

"Is that what you call this thing?"

"It is a perfectly good toolbox." She gave him her snippiest look.

"Seychelle." His tone said it all. "It's pink."

She raised her eyebrow. "I'm really becoming concerned over your lack of imagination when it comes to color. I've noticed your motorcycle is an unrelenting black. And then there's your clothes. All black again. There's a theme here. Black. You need color in your life, Savage."

Doris giggled again, drawing Savage's attention. "Miss Doris," he said, "Czar and Blythe's girls have jars and collect money when any member of Torpedo Ink swears. They have enough to go to college, I think, and then some. It's a good idea that you get yourself a jar about now."

Savage turned his complete focus back on Seychelle. "My motorcycle is *unrelenting* black? You're attacking my bike? My ride happens to be a 2015 Night Rod Special, not all black—it has gunmetal-gray trim, not to mention the gray skull."

There was a dark promise of retaliation in his voice. On his face. In his eyes. She liked sparring with him, but he could be intense. His Harley was his baby.

"You're attacking my toolbox."

"Babe. Really?"

"And you've never once suggested I get a jar for your foul mouth."

"You don't get a jar because you cause the swearing. Miss Doris makes cookies and she can use the money for bingo. Hand me one, babe, the chocolate chip. They smell great." He held out his hand.

Seychelle gave an exaggerated sigh, snagged the smallest chocolate chip cookie on the plate and gave it to him.

"Who's to say I don't love my toolbox just as much as you love your Harley?"

Instantly, Savage's expression softened. "Did someone special give you the tools, baby?"

She was teasing him. She didn't want him to feel bad.

Immediately, she shook her head. "No, I purposely bought pink so I could easily identify my tools when I took them to other people's homes. I didn't want to mix them up." In other words, she'd had tools taken multiple times and she didn't want to keep having to buy more, but she wasn't saying that in front of Doris. It would be repeated to every single one of the men and women who played bingo on Thursday nights. Doris would take it upon herself to reprimand anyone who came near Seychelle's tools.

"I bought the tools myself and I taught myself to use them. I'm fixing Doris's stairs before she falls through," she informed him, lifting her chin at him.

Savage took his time eating the cookie, all the while focusing on her face. "I think we'll continue this conversation at home, along with the one about letting me know where you are so I don't worry so much."

She narrowed her eyes at him suspiciously. "That reminds me. How did you find me? I didn't tell you I was with Doris."

"I've got eyes everywhere. You should know that."

Which didn't tell her anything. She glanced down at her phone. Was there some kind of tracking program on it? How had he really found her?

He finished the cookie, clearly enjoying every bite, ignoring her suspicious glare. "Excellent, Miss Doris. I'll have to tell Alena about your cookies. She loves different recipes for chocolate chip, and these are right up there with hers."

"Everyone talks about Alena's baking," Doris said. "Inez Nelson over at the grocery store said no one is better, and she would know. And it's just Doris, none of this Miss." She let out a little gasp. "I know who you are now. Inez told me all about you. You helped Donny Ruttermyer out when he got into trouble. That was so sweet of you."

"Savage is always sweet," Seychelle said, just to annoy him, her gaze glued to his face. She saw the flicker of heat in his eyes and knew it embarrassed him to be caught doing something nice. He turned those laser-cutting eyes on her, daring her to keep teasing him. Naturally, she couldn't stop herself. "Who is Donny Ruttermyer, Doris?" She asked the question deliberately, because it was the last thing he wanted her to do. She sent him a little taunting grin.

Savage let his burning gaze drift over her face and down her body in a slow, heated perusal that nearly made her catch fire. She felt as if he'd purposely ignited a wildfire deep inside of her.

"Goin' to get yourself in more trouble than you're already in, woman."

"Donny has Down syndrome and lives in the little apartment across the street from the grocery store, right above Donna's Gift Shop," Doris explained. "He's a good boy and usually is pretty good at taking care of himself. Inez and Donna Baker look after him. Jackson Deveau, the deputy sheriff, helps him most of the time, but Donny got into some trouble with his checkbook and Jackson wasn't around. Donny got very upset and no one could calm him down, so Inez sent for Savage. He took care of it right away."

"Why would Inez send for Savage?" Seychelle asked, all teasing gone. That didn't make any sense at all, and she really wanted to know.

Savage leaned back, gripping her bare ankle beneath her jeans with one hand while he snagged two more cookies off the plate with the other. His palm began to slide up and down over her calf and the scars there. He seemed to do that a lot, and she realized for the first time that not only did it soothe him, but he actually fed her energy that others drained from her. He didn't just take from her. He gave to her. He'd done it when they were alone together in the bedroom. She sat up straight, going very still as realization hit. That was part of the reason she found his company so exhilarating. He wasn't just taking.

"A couple of years ago, Czar and the others came to town and there were horrid men from another club in Inez's store destroying the place. They smashed things and were

pushing Donny around. They weren't going to pay for anything either," Doris said.

"We can change the subject anytime, Doris," Savage said.

Seychelle had missed him so much. Missed the way he
made her laugh. Missed the way he made her feel so alive.
The energy he provided. And she hadn't even realized until
this very moment, sitting on the porch with Doris, that Savage gave her back what those in need took from her. As
revelations went, it was a pretty big one. Huge. She had
always been the caregiver. The nurturer.

The idea that Savage didn't just take made her feel
strange. Self-conscious. As if she was taking from him
something she shouldn't be. Did he know? Was that why he
was always rubbing her leg? The scars that connected
them? She thought of her scars that way. His hand, under
her jeans, continued to slide up and down her leg slowly,
the pads of his fingers tracing the ridges and whorls of the
raised scars. She thought he'd done that for himself, and
she'd loved it. Now she didn't know what to think. She
nearly pulled away from him, but was afraid if she did, he'd
be hurt. She wasn't positive how she knew that, but she did,
just as she knew the more time she spent with him, the
more danger of getting her heart shredded.

"No, no, Savage. People need to know that you boys were
good to Inez and Donny. Czar, Savage and the others took
those bad ones out of the store and into the street, Seychelle.
Taught them a lesson too, right before the cops showed up.
Donny hero-worships those boys, and Savage in particular."

Savage let out a little groan. "Seriously, Doris? Half of
Torpedo Ink was there, not just me. I beat the shit out of
someone and you think that's a good thing?"

"Yes, I do," Doris said staunchly. "Sometimes there's
nothing else to be done. Those men would have hurt Inez
and Donny."

Savage heaved a sigh and shook his head. "Inez talks too
much."

"I think Doris is right," Seychelle declared, meaning it. "You do good things. You might look different, but you do very good things. He saved a little boy's life a few weeks ago. That's how we met. Dropped his bike in the road, scooped up the kid out from a truck coming straight at them and ran. Everyone else was just frozen and screaming."

"Oh my," Doris said. "Does Inez know about this?" She sounded breathless. "She always knows everything first, but she never said a word." There was no doubt Doris planned to tell every single one of her friends at bingo or cards.

"If she doesn't, don't tell her that bullshit story," Savage snapped. "It isn't true."

Savage's fingers never stopped moving on Seychelle's leg. The feel of his skin against hers was mesmerizing. Every stroke felt like a caress. Her nerve endings were raw, and his touch sent little sparks of electricity up and down her leg. She wasn't certain if it felt good or if it hurt, but it made her feel very connected to him, and she didn't want him to stop.

"It's true. You did lay down your bike and you did scoop that boy up and run to get him out of the path of the truck," Seychelle pointed out. She didn't want him to ever forget that he had saved that child. He would have given his life for that boy.

"And you shoved us both out of the way and took the hit," Savage said, his fingers suddenly gripping her calf like a vise.

He tilted his head back to look up at her, his glacier-blue eyes meeting hers, focusing completely on her in that way he had. He made her feel that he saw only her—that only she mattered to him. Her stomach did a slow somersault. Seychelle knew she was extremely susceptible to him, the need for him so deep, so physical, she knew she would have to guard her heart carefully if she was around him for even the briefest of times.

The moment she was near him, the craving for him seemed to grow. Now, knowing that he did for her what no one else in the world had ever done, what maybe no one else ever could do, added an extra layer of need to her addiction to him. He gave back to her. He nurtured her. And he had that draw of darkness in him that her body responded to. That was doubly dangerous to her.

At once, Doris's entire demeanor changed. She looked much older, the lines in her face deepening. "Seychelle." Doris breathed her name. "You were hit by a truck? Were you hurt? You never said a word to any of us." She put down the teacup, because her hands shook so badly she'd spilled some of the contents. "I couldn't bear to lose you, honey. You should have told me. This is terrible."

Savage began his slow massage again, up and down Seychelle's leg, from ankle to knee, his palm sliding over the raised scars. "Didn't mean to upset you, Doris. She's just fine. That's how we met and how she became my fiancée. Right then."

Seychelle could have kissed him. He knew exactly what to say to distract Doris.

"*Fake* fiancée, Doris," she reminded.

"Why fake, Seychelle?" Doris asked. "He seems like quite a catch, and you're not getting any younger. You run off anyone in the least interested in you."

"He's bossy. Really, really bossy," Seychelle pointed out. "You have no idea how bossy he can be."

Savage turned his head alertly toward Doris. "She have quite a few men interested?"

Doris nodded vigorously. "There's not a lot of women that look like Seychelle in town. She's a real looker and so sweet too. She walks down the street, and the next thing you know, they're coming out of the woodwork."

"Seriously? Just stop, Doris, we were talking about Savage, not me," Seychelle said, but she couldn't help laughing. How did he do that? One minute all the teasing was about him and the next the spotlight was on her. "In case you hadn't noticed, he's eating all your cookies and I can guarantee he won't gain an ounce of weight. Not one single ounce. I had two cookies and I'm going to have to jog for miles to keep from gaining ten pounds."

"I like that you're not a stick, woman." Savage sounded exasperated. "And I don't think you ate while you were away. You lost at least three pounds."

She had, but he couldn't know that. She made a face at him, and he grinned at her and then toed the toolbox.

"What's in that thing?"

"Tools, and don't make fun of my toolbox."

He leaned toward it, his hand slipping off her leg, leaving her feeling deprived. It was strange how much she found she had missed him. Not just verbally sparring with him, but his touch. She narrowed her eyes at him as he gingerly opened the toolbox as if it might bite him.

"Babe." One word. He looked up at her. "Really? What the fuck is this supposed to be?" He pulled out one of her favorite tools.

The handle was pink. She really liked it, not only because it fit nicely in her hand but because of the way the rubber felt. "It's a hammer, you moron. A perfectly good hammer. Since clearly you aren't in the least familiar with tools, I can go over them for you, name them and their uses if you'd like."

"Doris, you may need to put your hands over your ears and eyes for a minute so you can't testify in court."

"Oh dear, are you going to threaten her?"

"I do want to strangle her occasionally," Savage admitted, "but right now, I thought pulling her across my knees and paddling her sweet little ass would give me more satisfaction. Unfortunately, the snoop across the street is staring at us with a pair of binoculars, and she'd definitely call the cops on me."

Doris gasped and glared up at the curtains that were

peeled back from the upstairs window facing her house from the one across the street. "Sahara Higgens is a terrible person. She's always so jealous when Seychelle comes to visit me, and she spies on us."

Seychelle followed her gaze up to the second-story window. "Does she live alone?"

"Yes, she does. Her boyfriend left her a couple of months ago for someone much younger, and who could blame him? He's so sweet and tried so hard, but she was always doing everything she could to mess his life up. Now she's a bitter, nasty woman. She won't come to bingo or join our sewing circle or even come out of her house. Well, it's really *his* house. He lets her live there, even though it's causing friction in his new relationship, and she's so ungrateful. He should just evict her. Inez has to have Donny deliver her groceries."

Seychelle bit at her lower lip. That didn't sound good to her. Something about the way Doris's voice sounded when she was telling her about her neighbor bothered Seychelle— sent up a big red flag. "Does she have children, Doris?"

"No, he said she was too vain and didn't want to mess up her figure."

Seychelle shook her head several times, rejecting the idea of what Doris was saying. Her mind just couldn't accept that verdict. Doris sounded like a parrot, as if what she was telling them had been told to her over and over until it was forced into her brain, almost like hypnotism. "How old is she?"

"Maybe thirty."

"*Thirty?* I thought you were going to say your age," Seychelle said. "Her boyfriend left her for someone much younger? How old is he?"

"Well, honey, he hit on you several times. Brandon Campbell. I couldn't believe you turned him down. He's so handsome and sweet. He would always come over when she had her screaming fits and apologize to me. We'd sit and drink tea together. He'd ask my advice on what to do with Sahara, how best to handle her. He's still so good, comes to see her a lot of the time, trying to reason with her. I thought for certain you'd want to go out with him."

Savage had his piercing blue eyes on Seychelle's face. She knew she couldn't keep her dislike from showing on her face. Brandon Campbell was an arrogant bully. Extremely good-looking, charming, almost mesmerizing like a cobra, he'd definitely tried to get her to date him. Or at least sleep with him. When she hadn't, he had been very cutting to her. She'd seen right through him. He also had a psychic gift that he used, a subtle persuasion, and he didn't use it in a good way.

"How old was the woman he tossed his old girlfriend out for?" Savage asked.

"I think she had just graduated from high school," Doris said vaguely. "They aren't married. They live together."

"Isn't he pushing forty?" Seychelle asked.

"Oh, no, dear," Doris shook her head. "He isn't that old."

Seychelle inclined her head. "I'm afraid he is, Doris. He's a total creeper. You can't believe a man just because he comes off all charming sometimes. That woman he told you all about, she might just need a friend or two." She indicated the house across the street. "You say she has her groceries delivered? Does that mean you never see her leave the house?"

"Now that you mention it, no. She never comes out." Doris stared at the house for some time. "Did Brandon do something to you? Is that why you never went out with him? I've never heard you say a bad word about anyone, Seychelle."

"I didn't exactly say anything bad, only that you can't believe everything a man says just because he comes off as charming. He wasn't very nice when I turned him down."

Savage had somehow managed to slide back onto the porch until he was between her thighs. He'd done so when he'd scooped up several cookies. Laying his head back in her lap, he stared at the windows across the street. "Where does this creeper live now, Seychelle?"

The question was delivered in his very low voice. Very soft. Something about the tone sent a chill down Seychelle's spine. Looking at him, he appeared as relaxed as could be. Legs stretched out, one arm casually circling Seychelle's left thigh while the other was propped on her right one so he could feed himself the cookies. She wasn't buying into that seemingly tranquil pose, not for a moment. She could feel that well of violence in him rising like a red tide.

"Baby." He turned his head, his blue eyes meeting hers. "Asked you a question."

Her heart stuttered. Those eyes pierced right through her. Savage could look very scary when he chose. The arm circling her thigh shifted, and his palm slid back and forth in a mesmerizing glide on the back of her leg, as if he could soothe her, countering the absolute demand in his eyes.

"Not going to ask again, Seychelle."

"I don't keep track of him. I have absolutely no idea where that man lives."

"He bother you? Even after he decides to live with this child out of high school? He still come around and bother you? Is that why you call him a creeper?" His blue eyes never left her face. His posture never changed from that lazy panther relaxing on the porch. His voice was pitched low, almost gentle, but she caught the underlying menace, that ever-present rage swirling too close to the surface.

"I made it clear, Savage." She leaned down and deliberately took a bite out of the cookie he held in his hand. "It's getting late and I have to get working on the porch. I don't want Doris falling through the stairs. The second step is rotted almost all the way through."

"I'll take a look at it, but we're going to have to stick a couple of decent tools in this toolbox if you're going to insist on going around fixing things." He sat up. "And the conversation isn't over. You're racking up all kinds of trouble, baby."

"What does that mean?" Seychelle asked.

"Just don't want you saying I didn't warn you."

"I don't have a clue what you're talking about half the time." She found herself speaking to his back as he opened the toolbox again and peered inside. He ignored her, swearing under his breath at the multitude of pink tools inside the box.

Seychelle looked up at Doris. "Stop fanning yourself. Do you have any idea what he's talking about?"

"Does it really matter, dear? He's magnificent, and you're engaged to him." Doris looked very smug as she looked at the empty cookie plate. "I do wish it were bingo night."

"You *can't* tell your friends I have a fake fiancé." Seychelle had the unexpected urge to kick Savage right in the middle of that very broad back. She couldn't take her eyes off him as he stripped away the rotted top boards from the stairs. He did it easily, with no wasted effort.

"Not fake, Doris," Savage said without looking up. "Ice is working on the ring. I told him exactly what I wanted for her, Doris. She's got those eyes. I know everyone wants traditional diamonds." He yanked on a board on the next stair down, swore and shook his head. "Told Ice I wanted something to match her eyes. He showed me these killer blue diamonds. Dark, almost teal blue. Never saw anything like them. Just like her eyes."

"You'd better be making that up." Seychelle turned her blue eyes on Doris. "He's totally making that up to make me crazy."

"Babe." He gave her his one-word response, which he seemed to think spoke volumes.

She rolled her eyes. Doris fanned herself again. She was absolutely no help, and she clearly was going to repeat every word of the conversation to her friends.

"Seychelle, come look at this. It's all rotted. All of this has to be replaced. If it isn't, Doris is going to have an accident on her porch. I'm going to get the brothers out here tomorrow to take the porch apart. I'll measure everything now with your bullshit pink tape measure. We've got wood lying around the clubhouse takin' up space. It's a small enough job that we should be able to knock it out in an afternoon, if that's all right with you, ma'am." Savage glanced over his shoulder at Doris for confirmation. "Master and the others will be glad to get rid of the lumber. They get so much extra from all their jobs, and frankly, we don't have a place to store it. You'd be doin' us a favor."

Doris raised a hand to her hair. Seychelle could see it was trembling. She had a lot of pride. "If you're certain they need to get rid of the lumber. I can't pay them for it. It looks like it would be a lot."

Seychelle felt herself slipping just a little more down that inevitable path toward Savage. She didn't want to go there. She knew it was too dangerous, but the way he leveled his cool blue eyes at Doris and shrugged had her heart stuttering.

"You should see the stacks of lumber we have layin' around the place, ma'am, not only at the clubhouse, but it's spillin' over to Player's house now."

"Savage." Doris conceded with a nod. "May I get you some tea?"

Savage winced. "Don't drink the stuff, Doris. Blythe tried to convince me it wasn't poison, but so far, I think she's full of . . ." He broke off. "Let's just say no, thanks." He beckoned to Seychelle, and she put down her teacup and moved closer to examine the boards that he'd uncovered beneath the stairs.

Savage waited until she sat on the porch before he dug at the exposed network of wood with the claw part of the hammer, pulling it apart easily. "It's rotted. The lumber should have been treated and sealed. I'll talk to Master and

Player. They're good with this kind of thing. You don't want Doris or any of her guests falling through."

He wrapped his hand around Seychelle's ankle beneath the hem of her jeans, touching her bare skin, and the moment he did, a thrill shot through her, proving just how susceptible to him she really was.

"Doris, do you have another entrance you can use? One safer than this?" Savage's hand moved up and down Seychelle's calf while he questioned the older woman, instantly establishing a connection between them again.

"Through the kitchen. The back door leads to a porch."

"After we measure, I'd like to check that porch as well, just to make certain it's safe, if you don't mind. Seychelle, you do have a paper and pen or pencils in here, right?" He scowled down into the toolbox as if it might bite him if he put his hand inside.

"You're *such* a baby." She pulled a pencil and notepad from an inner pocket.

He groaned. "Who knew they made pink pencils and notepads? And why aren't you afraid of me the way everyone else is?" He shook his head and knelt to use the tape measure.

He had to repeat himself three times because she was fascinated with the way his muscles rippled when he was crawling around on the porch. The faintest hint of a smile lit his eyes, but he kept barking out measurements and then had Doris take them through her house to the back porch, which turned out to be in just as bad a shape as the front one. He measured that as well.

"We'll be back tomorrow, Doris," he promised, "but I've got a steak and some tofu marinating, so I need to get Seychelle home, if you don't mind."

"Not at all, Savage. It was wonderful to meet you. No need for you boys to worry about food—I can make something."

"Alena will not be happy if you do that, other than make

your cookies. She's going to want to meet you, and she always brings food. Tons of it, but when I tell her about your amazing cookies, she's definitely going to want to taste them," Savage assured her. "She gets her feelings hurt if she isn't the one bringing the food. I hope you don't mind letting her cook."

"No, of course not. I just need to do something when you're helping me," Doris said.

"You're helping us. Czar's going to be happy the lumber's gone. It's a fire hazard. And Alena gets to show off her cooking as well as meet you. You're doing us a huge favor, whether it feels that way or not. Expect a big turnout. The club will use this as an excuse to have a barbecue together. Another reason to thank you."

Doris looked so happy she might burst into tears. She nodded several times, her lips trembling, but she didn't say anything.

"Thanks for looking after Seychelle for me. She's a bit of a handful sometimes." He carefully replaced the tools, took Seychelle's hand and tugged until she went with him to her car.

"I'll meet you at home, babe."

Great. Now he was referring to her house as home right in front of Doris. She didn't know how to feel about that. Correction, she knew how she felt, but she also knew how she *should* feel.

FIVE

—⚡—

"Are you going to ask me how I got in the house to marinate my steak and your tofu and put the baked potatoes in the oven, Seychelle?" Savage turned his steak on the grill and flicked a quick look at her. Her tofu was on a separate mini grill.

She sat wrapped in a blanket, legs pulled up the way she liked on the chair so her chin could rest on her knees, watching him grill the meal. She'd already made the salad for them and had come outside dressed in her pajamas and the blanket.

"I can't believe you know I don't eat meat."

Was there a little challenge in her voice? He sent her a small smile. "Was in your home, babe. There wasn't much in your refrigerator. Definitely no meat. Tofu for certain. I'm observant when it comes to you." He'd made it his business to know as much as he could about her because she mattered to him. "You were going to tell me how I managed to get into your house while you were gone with the new locks I installed."

"I imagine you walked in. Or you dove in through the bedroom window. I was airing out the house. I did have the screen closed."

That long sexy hair of hers slid down one side of her face in a way that made him want to bury his fists in it and yank her face to his. She had just enough sass in her voice to let him know she knew she'd been wrong to leave her house open while she was out, but she wasn't going to admit it to him. He'd installed the damn locks for her, but she'd just walked off and left the house open. The screen might have been closed, but it hadn't been locked.

She'd gone off for a week and hadn't told anyone where she was—least of all him. Nor had she said when she'd gotten back. She'd ignored 90 percent of his texts until he'd said he was worried about her. She'd answered him then. He should have started right there.

"Yeah, babe. Walked right in, just like any fucker could have done. Like that pretend agent, Joseph Arnold, you tangled with. Spotted him at the local coffee shop with your old friend Hank, the guitar player who can't tune his own guitar. I imagine they'll be dropping by later for a visit. If not today, then in a couple of days."

Joseph Arnold had been around the headlands walking with a camera. Standing not far from her cottage, pretending to watch the ocean, but he was more interested in what was going on behind him in the empty house. The supposed music scout hadn't noticed Savage or any of the Torpedo Ink members, and eventually, after snapping pictures, he had joined Hank back at the coffee shop, acting as if he hadn't known where Seychelle resided.

Her color changed slightly. If it was possible, she went even more pale than she was naturally. "They don't know where I live," she denied. "I was careful."

She looked scared to him. Her long lashes swept down to veil her eyes. He speared his steak onto a plate and then put her tofu onto a separate plate, turned off the gas to both grills and walked over to her.

"Tell me about Brandon Campbell. What does he look like? Why don't you like him? What makes you think he's not a nice man? Because I could tell you thought everything he said to Doris about that woman was pure bullshit."

She was silent, rubbing her chin on the blanket, a little frown he found adorable on her face while she thought about what she was going to tell him. He liked that she always thought things through.

"He's extremely good-looking. Dark hair and eyes. Dresses nice but not over the top. He looks like he goes to the gym, keeps himself in shape. He's the kind of man women would look at when he walks into a room, and he knows it. He's very confident." She hesitated.

"Just say it."

"Do you believe in psychic talents?"

Savage regarded her silently. She was wrapped in her blanket, for the first time looking at him as if she was afraid he might disappoint her.

"Yeah, babe. I know psychic talents are a real thing. I think most people have them, they just don't develop them. Why?"

She looked relieved. "Because Brandon Campbell has one and uses it as a kind of persuasion, almost, in my opinion, like a date-rape drug. He influences those he talks to, swaying them to do whatever he wants, to believe whatever he wants them to believe. He definitely is capable of controlling someone or taking away their self-esteem. I think he persuades Doris to believe anything he says. I think he's controlling that woman in his house. He definitely tried to use his voice on me when he asked me out."

Savage's gut tightened into a thousand knots. *He* was capable of controlling with his voice. Persuading. Training. He could use it, and he had. Often. Over and over. He could hear the condemnation in her voice when she talked about Brandon Campbell. What was she going to think about him? He was far, far worse.

"Come on, babe, let's eat while it's hot."

"Do you think Hank and Joseph are going to come by my home this evening?"

"They aren't here right now, and we're not going to waste a good meal worrying about them." But he wasn't leaving her tonight, no matter what she said. He had a bad feeling she was going to be paid a visit. A third man had been sitting at the coffee shop with Hank and Joseph. He looked like a real charmer to Savage. He looked exactly like the man she'd just described as Brandon Campbell. What were the odds that Campbell would meet up with Arnold and Hank?

Even after Savage had his little "talk" with his sassy little lady, if he had to spend the night outside in the cold, he planned to stay right where he was. He held his hand out to Seychelle. She took it without hesitation and stepped onto her porch with her bare feet. He just shook his head. She was already cold in the foggy air, but she persisted in not wearing shoes.

"It was nice of you to cook dinner," Seychelle ventured, placing two bowls of salad on the table for them.

He sat down across from her, pissed at her. Pissed at himself. He knew he shouldn't be there. He'd left determined not to come back. If he stuck around, he wasn't going to be able to give her up. She was too big of a temptation. He'd lasted twenty-four fuckin' hours and then he'd come back to her—but she hadn't been there.

He glared at her as he cut up his steak and watched her carefully butter her potato. "A week. Seven fuckin' days. You just took off without a word." She'd lasted a week. He hadn't lasted twenty-four hours. Hell. He was totally obsessed. Like some stalker he'd have to hunt down and kill if they acted the same. "Lost a lot of sleep over you."

Her lashes lifted, and her gaze collided with his. "You're really angry with me."

"Damn straight. You scared me. I don't get scared. Nothing scares me. You disappearing like that, without one fucking word to anyone? Not answering when I called or texted? Yeah, baby, I'm fucking pissed."

He ate the steak, contemplating what he was going to do with her, because he wasn't giving her up. Figuring out how to get her to understand what he was and what he needed and how she was going to have to agree to be all that was a huge fuckin' problem—especially after what she'd just said about Campbell.

Seychelle sat across from him looking like an angel. She smelled like heaven. She was so beautiful he could barely breathe just looking at her. "Why'd you take off like that?"

"You know why." Her voice was very low. She ate a bite of salad.

"If I knew, I wouldn't be asking you, now, would I? Didn't I tell you I prefer answers?"

She frowned, and again her lashes lifted, her blue eyes meeting his. "You scare me. I asked you straight out if being friends with you was going to end up with me being hurt. You know it will. Physical hurt isn't the same as emotional, Savage. I'm not built to take a lot of emotional pain. I've gone through enough for a lifetime."

He held her gaze for a long time. Letting her see he wasn't going anywhere. She didn't want him to go. She was having a difficult time overcoming fear. He couldn't blame her. She saw things in him others didn't. They saw the outside of him and were scared. She not only saw the outside, but she caught glimpses of other, dangerous traits.

"You don't want me going anywhere." He made the statement for her.

"Maybe not," she conceded.

"You're not a coward." He indicated her plate. "Eat your food, babe. Should be great—it's Alena's recipe, and she's always the best. You lost weight while you were gone. And tell the truth about wanting me to stay. Just admit it to yourself and admit it to me. I need to hear you say it. It might go a little way toward getting you out of trouble, although I doubt it."

Her blue eyes met his again. She must have finally seen that he meant that shit. He was fighting to keep himself under control. She really had scared him, and that wasn't a good thing to do. He hadn't realized it was even possible. Her lashes veiled her expression.

"Fine. You're right. I don't want you going anywhere. I don't know why. You're as annoying as hell." She started eating. "And the tofu is wonderful."

She made him want to smile. It wasn't getting her out of trouble; in fact, he was planning on asking more questions once they got in bed. Seeing if she was up for a round of sinful daring. She didn't back down from a challenge. He needed to start teaching her. Training her. She was an incredible human being. Incredible. How had he managed to find her? How come he wasn't strong enough to save her? He had thought he was. He'd left her thinking he was. But then she hadn't answered his text and the bottom had dropped out of his world.

"You're frowning, Savage."

"Did you start smoking again?"

"No. I wanted to. I thought about it, but I'd already quit, so it seemed silly. What are we doing? Really, Savage, what are we doing?"

He watched her eat. She was beautiful even when she ate. Delicate. Refined. "You got under my skin, woman. Was going to do the right thing and leave you alone. I know you're too damn good for me, but I couldn't stand not having some connection to you. Just a small one."

Her lashes lifted again. A quick glance. His statement meant something. He could give her truth. It was all he had to give her.

"That's a nice thing to say. I have to admit, I liked hearing from you, even though I'd made up my mind it was for the best we didn't see each other." She ate another bite of salad.

"You didn't answer right away."

"I had to think about it."

"Babe, you know me. We have a strange connection and you see inside me. You know what kind of man I am. You don't do that to me. When I reach out to you because I'm looking to see you're all right, you fucking answer me or there's going to be trouble. Consequences. And don't tell me we barely know one another. You know what I'm like even when you don't want to."

Seychelle pushed the food around on her plate, sat back and picked up her drink. "We weren't even going to be friends."

"We were always going to be friends. Don't kid yourself. It didn't matter whether or not I was here with you, we were going to be friends. I told you, I have Torpedo Ink and I have you." He indicated her plate. "Are you finished?"

She nodded and stood up. "Thank you for cooking tonight. I'll do the dishes if you want to clean the grills." She frowned. "Where did those grills come from?"

"Transporter and Mechanic dropped them off for me. Once I knew you were back in town, I knew I'd need them. They're small, but they get the job done." He liked watching her move around, filling the sink, doing little things that were domestic. He didn't know why. He did his own dishes as a rule and never considered it anything but a task.

Watching Seychelle, doing dishes became something altogether different. He leaned back in the chair, eyes half-closed, legs stretched out in front of him, and found himself content. At peace. For just those few moments, with the sound of the ocean in the background and the scent of this woman drifting through the small room, filling his lungs, the demons always howling for freedom had quieted.

"Tell me what's really wrong, Savage. I don't like you so upset."

Seychelle's voice was that pure tone, like an angel's, slipping beneath every guard until she wrapped herself inside him. That was how she got in. He rubbed his hand over his aching chest. He was a big man with a lot of muscle, but still, she got in.

He was used to pain. Taking it. Giving it. He never let pain get to him. He never thought anything could take pain away or give it to him in a way that would distress him to the point that he couldn't eat or sleep. Or even think clearly. She'd done that to him.

Savage didn't answer her right away, contemplating what he could say. He would never give Seychelle less than the truth. In this case, he wasn't certain he knew the truth, only that he had to have her in his life. That was terrifying when nothing ever scared him. He couldn't afford to be out of control. He couldn't have anything in his life be outside of his control. He was too dangerous. He lived carefully. He was regimented in the way he lived. He had to be, in order for everyone around him to be safe.

She glanced at him over her shoulder, that hair of hers, all golden and platinum, soft silky strands, flying as she turned her head. His stomach dropped. It shocked him that she could do that to him without even trying. It wasn't like she was trying to be sensual. She wasn't trying to seduce him, yet she was the most seductive woman he'd ever met.

Looking at her, he couldn't stop his mind from seeing the erotic images of her bent over the table while he stripped those little shorts off her body, baring her cheeks to him. She had pristine skin. Flawless. A perfect canvas for a man like him. He'd dreamt about her, tied, body stretched out, completely naked, tears in her eyes, that liquid his. All his. She would wait. Unable to see him as he stood behind her. Never knowing when the lash would fall. When it would land across her, leaving his marks on her. She wouldn't make a sound because it wasn't allowed. Only her tears. Those were his. Those she could give him.

Just the thought put so much steel in his cock he could barely contain the erection. His jeans were stretched so tight the material hurt. His skin hurt where the scars were tight, but they gave way to the scorching-hot blood filling his cock at the thought of having his own woman willing to put herself in his hands. Giving herself to him. Surrendering to him when his cravings grew so dark there was no containing them.

In all the years of needing relief from his demons, he'd never once wanted or looked for a woman of his own. Until now. Until Seychelle. Now he couldn't conceive of another woman meeting his needs or satisfying his dark addictions.

"There are too many things wrong to even start," he admitted. His voice came out low. Velvet soft. Whispering over her. He could see the results, the way goose bumps rose on her skin. She was very susceptible to him. Receptive to his voice. She was as connected to him as he was to her.

Deliberately, he dropped his hand over his cock, massaging the terrible throbbing ache. It hurt like hell. Made him feel alive. His reaction to her was real. His erection was real. He hadn't commanded it. He hadn't put stripes on a woman's body to get an arousal. Just the images in his mind of them on her skin, the sight of the scars on her leg, and his cock was fuller and hotter than it had ever been.

There was a part of him that knew—if she'd been his woman—he would have just stood up, caught her by all that glorious golden hair and brought her to her knees right in front of him. Or he would have taken her on her hands and knees and pounded into her, relieved the brutal, vicious, *glorious* ache in his cock.

Her gaze followed his hand, just as he knew it would. He saw the way her nipples peaked beneath the racer-back tank she wore at night. She had lush, generous tits. Full and round. He wanted to see her nipples; they appeared as if they were generous as well, the kind he could spend time with. He had all kinds of fantasies about nipple play since he'd met her.

The tip of Seychelle's tongue touched her lips, wetting them so they glistened in the light spilling in from the window. The ocean cast a silvery tone to her hair and a glow over her body.

"I told you I knew all sorts of sinful, dirty things. Do you want to learn any of them? I'm in the mood to teach some of them to you if you're not afraid to learn."

It was a challenge, delivered in a low, sexy voice. Deliberate. Velvet soft. His voice mesmerizing. She knew his voice could compel, and she was susceptible. She had a choice: to let herself fall under his spell or tell him to go to hell. He waited, his lungs burning. Raw. His face an expressionless mask. Eyes, twin blue flames.

Her gaze jumped from his hand massaging his cock to his eyes. That was a mistake on her part, because he could hold her captive with his gaze. She should have remembered that. Her tits rose and fell with every ragged breath she drew. He had to be so careful. He didn't want to lose her, and he didn't want to lose control. Demons shrieked at him. The monster in him rose fast, howling to be let loose.

"The dishes can dry all on their own. Put the towel down." He waited to see if she would obey him. That was always the first step. The hardest.

She stood spellbound as he unzipped his jeans. Casual. She had no idea what he was going to do. Fear crept into her eyes, but she put the towel aside and stood in front of him, waiting. *Bog*, she was wonderful. So courageous. He hadn't even earned her trust. He intended to do just that.

"Do you use toys to get yourself off?" He kept his voice low. Casual.

He'd talked about jerking off in the hospital. She'd been under the influence of pain medication and maybe she wouldn't remember. He was commando under his jeans, and the relief to his cock was tremendous. The cool night air hit his shaft, those tight bands that were stretched so wide the pain was part of the pounding pleasure. He thought it was possible his cock might explode, it was stretched so thick with rich hot blood. He wrapped his fist around the pulsing shaft and waited for her answer.

"I have a toy," she whispered. "It fits over my clit." Her fascinated gaze was fixed on his fist, lazily beginning to pump his cock.

"Have you ever gotten off with it?"

She shook her head. Once more her tongue moistened her lips, and his cock nearly jumped out of his hand in response.

"Babe, get it out. You're going to need it."

She stood very still as if she might not do what he said. He didn't tell her again. He just stayed sprawled out in the chair, cock in hand, watching the expression on her face. The hunger in her eyes. There was so much mystery to Seychelle. So much about her he didn't understand.

She should have just kicked him the hell out, but she never did. She laughed most of the time when he was around. She never took offense at anything he said or did. She was the most peaceful person he'd ever been around. And then there was this . . . She gave him this—her trust when he hadn't earned it. She seemed like a little angel, and yet there was such a wicked side to her.

"It won't work." She turned away from him and went into the bedroom to the bedside drawer. He could still see her clearly through the doorway from his chair.

"Do you have the batteries in upside down?" He let his amusement show.

"Very funny." The return was sarcastic, but there was laughter in her voice. That damn fuckin' dimple of hers appeared, and his cock twitched hard in response. She held up the little toy. "I've tried it several times. I never get off."

"Even after you met me? No fantasies?"

"I'll admit, I didn't bring it with me when I left for the week. I definitely should have."

It was a mistake on her part to remind him of the week from hell he'd had while she was gone. "Are you slick now, just at the idea of doing something dirty with me?"

"Of course." She didn't lie, but then, she never did with him.

"Grab two of the pillows. Put them in the middle of the bed. Take off your shorts. If you want, you can take off your tank as well. If you're more comfortable, you can leave it on."

Savage watched his little angel walk to the edge of the bed, shimmy out of her shorts and lay the two pillows in the middle of the bed. She had that toy in her hand. Her hips were perfect. Curved from her small waist, forming the lower half of a wonderful hourglass. Her skin was just exactly as he knew it would be—a pristine canvas.

He nearly groaned aloud. Fire radiated up his groin and spread through his body. He would never be able to get that vision out of his head now that he'd seen it. Now that he knew exactly what was hidden beneath her clothing. Like her tits, she had generous hips and that sweet ass. He had done his best not to fixate on her body or her skin, but it was far too late now. His balls grew hot and tight, boiling with the need to be free.

"Crawl onto the bed, baby. You need to lie belly down, hips over the pillows. Fit that little toy over your clit and turn it on the lowest setting. I'll be right there." If he could walk. "I don't want you turning around. I just want you lying there, waiting for me. Anticipation is half the fun."

He didn't take his eyes off her as he pulled his shirt over his head and tossed it aside. She didn't hesitate this time, climbing up onto the bed, knees and hands placed carefully, her gorgeous ass swaying as she crawled to the center of the mattress. The two pillows pushed her bottom into the air, presenting her perfectly to him.

Savage took his boots off, and then shoved his jeans off, making his way slowly to the bed. She was so beautiful waiting there for him. Laid out for him. She obeyed him. Not once did she glance back to see what he was doing, and he was deliberately silent. She had discipline. She'd need it if he really did what his mind kept telling him to—make her his. He knew he shouldn't, but why the hell had fate thrown her in his path if not to give her to him?

He slid onto the bed beside her, turning his body so that he had a little bit of room. He was going to need it. "You do know that you scared the hell out of me, right, baby? No one has ever done that. Not since I was a little kid."

He rubbed her gorgeous bare cheeks in a circular motion. Let his hand slide just a little close to her entrance to feel her heat. He wanted to taste her. Pump his cock hard into her. He knew better. One small victory at a time. This one was the most important right now.

"You gotta pay for that shit, Seychelle. That, and not answering me. I didn't like that. When I call you, when I text, you answer me first thing. I don't fuckin' care what you're doing, you stop and answer me so I know you're safe. You're not to make a sound unless you come. Not one sound. Turn that little toy to medium."

He leaned down and nuzzled her bottom. First one cheek and then the other, allowing the bristles along his jaw to rub her tender skin. Without warning, he swatted her hard. Over and over. At first he switched cheeks and ensured he never hit the same place twice. Her cheeks turned bright red with his handprints. She started to struggle instinctively, just a little, but she didn't cry out.

Demons roared. His body went crazy. Joy surged through him. He hadn't felt this way in years—if ever. *Never*, whispered the devil. *Never*. This was real. This was the way he was meant to feel. This was why his cock was so hard, so full, in spite of the scars.

"Kick it up, baby, the vibrator, kick it up higher," he instructed. She had to stay with him. She had to keep going. He rubbed his hand over those marks. His marks. On her. Seychelle. His woman.

She settled, her hips bucking, and he pressed his body tighter against her, his cock so hot he knew she felt him like a brand. His fist jerked hard in time with her frantic hips. He could see his seed marking her white skin, long strings of pearly white leaking from the sensitive crown, a small preview of what was to come. Threads tying them together.

The sight of her ass red with his prints was so arousing to him, he increased the pace and the strength of his strikes, this time repeating them on the places he'd already smacked her so that the color turned the shade he craved to see. Her body shuddered, writhing, her breathing changing from ragged to labored to strangled as she moaned in a long desperate cry of pleasure that went on and on.

He fisted his cock and pumped hard. It was frantic and wild. Out of control. It didn't take much. He erupted like a volcano, long ropes of hot seed spurting over her bloodred ass. He came hard, violently, a long, brutal orgasm that went on forever. Heaven and hell. So perfect.

There was absolute satisfaction in knowing those dark red handprints he'd left on her would stay for a long while. "Turn your head toward me." He kept his voice low. Velvet soft. Commanding. She'd come just as hard as he had. He wanted to write his name all over her. More importantly, her tears belonged to him. They would always belong to him.

Reluctantly, she obeyed him, lifting her head slightly and turning it. Long strands of silky-soft hair fell over her face. He smoothed it back and leaned into her, his lips moving from her chin to her eyes, catching every tear as another shudder of pleasure went through her body. Ripple after ripple, little aftershocks. He wanted to be in her, feeling every one with her, but he had the satisfaction of knowing she'd given him her surrender. And her trust. And this—her tears.

He tasted every one. Salt, wild strawberries and honey dripping down her face. "Was that dirty and sinful enough for you, baby?" he whispered in her ear, his lips moving over that perfect little shell. He caught her lobe in his teeth and tugged.

"I think it was, Savage, thank you very much. I think. If I can stop crying. It hurt. And it felt fantastic."

He kissed his way down her neck, because he couldn't help himself. He bit that soft skin, but gently, not the way he wanted or needed to. "Which was it? Hurt or fantastic?"

She was silent for a moment, her blue eyes still liquid. Her lashes spiky. The sight set his heart tripping and his body stirring.

"I'm not certain. Both. Mixed together. I couldn't separate them. The feeling was explosive, but terrifying at the same time."

"Makes you feel alive, doesn't it?" He flashed a grin and pressed a kiss to the corner of her mouth. "Those tears are always mine, Seychelle. You remember that."

She didn't reply, her blue gaze drifting over his face, seeing things she shouldn't see. She always had.

"Give me the toy and don't move. I'll clean you up and take care of you." He held out his hand, giving her no choice.

She gave him the vibrator. It fit in his palm and he slid off the bed and went to her bathroom. She would have antibacterial soap to clean her toy with. Sure enough, it was right there, under her sink. He cleaned the toy himself, and then got a warm cloth for her. He was dick enough not to want to wash himself off of her. He liked claiming her. For him it wasn't about teaching her down-and-dirty sex. It was about putting his stamp on her. Proclaiming to the world—and to her—that she belonged to him.

Savage was very gentle as he washed her clean. He didn't feel gentle. That devil in him rejoiced at the marks on her. He dried her off with a towel very thoroughly. He found arnica lotion under her sink and grabbed that as well. "I'm going to rub lotion on your bottom so you hopefully don't bruise."

"I'd like to think you got carried away in the heat of the moment, but I don't think you did," Seychelle murmured. Her voice was muffled by the sheets. "You were really upset about me disappearing on you, weren't you?"

"It was both." He began rubbing lotion into the marks on her ass. The handprints were beautiful. Very defined. He loved seeing them there. He massaged a little deeper, using a circular motion, pushing the lotion into the heat of his prints, his stamp on her. He wanted to make certain he didn't leave any lasting effects on her, no matter how much the monster in him howled for that very thing. "Your ass is gorgeous, baby. Just like everything about you."

He needed to distract her from the question she was asking. He was very conflicted about Seychelle—about himself and how to fit her into his life. He knew what he was and had accepted himself and had for years. He bent his head and brushed a kiss into the heat of those dark red, now almost purple prints. He loved seeing them on her just the way he loved the scars on her leg. They were his. She'd given him those scars. She'd offered up the perfection of her pristine ass, never once pulling away from him, even when he was far too rough for her innocence. And she'd responded to his roughness. Exploded. Detonated. That was dangerous.

"Why did you let me get so tough on you?" He kept his hands gentle. Needing to be gentle with her, even though the monster in him roared with happiness. He smoothed the lotion over the roundness of her cheeks, following the dark red prints to the sensitive seam connecting her cheeks to her thighs.

She didn't answer him, her blue eyes drifting over his face. Sometimes he swore she saw right into him, into places so deep he didn't even see.

"You going to answer me?" he finally asked, because if she wasn't answering, that meant something.

"I'm thinking about it. I need to shower. I like to go for a walk after dinner. Finding out I like dirty and sinful a little too much is shocking, especially when it involves you smacking me when I'm using a toy. I have to spend a little time contemplating that."

"Are you going to get embarrassed on me and throw me out?"

"No. Should I? I asked to learn something dirty and sinful, and you gave me what I asked for. Something."

"Something simple," he clarified, hoping to intrigue her. He pulled away from her. The now dark purple prints on her beautiful, perfect bottom were beginning to make the monster in him crave more. He rolled off the bed and set the bottle of lotion on the nightstand. She'd need more to ensure she didn't bruise.

"Great. Now I'm going to have to wonder: If that was simplistic, what would be even more?"

He gave her a grin over his shoulder as he pulled on his jeans. "Something a little dirtier and just a little more sinful. You'll have to tell me what you want to learn next time. I'll get those grills cleaned while you take your shower. We can walk afterward."

He wasn't going to let her separate herself from him if he could help it. Even if he had to find a way to give her up as a partner, he knew he would need her in his life. He just had to figure out how to keep her safe. He was already close to the end of one of his cycles. He could feel the darkness rising in him like the inevitable tide. It was bound to swamp both of them if he let it.

Savage resisted giving her a swat on her gorgeous ass, but it took discipline to walk to the table, recover his boots and make his way outside. He heard the shower go on a few minutes later. That woman. Why in the hell did a woman like her put up with him? They had a connection, a deep one forged when she'd saved his life, delivering herself up like a sacrificial lamb. Hell. He already thought of her as his. That was so fucking dangerous.

Seychelle came out of the house looking like an angel. Dressed in soft leggings that clung to hourglass hips and thighs. Lavender with little sprigs of flowers running down them. He wanted to smile when he saw the pattern because it was so completely absurd but so utterly perfect on her. Her T-shirt was ribbed, a soft pastel that matched the darker purple of the floral roses scattered in the leggings. A heavy knitted cardigan fell to her knees, but was open.

Savage held out his hand to her and waited until she took it. There was just the slightest hesitancy, but then she stepped forward and allowed him to close his much larger hand around hers. That hesitancy worried him. Seychelle, for all her innocence, wasn't a woman inhibited in any way, especially with him. She wasn't embarrassed by what they'd done, and she'd fully participated. She was receptive to him whether she wanted to be or not.

"You going to be warm enough? The fog's rolled in."

He began walking toward the bluffs across the street. The mist was heavy, rolling in off the ocean, a heavy gray film that was going to obscure vision on the roads soon. He brought her closer to the warmth of his body, tucking her under his shoulder, matching his longer strides to her shorter steps.

"This sweater is surprisingly warm." She was silent a moment. "My mother made it. She made three different sizes of the same cardigan because I said how much I loved it."

There was an ache in her voice, and he tightened his arm around her. She was giving him things he knew instinctively she didn't give anyone else, just as he gave her things he never gave to anyone else.

"I was nine when I told her I loved the pattern."

"She loved you a hell of a lot, *moy angel*. I know you

didn't have her for very long, but she loved you. That matters."

He made the mistake of looking down at her. Those eyes saw too much. That woman could see inside him when no one else could. Damn her. Damn him for being so fucking exposed. He didn't know how she got in like she did. He didn't want her sacrificing herself for him because she pitied him, but then who the hell was he kidding? He'd take her any damn way he could get her. But he wanted her to want to be with him for him.

"It does matter, Savage," she answered softly. "Thank you for reminding me. I think I need that every now and then." She gestured toward the wild sea. "That's so crazy tonight. I love how it's always changing."

The ocean was roaring, throwing white waves high into the air, slashing at the sea stacks and bluffs. The wind tugged at the high grass on either side of them as they walked along the narrow dirt trail. The grass bent first one way and then the other, rolling like the waves.

"If you had to choose between a mediocre marriage where you're comfortable but not really in love but you have children, or one where you're both wildly in love but can't have children, which would you choose?" Savage asked.

Seychelle was quiet, thinking it over. "Comfortable but not in love. No children but wildly in love. I've always thought I would want children, but I know I want to be loved. I also know it's very important to me to love the man I'm with. I'd have to choose being wildly in love. That sounds like I'd be living in a fantasy world, but I know myself and I wouldn't be very happy if I knew that the man I was with didn't really love me, nor I him." She looked up at him. "Same question."

"I want my woman to love me, and I'd never take on a woman without loving her. Why do you prefer to hang out with older people?" He rubbed the pad of his thumb over her knuckles.

"Often, they're lonely and they need someone to care, and I like to listen to their stories."

He remained silent, knowing there was more. She was struggling to find the words. Struggling to decide whether or not to tell him.

"I don't have control. I was never able to learn it. I try every day, but I just don't have the ability to control certain things I need to when I'm around people. The older people give me a kind of peace most of the time. I don't know any other way to explain it."

There was no doubt in Savage's mind that every word was chosen with care. He needed to think about her answer. She'd revealed something of extreme importance to him.

"Why a motorcycle club?"

"Freedom. We needed to feel free, and there isn't a better way to feel free than on a motorcycle going down the highway."

He brought her hand to his mouth and scraped his teeth along her knuckles, his gaze fixed on the powerful waves rushing toward the bluffs, thundering and roaring, with a vicious storm roiling beneath the surface. His life was like that. "Have you always felt you were unable to be in control?"

"Yes." She answered without hesitation. "Why do you suppose, when I've never responded before to sexual stimulation, I responded tonight to the combination of pleasure and pain?"

It was his turn to take his time and think carefully before he responded. "To answer your question, I have to ask another question. Is that fair with our rules? Will I get a pass?"

"Yes."

"When you read or watch movies, what kinds of books or movies most get you off?"

She frowned. "No movies. Sometimes the darker porn works. Books sometimes are interesting, but not enough to get me off."

She was absolutely perfect for him. Honest. Able to communicate. Be direct.

"I think the situation was different, exciting, sinful and dirty, just the way we talked about. A fantasy you'd never had with anyone, and you were daring enough to try it," Savage said. "What do you think appealed to you about the situation?"

"It made me feel alive. Hotter than hell. Bad."

There was more. He knew there was, she just abruptly cut it off.

"Would you go for it again if you had the chance to learn more dirty, sinful things with me?" Savage asked.

Seychelle again spent a few moments giving his question some thought. He was very grateful he was as disciplined as he was. Her answer meant too much to him. He turned her away from the bluffs, back toward her cottage. The wind was just a little too biting.

"Given the opportunity, yes. Absolutely. Who else am I going to take advantage of?" She sent him a sassy grin. "What would you do if your wife cheated on you?"

He answered without hesitation. "Hunt down the man she cheated with. If he was a friend who knew me and betrayed me, I'd kill him, but he'd take a fuckin' long time to die. If it was some poor bastard who didn't know he was messing with the wrong woman, I'd beat him within an inch of his life and tell him not to come back. Then I'd go to my wife and find out what the hell went wrong and why she didn't come and talk to me about it. Then she'd be punished."

"Punished?" Her gaze jumped to his again.

"Punished." Savage repeated the word without hesitation. "Never pretended I was one of those really nice men, baby. You knew that from the first time we met."

They were close to the cottage. He had texted his brothers to come, keep an eye on things, and as they approached the narrow street that was really no more than an alleyway between her cottage and the field overlooking the bluffs, his cell vibrated. He pulled the phone from his pocket and glanced down.

Stalker-scout Joseph Arnold and the asshole guitar player who couldn't tune his own guitar, Hank Waitright, had walked right into Seychelle's house as if they owned the place and were waiting for her. Savage angled himself and Seychelle as they approached the house so they couldn't be seen from the doorway or window.

"Babe, go on in. I'll be right there. I want to make sure my bike's locked up. I put it in the garage, but I didn't secure it in case you kicked me out."

She rolled her eyes. "I've never kicked you out."

"You've thought about it."

Seychelle smiled. "That's true. But now you're showing me really dirty, sinful things, so I guess I'll have to keep you around for a little longer."

He watched her walk right up to the door, no hesitation. Head up. That golden hair swinging. Her hips. He knew she carried his prints on her skin, and just that knowledge had his cock aching. He liked the feeling. She said she felt alive. That was the way she made him feel every minute.

She froze just inside the door with it still open. She was smart, his woman, and she didn't turn around to alert the two to the fact that she wasn't alone. She simply left the door ajar as she moved farther into the house. Savage picked up the pace. Destroyer, Maestro and Keys, three of his Torpedo Ink brothers, came around the sides of the house and just stood by the outside of the door, waiting.

"Get the hell out of my house," Seychelle said. Her voice was low but angry. Savage had never heard her speak in that tone.

"I don't think you're in any position to order us to do anything," Hank said. "You're going to do what we say or you're going to find yourself in a very bad way, Seychelle. We could really fuck you up and no one would know."

Savage decided it was a good time to make himself

known. He stepped out of the doorway, fully into the room, coming behind Seychelle and gently moving her aside so he faced the two men, who had made themselves right at home. They were sitting in the two most comfortable armchairs she had.

"I'd be interested in knowing how you plan to fuck my woman up, Hank." He spoke quietly. Very softly. That should have told both of them they were fucked. He could see Joseph got it, Hank not so much, but then Joseph had already felt Savage's fists pounding his body before.

"I'm calling the cops," Seychelle said. Her voice was shaking.

"No, baby. You don't want to do that," Savage said, keeping his voice low. Calm. Very steady but commanding. "I'll handle them."

The two men stared at him. Joseph looked scared. Hank looked defiant.

"They broke into my house," she said.

"Yeah, they did, but it's best never to call the cops. If these two end up dead, we don't want a trail leading back to us."

Her hand twisted in his shirt.

Savage pulled her into his arms. "Seychelle. You're safe. The brothers are right outside. These two are going to apologize to you right now and tell you they aren't coming back."

"Fuck you," Hank burst out.

"Or they might apologize later. Either way, they won't be coming back," Savage amended, keeping his voice gentle. "You get ready for bed and I'll be right back." He kissed the top of her head, his arms tight around her. "Gentlemen, do either of you have anything to say to Seychelle before you leave?"

Joseph shook his head and started toward the door. Hank flipped them off and all but pushed the music scout out of his way to get to the door. Destroyer stood on the other side looking grim-faced. He held the door open for the two men. Beside him, Maestro and Keys indicated for the two men to keep walking when they both hesitated.

"I'll be right back, angel." Savage kissed the corner of her mouth and then caught her chin, forcing her head up so she was looking into his eyes. "Get ready for bed. I'll expect you to be in bed when I come back inside." He waited for her to nod before he went to join the others.

Savage followed Joseph and Hank out and carefully closed the door. He didn't look at either man as they turned to face him. He looked at Destroyer. Destroyer was a tall, imposing man with wide shoulders, all muscle, once handsome, now covered in scars and tattoos. He wore his hair long, his dark eyes flat and cold. Maestro stood to the left of the door with Keys beside him. Keys had hazel eyes and dark hair, while Maestro had dark hair streaked with silver. Savage nodded to them, pulling on his gloves as he stalked past them.

Hank turned toward them. "You don't scare me, fucker . . ."

Savage hit him in the stomach so hard Hank collapsed in on himself. His knee caught the guitarist under the chin, straightening him back up. He proceeded to beat him viciously until Keys stepped in. Savage turned and hit Joseph. When he staggered back and went down, a hairbrush slid from his pocket onto the ground. Both men looked at it. Joseph made a grab for it, but Savage's hand got there first.

"What were you doing with this?"

"She wanted me to have it."

Savage looked up at Maestro and then Destroyer, shaking his head. The brush had belonged to Seychelle's mother. Seychelle kept it on her nightstand, but she didn't use it. He handed it to Maestro, and as he did, Joseph let out an animalistic growl and swung his fist at Savage's jaw. Savage slipped the punch easily and proceeded to beat the man nearly unconscious. Again, it was Keys who stopped him before he went too far.

"Take them to their car. Get them away from here. This is their only chance. And get their phones to Code."

"You know Arnold is never going to stop," Maestro said. "That was pure bullshit with the brush. Fantasy stalker mentality. He was fixated on her long before he approached her as a scout. They have to have some kind of history."

Savage nodded. "I'll figure it out. Thanks for the help tonight."

He watched Destroyer heft Joseph Arnold to his shoulder, and Maestro followed suit with Hank Waitright. They disappeared into the fog and he went inside the cottage, flexing his fingers before locking the door. Seychelle was in bed. He put the hairbrush back on her nightstand.

"Arnold stole it. Had it in his pocket," he said, his voice gruff. She looked so horrified he couldn't scold her for leaving her place so easily broken into. He just stripped and padded barefoot and naked into the bathroom. "Tell me about you and Joseph. How did you meet?" He turned the shower on.

"He was at a bar in San Francisco where I was singing. It was a little dive, really, but I liked it."

Of course. Savage suppressed a groan. Anyone hearing her voice would be enthralled. She had magic. She could cast a spell.

"He bought me a drink."

"Tell me you didn't drink it." Knowing Joseph Arnold, the man would have put a drug in her drink. No question, he would have.

"No, I'm not that fond of alcohol. I did sit and talk with him. He appeared charming at first, but the longer I sat and talked with him, the less I wanted to go out with him. That's always the way. I'm attracted on the surface, but then I'm with a man for a few minutes and that attraction just disappears."

"He asked you out." He made it a statement.

He turned off the water and stepped out of the shower, snagging a towel and drying himself off. Normally, he would have put on a pair of jeans, but it was a little too late for that. He just walked to the bed and slid under the sheet. She wasn't under the covers. She sat in her usual position at the headboard. He reached up and caught her hips, tugging until she sprawled out, lying on her back.

Savage rolled over and pillowed his head on her belly, wrapping his arms around her hips. It was fast becoming his favorite place to sleep. "You told him no, and he didn't like that, did he?"

Seychelle's fingers went to his scalp, immediately beginning to massage his head. "No, he definitely didn't like it. He asked me out numerous times. He got . . . pushy. I quit singing with the band to get away from him. It wasn't a big deal. They weren't a great band, and I never stuck around for very long. I hadn't moved up here at that time. I was . . . tired."

He tipped his head up to look at her. "What do you mean, 'tired'?"

Her fingers never stopped moving in that circular motion that felt like caring to him. He found himself tracing those same patterns into her hip and then down her thigh.

"After my father passed away, I was worn out. Sometimes I'd join a band because I needed the company, but it took a long time to get back on my feet, and singing was draining."

"Arnold always found you?"

"He did. Eventually, he came up with the scout gig. If he really is one, he can't be very good at it. He just needs to hear the word *no*. He doesn't seem to know what it means."

Savage knew Joseph Arnold wasn't going to ever hear it where Seychelle was concerned.

"You locked the windows and back door, but you deliberately didn't remind me to lock the front door, didn't you, Savage? You knew they were going to come to my house." Seychelle continued to massage his scalp, her fingers magic.

"Yeah." He shrugged. "At least I thought it was a good bet they'd come. I had a good guess that third man they were talking to in the coffee shop was Brandon Campbell, that man you and Doris were talking about. I just had this gut feeling. I thought maybe he was watching your house and directed the two of them here. The description fit. Arnold had been here earlier, watching the place. I think he was taking photographs. You ever have anything disappear from any of the places you were living after you met Arnold? Anything at all? Something small?"

He felt the little shiver that went through her body, and he tightened his hold around her hips. His hand moved over her thigh, rubbing along the scars that belonged to him, tracing each one of them. He knew them by heart now.

"Yes. A few items. A toothbrush. A book I liked on wildcats. A candle. A pair of my red lace panties that were part of a matching set. I still have the bra."

Savage swore under his breath and kept caressing the scars on her leg. Joseph Arnold was definitely a first-class stalker of the worst kind.

"You and your friends beat the crap out of them, didn't you?"

"Technically, *I* did. My brothers just watched and made certain there were no witnesses and that their cell phones were not going to record the event. They also confiscated the phones so we could ensure you were safe. Just in case."

"I don't know what that means."

"I don't like the fact that Joseph Arnold keeps coming back around when you've told him no over and over. When you sang at the bar in Willits, it clearly hadn't been your first confrontation with him. I beat the crap out of him and yet he came back. Hank is a punk, but he's no real threat, and I doubt if we'll be seeing him anymore. Arnold really is a problem. I want to know how much of one. Code can take a look at his phone and tell us if he's been watching you. I'm a scary man, Seychelle. Most people take one look at me and they don't ever want to mess with me once, let alone a second time. After what you just told me, I think he's a major problem."

"He didn't know I lived here until someone told him."
She turned her body slightly, easing over onto one hip. "I
hope you're wrong and it wasn't Brandon."

Savage accommodated the change, sliding his head to the
side, his hand moving around to her bottom. He heard the
slight tremble in her voice. "You haven't lived here that long,
Seychelle, and Arnold did know you were here. He was taking pictures earlier." Her fingers felt good on his head. Even
when she shifted her weight off her butt, she never stopped
massaging his scalp. For such a small woman, she had surprising strength in her hands. "Both of them know I'm here
with you now." He wanted to reassure her.

She was silent again, and he wished he knew what she
was thinking. Sometimes he felt very connected to her, and
then in the next moment, she eluded him, sliding away. He
rubbed her thigh, brought his palm up to her hip and then
slid it around to her bottom again. His heart clenched hard
in his chest. He had spanked her hard. Maybe too hard for
her first time. Did he really want that for her? Did he really
want a monster like him for her?

Tomorrow he was going to talk to Absinthe, one of his
brothers in the club. There were few people smarter than
Absinthe. He had to figure out exactly what he was going
to do before he made his next move with Seychelle.

SIX

Savage stood for a long time in silence, staring at the bubbles flowing upward endlessly between the thick glass of the wall in front of the glass room Scarlet had given Absinthe. It was there for her man to go to when he needed silence. A place where his demons couldn't reach him. He could relax and just let his mind be at peace.

Savage had such a place. He'd discovered it by accident. His place was a woman named Seychelle. When he was with her, she held back the terrible well of demons that howled and raged at him to open that endless vault of violence inside of him and visit it on others.

He sighed, uncertain what he was even doing there. He already knew the answers to the questions he was going to ask Absinthe. He'd spent a great deal of his time researching, but Absinthe was the smartest person he knew. By coming to Absinthe, he was revealing how desperate he truly was.

He turned to face his brother, a little dismayed that Scarlet, Absinthe's wife, was with him. Savage knew she would be, but still, he didn't like it. He kept all expression from his face. Absinthe indicated the chairs in the living room. Lana, another Torpedo Ink sister, had chosen those chairs. They gave off Lana's comforting vibes. Savage needed that comfort. He took the chair across from the two sitting across from him.

"Can I get you something to drink, Savage?" Scarlet asked.

His first inclination was to say no, but it was a way to get her out of the room if only for a few minutes. "Thanks, Scarlet." What the hell would keep her gone the longest? "Coffee sounds good right about now."

She looked surprised. "No problem." She got up and left the room.

"I thought you were going to be on the work crew heading into Sea Haven this morning," Absinthe said. "Scarlet and I were just getting ready to head out when we got your text."

"Yeah. I'm going after we talk. Just wanted to ask you a couple of questions. This woman, Seychelle. The singer. I suppose everyone knows about her. And they've got to be worried."

"It isn't any secret that you've been hanging with her, Savage. It's a little out of character for you. So yeah, there's some concern there."

Savage took a deep breath and just asked, "Will really loving someone change what I am? What I have to have?"

He knew the answer because he *craved* being with Seychelle, having her tied, his whip marking her skin. He dreamt of it. Was obsessed with the idea of it. Still, he despised himself. Loathed what he was, loathed his needs. He wanted to see red marks on her. He'd reveled in his handprints on her bottom, and that just made him crave to see the gorgeous patterns he could put on her pristine skin. He wanted the real thing in his hands. Not some pretend whip one bought in a toy shop, but one he could wield like the master he was.

Absinthe held his gaze for a long time. "You know you're not a true sadist, right, Savage? You don't need to humiliate a woman, or anyone for that matter. You don't need to constantly cause pain. You have a cycle. That's unusual."

Savage shook his head. "That's not true. To be aroused, I need to cause pain. The level of pain can be different. The need is always present when it comes to sex. You're stalling. Just answer the question, Absinthe."

"You already know the answer. I can maybe lessen the demand for you over time. Help with it, but I don't know for certain if I can really do even that. I'm willing to try. I will say, if you want to be with this woman, you have to be honest with her. You have to lay it out for her. Tell her what you need. It isn't easy. I had to be honest with Scarlet about my fetishes."

Savage stared at Absinthe, trying to decide if he was attempting to be funny or not. "Are you seriously comparing you talking to Scarlet about your need to have her dress like a kitten occasionally to me having to tell Seychelle I want to use a real whip on her in order for me to get off? You think that's going to go over very well?" He stood up and paced across the room, afraid of Absinthe seeing his expression.

"Savage, you're not remembering who you are. You were able to get those girls to enjoy what was done to them. If she consents because she returns feelings for you, you can help her get to a place where she responds to the things you need."

Savage stood in front of that wall of bubbles rising slowly toward the ceiling and then rolling back toward the floor. "I have no doubt I can do that, Absinthe." He knew he could. Absolutely he could. "But is it right?" He turned back to face his Torpedo Ink brother. "Every fucking day, I have to look at myself in the mirror. I don't want her to look at herself and hate who she is."

"Why should she do that if she's giving a gift to a man she loves?"

Savage pulled in a breath because he'd run out of air. His

lungs felt raw. Burning. He despised that he was a monster and there was no way to be anything else. He had to remind himself Absinthe had no idea what it was like to be him. To have to see a woman's skin marked to be aroused. To want *his* woman to have tears running down her face for him. To need her to suffer for him. That was about as fucked up as it could possibly get.

There was no doubt that he could "train" Seychelle. She already had a proclivity in that direction. They had unbelievable chemistry, but there was so much more between them. It went far deeper than that, and both of them knew it, which was why she was so leery. She was susceptible to his voice. To him. And she'd told him about Brandon Campbell and what a dick he was. About his psychic talent and how he used it against women.

"You were a child; we were all just children," Absinthe said, pushing both hands through his hair. "We were just trying to survive."

"I survived by teaching girls to accept pain with sex. To like it," Savage said. "I was so fucking good at it, they branded me. They put that shit into my skin permanently, just the way they branded it into my soul so that I needed it."

"If you hadn't trained those girls to accept or even like pain with sex, they would have been tortured repeatedly. Reaper would have been killed. Alena and Lana would have been. Hell, Savage, the sacrifices you made saved us over and over. None of us had choices. We lived in hell and we got out alive. None of us are ever going to be what the world calls normal. We live with what they did to us, and the women who love us have to live with it as well. That's what we ask of them."

"How are we supposed to do that?"

"It's called free will, Savage. It's her choice. You shouldn't make that choice for her. If you think she cares at all for you, you have to lay it out for her, not walk away from her. If you don't at least give her the chance to say no, she'll never know why you walked away in the first place. She'll always think she was never good enough for you."

Savage swore under his breath. Absinthe had no idea what he was talking about. He didn't know the extent of what Savage would be asking of Seychelle. Once he trained her to need pain, to crave it, she wouldn't magically get over it if something happened to him. She would always be that way, with or without him to take care of her.

"You have to give her back something of equal value to what she gives you," Absinthe added quietly. Before Savage could protest, he held up his hand. "I'm not saying you have to think it's equal. Only she has to think that. You have to find something that matters to her. And you have to give her back everything she's giving you."

There wasn't anything here for him. Nothing was ever going to change for him. He was always going to be a monster, craving things others found abhorrent—others knew were wrong. Absinthe could talk about laying that shit out to a woman one fell in love with, asking her to join him in a life of pure hell, knowing what he was asking of her, what he was going to do to her . . .

Shit. What was he going to do? Give her up? Never see her again? She was already so deep inside him. She'd crawled right in and wrapped herself around his heart. He didn't know how or why. It made no sense to him, when he barely knew her. Except she was honest and direct and she saw him. Saw inside of him and didn't flinch away. She might be scared, but no matter what he said or did, those blue eyes of hers would meet his when he called her name.

Savage knew nothing was going to change who he was, and no one, not even the smartest man on the planet, was going to make it happen, not even if they both willed it. "Not sure I want to thank you, Absinthe, but you gave me your best advice. I'd better get back to Sea Haven. That woman can get into trouble in a heartbeat. Tell Scarlet I had to get back to building the porches, since I initiated it."

He couldn't stay there. Abruptly, he spun around and stalked out, lifting his chin at Scarlet as she came toward him in the hall. She'd most likely taken her time making the coffee, giving him time to be alone with her husband. She was intuitive when it came to the Torpedo Ink brethren, and she respected the members of the club. Savage held Scarlet in high regard. She was an asset to the club as well as being perfect for Absinthe. He was happy for his brother, that Absinthe had found the right woman for his wife, but comparing Absinthe's fetish to his monstrous cravings was simply ludicrous.

He took the ride not to Sea Haven to work on Doris's porch but to Caspar and the house he'd bought the moment he'd laid eyes on Seychelle. He'd found it a couple of years earlier. It had been everything he could want, but the price was steep, and what the hell was he going to do with a house? He knew eventually he was going to have to take that last ride in order to keep his brother or Czar from having to put a bullet in his head.

This house was for her. Seychelle. It was beautiful. The property was beautiful with the views. He'd put in a state-of-the-art security system. He'd taken his time, watching her, learning the things she liked and finding furniture he thought she would love. He walked through the house to the master bedroom, where the very large sliding glass door revealed a deck that led to a private courtyard. He stood at the glass door, looking out into the courtyard, where he had set up multiple targets—mannequins. He practiced his craft every single day. Now he practiced more than once a day.

Like the other men of Torpedo Ink, he had to command his body to work when he was desperate for relief. He could flog a woman and let her blow him and he'd be okay for a short while if he was lucky. But he never could do this—be who he was. Become Savage the whip master. The real man. He wouldn't give that to just anyone. The moment he lay on the hospital bed beside Seychelle, he thought of nothing else. He thought of no one else. He would give this part of him to one woman. The only woman. She would have to accept the real man, and deep down, where rage and pain came together in a black-and-red swirling mass of raw, violent energy, he knew the only woman he had a shot with was Seychelle.

He stood for a long time looking at the mannequins and the patterns he'd cut into the thin paper he'd covered them with. He didn't want to admit, even to himself, that minute by minute, thinking of having his own woman accepting him totally, and giving him her tears freely, just as she'd given them to him that first night in her hospital room, aroused him like nothing else ever had. He had so many sins damning his soul that asking her to love him was just adding to them. Still . . .

He sighed, shook his head and turned to go find her. The ride on his Harley helped calm the turbulence raging in his gut as he moved with the machine, the wind battering at him the way his thoughts did. He had always known there was only one way to end it. He had always held that option open to himself, knowing if the rage in him got too bad and he couldn't bleed it off enough to relieve the pressure, he'd take that option before he ever hurt an innocent. Now there was Seychelle. He just had to work it out in his mind. Find a balance.

She wasn't at the cottage. Her car was gone. Little Miss Independence. He knew she would have already gone to Doris Fendris's home to make certain the woman was doing okay with all the bikers showing up with tools and wood to fix both porches for her. They were going to have the work done fast, and it would be done right. He knew Doris would be in her element, ready to lord it over her friends—especially Inez.

There was a row of bikes parked in front of Doris's home, and Savage backed his Harley into the spot at the end. Glitch, one of the prospects, nodded to him. Savage sat straddling his motorcycle. He didn't look up. He wanted to hear her first. He knew right where she'd be—with Doris, out front. Probably sitting in the ridiculous lawn furniture that looked as if it had seen better days. He'd seen it the day before, when he'd come to collect his woman.

There it was. The single sound he was waiting for. Laughter. Magical. Soft, yet the sound carried. He looked up, and sure enough there were the notes, gold, drifting through the blue sky. His heart clenched hard in his chest. How the hell was he supposed to give that up? Worse, how was he supposed to drag her down to his level? Ask her to let him hurt her? Cursing under his breath, he swung his leg off his bike and started up the walkway toward her. As long as she was in the world, he'd be drawn to her.

Jackson Deveau, the deputy sheriff—clearly off duty, wearing casual clothes, jeans and a tee and eating Alena's famous chicken—came walking toward him. He stopped right in front of Savage, preventing him from passing on the narrow sidewalk, clearly inclined to talk, when the man rarely said a damn word.

"Nice thing you did here, Savage."

"Didn't do it. That was all Seychelle."

"Not the way I heard it. You walk on water, according to Doris Fendris. She said you came in and ordered the wood for her and had your brothers working to put the porches and stairs in today, right along with feeding the crew."

Savage nodded. "I think that might be as true as the story circulating about you and the Dardens. The way I heard it, Clyde Darden has this special greenhouse where he grows prize flowers he names after real-life heroes. He's got this real hot one, flame red, very rare and unusual. I know because although he said the place is sacred, he let little Zoe go in. Said he named that flower Jackson Fire and won the grand prize with it."

"Oh, for God's sake, now you're just making shit up," Jackson burst out. "Clyde never said that."

"I think Doris was making that shit up too," Savage pointed out.

Jackson nodded. "I see your point. This chicken is damn good. I'm taking Elle to Alena's restaurant tonight. Already have reservations. She's been looking forward to going for weeks."

"Got something to say to me, spit it out, Deveau," Savage said. He wasn't buying into the small talk. Jackson wasn't a man to make small talk. As a rule, he didn't string five words together, but there he was, blocking the sidewalk.

Jackson nodded toward Seychelle. "It's obvious the way you look at the woman how you feel about her, but I can see you made up your mind you're not going there."

Savage couldn't believe he was that damn easy to read. And he wasn't so certain Deveau was right. "She deserves a hell of a lot better than me, if it's any of your fuckin' business."

Jackson studied him. "Don't be in such a hurry to give that woman up, Savage. You think I deserve to be with Elle? If that had anything to do with it, I'd be nowhere near her."

Savage shook his head. There was no explaining to Jackson what he was.

"You ever think maybe she needs you? Look at her. Really take a look at her. This world is a place that's going to eat someone like her, chew her up and spit her out. She's not like either of us. She's never going to develop a protective shell. She's never going to be able to find a way to shield herself against the sharks of the world. She won't even see them coming until it's too late. You, however, just like me, can see them while they're still just shadows. Think about it, Savage, before you leave her hanging out there alone."

Deveau took another bite of his chicken, stepped around Savage and walked away. Savage cursed again under his breath and made his way into Doris's yard. It was small, the grass just a little overgrown. Doris, Seychelle, Alena and Blythe sat on four rattan lawn chairs surrounding a table. A little distance from them was another table with lawn chairs clearly brought from the clubhouse. Lana, Anya, Breezy, Soleil and Inez sat together at that table.

A wealth of food was laid out at each table for the Torpedo Ink members to grab when they were hungry. Several coolers filled with ice and drinks were at the ends of the tables and chairs for anyone to grab water or beer if they wanted something to drink.

Savage went straight to Seychelle. He knew he was late and should have picked up a hammer and joined in the work, but he'd left early to get to Absinthe's. Too early. He knew Seychelle had felt him disconnecting from her. Dropping a hand on her shoulder, he leaned down to brush a kiss on her temple. The moment his lips came in contact with her skin, his gut tightened into knots and his heart ached.

Doris grinned at him. "It looks so good already, Savage. I can't believe how fast the porch is going up. I haven't even seen the back. And Alena and the others brought all this food."

He nodded, keeping an expressionless face. "Yeah, they like to show off."

She giggled. "You're so outrageous."

"I brought you iced tea," Blythe said. "I made it just for you. Your favorite."

"I'd give you the finger, but even though Czar's in the back, he's bound to have eyes on you," Savage said. "Catch you ladies later."

He made his way around to the back porch, needing to separate himself from Seychelle. Just looking at her took his resolve away. She was dressed in leggings. She normally wore jeans, but he knew her spectacular ass was most likely still a little sore from the night before. Just the thought of his marks on her skin and how they got there sent his body into a frenzy of hot, sparking arousal.

Her simple tank framed her full breasts and those perfect nipples he had far too many fantasies about. She wore her hair up in a ponytail. Even that put thoughts in his head that shouldn't be there. He knew more ways to weave hair into ties that would keep her very still while he wielded his own magic with his whip. He was a master with a whip. Shit. He had to stop thinking about it.

He had drawers of custom-made, perfectly balanced whips in his home, just waiting. Untouched. He never thought he'd ever use them. Beautifully crafted. Each one of them. Signal whip. Gallery whip. Bullwhip. Snake whip. He had them all. Short. Long. He could lay down just about any pattern he chose with those whips. He could write his fuckin' name with a whip and never break skin, just leave beautiful welts that would last for days. Very few could wield a whip and not break skin, not when they were laying down a pattern. And not when they were fully aroused.

The others greeted him as he joined them, Master indicating where he wanted him working. Czar moved over to him as he was pounding nails into a long board, finishing up the porch before the railing could be added.

"This was a good thing you did, Savage. Not only good for Doris, but for our club."

Savage glanced up. "It was Seychelle. She was trying to fix the stairs, but both porches were rotted. I was worried Doris was going to fall through. Seychelle visits quite a few of the elderly in town." He sighed. "Most likely she'll have us fixing all their porches. And I'll be fixing whatever's broken in their homes. I'll pay for materials."

"The club will pay for the materials. This is the break we've been looking for. We needed an in with the community, and your woman inadvertently gave us one. This could be big for us. After word got out that we guarded Zyah's grandmother and her friend Lizz from the thieves, this is going to go a long way to cement goodwill in the community, and that's what we've needed. Lumber and nails and a little hard work isn't going to hurt us if in the end we achieve what we've wanted. We'll have a safe place where the citizens are willing to look out for us the same way we look out for them."

Savage glanced to the left. A couple sat on their porch

watching. The house on the right held another couple. Both looked to be in their late sixties and were drinking coffee, watching the show. They smiled and waved. Czar lifted a hand in return. Savage used a nail gun to drive several nails into a board.

The front porch had to be finished because the other Torpedo Ink members were in the back working to get the steps finished. The railing was already done and ready to be attached.

"Glad you think this will help." He stood up and signaled to Master that the last of the porch was in place and the railing could be put on. "Need to check on Seychelle." He was uncomfortable having Czar, or anyone else, praise him when he felt Seychelle had been the one to notice that Doris needed help. He never would have stopped by the woman's home had it not been for Seychelle.

Savage hurried around to the front, where Ice and Storm were playing with Czar's children while Reaper kept a close eye on them. Doris was talking with Blythe, Inez and Marie Darden, but Seychelle was nowhere in sight.

"It's impossible to know what to get Jackson for his birthday," Inez complained as Savage walked up on them. "He's always telling me not to get him anything, but he's the most generous man. I don't like it when I can't think of anything he'd really love. Do you have any ideas?" She looked around at the other women.

"Funny you should say that, Inez," Savage said, keeping his features perfectly expressionless, the way he always did. "Jackson and I were just having a conversation about Clyde Darden and his greenhouse, where he grows his prizewinning hybrids. At least I think that's what you call them. Clyde showed them to Zoe once. In any case, Clyde sometimes names them after people. Jackson was very enthusiastic about his greenhouse. Well, as enthusiastic as Jackson gets," he amended. "Said something about a fiery red flower

Clyde was working on that Jackson wished was named Jackson's Fire or some such thing. I don't know."

"Oh dear," Marie said. "I did forget about that, Inez. Jackson helps Clyde all the time with the greenhouse. If it wasn't for him, Clyde wouldn't be able to keep the greenhouse going half the time. He's fixed the watering system. Last year, he removed all the beds and completely replanted for Clyde when he was unable to do it."

"Does Clyde have a really special hybrid he's growing this year?" Doris asked. "If he does, Inez, maybe if we all went in together and helped pay for the entry fees, Clyde could take it around to the various shows and get a win."

"Does he have a red hybrid he's working on?" Blythe asked. "That sounds so perfect."

"Do you think he'd name it after Jackson?" Inez asked. "If we all pitched in to help him pay for the fees and travel?"

"I think that would be an excellent birthday gift," Marie said. "Clyde would love to pay Jackson back for all the things he's done for us. What a wonderful idea, Inez."

"Blythe, where did my woman go?" Savage asked, feeling pleased with himself. The cop was never going to live down having a prizewinning flower named after him. Inez's group of women would bring it up at every opportunity, especially if the flower won anything.

Blythe, immersed in the conversation, had to refocus, frowning a little. She glanced toward the house across the street. "She said she saw someone coming from the house across the street. We were all laughing and she just kind of went quiet on us. When I asked her about it, that's when she said she saw someone leave the neighbor's house and she just had this feeling."

Instantly, all good humor was gone. Savage turned and looked at the two-story house with the heavy drapes drawn across the windows. "She went over there?"

Blythe's frown deepened. "I said I'd go with her, but she

said the woman was shy and wouldn't talk unless she was alone."

Savage pulled out his phone, already striding across the street, texting as he did so. **Coming over. Get to the door now, Seychelle.**

He told himself he would know if something was wrong with her. They were connected so closely together, right? But he'd deliberately pulled away. Put distance between them because he needed to think about whether or not he should bring her into his world. His gut was suddenly churning, tied into knots.

Moving slow. Getting to door.

Why the hell would she be moving slow? At least she hadn't objected to going to the door. Even that worried him. She didn't like him ordering her around, not when she was visiting her friends. Technically, she couldn't call this neighbor of Doris's a friend—yet.

He heard something scratch at the door, and then it was open and Seychelle was there. She looked pale as she came toward him, stumbling a little, pulling the door closed behind her. Savage wrapped his arms around her.

"What the hell, baby? Are you hurt?"

She leaned into him, one arm circling his waist. "No. Just a little weak. I think my blood sugar is too low. I need to rest. Can we sit on the curb?"

They weren't sitting on the damn curb. He scooped her up and carried her across the street. "Tell me what happened." It was a demand. He didn't care if his voice came out more of a growling command than a question.

"Not where anyone can hear us." She buried her face against his neck. "Can you just please take me home? I'm really, really tired."

At least she was going to tell him. "Do you have your car keys on you?"

"I left them on the floor of my car."

He tried not to let his head explode. She had no concept

of personal safety. None. Zero. Not with her house and not with her car. He clenched his teeth against giving her a lecture, mostly because she was exhausted. Not just physically drained, she was mentally drained as well. When he put her on the seat of the car, she didn't even reach for her seat belt, nor did she object when he belted her in. He debated whether or not to text Steele, but she didn't appear to have any physical injuries on her. Seychelle fell asleep in the short time it took to reach her cottage. Thankfully, she had actually locked the place up.

He knew he had a short window of time and then he was going to have to leave her, even if it was just for a few days. She kept the monster at bay, but he could feel the rage in him building in spite of her delaying that burning need in him. He didn't dare take too many chances being around her—and he didn't dare play any more sexual games with her, no matter how much his body demanded it.

The thought of touching another woman was abhorrent to him. It made him feel physically ill. There was no time to get Seychelle ready even if he did make up his mind to lay it all out for her. He couldn't take the chance that she'd look at him the way she should—like he was an evil monster and she shouldn't have anything to do with him. That was the real reason he was being such a coward. He was afraid she'd reject him totally and he wouldn't even have this part of her. He didn't want to lose what he had.

Savage scooped her up and carried her inside, unlocking the keypad with his own code he'd programmed in. She murmured a little protest when he put her on the bed in a sitting position.

"Stay there. I'm going to get you a glass of water and you're going to tell me what happened." He'd forgo the car lecture and every other lecture, but he needed to know what had gone on in that house. She'd been laughing with the other women, perfectly fine, when he'd left her. Now she was pale, almost to the point of gray, and her energy was zero.

Seychelle moistened her lips and pushed back her hair. "I saw Brandon come out of her house. Sahara's house. Well, I don't know who owns it. According to Sahara, he has the right to come and go whenever he wants. Of course that means he has the right to fuck her whenever he wants as well. No matter that he lives with that young girl. And he compares Sahara to her the entire time. Tells her that she's let herself go. That she's fat and no one would ever want her. That she's so lucky he bothers with her."

"He sounds wonderful."

"That's the problem. She believes every word he says because he uses his voice to persuade her. If he leaves her alone long enough, she begins to do things for herself. She starts to remember the woman she was, but he always comes back, and he takes everything away again. I'm afraid for her."

The weariness in her voice made Savage afraid for Seychelle. She seemed like she had slid down a bit in the bed. He pulled off his boots and climbed onto the bed beside her, lifting her and then placing her between his thighs. He wrapped his arms around her. She felt cold to him.

"Did he hurt her? Physically? Clearly, he did emotionally. Did he hurt her physically?"

A little shudder went through Seychelle's body. "Yes. When he insists on having sex with her. But no, he never hits her. He threatens her and she cowers down. But then he tells her she isn't worth even hitting. She isn't worth what he would do to a dog. She told me she apologizes for all the trouble she gives him. She told him she would leave, but then he gets mad and says she's ungrateful to him for all he's done for her. When he leaves, if he's been really mean, she hurts herself." She whispered the last like a confession.

Savage rocked her to try to comfort her. "I've got you, baby. I'm sorry you had to see her like that. No one deserves that. What can we do for her? Does she have a family? Can we call them and bring them here?"

"She wants to go home, but she's afraid to. He separated her from all her friends. From her family."

"That's a typical abuser. Once he's got her separated, he can do whatever he wants with her. She has nowhere to go. No one to talk to."

"In this case, he's poisoned everyone against her. Even Doris is conditioned to think Sahara's the one abusing poor Brandon. He has the ability to turn everyone against her, making them believe she's mentally ill. She believes him, Savage. He's so evil. He takes pleasure in making her believe that she's ugly and unworthy, that her own family doesn't love or want her. He doesn't have to physically hurt her. She hurts herself."

There was a little sob in her voice that broke his heart. He didn't even know he had a heart that could break. "Baby, don't." He whispered it against her ear. "We'll fix it. We'll find a way to help her."

"I think it's too late. Even if we can get her out of there, if he finds her, she'll go back to him if she hears his voice. He's programmed her. She can't break away. I couldn't get her away." This time there was guilt, even shame, in her voice.

Savage tightened his arms. "Seychelle. This woman has been with him for years. One visit isn't going to undo everything he's done. You know that. You aren't thinking clearly. You just panicked because she's in a bad way and you always want to help. We'll take care of it. Did you manage to get her parents' names and number?"

She shook her head. "Almost. At the last minute she wouldn't give it to me. I had her at the phone, ready to call her mother, and then she was sobbing, and she wouldn't do it."

"What about a name? Her parents' names. First and last. Are they together?"

"Yes, her parents are still together. She talked about them very lovingly. Valerie and Harry Higgens. They live somewhere in Oregon, but I have no idea where. It's a big state."

"But, baby, I told you about Code. He's our ace in the

hole. How do you think I know where you are all the time?" He pulled out his phone and held it out in front of them both, texting fast, one-handed. He used their encryption that told Code it was a priority. He gave the data he had on the couple, which wasn't much. "Tell me anything else you have. What kind of work, anything at all she might have talked about?"

"Valerie was a teacher. Sixth grade, I think. She won awards. She's retired now, although she does substitute. And she will tutor. Harry owned a feed store, but he sold it and retired as well. They bought a little property and he keeps bees. He's very passionate about being a beekeeper, and they have lavender fields on their property. He sells lavender honey."

Savage quickly relayed the information.

"How did you learn to text that fast?"

He nuzzled her neck. She always smelled delicious. He didn't need to be a beekeeper to have honey. Her hair was honey colored, and she smelled like a mixture of wild strawberries and honey. "When we were kids, we used to tap on our thighs or arms or shoulders, whatever was handy. We had to be fast so no one would see. We used our own code. We still use it."

"You really were raised in a prison? All of you? Every member of Torpedo Ink? Is that why you're all so close? I can see it when you're together."

"It was a kind of prison. It was supposed to be a school. At the time, there was a man by the name of Sorbacov who backed a certain candidate for the presidency. Each of us had parents or grandparents, someone raising us, who were opposed to that man. Sorbacov was very powerful and he had access to a branch of the military that was secretive. He commanded those soldiers to murder the parents of his opponents and take the children to be trained as assets for the country."

He felt her shock. It was like a terrible wave that raced through her body, nearly buckling her. She turned in his arms to look at him. Her blue eyes went dark with sorrow for him.

"That's the most horrific thing I've ever heard, Savage. They *murdered* your parents?"

"They did. They took my older sisters, Reaper and me to their school to be trained. My sisters died there."

He didn't tell her they were raped and beaten to death. Or that they had been thrown down the stairs into the basement to die slowly in front of their traumatized baby brothers, who had also been raped and beaten. She didn't need to hear that shit. She was too compassionate as it was. She felt every damn thing anyone told her.

"We were all in the same boat, so to speak. Czar was our savior. He was determined we were going to learn to stay human beings. We didn't have adults to teach us all the rules of polite society, but we made up our code of honor and we stick to it."

Savage distanced himself from the story, telling it as if it had happened to someone else. He wasn't going to open that door, not when Seychelle was around him. He couldn't take a chance that she would hear the screams and see blood trickling like little intriguing beacons. Rivulets, tiny streaks of red on perfect canvas. Or how those screams were quieted. How the red streaks were tamed over time and the patterns turned into something else, something beautiful and pleasurable but equally as monstrous.

If he asked her to stay with him, to love him and be a partner to him, he would have to disclose everything to her. She would have to know the worst of him. It wouldn't be a play dungeon for her. Her life would be the same horrific cycle as his. She was shivering in his arms right now. He was rocking her and holding her tight, comforting her because she had seen evil, but the one doing the comforting was the devil.

He wanted her so bad, the taste of wild strawberry and honey mixed with the salt of her tears was in his mouth. On his tongue. Down his throat. The memory of his handprints on the perfection of her sweet ass was burned into his mind. That shade of dark purplish red he'd brought out on her skin. She colored so easily. His cock was a fuckin' steel rod, the monster roaring with demands just having the image in his head. Lust pounded through his bloodstream, a violent, hot wave, the red ribbon banding strong and brutal. She was the one. The only. She was *his*. He was hers. Soul to soul. He knew it. What did a monster have in common with an angel?

"You were all children."

"Most of us were toddlers when we were taken. We learned our lessons fast." His phone was already vibrating. Going crazy with Code's information. "Look at this man. He's so damn good. All of what? Five minutes max? Under five? He's got their location in Oregon, address and phone number. We can call them, baby. Talk to them. Sound them out, see if they really are good people. Absinthe, one of my brothers, he can hear the truth. No one can get past him."

"Sahara sounded as if they were very loving parents. She was very close to them at one time, but little by little that went away. She moved here to be with Brandon, but then he took her phone away and gave her a different cell. He could see her text messages, and anyone she called. He didn't want her calling unless he was there. He timed her calls. Eventually, when her mother started asking too many questions, mostly because Sahara would say alarming things now and then, Brandon persuaded her to block her parents. They can't get through to her by phone or email or any type of social media. They sent the cops to do a wellness checkup, and she told them she'd had a fight with her parents and didn't want to talk to them."

"You believe if you call them yourself, they'll be receptive to the call?"

"I do. But I don't know what I'd say. Sahara would probably lie to them if they tried to talk to her. She's so brainwashed at this point."

"What if they just drove straight here from Oregon and our club guarded her house? You go in with the parents, pack her bag and get her to come out, get in the car and go. You'd have to take the phone away from her. Her parents would have to know she'd need a place with no way for him to get in touch with her until she was strong enough to resist him."

Seychelle thought it over, frowning, her teeth biting down over and over on her lower lip. "I think, if her parents cooperated, we could make it work, but honestly, Savage, we're running out of time. He's got her to the point where she might really harm herself. She's very confused."

"Then let's not waste any time. You make the call. I'll just sit here, hold you and listen. If they aren't receptive, I'll call Czar and we'll move her somewhere she'll be safe. I promise, baby, we'll get her out of the situation."

"Thanks for believing me when there's no proof."

"I don't need any proof other than your word. You went into the house. You saw her. Take the phone and make the call. See what they have to say."

She took his phone, glancing over her shoulder at him with a look he didn't deserve but wished he could see for the rest of his life. Her knight in shining armor. More than that. She looked at him like the sun rose and set with him. He didn't deserve it, but he wanted to see it every damn day—for the rest of his life.

SEVEN

The call to Sahara's parents was met with joyful tears that turned to worry once they heard everything Seychelle had to tell them. They indicated they would drive out as soon as they could get someone to watch over their farm. Savage took the phone and quietly made arrangements to have them come to the Caspar Inn, where Brandon would have no inkling that Sahara's parents were anywhere close.

Nearly two weeks later, when Sahara's parents were in Caspar, Seychelle visited Doris and casually found out when Brandon had last been by the house to see Sahara and if Doris had noticed any kind of a pattern to his visits. Doris was very chatty. She said Brandon wouldn't be around for another couple of days, but he would be checking on Sahara soon enough. Immediately, Seychelle texted Savage, who let his club know. They contacted Sahara's parents to come immediately. Members of the club escorted them to Sahara's home.

Seychelle went to visit Sahara while Savage sat with Doris, ensuring that she didn't contact Brandon, just in case he had programmed her to let him know if Sahara had any visitors. Sahara hadn't seen Brandon for almost two weeks, and she was much more amenable to packing a small bag.

When her parents came to the door, Sahara had a total breakdown and Czar carried her to the car and put her in it. She was surrounded by the club members, so it was difficult for anyone driving by on the road to see what was going on. Savage had asked Doris for a cup of coffee, and she was in the house when Seychelle emerged with Sahara. By the time Doris returned, the car was gone, escorted out of town by the club members, and Seychelle was seated once more on Doris's porch.

They could only hope that Brandon didn't find a way to contact Sahara or that she didn't try to go back to him. Later, Doris told her Brandon was worried that Sahara had run off. Her phone had been left behind and he had no way to contact her. He asked Doris if she'd seen anything. She mentioned that Seychelle had visited with Sahara. Seychelle knew Savage was concerned that Brandon might come to the cottage, using her visit as an excuse.

Still, as worried as Savage seemed, Seychelle knew she'd lost him. It wasn't like Savage didn't come every night. He did. She'd wake up to him stretching out on her bed, his arm slung around her waist, and everything in her would settle, but they were back to being just friends. There were no more sinful, dirty lessons. He was very, very careful with her.

She knew he cared for her, but he had backed off, making it clear she gave him peace, just like when they'd first met. He liked spending time with her. He even needed it. She knew better than to let him stay with her, but he was so tempting. It wasn't just his body, and he was rock hard—all of him—just apparently not for her.

She wasn't going to live a long life. That was the bottom line. She didn't have that advantage. There wasn't a rosy future for her. When Savage had asked the question about whether or not she would rather be in a comfortable relationship and have children or have a man love her wildly, she knew she wanted to be loved. She needed to be loved. She wanted to love someone with insane, crazy intensity. She'd found that man. She knew she had.

Savage deserved to be loved. He didn't think he did. She could see into him, into a place where he was vulnerable, a place he didn't even see because he kept it locked up so tight. Somehow, when she'd saved his life, they'd made some kind of connection she couldn't explain, and she didn't even care to, but she knew he was a good man and that he could have been the right man for her.

In spite of not having had relationships, she wanted to try everything with her partner. She wanted to live life large. She wanted to die with no regrets. After her parents had died, she'd been so ill. So exhausted. She'd been barely able to walk across the floor, and she'd gone to a doctor. After running a multitude of tests on her, he'd given her the bad news—she had the internal organs of an old woman. Her heart was worn out. She didn't have heart disease like her father, but she might as well have. Her body wasn't going to last long.

She took vitamins. She ate right. She walked. She did the best she could to prolong her life. She noticed that when she sang in bars with bands, that feeling of being drained often came over her, just the way it did when she had tried to help Sahara recently. She chose crappy bands so she wouldn't want to sing with them for very long.

She knew Savage thought he was the only reason she hadn't gone to the bar in Caspar and auditioned with the band there, but she had a feeling the musicians were very good. She knew if she heard them, it would be difficult to resist joining them. She'd never really had the opportunity to be with a good band, but she couldn't stop herself from reaching out to people in the audience if they were really ill.

She'd admitted to Savage that she had no control. She just hadn't told him what exactly she had no control over. It was a terrible compulsion she couldn't overcome, to try to relieve suffering when people were sick. She suspected that was what was shortening her life, but she just couldn't stop herself, so she limited her singing gigs and the amount of time she spent with people she didn't know, especially crowds.

She wanted to date. She wanted to have crazy, wild sexual experiences, but when she met men, they weren't in any way exciting to her. She found she didn't respond physically to the men she encountered. Everything was so different with Savage. Every nerve ending in her body went on high alert when he was in the same room with her. If he touched her, just a whisper of a touch, it was like a small splash of hot wax on her skin. When he spanked her . . . that was pure fire.

Savage felt as if he needed her. The pain he caused was heartfelt, emotional, but he didn't deplete her body. He filled her up. He gave her energy. Exhilarated her in ways she didn't yet understand.

The nights with him were always fun. He wanted to play that silly game of honest questions. Sometimes he asked her what she'd had for dinner, and if she hadn't eaten more than a piece of fruit, which was pretty much her standard dinner, he would smack her on the butt, get up and go to her fridge to find eggs, cheese and mushrooms. He always complained that she didn't eat meat, but he was teasing her. He brought meat for himself and he always cooked his food separately. He was thoughtful in ways she didn't expect.

Seychelle found herself looking at Savage the way she did most times he came, so happy inside she didn't know if she should allow their strange friendship to continue. He never told her when he was going to show up, he just did. Right now, he was scrambling eggs with cheese, and this time he had added hash browns to the mix. She knew he was always worried that she wasn't eating enough, which was silly.

"You know I'm going to gain weight if you keep insisting I eat in the evening," she pointed out. "I make it a practice never to eat after six o'clock."

He didn't turn around. "That's bullshit."

"It isn't. In case you haven't bothered to notice, I'm already carrying a few extra pounds." She might as well point it out. He had sharp eyes. She couldn't imagine that he hadn't catalogued that fact. "If I eat at night, I'm going to just pack on more weight, Savage."

"You have a perfect figure, Seychelle, and you have to know it. No man wants a fuckin' stick in his bed. You've got great tits and an ass most men would kill for their woman to have. You need to eat. You want to go for a walk after we eat, just say so, I'm up for that. We can walk on the headlands. We do most nights anyway."

Savage always threw out compliments so casually, as if they were facts and he was just stating them. He almost sounded annoyed, and he was getting more irritable as each day passed. He definitely wasn't trying to flatter her.

"Nice of you to think so, Savage. I never thought about it that way. I guess I'll eat the eggs and go for the walk with you." She kept the challenge out of her voice. The last few nights he'd come, he'd just wanted to lie on the bed with her. The entire last week he'd gotten edgier.

She felt the difference in him when he got close to her. He felt more dangerous. His skin was hotter. His rage closer to the surface. His blue eyes actually had gone from being flat and cold to holding flames that burned with a fire she found she dreaded. That well of rage in him was growing, and it wasn't good. No matter what she did, she couldn't stop it. She slowed it down. She soothed him. She sometimes made those flames fall back to smaller embers, but they flared right back up, burning hotter than ever the moment her hands were off him.

Seychelle was just a little nervous around him when before she hadn't been at all. She felt the house was too small for him and he was a bit like a tiger in a cage, pacing restlessly, and she was his meal. The need for violence rode him hard. She could see it in him. Feel it on him. It was like a vicious animal alive in him, ripping at his insides, shredding his intestines with cruel, spiteful claws, demanding its pound of flesh.

The Whip Master. The Master of Pain. She didn't dare

touch him when he was like this, and yet everything she was demanded that she do so to ease that terrible need for violence. For hurting another human being. He looked at her with his blue eyes as if only she was right for him, and she not only wanted to be that woman for him, she needed to be.

"Honey, are you going to tell me what's wrong?" She held her breath, afraid he would. Afraid he wouldn't. In spite of his abruptness, he treated her gently as a rule, but she didn't know how he would be when he was like this, and there was a part of her that was afraid of finding out. She didn't want to lose him, and yet she knew she didn't dare grow any closer.

He glanced at her over his shoulder, his eyes meeting hers, and those blue flames leapt and burned, scorching her before he turned back to the eggs.

"Sometimes I can go through some pretty bad patches, baby, nothing I haven't been through before. Just gets a little rough. That's why I'm hanging around so much. Does it bother you, having me staying so long?"

He had been—not just nights, he'd been there mornings and even, a few times, into the afternoon. He didn't talk much, just watched her play the guitar or walked with her on the headlands or into Sea Haven. She spent time visiting several elderly couples and two widows, bringing them groceries, and he went with her on her visits. Again, he didn't say much, but he carried the groceries in and put them away.

At the home of Rebecca Jetspun, a widow, he'd gotten under the sink and repaired a leak while she'd visited. At the home of one of the couples, Dirk and Harriet Meadows, he did the dishes and cleaned the kitchen until it was sparkling while she sat and visited. Dirk had a hip replacement and was going through his therapy and not the best of company for his wife. Harriet was very glad to see Seychelle. Savage just shook his head when Harriet tried to pay him.

Penelope and Forest Potts needed extensive weeding done in their greenhouse. The couple had gotten sick and hadn't been able to keep up with their vegetable garden. It was their food source. They canned for the winter. Savage took care of it while Seychelle visited with them and took down what they might need on her next visit.

Eden Ravard was a favorite, and one neither of them minded visiting. She loved to play cards and was always upbeat, even when her entire kitchen flooded and Savage waded through two inches of water to shut down the main, pump out the water and then fix the pipe. That had been a total disaster, and two of his brothers from Torpedo Ink had come to help.

"You're taking too long to answer me, baby." Savage looked at her over his shoulder. "Are you getting sick of having me around?"

"Of course not. I like having you here with me. You're so good to all my friends."

He waved her toward the kitchen table. She had already set out two dinner plates. He pushed eggs and potatoes onto her plate and then his. The bacon and cheese were already scrambled into his eggs. Now that the aroma of actual food wafted throughout her house, she found she was really hungry.

"I like how you call them all your friends. You haven't even been in Sea Haven that long and you already know all the elderly people who need extra assistance. I went back to the club and told Czar we should have been on that. He was already happy with us helping Doris with her porch. Give us a better rep."

"That's not why you helped them."

"You don't know that."

"Others don't know, Savage," she said. "I do." She forked the eggs into her mouth and savored the flavor. The man could cook. Really. Anything. "You didn't think twice about helping them, and it wasn't because you were looking for goodwill in return."

"You have to stop thinking I'm a good man. I'm not."

"You have to stop thinking you're all bad. You're not," she countered.

"Damn it, Seychelle, has it occurred to you that maybe I'm trying to save your ass?"

Her eyebrow shot up. "Just how are you doing that? By coming here all the time and crawling into my bed? By showing me how sweet you are? How are you saving me? You're seducing me, Savage, little by little. You know you are, so just own it."

She ate the eggs because they were protein and they tasted so good she couldn't help herself. She debated about the potatoes. Carbs. Calories. She had hips. A butt. Breasts. She wasn't buying into his compliments. He might like her figure now, but a few more pounds and he'd be looking elsewhere. Who was she kidding? He might come to her every other night and crawl into her bed, but he wasn't interested in having sex with her. What did that tell a woman?

He wasn't attracted. He might have a permanent erection, because she could see it, but it wasn't for her. It wasn't about her. She hadn't put it there in spite of the fact that she thought she had at first. He came to her because she did what no other woman could do—she took away the rage in him. She soothed him enough that he could sleep when nothing else could get him there. This was about something other than physical attraction, and she knew if she fell for this man, he would need someone else besides her—other women. There would always be other women.

"I know," he said. "I'm always at war with myself. You're so damn honest, Seychelle, and you don't pull your punches. You tell the truth, and you make me face up to mine as well. That truth being, if I wasn't trying to save you, I'd just move in."

She laughed. "The house isn't big enough, and I swear, Savage, I'd gain so much weight I'd have to take up running, and I'm just too lazy for that."

"We're not talking about your weight again. Eat the potatoes and we'll go for a walk. You don't eat enough to keep a bird alive and you walk all over town."

That was true. She liked walking, and Sea Haven wasn't that big, although it was sloped, so she always felt like she was walking uphill when she was visiting her ladies.

"When are you going to come to a Thursday-night jam with the brothers?"

He hadn't asked her in a while. She sighed. "I don't know. I'm thinking about it. I thought they might have found another singer by now."

"They have their hearts set on you. You sing like a fuckin' angel."

"I don't think you can say *angel* and *fuck* in the same sentence without some kind of repercussions, Savage."

"Babe. Really? I'm going to hell, if that's what you're implying, so I can say or do any damn thing I want here on earth."

"You could try not to go to hell," she suggested, and took a cautious bite of the potatoes. It was a major mistake. She knew it would be. They tasted so good. Perfect. Of course they were perfect. He was leading her down a path she knew better than to take, and he was even getting her to eat food she knew better than to eat. If she wasn't careful, she'd be going straight to hell with him.

He was giving her too much of himself—the real man, not the one that was steeped in violence. She had the one no one else knew. He was her best friend. They shared laughter and silly things. They shared truth, no matter how embarrassing or painful. They took care of the elderly and enjoyed their stories. Simple things mattered, like eating eggs and then walking together on the headlands with the wind blowing in their faces.

"You know I have no choice."

There was so much sadness in his voice, she wanted to go to him and put her arms around him. It was all she could do to stay in the chair. It was definitely getting harder to keep herself from being all in with him. That deep well of self-loathing in him disturbed her. She knew he fought every day with himself just to stay alive. She tried to give him as much of herself as she could without compromising her heart, but she knew it wasn't enough. On some level, he knew it too.

"You finished?" Savage stood up abruptly and took her plate, not even commenting on the fact that she hadn't really eaten all the hash browns. Normally, he never would have let her get away with that. He put both plates in the sink, something else he never did, and he took her hand. "Let's go. I need to get some fresh air."

He didn't say another word, just handed her a jacket, pulled on his own and shoved open the door before taking her hand again. She let him. She saw inside him now. It wasn't a surprise to her that sex, violence and pain were all wrapped together in one terrible knot that was tight and bright red with blood dripping down flesh from stripes etched into skin. She absorbed it calmly, not shrinking away like she knew he expected her to do.

She'd never come across anyone like Savage before. He was the epitome of the kind of man a woman like Seychelle should never go near. He was like the flame and she was the moth, drawing ever nearer and nearer. She walked with him, easily falling into step, and he pulled her closer to his warmth, right under his shoulder, until her body was tight against his.

He moved smoothly, no jarring steps in spite of the uneven ground. He was protective, making certain she didn't step off the narrow trail, so that if necessary, he was the one smashing a plant with his heavy motorcycle boots.

They walked in silence and let the wind coming off the ocean tug at their clothes and hair. She was grateful for the continuous assault of the cool breeze that bit at her face and whipped at her eyes so that when tears leaked out, there was another reason other than the slashing pain of the need for whips tearing into skin.

Just as abruptly as Savage had gathered their plates, he swung Seychelle around and all but dragged her back to her house. At the door, he caught her face in his hand, nearly squeezing her jaw between his thumb and forefinger while his eyes blazed down at her like two living flames.

"Can't stay tonight, babe. It's not safe for you."

He leaned down and took her mouth. He wasn't the least bit gentle. His mouth was hard and hot. It was a takeover. An invasion. It was pure hell, flames and wicked heat pouring into her. Rough. He bit her lower lip, a sting his tongue soothed, and she felt an answering fire raging through her veins and pooling low. He stepped back, his hands on her shoulders, steadying her.

"Where are you going?" The query came out a whisper because it was all she could manage.

"San Francisco. Fight club. A couple of the brothers will go with me." He shrugged. "They'll make sure I keep it under control."

He didn't look like it was going to be under control. He looked . . . destroyed.

She shook her head. "Don't go, Savage. I've got a really bad feeling. Stay with me. I can find a way to make it better for you."

He shook his head. "When I'm like this, it's bad. I can't be around you. I want you to promise me you'll stay close to home. Be alert and remember to lock your door."

"Savage, don't go. I really do have a bad feeling." She did. She wanted to hang on to him. Hold him close. She knew something terrible was going to happen if he left her.

"I'll be back in a day or two. You've got that worried look on your face." He bent his head again, and this time he brushed light kisses over her eyes and along the corners of her mouth. One over the little mark on her lip. "Be good."

She stood there, watching him swing his leg over his Harley, listening to the now-familiar roar of the pipes, and he was gone, heading south toward the city. She hoped he remembered to text a couple of his brothers, because he was going to need them. The chaos in his mind told her that.

She did the dishes and tried not to think what he would

be doing all night, but she knew. He would fight one competitor after another. She'd caught glimpses of those brutal battles in his mind. She knew he needed them to calm those ferocious demons that rode him so hard at times.

Lying in bed, she let herself cry for him. She should have tried harder with him, instead of protecting herself. She knew he'd lost hope a long time before he met her, and then, when he was with her, he had renewed optimism, an idea that maybe she could actually bring him peace. She didn't know how it was possible to do so and remain intact. She hadn't figured that out yet, but she wanted to.

By morning she was exhausted, and she spent most of the following day wandering along the headlands and the beaches at Little River, avoiding people. She walked aimlessly, and the entire time she had this odd sensation that someone was watching her. It gave her an eerie feeling, but she was too distraught over losing Savage to care about trying to figure out why she had such a strange, creepy vibe. She put it down to being so emotional when she stopped several times to take a good, long look around her and didn't spot a single soul out on the headlands watching anything but the relentless sea.

By evening she was back in her little house. The moment she entered, her home felt strange, as if someone had been inside. She checked every corner, the closets, the shower—nothing seemed out of place, but the strange jangling of her nerves continued far into the night as she sat alone on her bed. She felt more alone than she ever had now that Savage didn't come. She found herself just staring at the four walls, wishing she knew what to do. For him. For herself. Because when he wasn't with her, she felt like she was living a half life.

━━━

Doris Fendris had been a widow for six years. She had three children, none of whom lived in Sea Haven and only one of whom visited her on what could be considered a regular basis, which meant her daughter came approximately every six weeks on a Sunday. She called every other Sunday and talked to her mother for about fifteen minutes. Doris always looked forward to her calls and chatted with Seychelle about everything her daughter had to say.

Doris called Seychelle late Monday night in tears, saying she'd taken a fall and needed help. She didn't want an ambulance, but could Seychelle come over? There was a part of Seychelle that knew better. She really did, but she went over anyway because she never could stop herself even when she knew the consequences. She had enough sense to park her car right in front of Doris's house and hurry up the walkway to the retro pink door she found obnoxious but strangely Doris loved. It was unlocked, which was also all Doris.

The moment Seychelle walked in, pain hit her hard. Her head felt as if it had exploded, the pain vicious, swamping her. The pain was so severe, wholly encompassing, and it drove her to her knees. Her ankle buckled completely, and she went down to the floor. Seychelle pressed both fists to her chest over her wildly beating heart, took a deep breath and then dragged herself out the door. It was a full minute before she was able to stand on the porch and take several deep breaths before calling out to Doris.

"I'm here on the front porch. Doris, do you need an ambulance?"

The sound of sobbing greeted her query. It was loud and keening, tearing at Seychelle's heartstrings. She took another deep breath and forced herself to step inside again. Seychelle had to fight to keep from vomiting. The pain in her head was that severe, her eyesight suddenly blurring.

She found Doris lying half in and half out of the living room, with the phone beside her on the floor. Tears poured down her face. She sat with her back to the couch, sobbing, pressing her hands to her temples as if trying to keep her head from coming apart. One leg was stretched out and the other tucked up under her.

"Migraine. Vicious. One of the worst I've had yet," Doris managed to get out.

Seychelle didn't need to be told. She felt the pain pounding through her head. There was no doubt it was going to take her down very soon. She ran her hands gently over Doris's leg to search for damage. There was bruising on her calf and swelling on her ankle.

"You have to calm down and let me help you, Doris," she said softly, trying to find composure herself in the midst of the storm. "Tell me what happened."

"It's my daughter," Doris said, when she finally managed to speak after Seychelle had gotten her water and tissues. "She called and said her husband doesn't like her coming so much, and she wants me to sell my house and move closer to her. Maybe into a home where someone caretakes me. She loves to visit and so do the kids, but he can't be bothered, and it annoys him if she comes here alone, because she isn't there to fix his dinners. She only comes once every six weeks, but she still chooses him over me."

Another fresh flood of tears. "I won't move there. I love it here. She knows that, and he won't let her come see me anyway. How can she decide to stay with him?"

Doris began to cry again like her heart was breaking, and Seychelle knew that it was. Her sons lived several states away from their mother. She didn't expect them to visit very often, but her daughter had always been her best friend, and she adored her grandchildren. She knew she wouldn't see them anymore unless her daughter chose to leave her selfish husband.

The stress of the call had brought on the terrible migraine she had been subjected to on and off throughout her life. The vicious headaches came on fast, very severe, taking her vision and making her sick; the migraine had made her disoriented. Crying, she had twisted her ankle and fallen.

It took effort to get Doris off the floor, into her nightclothes and into bed. Seychelle made certain Doris took her migraine medication and drank plenty of water. All the while as she did so, Seychelle began to take on more of her pain. She drew it slowly from the older woman, afraid Doris would have a heart attack and die in the night from the stress of the choice her daughter had made.

The more Doris's pain poured into her, the sicker it made Seychelle until, like when she'd first arrived, she could barely stand up. She doubled over beside the bed and then found herself on her knees. That sobered Doris up immediately. She leaned forward in the pristine white cotton gown that Seychelle had helped her into.

"Are you all right, dear? Should I call someone?"

Seychelle shook her head. Who was there to call? She indicated for Doris to rest and dragged herself to her feet, using the furniture to pull herself up. This was going to be bad. Already her vision was so blurred she could barely make Doris out, and she was right in front of her. Her head pounded and her stomach was churning. In another few minutes she was going to black out if she was lucky; if she wasn't, she was going to be very, very sick.

She staggered into the living room and found herself on her hands and knees, crawling to the front door. Managing to get out of the house by falling through the door frame, she jerked the door closed after her and rested against it, her heart pounding. There was no way she could drive her car home. The only person she could think to call was Savage. He'd programmed his number into her phone, but she'd never used it—not once in the weeks they'd been friends. Weird friends, but friends.

She had no idea if he was back from San Francisco or, if he was, whether he'd really come for her, but she didn't have much choice. He'd been gone three days. It was possible he was home, but he hadn't contacted her. If he didn't come for her, she'd be riding this out on Doris's front porch, and it was really cold outside. She was *so* sick. She was going to vomit, and she didn't want to do that on the porch.

With shaky fingers, she texted him. **Need help, very sick at Doris's, can't drive home. Can you get me home? On front porch.** The answer came back immediately. **On my way.**

She closed her eyes. She didn't want him to see her like this. She knew he was trying to figure out the way her gifts worked. She couldn't tell him, because she didn't fully comprehend how they worked, but she was fairly certain that having taken on her parents' illnesses to prolong their lives and now helping others the way she was doing was slowly killing her. She just couldn't fight the compulsion.

It seemed like hours passed, because she was in agony, but she knew it was only a few minutes before Savage was crouched down beside her, sweeping the hair from her face with gentle fingers. Her heart contracted at the look on his face. So gentle. The caring there. She could see it so plainly, and everything in her responded to it. No one had ever looked at her the way he did—as if she was his world.

"Do I need to take you to a hospital?"

She shook her head. "Just sick. A migraine. Very bad. My ankle." She had to reply through clenched teeth. If she opened her mouth, she'd get sick all over him. "Home, please."

"Keys?"

She nodded toward her pocket. He didn't hesitate but reached into her jacket and tugged them out. She heard the second motorcycle arrive and put her head down, embarrassed that anyone else would see her curled up in the fetal position, rocking back and forth on an elderly woman's front porch.

"Just Ink and Mechanic bringing my bike to your house for me," Savage said. "I'm driving your car."

That made sense, but her head was pounding so hard she couldn't think clearly. Nor could she see properly. She was grateful he'd come for her. Savage. She'd fallen so hard, so fast. She knew it was too soon and far, far too much. She was giving him all of her because she was the type of woman who, once she made up her mind, couldn't hold anything back. She gave every part of herself to him. She was all in. All his. Heart and soul.

Savage gathered her up, lifting her into his arms, cradling her close to his chest as if she was the most precious cargo in the world. For one second, she was dizzy with love. With the most amazing, wonderful feeling, almost a euphoria, in spite of her lurching stomach and pounding head.

And then it hit her. The woman. The smell of her. The scent of the woman's sexual lust mixed with Savage's raw, violent, sexual scent. His mingling with the woman's. The color red slashed across her vision.

Betrayal was a red-hot poker, as crimson and as bright as those streaks in her vision, only this was a knife stabbing over and over through her heart. The reality of betrayal was brutal and visceral, shredding her, ripping her to pieces, just as she'd known it would. It hurt worse than if he'd beaten her. That terrible stabbing continued over and over, driving through her body until she felt every single hole, until there was nothing left of her flesh on the bones. It hurt worse than the very real physical pain of that vicious jack-hammer drilling at her head in the form of a migraine.

Seychelle struggled. Fought him. Tried desperately to get out of his arms. She had to get away from him. His touch was killing her, stripping her down to nothing but raw, visceral pain.

"Stop it, Seychelle. Be still. I have to get you to the car." He spat the command through clenched teeth.

They shared the vision of the woman on her knees, her naked body striped with his mark, his brand, her mouth eagerly devouring his cock. He was there with her, just as upset as she was. Just as horrified. As disgusted. As fiercely rejecting the truth that was in that highly detailed vision between them because he'd come straight from the woman to Seychelle. He hadn't even taken the time to do more than empty himself down her throat, pull away, jerk up his jeans and run for his motorcycle.

"Damn it. Stop it."

She'd landed a punch to his jaw. It wasn't hard, because she couldn't find the necessary strength when she was so sick, but at least he had the door to the car open, and he all but dumped her on the front seat. She curled up in the fetal position and rocked herself, closing her eyes, trying not to think. Trying to force herself to just count. She needed to get home. Find peace.

"Baby, listen to me. I know you're hurt. I know this fucking hurt you."

The car was in motion and he was talking. That voice. The one that could wrap her in velvet and smooth over every abrasion and cut on her skin. Those scars she wore for him. Nothing could soothe this away. Nothing. She had no skin left; he'd torn it all off her.

"It would have hurt a lot more if this had been done to you."

She wanted to cover her ears. She *felt* the victory in the woman. The greed. The hot need for sex. She was practically begging him. The worst of it all was, Seychelle knew Savage could have cared less about the woman. He didn't know her name. He didn't want to know her name. She was absolutely nothing to him. He'd found a woman more physically attractive, had sex with her and didn't even know her name or care one thing about her. He'd given her that side of himself, depraved, sick and violent—it was still Savage, *her* Savage, and he'd given that man to someone else. Not her.

She detested that she felt so betrayed. She detested that she was so weak, that she loved him so much she was that hurt. She wanted him gone. She kept counting over and over in her head to drown out the sound of his voice, refusing to hear what he said. She could smell him, smell the woman, the mixture of sex and the coppery taint of blood. Thankfully, he wasn't touching her, so she didn't have to feel his emotions or the woman's. She just had to feel sick and shiver with the pain of Doris's vicious migraine and twisted ankle and the knowledge of Savage's betrayal until her body would finally reject everything.

The car slowed. Behind them, she heard the sound of the motorcycles. Her hand fumbled for the door handle the moment the car was turned off. She managed to get the door open, but there was no way to walk. When she tried, she was too dizzy to take a step, and her ankle collapsed under her.

"I'm taking you into the house."

"You can't touch me." Seychelle backed up to the car, pressed hard against it for balance and forced herself to look at him. Savage. God. She was so in love with him. What was wrong with her that she'd let herself step off that cliff? She'd promised herself she wouldn't, and yet she must have, to hurt so bad.

"It can't be helped. It's only a few steps, and you know the worst. I'll get you inside and we'll talk."

They weren't talking. There was no talking his way around this one. This had been her greatest fear. She'd wondered if she could handle it. She had almost persuaded herself that she could. Now she knew she couldn't. There was no way.

She didn't argue with him. There was no arguing with Savage when he made up his mind. He had that look on his face. He came at her, caught her up and strode toward the front door. Seychelle did her best to keep her mind blank. To not inhale. To not breathe. She concentrated on counting. She didn't want to feel his emotions. Or her emotions.

Savage put her on the bed, and she scrambled to the familiar headboard, grateful that she'd taken the time to make every single space in her home count. The crystals sang to her, and sitting right there, in that exact spot, always made her feel so much better. Only, nothing helped. Nothing would ever help again.

She moistened her lips and forced herself to say the one thing that would make him have to leave. The one thing she knew he couldn't ignore. "I want you to leave, Savage, and I don't want you ever to come back. I mean it. We're not friends. We're not ever going back to being friends. I can't do this, so you have to go."

Savage stood across from her, and he looked as devastated as she felt. She didn't expect that. He shook his head. "Don't. Seychelle, don't. I know this hurts. I know it's fucked up. I'm fucked up. You knew that. I never hid it. I did this to keep you from getting hurt."

She knew that. God help her, she knew that. And she'd known he'd say that.

"I'm not the only one fucked up, Seychelle. You need me as much as I need you. You don't want it to be true because it scares the crap out of you. I scare you. What's between us scares you, and it should. It's raw and violent, and it can get out of control. The thing is, look at you. Look at what happened to you. If you were my woman, that wouldn't happen. Not ever. You want to know why? Because I would make absolutely certain I knew what was happening and I'd stop it. I'd teach you how to control it."

"Unless it was all about you."

He shook his head. "That's where you're wrong, baby. *Especially* when it's about me. I'm that scary and that violent. We both know that. That's when you have to be your strongest, and you make the choice, not me. That's when you control what you take on. But you have to learn, because right now, you're wide open and everything hurts you."

She pulled her legs tighter to her chest. "You hurt me, Savage. Like no one else, and you'll keep doing it. I can take a lot, but I can't take that. You have to go. You're tearing me up, and I can't recover. There's no way back for me."

There was a long silence. Savage shook his head. "Seychelle. Baby. Think carefully before you do this. You throw me out and you mean it, there's no way for me to come back from it. We have a code. Torpedo Ink has a code. We live it. We breathe it. I am Torpedo Ink. You say you mean it, I have to leave and I can't come back."

"I do mean it. You have to go. I don't want you back." She had to say it fast before she couldn't say it. It was self-preservation, the only way to survive.

Again, there was a long silence. His voice was raw when he answered her. "Here's the bottom line, Seychelle. You've made it impossible for me to come back inside your home. I have no choice but to leave, because you're making it clear that's what you want. But if you ever change your mind and you come to the club for any reason . . . *Any reason*. Be fuckin' clear on that. You show up on a Thursday to rehearse with the band, you're declaring to me that you want me. That you're coming to me and you're mine. There's no going back from that decision. Are we clear?"

She couldn't imagine that he'd think she was going to sing with his band. What? And watch women hang all over him?

"I don't come inside your house. I'll respect that. This is your space. But you respect mine. You don't decide the clubhouse needs to be cleaned. You don't cater a party or come to one. You don't go into the laundry business."

"You've lost your mind," she whispered. Maybe he had. She felt a little as if she'd lost hers.

"I just want you to understand, Seychelle, because I mean every fuckin' word I'm saying to you. You come to my territory for any reason, then all bets are off, and you belong to me. Do you understand what that would mean? You show up, you're making the choice to be with me. That's how I'm taking it. That's what you're declaring. And there won't be any going back from it."

She wasn't a child. He couldn't be making himself any clearer. She definitely understood every single word he said. It wasn't like she was going to choose to go sing with his band. Or clean his clubhouse. Or wash his clothes. Or watch some woman blow him.

"I think I got it, Savage." Her throat was so raw, it burned when she whispered to him.

"I'm not just going to leave you like this. I've texted Steele, and he's on his way. Once he tells me you're good, then I'll go. He's our doc."

Fear coursed through her, bright and hot. She didn't want

a doctor examining her, not again. Never again. She didn't want someone telling her—or him—her days were numbered. She didn't need to hear that. She knew she looked scared. She could tell he saw too much just by the look on his face when she involuntarily pulled back, making herself small and giving a little cry of pain, both hands covering her temples and then her eyes.

Savage dimmed the lights immediately. He pulled her favorite tank she wore to bed from her drawer along with her little shorts, and impersonally pulled her shirt from over her head and then got rid of her bra. Without a word, he dressed her in her pajamas. Seychelle ignored him, rolling onto her side. She didn't want to look at him. Her vision was so blurred anyway, trying to focus on anything, especially Savage, just made her sicker.

Eventually, she became aware of a second man in the room, sitting next to her on the bed, murmuring softly to Savage. She shivered violently, continually, her teeth chattering. She recognized those signs. Her body tried to rid itself of the toxic diseases she'd taken on from another party. Steele's hands were cool on her temples. Then her ankle. He stroked his fingers over her skin. She ignored both men, wishing they'd just go away.

She must have said it aloud.

"I heard you," Savage said.

Tears blurred her vision. "Please don't come back."

He brushed the tears from her face. "You remember what I said. Every word I said, Seychelle. If you come to me, there's no taking that back." Savage didn't leave immediately. He stood there a long time and then framed her face with both hands. "I swear to you, I gave you the best of me." He brushed a kiss across her lips, and then he was gone, taking her heart and soul with him. Taking everything and leaving her with nothing.

EIGHT

Savage didn't like one single thing Steele had to say to him about what he found when he examined Seychelle. Steele had psychic talents. He had the ability to heal and the capability to do surgery psychically. He'd saved Player, one of the Torpedo Ink brothers, when no brain surgeon could have done so. He was a powerful doctor, a surgeon, healing both physically or psychically, and yet he didn't hold out much hope for Seychelle.

"She's a psychic healer, Savage," Steele told him with a sigh, pushing a hand through his hair as they walked out the door of the cottage together. "I'm sorry, brother. I wish I had something good to tell you, but I don't. She doesn't heal others in the same way I do. She takes on the actual illness or injury, and I don't do that. It could kill her. It is killing her. Her body is wearing out. She can't keep it up, not at the rate she's going."

Savage's breath caught in his lungs. "What the fuck does that mean?"

"Her heart is damaged. She doesn't have heart disease, but she must have tried to heal someone with heart disease, or she took it on. There are signs of all kinds of other illnesses.

She has to stop and let her body rest, Savage. Seriously. That girl is worn out."

Savage hung his head. He should have seen it. All along the signs were there. Seychelle did need him. Physical pain wasn't the same as taking on disease. He'd been so worried about what he might do to her, what she might think of him, and all along she was killing herself slowly, allowing those around her to kill her because she couldn't stop herself. That was what she meant by her lack of control. Now it was too late. Torpedo Ink had a code. He couldn't go back to her until she invited him back. Unless she came to him. In the meantime, he had to find ways to keep her safe.

He had the brothers watch over her the next few days while he thought about the best way to find out about her gift and how to help her. He had heard rumors that Blythe's cousin Libby Drake was a healer. She was a doctor as well, but she was reputed to have the psychic gift of healing. Libby Drake came from the infamous Drake family, a notorious family in Sea Haven many locals thought of as royalty.

A few years earlier there had been a write-up in a magazine about Libby. Whether it was true or not, only Blythe could tell him. He didn't ask favors of others, but only Seychelle mattered to him, not his ego. He needed this for his woman. Even if she never let him back into her life, he had to find out how to help. He texted Blythe.

Need you to get in touch with your cousin Libby Drake. Need a sit-down with her.

It took a long time before she answered him. As a rule, Blythe got back to any member of Torpedo Ink immediately. The fact that it was Savage, who never texted her, would make her want to answer even faster.

I don't like letting you down, but the Drakes are secretive and I'm protective of them just as I'm protective of you. Why do you need Libby?

Blythe was straight-up asking. Either he had to tell her, or she wasn't going to take any chances with her cousin. He didn't blame her. In fact, he respected her all the more. It meant she would be equally as fierce protecting Seychelle.

Suspect Seychelle has the same gift. Need to know how it works. Steele examined her, Czar can confirm if need be. Worried. Have to know how to take care of her. I don't need Libby to heal her. Just need advice. Give favor in return if needed. Word of honor whatever is said between us stays that way. Need way to help Seychelle.

Libby is shy speaking to outsiders about her gift. It isn't done. Don't get your hopes up and don't take it personally if she refuses. Will ask.

Savage paced up and down all night waiting for Blythe's answer to his request. His brothers Storm and Keys, the two watching over Seychelle, said she hadn't moved from her bed, other than to use the bathroom. She wasn't even taking her normal walks on the headlands. He detested that he wasn't there to take care of her. It took three days before the answer came. Three long days and nights. Savage was afraid he might lose his fucking mind.

It turned out Libby was pulling her shift at the hospital and doing volunteer work as well. She also had to think his request over very carefully, and Tyson Derrick, her husband, wanted to investigate him—meaning talk to Jonas Harrington and Jackson Deveau. Both men were her brothers-in-law. Savage couldn't blame Tyson. He would have done the same thing to protect his woman. But that was three more nights without much in the way of sleep.

He'd taken the ride to Sea Haven all three nights and sat outside Seychelle's bedroom window, his ass on the ground, back to the wall, eyes closed, hoping she knew he was close. Two of those nights the fog rolled in, turning the world into a deep gray mist, and he turned his face up like a sacrifice. The fourth day he got a text that Libby would meet him at Czar's residence while the kids were away at Maxim and Airiana's home. Maxim was one of Czar's birth brothers, who owned the large farm with him.

Savage wasn't happy that they were meeting at Czar's home, but he'd take the meet anywhere. He was just grateful he'd get one. The Drake family consisted of seven sisters, all with tremendous psychic talents. The small village of Sea Haven tended to attract those with gifts, or hidden talents. The Drake sisters were considered to be the most powerful of all those living in the area, but who really knew?

Jonas Harrington, the local sheriff, was married to Hannah Drake. She owned a tea and bath and body shop in town. Jackson Deveau, a deputy sheriff, was married to the youngest Drake sister, Elle. Savage knew very little about her, other than that she was considered to be the most powerful of all the Drake sisters. He hoped so. He hoped she gave Jackson hell as often as possible.

Libby Drake Derrick had the body of a ballet dancer. She wore her thick, jet-black hair short, curving around the chin of her delicate face. The color of her hair really showed off the intensity of her vivid green eyes. Tyson Derrick, her husband, a brilliant biochemist, was an unexpectedly muscular man with wavy black hair and piercing blue eyes. He gave off a protective vibe as he sat beside his wife, although his handshake was direct and without any stupid manly games.

Savage could feel the subtle power coming off of Libby Drake the moment she walked into the room. He had grown up with psychic talent, and there was no mistaking the energy. With Libby, that energy was so strong it could barely be contained. She was a woman it would be impossible to withhold secrets from. She would be stripping him raw in seconds, seeing inside him, straight to the monster, if he sat in the same room with her for very long.

He didn't hesitate. This wasn't about him. This was about Seychelle and finding a way to save her life. If Libby Drake saw that he needed to wield a whip to be aroused and she was disgusted by him, he would take that. The information she had was too important for him to be worried about what anyone thought of him. They stared at each other, each sizing the other up. She was very aware he knew she could see inside of him and didn't care.

"Thank you for seeing me, Mrs. Derrick." He was formal. Polite. He didn't know how to be with her. He wasn't a man used to moving in her circles. He stayed in the shadows and came out when someone needed to disappear.

"Please call me Libby. I much prefer that we're not formal." She flashed him a gentle but very real smile. "Blythe is my cousin, and it's been very nice getting to know Czar and her family. I'm happy that I can finally start to meet some of Czar's family."

Savage wasn't certain he was the best one of the Torpedo Ink members for her to start with, but he forced himself to meet her eyes and nod. "Czar's got a lot of family members, but I've heard you do as well."

Libby acknowledged the truth of his statement with a small smile. "Blythe told me your friend has a talent similar to mine and you're looking for information on how best to help her."

Savage nodded. "Seychelle is extraordinary. She isn't a doctor, and she hasn't had any medical training. Both of her parents had long-term illnesses: her mother, a form of blood cancer, and her father, heart disease. She didn't even realize she was taking that on herself to prolong their lives. She doesn't seem to be able to stop herself from doing it, and she's wearing herself out. I don't understand how it works, and I don't know how to help her. I'm afraid I'm going to lose her."

Tyson threaded his fingers through his wife's, and she smiled up at him before once more turning her attention to Savage.

"My talent works much the same as yours. It's a compulsion I can't stop. If Seychelle is like I am, she can't stop any more than I am able to or you can. I imagine yours started at a very young age. You've been shouldering the anger and rage for the others, as much as you could manage, for years, right? You can't stop yourself now, even if you wanted to. It's too ingrained in you. Whenever the people you love most are too close to their limit of pain with anger at betrayal or whatever, and you're with them, you just take it on. That's what happens with a healer's gift. At least our kind of gift. Tyson has to keep me in check. My sisters did before him."

"Wait." Czar surged to his feet. "What the hell did you just say, Libby? Does she mean us? Torpedo Ink? What do you mean, Savage takes on our pain? What does she mean by that, Savage?" There was pure shock in his voice. On his face.

Blythe put a restraining hand on Czar's wrist, but there was nothing that was going to stop him as he paced across the room, every step portraying hurt, guilt and bewilderment. "I need someone to tell me right now what that means." He swung around to face Savage. "You've been shouldering that for me all this time and I didn't know?"

Libby looked confused. Her eyes met Savage's. "I'm so sorry. I thought everyone knew about your ability."

"What ability? Apparently, the president of your club, your brother, doesn't know about your ability, Savage," Czar bit out. His incomprehension began to give way to temper, the one thing that allowed him to cover up his real feelings. "Maybe you want to enlighten me."

"Not at this time," Savage said calmly. "Right now, Libby is going to tell me what I can do to help Seychelle. After that, Czar, I'll be happy to fill you in, if you really think it's necessary."

"Yeah, Savage. I really think it's necessary." Czar stood for a few moments staring out the window, and then he sank into the chair beside Blythe. She took his hand, her fingers sliding over his soothingly.

Once Czar was seated, Savage continued, "If you explain how it actually works, Libby, and I understand it, then maybe Tyson can explain how he stops you."

"That's easy enough." Tyson grinned at him, kissed Libby's hand and brought it to his chest. "Caveman style is sometimes the only way. Other times I just say her name and she knows that's the only warning she's going to get before the caveman appears. We try to have code words. Signals."

Libby nodded. "I take on the actual illness. If your Seychelle is attempting to help someone with a heart condition, she's actually taking on that heart condition. Potentially, that can kill her. I'm a doctor. I've learned that I can't do certain things. I know going into things I have to say no, and if the compulsion is overwhelming, I can't even enter the room unless I have backup with me to stop me from doing it. Seychelle is going in blind. She has no training. She may not know what she's taking on. From what you just told me, she had very sick parents, and she must have prolonged their lives by exchanging her own health without even knowing it."

Libby leaned toward Savage. "She is very lucky to be alive. More than once, even with my sisters aiding me—and they are extremely powerful—I nearly died. This type of exchange can be deadly. What you do is violent and deadly. Any gift of this magnitude has consequences. We pay a price, all of us. It's an exchange, Savage. When we use our gifts, we're agreeing to pay that price. She is probably becoming aware now that she's trading her life for those she's helping, but she can't stop what she's doing because it's too late. She doesn't know how any more than you do, or I do."

Savage scrubbed his hands over his face. Seychelle was in her house right now, wide open, unprotected, because he'd fucked up. He should have laid it all out. Still, he'd been at the end of a cycle. He wouldn't have had time to prepare her for what she would have to go through with him, even if she agreed to belong to him. He'd been at his worst. No matter what, it would have been too dangerous to be with him. In that moment he despised what and who he was more than he ever had. He thought he'd come to terms with it long ago, but now, all over again, he loathed himself.

"Can she recover? Is there a way I can keep her safe?"

Libby glanced at the others in the room. "I would like to speak with Savage alone."

Tyson frowned at her, clearly wanting to protest. Czar did the same. Blythe stood up immediately, prompting the two men to do so as well. Reluctantly, they followed Blythe out. She was the one to close the door.

There was silence as the two of them looked at each other. Savage didn't flinch under her steady gaze.

"If I can see you, she can," Libby said. Her voice was still that same soft, accepting tone. Clearly, she wasn't probing too deep. "I doubt if she's adept enough yet to see more than flashes, but it would be enough to see what you've done for the others. You shoulder their emotional pain, Savage, and it's tremendous. Not just when you were children, but even now. There's rage. Sheer rage. Hurt. Terror. So many emotions all blended together. You take those burdens on so they're bearable for the others. She sees that in you, and that's why she's so drawn to you. Not just the healer in her—and she can't take that on—but the woman in her."

He was aware of what Libby was telling him on some level. The monster in him was counting on it.

"You're worried about your lifestyle impacting her health," Libby said, getting straight to the point. "She doesn't have to heal you. Physical pain isn't the same thing as sickness, Savage. What she chooses to suffer on your behalf, or if she chooses to find pleasure in the sexual practices with you, is up to her. Those things will not in any way affect her health."

"You're positive? My lifestyle can be . . . rough."

"You know better than I do that what she will need is rest and care. Lots of it. You will have to see to those things, no matter what lifestyle you have with her."

Savage knew that already. His intention was to give Seychelle more care than she'd ever had in her life. So much she'd probably feel smothered.

Libby leaned in close. "I can see that you love this woman and you intend to care for her. If that's the case, you have to build such trust between you that she will accept your word instantly. I was lucky to have my sisters to guide me. If I screwed up, I knew I endangered them as well as myself. Your woman doesn't have those guidelines. She's doing all of this blind. She has instincts and a tremendous compulsion just like you have. Think about trying to stop what you do. You're a force of nature. You don't want her to think you're a dictator. I can't emphasize this to you enough. If you don't get her to understand and willingly follow your guidance, she's going to die. That's the bottom line. If you can't convince her that you *have* to step in to save her life, then you'll lose her. I'm willing to speak to her if you need me to. I'll give you my cell phone number."

"Thanks. She loves to sing. She wants to sing with bands some of the time, but when she does, there are people who are sick. I had a headache the other night and she took it away. The next thing I knew, she had it. When I realized what she'd done, I was so fucking pissed I could barely see straight. She loves singing. Loves it. But when she's up there, she can't help herself . . ." He trailed off, shaking his head. "If I take that away, if I take everything she loves from her, what does she have?"

"You can't take that away. You have to communicate. She has to trust you implicitly. You have to do exactly what Tyson said. Have signs, code words, and if that doesn't work, then you become the caveman. Her band can be clued in, be part of her protection. They can help. As for taking away a headache, Savage, she has to be a healer. That's her gift, and you have to let her do the small things that won't kill her. Especially for you. For the people she cares about. Little things aren't going to harm her, and she'll grow in control."

"So, eventually, she'll be able to control her impulse to heal people?"

Libby shook her head. "No, she'll have a little more control in that she'll be able to reach out to you and tell you she's in trouble. Can you stop yourself from taking on the emotional pain or the anger and rage of the others in your club?"

"No, I can't stop," he admitted. "I know to gain Sey-chelle's trust, I have to be completely honest with her. I don't want her to blame the others for the buildup of violence and rage that happens in me." He rubbed both his hands over his head in agitation, wanting to pound his fists into the wall. For a moment the walls actually breathed in and out with him. "I can't change what's in me, Libby."

"Has she asked you to?"

The moment she spoke in that soft, sweet tone, the terrible buildup of anger in him settled back in the well. He shook his head. "No, Seychelle isn't like that. She's . . . extraordinary."

Libby smiled at him. "You've used that word before."

"You're absolutely certain that the things I need sexually won't contribute to her becoming ill?"

Libby shook her head. "Those are two different things. I can't stress enough that she has to take care of herself. Resting. Eating right. The right kind of exercise. She probably is already doing that, or she wouldn't have lasted this long, but you need to be on board with that. If you really love this woman, Savage, you have to watch her the way Tyson watches over me. If you don't love her enough to do that, walk away from her now."

"Do you get upset with him when he tells you 'Enough'?"

"Every single time when the compulsion is very strong," she answered honestly. "Would you like it if Seychelle told you to stop when you needed to help out your brothers in the club?"

Savage hadn't thought of that. He wouldn't like it, nor would he be able to stop. He shook his head. "I see what you're saying." He couldn't help but like her. "I can't thank you enough. Blythe told me you're a very private person and this would be difficult for you, so it's even more appreciated. I understand wanting privacy more than most people."

"I'm really sorry about revealing your talent to Czar and Blythe. I had no idea they didn't know. Czar seems to be aware of every talent. He has a gift that way. How yours escaped him is beyond me. It's very powerful, especially when you're close to him. You use it on him quite often, don't you?"

Savage considered carefully what he was going to say. She was Blythe's cousin, and she could see into people, but he had no idea how much she actually knew of their childhood. The Drake sisters had stood with them when they had come to Sea Haven in the hopes of taking down a major human trafficking ring and killing the man who was determined to murder the youngest Drake sister and her husband, Jackson.

Savage chose his words with care. "Czar sacrificed a lot for all of us. When we were kids, the weight of us was crushing on him. Seeing all of us, the way he had to, unable to stop what was happening. Someone had to help him. I didn't know I was doing it at first, and then when I realized I could, I started trying to develop my ability. I wanted it to be very strong so I could help him. I was so much younger, and he seemed larger than life." He shrugged, a roll of his shoulders. "I don't want to keep you, Libby. I really appreciate your time. I have a long way to go to help Seychelle, but I'll find a way to get her back."

"I have no doubt you will." Libby offered her hand as she stood up.

Savage knew touching her was dangerous to both of them. He could read her almost as easily as she could read him, but he figured she already knew the worst of him, so why the hell not? Libby's healing power was immense. It was tied to her sisters, giving her a huge well of energy to draw on should there be need. She gave him a sweet smile and left him there in the room to go join the others.

Savage considered trying to make a break for it out the back door, but he knew no matter what, he'd have to face Czar, and it was just better to get things over. He waited a little impatiently for him, staring out the window, watching Tyson open the door of his sleek Corvette for Libby. Tyson was a brainiac. The real deal. He also was a bit of an adrenaline junkie if the rumors were true, but the way he hovered over his wife showed he was definitely into her. Savage liked that. Libby Drake deserved a husband who loved her.

"You want to tell me what's going on, Savage?" Czar greeted as he entered the room. It was an order.

Savage turned to face the man who had saved all of them—all the original members of Torpedo Ink. Without him, there would have been no survival. He didn't pretend not to understand. He would never disrespect Czar that way.

"It's a small talent I discovered as a child. I wanted to find a way to help you—to help everyone. I didn't feel I had much to offer. I'd come back ripped to pieces and all of you would have to take care of me. I could feel your anger, the rage building in you because you felt so helpless. It wasn't your fault. You couldn't stop what was happening, but you took it on your shoulders. Everything that was happening to each of us."

"You were a fucking toddler, Savage, when they started on you," Czar bit out.

Savage nodded. "I realize that. My world had been turned upside down. Reaper was in bad shape. They murdered my sisters. Everything around me was blood and pain. I needed to focus on something, and you were the only thing that made sense. You fought back. Even then, the idea of fighting back gave me hope when nothing else could. So I practiced on developing that talent because it was all I could do when I was so scared something would happen to you."

"How could I not know?"

"Probably because I wasn't very good at it," Savage replied with a humorless smile, but the rage was building in his eyes. In his gut. Already he was pulling it from Czar in the way he had been doing all his life. There was no way to stop it, no way to control it—he'd been doing it since he was a little child. Too many years had gone by, and it was so ingrained in him he practically bled the rage from the others in steady streams.

"I had no way of knowing back then, although I think even as a child, I realized the tremendous amount of weight you carried. The basement was enormous, and many of the others were older. It was like a jungle down there with so many territories. Everyone owning their own piece, like gangs. You were the youngest and yet the strongest, holding one of the best spots. You had to make decisions, turning away children that wanted to be with us, children we wanted to have join our group. Sometimes we'd be angry about your decision. That was so hard on you, but in the end, you were always right about them. They ratted on everyone."

Every day had been a lesson in survival. Czar had been so young and yet he'd guided them through the pitfalls of the older boys trying to steal food, encroach on the meager territory they had. Viktor had chosen what had seemed to the others as one of the worst spots in the basement, but it was below the kitchen and the ovens, so in the freezing of the winter, they had some heat. He planned out everything carefully and chose each person to join their group—only the ones he knew would stay loyal no matter what.

Czar studied Savage's face for a long time. "I think you were very good at what you did, and you got even better as time went on. The girls you trained?"

Savage shook his head. "Physical pain isn't the same as emotional, and by that time, they'd already conditioned me to need both from them. It was too late for me and them. I just had to get them to a place where they accepted what was happening to them."

"You did your best, Savage, one hour at a time, like we all did," Czar said. "I wish I'd known what you were doing. You already carried a heavy enough burden. Crawling through the vents with Reaper, our appointed assassin, when we knew they were going to kill one of us. Those bastards forcing you to use those whips. It was bad enough what they did to all of us, but . . ." He trailed off. "No matter what I did, I couldn't protect any of you."

"We were all kids, you included. It's all good now, Czar." But Savage knew it wasn't. Unless he was able to convince Seychelle to give him another chance, nothing in his life was ever going to be right again. He wouldn't give up. When he wanted something, he kept going until he got it. Her life was too important. If she absolutely refused to take him back even as a friend, he had to find a way to get her in touch with Libby.

For the next three weeks, Savage found it impossible to stay away from Seychelle. He couldn't sleep more than a few minutes at a time. The nightmares were worse than ever. He spent as long as he could pacing in his room at the clubhouse and then he rode to her cottage. He would sit on his bike for several minutes, listening to the sound of the ocean as the waves battered the rocks and cliffs. The frogs would start up. The crickets would call to one another. That was his signal to get off his bike and walk over to the side of her house.

He sat under her bedroom window. That wasn't violating the code. He didn't go inside. He just sat there. The first night, the bedroom window was closed. He knew she heard and recognized his Harley. She couldn't fail to recognize it. After the first night, her window was open, and he swore she was awake, and he could breathe her scent into his lungs. He imagined her sitting just on the other side of the wall, breathing him in at the same time. Hurting like he was. Those were the best and the worst nights. He was hurting. But he knew she was hurting because she stayed to herself, according to his brothers watching over her. She didn't eat much, and she walked alone along the headlands. She cried herself to sleep.

Each morning, after he'd been there, she went outside and looked at the tracks where his motorcycle had been. She always picked up his offering to her—a perfect red rose with a long stem and no thorns. That long stem was intertwined with the stem of a dark rose that did have many thorns. She couldn't fail to understand what he was trying to tell her. She put all twenty-one pairs into a vase.

Nearly a month had gone by, and she'd stayed alone in her cottage, just walking the headlands, playing her guitar and crying. During that time, the club members reported to Savage daily. He didn't like their reports.

The first week, Joseph Arnold walked along the headlands with a camera every few days, mostly aiming the camera away from the ocean and toward Seychelle's cottage. He didn't go near the place or Seychelle. Had he done so, the club members would have stopped him. Eventually, he disappeared.

The third week, Brandon Campbell drove Doris to the cottage to see Seychelle. She had the good sense to sit outside in the chairs by the two grills Savage had left behind. He had no way of knowing if she knew Transporter and Mechanic were close, but she didn't let the visitors inside her home. Mechanic was close enough to record every word and send it to Savage. The video was very clear, and Savage reviewed it over and over, looking at Seychelle's face, listening to her voice, and then studying Brandon's expressions and voice.

"I've been so worried about you, Seychelle," Doris said. "I called and left you messages. You didn't pick up. I asked Brandon to drop by just to make certain you were okay, and he did twice. He said you didn't answer the door."

Seychelle turned her head to look at Brandon, her blue eyes lifeless. She was looking directly into the camera. "How strange. I never heard you knock."

Mechanic interjected his own commentary. "That's because the son of a bitch is lying his ass off. He didn't stop by. He did watch the house from up the street three days in a row. Then he parked just across from her house two nights in a row and made out with some girl with his eyes open, watching the house. He never went near it."

Savage wondered what his game was. Seychelle's voice sounded as if she wasn't the least bit interested in the conversation. Ordinarily, that would have made him happy, but he wanted her alert. Just having Brandon show up with Doris should have raised red flags, but Seychelle barely gave the man a glance.

"Are you all right, Seychelle? You were so sick when you left my house," Doris persisted. "You've lost weight. Brandon, she's lost so much weight."

Seychelle attempted a smile at the older woman. "Brandon always pointed out how chubby I was. Actually, I believe he used the word *fat*. Isn't that what you said on every occasion we met? Fat? He said I needed to lose weight, so I guess something good came out of me being sick, right, Brandon?"

Her voice was very mild, so soft Savage could barely make it out, but just hearing that Campbell called his woman fat made him want to hunt the little bastard down and beat the crap out of him. Seychelle was gorgeous. Perfect. Ass and tits. A woman with real flesh on her. What the fuck did the man want, anyway?

Doris gasped and turned on Brandon, her hand going to her throat. "What a terrible thing to say."

"She misunderstood, Doris. Seychelle. Seriously, honey, you misunderstood what I was saying to you. You're a beautiful woman. You are. Right now, you're pale and you need someone looking after you. I haven't seen your boyfriend around."

"He's her fiancé," Doris corrected.

Savage liked that distinction being made, and he was very glad that Seychelle didn't deny it in front of Brandon.

"He's here at night. He's been away on business mostly, but Alena brought me soup, and his brothers from the club check in on me now and then," Seychelle said. Her voice didn't sound assuring. She sounded monotone. Tired.

Doris reached over and put her hand over Seychelle's. "Honey, why don't you come home with me and let me take care of you? You're always taking care of everyone else."

"I've been sick, but I'm getting better, Doris. I've always

had a problem getting over things. Poor immune system. It's genetic. I'm getting stronger, going for walks now. Thank you for the offer, though." Seychelle sent her another faint smile.

It was a little too vague for Savage's liking. He wanted to wrap his arms around her and hold her close. She looked far too pale, as if she was fading away.

"I do still tire easily though, Doris. I need to lie down. Thank you for checking on me."

Savage hated that she was so down. He'd done that.

Brandon cleared his throat. "I've been worried about Sahara. Doris tells me you went to see her the day she disappeared. I didn't even know you two were friends."

"You didn't? How strange. I thought Sahara told you everything. I saw her quite often." Seychelle turned her head again, looking him directly in the eyes. This time her blue eyes weren't so listless. They were that deep blue, almost mystical. Challenging. Her voice had a soft, musical quality to it.

Savage felt the knots in his stomach tighten. He would be going there every night and he wanted members of Torpedo Ink on her every second. He didn't like the way Brandon was looking at her. The man liked victims, and he didn't like women standing up to him. Right at that moment, Seychelle looked very fragile and worn. But her eyes and voice were saying something altogether different from her body. Her look all but told Brandon to fuck off.

"What was her state of mind that day?" Brandon looked as if he was truly concerned. "She'd been very upset, crying often. I was so worried about her. I had even told Doris I was afraid she would harm herself. She'd gone back to cutting herself. She did that years earlier, but I managed to get her to stop."

"She seemed very happy. She certainly didn't talk about harming herself. She'd been telling me for weeks that you wanted the house back. She said you needed it for your new girlfriend and she completely understood." That sweet musical note was building in her voice.

"It was so generous and kind of you to let her stay there rent-free, Brandon," Doris said.

"Rent-free?" Seychelle echoed. "She paid rent, Doris. Didn't Brandon tell you? Sahara has her own money. She illustrates children's books. There is a huge demand for her work. She has a very large bank account and paid for all the repairs on the house and the upkeep of it. I helped her go over all the invoices for tax purposes and sort everything out for her attorneys so everything would be in order for Brandon when she left. The books were right there for you on the kitchen counter, Brandon. The ones pertinent to the house. She had the roof repaired for you, and new plumbing put in. The heating system was upgraded. She retiled the upstairs bathrooms. Everything was paid for and all receipts were copied and left for you."

Her voice was different now, the notes much more musical and directed toward Doris, countering the mesmerizing effect Brandon's voice had on the older woman. Savage clenched his teeth. His woman was taking chances. Brandon might not hit women, but he liked to play his games with them. He'd been setting Sahara up, using his voice, trying to see what he could force her to do—how far down he could take her. Was he setting her up to commit suicide? Savage hadn't realized Sahara had money. Had he been talking her into making him the beneficiary of her money if she died? Had Seychelle just told him she'd helped Sahara change that?

Savage needed to find that out. Brandon might forgive and move on to other things, but if he was set on getting a payload, he might be angry enough to retaliate against Seychelle. Savage detested that he wasn't with her to watch over her himself. He knew he could rely on his brothers and sisters, but it left him feeling impotent and out of sorts.

Edgy. Angry. At himself. At the circumstances. Even at Seychelle, for not letting him explain.

If it wasn't bad enough that Brandon had wormed his way into Doris's life, he was now walking with his latest girlfriend along the road between Seychelle's cottage and the headlands. Ever since the conversation, three times a week, he had parked his car up the street and forced a very reluctant girlfriend to walk, no matter the weather, in the evening with him.

The girl appeared, according to the Torpedo Ink members who watched over Seychelle, to be very young and too thin, listless, yet eager to please Brandon, hurrying to do whatever he whispered to her. After she did it, he whispered again to her, and she would get tears in her eyes and look at the ground as if she hadn't met his expectations. They always walked past Seychelle's cottage, and he would stare at it, even as he kissed his girlfriend or acted as if he was nibbling on her neck.

Aside from Brandon coming three times a week to walk by the cottage, an older man of about fifty had appeared on the headlands with a camera, taking photographs of the birds, or appearing to do so. Then he photographed the cottages along the road where Seychelle lived. That wasn't necessarily a threat. The buildings were historic, and more than one person had painted and photographed them.

The man returned a few days later and set up an easel to paint, tucking photographs in the corners of his canvas, facing the cottages. His camera hung around his neck. That was unusual and a red flag for Keys, who happened to be watching over Seychelle that day. He kept his eyes on the "artist."

Seychelle emerged from her cottage to take a walk on the headlands around five that afternoon. The artist had lost the light. He hadn't packed up his equipment. He'd eaten. He'd dabbed a few strokes of paint here and there on the canvas, but for the most part he'd gotten up and paced or stretched. The moment Seychelle walked out her front door, the man came to life, putting down his paintbrush and catching up his camera.

He took several pictures of her as she walked across the street toward the narrow path leading to the bluffs. He had to turn away from her as she came toward him, but the moment she was parallel with him, he backed away to put distance between them and began snapping her picture. He took photographs of her standing on the bluff with her hair blowing wildly and then more as she returned to her cottage.

Keys followed the stranger to the local hotel and waited until he had gone to dinner before entering his hotel room. Evidently, the man was a private investigator. Keys turned over his name to Code and, with a little digging, Code discovered Joseph Arnold had hired him to take pictures of Seychelle and report on her movements.

Savage thought his head might explode. His woman sat in her cottage, totally oblivious to the danger. In fact, with Brandon, she invited it to her. He was grateful for his Torpedo Ink brethren. Each of them took shifts, even those who were married.

His woman was racking up indiscretions, things they were going to be dealing with once she was back under his wing, because he was determined he was getting her back. He was *willing* her back to him. Finding a way. They belonged. She knew it. He knew it. She was scared and hurt and had every reason to be. She just had to want to be with him more than both of those things.

NINE

Savage went to the bar every Thursday night hoping Seychelle would come to sing with Maestro and the others jamming. He sat at the same table, at the very back, nursing a beer, willing her to come to him. To give herself to him. He knew what the cost would be to her, and it would be enormous. Still, now he knew he had something to give her back.

She needed him every bit as much as he needed her. He didn't just need her. He wanted her. Her brightness. Her compassion. Her laughter. That directness that got to him every time. The way she was with the older people who counted on her. She gave and gave and didn't ask for anything in return. He knew he could give a lot to her. He wanted to.

He drummed his fingers on the table, knowing the cycle was starting all over again. If his woman was going to come to him and he had any chance of getting her ready for the monster in him, it had to be soon. *Bog*, it had to be soon. There were too many things coming together too fast, building up around the others and in him, to keep the rage at bay. Fucking Arnold and Campbell stalking Seychelle.

Various members of the club hurting or having nightmares when the past was getting too close.

He wrapped his fist around the neck of the bottle and took a slow drink of the cold liquid, letting it cool his throat, hoping it would ice down the fire gathering in his belly. All the while, his gaze never left the door. The bar was supposed to be somewhat quiet on Thursdays, but the band was too good, and more and more clubs were showing up.

Right now, they had four members of Venomous wearing their colors, and five of Headed for Hell. Both clubs could be a problem for Torpedo Ink as well as with each other. They'd postured at each other once, and Reaper had been there instantly. No one fucked with him, and the incident was over very quickly. That didn't mean it wouldn't start up again. The nine men were being watched closely.

The Venomous club had been chipping away at the borders of Diamondback territory, trying to carve a space for themselves by horning in on the strip clubs and drug trade. Plank, the president of the Mendocino chapter of the Diamondbacks, had come to Torpedo Ink and asked them to put a stop to it. It hadn't been difficult to figure out that Torpedo Ink was being set up.

The Diamondbacks used Torpedo Ink when they needed them, but they wanted something concrete on them—something to hold over their heads. So far, they had nothing, although they'd tried to set Torpedo Ink up when they'd asked them to burn down the strip businesses the Venomous club had stolen out from under the Diamondbacks and bring the manager patches to them. Torpedo Ink had looked into the situation and found out the Venomous club had murdered one of the women and regularly abused the others working for them in the strip clubs. The Diamondbacks had gotten the patches and the bodies and burned down clubs, but had not gotten any evidence that Torpedo Ink had anything to do with any of it.

The Torpedo Ink bar was packed with civilians as well as bikers. Most of the bikers were simply men and women who liked to ride. They weren't clubs that were going to give any-one trouble, but they liked to party. Drink a lot. Dance. As a rule, that was a good thing, but with the members of Venom-ous and Headed for Hell possibly looking for trouble, Savage thought the night could turn ugly really fast.

The door opened, allowing the cool air to shoot through the room, and Seychelle walked in. His heart nearly stopped beating. For a moment, he could only stare, frozen. Unbe-lieving. He never really thought she would come. He hadn't thought it was possible, but there she was, looking so beauti-ful she took his breath. She looked young and so damn in-nocent his body reacted. Or maybe it was because her body belonged to him. Those curves. That face. Her mouth.

She wore her favorite pair of jeans. Vintage. Faded blue with two frayed holes he knew intimately. One on her back pocket and one on her left thigh. Those jeans clung to her sweet ass, cupping the perfect curves of her cheeks, giving him instant fantasies. Her simple tank top was a dark navy blue. It shouldn't have been sexy. There was no plunging neckline, no bra showing, but her tits were hard to contain. Round, firm and high, pushing against that thin material, straining to be free. She wore a little thin sweater, open, that didn't cover much of anything and only made a man want to see more. Just looking at her, his every nerve end-ing came to life, was acutely aware of her.

He studied her face, that gorgeous, flawless face. She was very pale. To anyone who didn't know her, she looked com-posed, but he knew every little nuance, every tiny tell she had, and she was scared out of her mind. This wasn't an easy decision, and she probably had it in her head she would run like hell if she saw him. That wasn't happening. She'd come because, like him, she needed. They needed each other.

Those nightly visits he couldn't stop had been just as much a compulsion for her as they had been for him. That open window. He could hear her crying some nights. She wasn't in bed when he walked up to the window; she was sitting on the floor under the window, waiting for him so she could breathe him in the way he was breathing her in. They belonged—however fucked up that was.

He knew he would have to bring her into his world as fast as possible. Already, nearly a month had passed, and he could feel the familiar violence beginning to build in him. He had time, but it was a limited amount. Seychelle would have to be entirely on board. *Bog*, but she was beautiful to him, and so courageous. She would need that courage to be his partner—to love him, and he wanted her to love him.

Savage stared at Seychelle as she took her first steps into the very pressing crowd, his mind trying to fully comprehend that she'd come, his lungs trying to draw in air when he couldn't really breathe. He did manage to get his arm into the air, and he sent a high-pitched whistle into the room that reverberated over the music and the crowd for less than a second. That would be enough of a signal to alert his fellow Torpedo Ink members that his woman had just walked in.

Reaper, his older brother, sat with him, as he had these last Thursday nights when Savage had come to the bar. Savage knew Reaper was concerned about his state of mind, afraid he might pick a fight and "accidentally" kill someone.

"You've got your mouth hangin' open, and your woman is goin' to get assaulted in this crowd lookin' like that," Reaper said. "What the fuck is wrong with you?" There was a trace of amusement in his voice, but not on his face. Maybe in his eyes. "Does she sing as good as she looks?"

Seychelle looked out of place in the bar. Too young. Too sweet. She didn't look around for him, and that pissed him off when he couldn't take his eyes off her. When he was practically devouring her.

"Sings like a fuckin' angel. Her voice, Reaper. It's something else."

Reaper's woman, Anya, was the bartender, along with Preacher, another member of Torpedo Ink. Anya glanced around the bar as she shook something ridiculous for three women who had come to shake their tits at the band members. She caught sight of Seychelle and flashed her a smile. She'd recognized that signal, the one they'd all been hoping for. She was Savage's sister-in-law, and she was extremely worried about him.

"Hey, girl. We've been waiting for you. Give her some room, guys, and keep your hands to yourself," Anya called out.

No one messed with or made a play for Anya unless they were new to the bar. Most everyone knew she belonged to Reaper and he wasn't pleasant if anyone got out of line. Savage felt equally possessive of Seychelle. The trait ran deep in the family. It hadn't occurred to him someone might decide to touch her. The place was crowded, and it was easy enough for a man to slide his hand over a woman's ass or tits as she walked by. Depending on what club they were in, some felt like it was their just due.

Savage stood up slowly, still blending in with the shadows. Reaper and he had perfected that art when they were children, all the better to stalk and kill the ones holding them prisoner. Now, standing, Savage could better see Seychelle's progress as she made her way to the bar. Anya waved her to the bar stool that Bannister, a regular, had vacated in order for her to have a seat. She was short, and her feet didn't quite hit the floor when she slid onto it. Zyah, Player's wife, sat on the other side of Seychelle.

The band members, Keys, Master, Maestro and Player, exchanged relieved smiles and then swung into one of their very popular songs. Each of them, in his own way, was a genius when it came to music and playing instruments. They were good—very good—far better than most bands, and it showed. They knew, as much as Seychelle was auditioning to see if she fit with them, they were auditioning for her. If she didn't like their music, they had little chance, especially since she was sitting on the fence because of Savage.

He had eyes only for her. On her face, just below her left cheekbone, there was a small scar. Over her left eye, bisecting her eyebrow, there was another one. Those belonged to him. They were so small, no one would notice them, but to him, they stood out and said something about her and the kind of woman she was. She'd gotten those scars saving his life.

He knew how to help her now that he understood how her gift worked, but stopping her from healing others when she couldn't control the compulsion was going to be difficult until she was on board with it. Savage wasn't the kind of man anyone said no to, least of all his woman. Still, he knew there had to be a balance—he had to give to her just as much as she was giving him. She hadn't run screaming from him. She had the courage necessary to face him, to show up at the bar even though she was terrified of the choice she was making.

First her foot moved to the beat of the music, and then her head. She couldn't help herself. She had that perfect pitch, and the music was alive in her. He could see her face light up, her hands patting out the rhythm on her thighs as she danced sitting right there on the bar stool. He doubted if she was aware of it, but it was sexy as all get-out.

There were eyes on her. Too many. He didn't like it. "Fuck." He whispered the word aloud. "We should have provided an armed escort."

"You give her a choice? Did you try to save this girl?" Reaper asked, watching her.

Yeah, he'd tried to save her, but how hard? He didn't know. But now he had an excuse, now there was her gift and what it was doing to her.

Savage shrugged. "I gave her a choice, Reaper. I told her this was my territory. Her house was hers. She threw me out. If she came here, she was mine. That was the deal. She came."

He felt his brother's eyes on him. Weighing him. He didn't like that. Reaper saw things others didn't, but the scrutiny didn't matter. Savage was there to further his claim on his woman, and no one could get in his way. She made the choice. That was their code.

"You absolutely certain she's the one?" Reaper asked, his voice gruff.

Savage's fucking chest hurt so bad, the pressure was enormous. Just looking at her made him happy. He pressed his hand over his aching heart just to reassure his brother without words.

Reaper nodded slowly. "You need help?"

Did he? Savage was certain he was borderline crazy. His only hope was the woman sitting on the bar stool, who hadn't once, not one single time, looked around the bar in order to try to spot him. He was going to have a word or two about that tonight, when they were lying together on her bed. Just the thought of being in her bed, of wrapping his arm around her hips, his head on her belly, hearing her voice in the darkness enfolding him in silk and velvet, was almost more than he could take.

His head hurt like a son of a bitch. It had for days—weeks. He had no idea what she did to bring him peace, but whenever he was alone with her, he felt different. Calm. Settled. Happy. Hell, just looking at her made him feel that way.

The song ended to the sound of applause. A few bikers raised their beer bottles. Seychelle slipped off the bar stool when Maestro beckoned for her to take the microphone. She was graceful when she walked. Her ass swayed invitingly. Her generous tits pushed at the very modest dark navy tank she wore. She hadn't dressed up for him. She wasn't wearing makeup on her skin. That smooth, soft skin on her face was all her. She'd enhanced her eyes, giving them a smoky effect, the same as the day he'd met her. He remembered that.

The band swung into a song after a brief consultation with her, and she began to sing. At first her voice was low, blending in with the soft beginning, and then the music and her voice began to swell, filling the bar with the promise of love. There was joy and laughter and then sorrow. Every emotion was felt through her incredible voice.

He knew her voice touched everyone. He wasn't an emotional man and yet somehow, like the other times he was with her, close to her, she tapped into some emotion buried so deep he hadn't known it was there. The sound slipped into one's body and eased aches or compounded them depending on what she was feeling as she sang the lyrics. She wove a magical web around them all. Mostly, he was certain, around him.

The second song was pure Seychelle. It was a song designed to bring peace and happiness to others. Savage never took his eyes from her. He felt her energy, her compassion and her need to help others, to lift them up when they were down. He saw the various expressions cross her face as her gaze touched on individuals in the crowd. That golden net began to climb the wall and over the ceiling, sliding down to touch this person or that.

The crowd was mesmerized by her. Stunned by her. That magic in her voice captivated them, but as Savage continued to scrutinize her every expression, her every move, he noticed she flinched occasionally, or hunched in just for a single second.

Puzzled, he tried to figure out what it was he was missing, and it was something very important. She turned her head, and he felt the instant impact of her eyes. She didn't smile, but her expression softened. His heart twisted. His head had been pounding all day and the loud noises in the bar hadn't helped. He almost missed the way a frown flitted across her face and she looked just a little strained for that split second, and then she looked away. His headache was gone.

Awareness rushed into him. He swore softly under his breath. He should have guessed. There was an exchange taking place, just as Libby said Seychelle would do, and he didn't like it. It was one thing to sing, but to start healing aches and pains in an entire crowd? Hell no. That was one thing he was putting a stop to.

Then, suddenly, she nearly faltered. She didn't miss a beat, but knowing her as he did, and knowing the band members, he was alerted instantly. At first he was afraid she'd taken on some illness that was so harmful it was destroying her, but it didn't seem to be that at all. To Savage, she was an open book, and she looked hurt—not physically but emotionally hurt. Upset. Devastated. So much so that every alarm he had went off.

Seychelle had never heard a band as good as the one playing. They were incredible. She couldn't believe they had invited her to sing with them. The crowd was great, the energy uplifting. Most of the people in the bar were there to have fun. Ailments were minor for once, and when she finally allowed herself to look at Savage, he was totally focused on her—very happy to see her. She'd been worried he might have changed his mind after a month.

It was silly to be so nervous over that when he'd come to her cottage nearly every single night and left her roses. He'd sent Alena with delicious meals she couldn't eat but was grateful for. He'd made certain his Torpedo Ink brothers had watched over her. Savage wasn't a man to do all that if he didn't want her. It was just that she was so confused over what their relationship really was. What it could be. What he wanted from her and what she could give him.

If felt good to be able to take away his headache. It was a small thing, but she liked being able to help him. She had missed him so much. It had felt as if she was living a half life without him. She'd taken her time, really thought a lot before she'd decided to come to him. She didn't know exactly what his lifestyle entailed or if she could handle it, but if he was willing to teach her and not have other women in his life . . . Maybe. She just didn't know. She just knew she was willing to chance finding out more. He was worth it. Sharing his life was worth it.

Looking at him, seeing his eyes so blue, looking like twin blue flames burning over her, claiming her, made her feel as if she belonged. She'd missed having that. She'd been adrift without him. She sang to him. Gave him joy. Gave him her happiness. Lifted the spirits of everyone in the bar.

A jarring note slipped into her web of silken fairy tales. A dark thread of truth to unravel her dreams. Lust. Craving. Twisted greed. Her gaze found that thread and followed it. The woman was dancing in front of the band, but she was dancing for one man—Savage. Her eyes were on him, carnal desire stark on her face. She was shaking her dark hair all around so that it shimmied under the lights. Seychelle recognized her immediately. She was broadcasting her thoughts loudly in time with the pulsing music, her pelvis thrusting suggestively toward Savage. She was with another woman, and that woman was staring at Savage as well, her expression almost as lecherous as her friend's.

When the last notes of the song died away, Seychelle handed the microphone to Maestro, flashed a smile to the crowd and stepped off the stage. Unfortunately, their backs to her, the two women inadvertently blocked her path leading to the back room and safety.

"See why I came all the way from San Francisco? I followed him here," the dark-haired woman said. "Everyone said he never came back twice, but I had him twice. I'll have him again, you just wait and see, Melinda."

"Shari, he's awesome. I wouldn't mind a go at that myself."

"Well, back off, he's all mine," Shari declared. "I'm going for permanent status."

Seychelle managed a polite smile as the band swung into the next song. "Excuse me."

Immediately, the two women parted to let her through. Seychelle was instantly mobbed, mostly by men, as she tried to make her way to the door. That was all she could think of. Getting out. What had she been thinking? Shari? Melinda? How many more was he going to have while she stood on a stage with the band and sang? She was crazy to think she could handle that. Absolutely crazy.

Savage had no idea what had upset Seychelle, but she was running. Heading toward the door, thinking she was going to get away from him. That wasn't happening. The moment Seychelle made her way into the crowd, she was mobbed by men. One had his hand on her back—a member of the Headed for Hell club—and his palm was slipping down toward her ass.

The crowd parted for Savage, always a good thing when he was willing to mow everyone down. He slung his arm around Seychelle and pulled her body into his, giving the interloper his killer eyes. He'd earned his reputation and then some.

The biker stood there a moment, then glanced around the bar looking for his buddies. Savage took the time to brush a kiss across Seychelle's mouth, but he didn't lose sight of his "rival." The man had been drinking and he had fallen under Seychelle's spell. Savage wasn't so certain he wanted her singing with the band after all.

She tasted too good and he didn't want to stop kissing her. She felt too good, her body soft and her skin like silk. He'd missed her. He'd been craving her, and he suddenly felt like a man starved. Her voice had gotten not only to him but to other men in the room, and he didn't like it. He especially didn't like the fact that she hadn't really kissed him back.

"Come on, babe, let's head to the back room. Maestro can come find you when he's finished. I want you out of this mob."

She didn't protest, or really look at him. She was trembling, clearly still very frightened and uncertain of her choice. She was upset, wearing that look of complete devastation, and he had no idea why. She'd come to him, and now she already wanted out. Savage was spoiling for a fight. Too many men surrounding them, wanting his woman, pushing at her, and Seychelle wasn't falling into his arms. If anything, she was holding herself away from him.

The idiot from the Headed for Hell club with the name Eliminator on the front of his vest, staring at her so hungrily, was about to get his ass handed to him if he didn't step the fuck out of the way.

Seychelle didn't move, even when Savage smoothed his hand over her hair. She didn't look at him, almost as if she hadn't noticed him.

"Babe." Savage exerted a little pressure on her back to force her forward.

"I don't know what I'm doing," she whispered, and turned her face up to his.

He stepped behind her, put both arms around her, locking her to him, and walked her straight to the side entrance to the back room. It was a long hallway with a door at the end. He ignored the three side doors along the walls and chose the end one, propelling her inside.

"Babe." He did his best to keep his voice gentle. "You're making a commitment to me. To us. That's what you're doing."

She shook her head. "They're so good. That band is incredibly good. I want to do this, but I don't know, Savage, I'm very confused. I need more time to think about all this. Your world is very different from mine. I'm tired. I'm just so tired."

Adrenaline rushed through his body, fear lacing the rage in a deep pool so that it splashed up red and dangerous. He made every effort to push those emotions aside. "You're done for the night, Seychelle, and if I'd realized what you were doing, I would have gotten you out of there after your first song."

He tried to keep his voice gentle, but he wasn't a gentle man. He sounded harsher than he'd intended. His hands held on to her waist, maybe a little tighter than necessary. She felt as if she might escape him at any moment. "Baby, you can't give away pieces of yourself and take on everyone's shit like that."

She squirmed until he released her, taking two steps away from him. "It just happens. I don't know I'm doing it until it's too late. I told you, I don't have control."

He closed the distance between them. "You can't do

what you just did in there and survive for very long." He studied her expression. "Fuck." He spat the word and pulled her closer to him, forcing her up onto her toes. "You already know that, don't you? You're not doing that again, do you understand me?"

"I told you, I can't control it. I do try to protect myself, Savage . . ." She broke off and shrugged, swaying. "I need to sit down."

He immediately guided her to a chair. He crouched down and tipped up her chin, at the same time gripping her ankle. He ran his thumb up her pale skin. That perfect canvas that now belonged to him. "I'll tell Maestro you're not going to take the job."

Her gaze jumped to his. "You won't tell them anything. I'm heading home. I'll think things over and decide for myself."

"Babe, you know that job's not right for you." He really didn't want her to take it. "Before you get all defiant on me, think about it. When you sing in a bar, does that happen every single time? You trying to help everyone like that? Or just once in a while?"

She looked down at her hands. They were shaking so much she couldn't control them. "I thought I could do this with you, but she was here tonight." She whispered it.

Savage frowned. "I don't know who you're talking about."

"The woman. She was here. And she isn't the only one." There was pain in her voice. Anguish, even.

He swore under his breath, his gut tightening. He knew exactly who she meant now. Sometimes the women he used fixated on him. It made no sense. He didn't remember them. He didn't know their names. He used them and walked away. The particular woman she was referring to had been in a kink club in San Francisco. He'd used her there a few months earlier.

He'd been in rough shape, needing a woman, and no one appealed to him, but then, they never did. It was far worse knowing he wanted only Seychelle now and realizing he couldn't have her. He'd found an older woman who liked pain and taken her to one of the private rooms. A couple of other women had tried to talk to him, telling him they remembered him from before, but he ignored them. He left after being with the older woman and came back to the clubhouse in Caspar.

Savage hadn't gone to see Seychelle because he was still edgy, his demons riding him hard. That's when the woman had walked into the clubhouse and all but begged him to show her his whip skills. He'd been a fool to oblige. He knew better, but all that mattered to him was finding his way to Seychelle. And then Seychelle had called him saying she was in trouble, and he'd run to her. It had been the worst mistake of his life as far as he was concerned. He'd lost Seychelle.

"Babe, we're past that. We have to be. We'll go home and talk it out. You knew what you were doing when you came here." He didn't want that woman to be any part of them ever again. Seychelle knew about her. She'd come anyway. That had to mean she was over it, right?

He'd warned her. She knew exactly what she was doing when she came to the bar, and she'd come there for him. Choosing him. She was scared, and that was acceptable—even expected. She'd probably forgotten what a bastard he was. But he wasn't letting her out of the deal.

            ➤

Seychelle shook her head as she stared at him. She was in *such* trouble when it came to Savage. She could barely resist him, and when it came to those dark places inside of him swirling with violence and rage, she thought she had a chance of handling that if he gave her time and explanations.

She had tried to hold out, and she had for weeks, but then she was so miserable that she couldn't breathe. She found herself waiting for the sound of his motorcycle. For the roses. For the breath she perceived they shared with the wall between them. She *lived* for those nights he came. She could barely stand getting out of her bed during the day when he wasn't there, afraid he might not come back that evening. It was a miserable way to live. The longer she was without him, the more the hurt and fear keeping her away had faded.

Seychelle worried about Savage until she was so desperate to see him, she knew she would have to go to the bar even if that meant swallowing her pride. Even if that meant being so terrified of what she was doing she couldn't comprehend the price she would pay. She had no idea why their connection had grown so strong, but it had, and she had no way to sever it. She had to find a way to get out from under him.

Her head hurt, and so did her heart. She felt battered. He had just dismissed her pain and fears over the women as if they were nothing. To him, they weren't important. To her, that issue was everything. There was no way for her to get past it if he refused to even acknowledge she had a right to feel the way she did. She rocked herself back and forth, making herself small, trying to think of what to do, but her headache was very painful, making it difficult.

The band members came in just as Savage straightened. "I'm getting her something cold to drink. Don't discuss her joining yet. No commitments. I'll be back."

Maestro sighed as he watched Savage walk away. "Seriously, woman? How did he get to you first?"

"He doesn't exactly own me," Seychelle denied, but she wasn't certain of anything right then. She was more confused about her feelings than ever.

Going to the bar had been the biggest mistake of her life. She really couldn't live without Savage. She couldn't eat. Or sleep. Or even breathe properly. But seeing the women and feeling the way they were lusting after him, their eyes following him, bright with almost fanatical carnal greed, she knew she wasn't strong enough to cope with him going off with other women the way he had. She had convinced herself she could do it. Savage was so casual about it. How did one get past it? Especially if she knew it would happen again and again?

"I'm not even with him, exactly," she said. Uncertain. Wanting to cry. Feeling sick inside and confused outside.

"She is. With me, I mean," Savage corrected, walking in so confidently. He handed her two white tablets. "For your headache." He took the bottle from her and unscrewed the cap. "Drink. And we're more than friends, and that's all the time."

Her heart jerked hard in her chest at his declaration. He wasn't going to let her go back on her word so easily. Still, she tried to play it casual, rolling her eyes. "He's being difficult. He likes to mess with everyone."

"Maestro, I know you want her to sing with you." Savage caught her hand and brought it to his thigh, his thumb sliding back and forth over the back of it. "Give us a little time. We'll go home and talk it over."

When he did that, pressed her hand tight against the muscle of his thigh and rubbed his thumb like he was stroking little caresses, she went damp. Her breasts instantly ached. She wanted him with every breath she took.

Seychelle just needed to run. Self-preservation was kicking in. "I've got to go home. Thanks for letting me sing with you tonight. You're the best musicians I've heard in years, maybe ever."

"Back at you, babe," Master said. "I haven't heard a voice like yours ever. Say yes."

The others murmured their agreement and walked out, leaving her alone with Savage.

Savage brought her hand to his mouth. He nibbled at the pads of her fingers and then scraped with his teeth. Her heart nearly stopped. Her sex clenched hard. He pressed a kiss into the center of her palm.

She tugged until Savage released her. Standing was difficult because he didn't back away. Her body was up against his, so tight she could feel every breath he took.

"Can you drive safely?"

She nodded, although she was shaking so much she wasn't positive, but she had to get out of there before she lost every single thing she'd fought so hard for. Her pride. Her independence.

"I'll walk you out to your car."

She was so weak with relief that he was letting her go that her legs nearly gave out. At the same time, she wanted to weep that he didn't care for her the way she did for him.

"Thank you." There was nothing else to say. She couldn't take it if he left her time and again for other women, and he would. She couldn't sing in the bar knowing those women had a part of him that really should belong to her. How could he so casually declare they were past that? She wasn't past it. She would never be past it.

She kept her head down as he went to the back door and opened it, showing her the exit from the meeting room at the end of the hall. It was dark outside. The band was playing again, and most everyone who had been smoking cigarettes or weed was drifting back inside.

Savage didn't say anything as they walked to the car, but he kept his arm around her shoulders. In some way that arm was comforting; in another, it felt like a heavy chain binding them together. She knew she was slightly hysterical, but she was going home and packing up and driving to another state as fast as she could. Nevada was looking very good to her. First, she was heading into Fort Bragg and buying a pack of cigarettes.

He took the keys from her hand and unlocked the driver-side lock with a simple button push, as if he'd been doing it for her his entire life. "I know you're scared, baby, but don't do anything foolish tonight. Just drive straight home and crawl into bed. You'll feel better once that headache disappears."

She didn't make the mistake of arguing; she just nodded her head. Savage caught her chin and lifted it, forcing her to meet his eyes. She didn't know why she felt so guilty and yet defiant at the same time.

Savage shook his head. "You could trust me a little to take care of you, Seychelle. Whatever you're thinking of doing is just making you miserable. You made the decision, and we'll make it work. I was miserable without you. You were the same without me. We'll find our way."

She didn't shake her head or protest. She was so close to getting away. Once she was out of his presence, she could break free of his spell. The door to her car was open, but he had the keys in his hand.

She wouldn't go home right away, just in case he went there to check on her. She could go to one of the bars in Fort Bragg, smoke to her heart's content, drink a few drinks and check into a motel, hide her car. That way, if he went to the house, he'd just give up by morning. She could go home, pack and get out. Drive away. What was tying her there besides her home? She could have a management company rent it out. If she was in Nevada, they couldn't find her. No one could. She'd keep going . . .

Savage sighed, framed Seychelle's face with both hands and brought his mouth very gently down on hers. His lips just rubbed softly over hers, like the lightest of caresses. He ran his tongue along the seam of her lips gently. Coaxing. She made the softest of sounds, but it got him in the gut. Maybe higher. Maybe in his chest.

He took his time—patience was everything, and he was rewarded when her lips parted, and he sank his tongue deep. He swept into her mouth, her taste nearly overwhelming him, so that a dark lust was desperately spinning out of control. Her mouth was hot and wild, her tongue tangling with his, sliding tentatively at first and then surer, dueling until he could barely breathe for the two of them.

He needed to see those sexy, sweet tears and the beautiful patterns that made his world right again. Just the thought turned him inside out. Hot flames poured through him, swirling like a storm through his veins to settle deep in his cock. She was turning him inside out.

When he lifted his head, she was clinging to him, chasing after his mouth shamelessly. He stroked caresses over her hair and down her back. "It isn't going to be so bad belonging to me, Seychelle. I'll be careful with you. After all this time thinking you didn't exist, I'm not about to drive you away. I'll introduce you to my world carefully. Once you know me, know the rules, you aren't going to have trouble."

Seychelle buried her fists in the front of his shirt, shaking her head, more panicked than ever, because she'd just proven to herself she couldn't resist him. She'd never resist that mouth. The way he kissed. The fire or his taste. It was probably already too late. She had to do something to distract herself, something terrible if she was going to save herself.

"You'll hurt me, Savage. In the end, you'll hurt me." She looked up at him, needing to see his eyes. "Won't you?"

"Probably."

He continued to stroke those caresses through her hair that made her weak with need for him. She knew he'd be honest, but she didn't want that answer. She wanted hope.

"I don't know the first thing about relationships, baby. That's going to set us both up for mistakes, but we'll work through it. You'll learn. I'll learn. That's what couples do."

"I thought we were going to be friends." She was feeling desperate to get away from him. Friendship would never work. She was too attracted to him. She needed to give him everything he wanted or needed, just as she'd done all her life with her parents. She gave and gave until there was nothing left of her, and they died anyway.

"We're going to be friends, honey. We already are. You know more about me than anyone but my brothers in Torpedo Ink. I know you're scared, but you have to trust me to take care of you."

She was scared. Not only of him, but of her own hidden desires. He brought things out in her that she was terrified to explore. She forced a nod, pressing her fingers to her lips to make certain she didn't try to kiss him again. She didn't seem to have any control at all around him.

Savage sighed again and stepped aside, letting her slip inside her car. The moment she was seated and she took the keys, he stepped back and closed her door.

She wanted to cry as she looked at him through the window while she started her car. It was the last time she was ever going to see him. He was a beautiful, gorgeous man, but far too broken for her to fix. She couldn't save him any more than she could have saved her parents or herself. She'd done everything for them, even taken on their illness, and in the end, she'd lost everything, just as she would lose Savage. The difference was, with Savage, she would lose her heart. Her soul. Everything she was.

TEN

Seychelle drove straight to the bar. She could walk to a motel from there. Motels were in abundance. Tourists came often for whale watching and film festivals and everything else Sea Haven and Fort Bragg had to offer. Then there was Alena's restaurant, Crow 287, fast becoming a huge draw for Caspar. There was everything there, but she was leaving.

She put her head down on the steering wheel and allowed herself to cry. She had come here hoping for a new start. She wanted to be independent and happy, but she wasn't either of those things. She was strong and disciplined in most areas of her life, but the fact that she couldn't stop herself from trying to heal other people's illnesses was slowly killing her. She was just worn out. There was no way to stop herself. She'd tried, but she just couldn't find any control. That meant living a very solitary existence. She didn't even know what she was doing, as evidenced by coming here to this bar. It made no sense and yet here she was.

Savage. She whispered his name. She couldn't imagine her life without him in it.

She had no control when it came to him. No more control than she had when it came to her strange gift—or curse—of attempting to heal others. She'd never felt so much for another human being. She'd never felt so alive. So passionate. So completely happy or sad. So . . . *everything* when she was with Savage. She had no balance anymore.

She caught glimpses of the violence in his life. Of darkness. He was worried about his dark sexual practices coming to light and that she would be disgusted. She was intrigued. She even, to some extent, fantasized about them. That was a hidden secret she barely wanted to admit to herself. Why she would be hot, slick and wanting whenever she thought about Savage and what he needed, she didn't know, especially when nothing else seemed to put her body in the mood. She wasn't entirely certain she wanted to explore that side of herself, although the thought was both thrilling and terrifying.

But other women? She couldn't do that. She just couldn't. No matter how much she loved him. How much she wanted to be with him. The emptiness she felt when she was away from him. Just feeling the raw lust those women had for him as they fixated on him had eaten away at her. She'd felt less of a woman than she ever had in her life, and Savage had dismissed her concerns and doubts so easily.

She stared at herself in the rearview mirror and then, making up her mind, she locked her car and went inside. There were mostly men sitting at the bar and a few couples occupying the tables. A country-western song was playing, and the lights were low. Exactly what she needed. She bought a pack of cigarettes and immediately went outside and lit one. She might have enjoyed it, but she felt a little like a guilty, defiant child instead of an adult making her own decisions—because lighting up the cigarette was just that: defiance. She didn't even want to smoke. Restless and unhappy, she crushed it under her foot, picked it up and tossed it in the trash can just outside the bar.

Back inside, she ordered a drink, and immediately one of the men at the bar insisted on paying for it. He slid from his bar stool to sit beside her. His name was Bill, and no, it wasn't her first time in the bar, but she didn't come here often. He gave out harmless vibes of loneliness, so she let him pay for her drink. He seemed a nice enough man, just trying to find his way the same way she was.

Two drinks later she was back outside with another cigarette. This smoke was much more enjoyable than the last one. Bill stood with her, still talking, but his vibe had gone from lonely to far more amorous. He was easy, though. Easy to talk to. It was easy to make decisions about whether or not she wanted to be with him. He'd tried to kiss her once, but she couldn't, not with her suddenly churning stomach threatening to empty itself all over him. Smoking outside was a better thing to do. She felt so sick. And the world kept tilting, first one way and then the other.

"Come on, baby, time to go home."

She blinked rapidly to bring the speaker into focus, because she knew that voice. So soft. Velvet soft but with steel under it. Savage stood there, gently removing her arm from Bill's grasp.

"She's with me," Bill said, but he stepped back.

"Actually, she's my woman, and touching her isn't allowed."

Again, that voice was very soft, but a little shiver went down Seychelle's spine. She stuck her chin out belligerently. "Actually, you can't stop me from being with Bill."

"Babe. Really? I could put Bill six feet under, and then I'm sure you wouldn't want to be with him. Corpses don't make good lovers. Let's get you home. You drank a little too much."

"I can't go home. I can't drive." She was certain of that. She could barely stand. She wasn't used to drinking, but she wasn't going to admit to that. The world was spinning, and so was her stomach.

Savage wrapped one arm around her waist and took the cigarette from her hand. "Where's the pack, Seychelle?"

She loved his voice. That soft, velvet brush along her skin. The sound sent a million butterflies winging their way through her body. Her stomach did a slow roll, and always, always when he spoke like that, she went damp and needy. Little fingers of desire danced up her thighs and down her spine. Just with his voice. She really had to tell him.

"I love your voice. It's so beautiful."

Savage smiled at her. "Thank you, baby, but I still need the pack. Give it to me."

She watched him crush the cigarette and put it in the trash can. He tossed the pack after it and then he walked her to her car. "It's good you didn't litter," she said solemnly, because really, littering was *so* wrong. "And I've been contemplating the corpse thing. That's just really *eeww.* I might have nightmares." She waved at Bill.

Savage shook his head as he opened the passenger-side door and snapped her seat belt in place. "You're going to be all right. I'll take care of you."

"You're kind of dreamy, Savage. Like dreamy gorgeous."

He tucked her hair behind her ear, a faint smile on his face. "Glad you think so, baby." He closed the door and rounded the hood. She watched him every step of the way as he got behind the wheel. He really was beautiful. As he drove the car from the parking lot, he signaled to someone behind them. She heard the familiar and now comforting roar of Harley pipes, and then they were on the highway, heading back to Sea Haven.

Savage knew he wasn't getting drunk sex, as intriguing as his body thought it was. His woman was a very sick drunk. She wasn't sloppy. Or clingy. Or even weepy. She was just plain sick. Savage had no idea why he found that so fuckin' amusing, but he did. She couldn't drink worth shit and he was going to put his foot down when it came to her drinking alone, without his club—or him—protecting her.

He spent some time with her in the bathroom, although she protested, embarrassed, not wanting him to see her like that. He had news for her: he was the kind of man to want to see his woman in every type of circumstance. He didn't leave her alone when she needed him. And she needed him. He'd never seen anyone so sick. He had the feeling it was less about how much she'd drunk and more about her being allergic.

"Do you think it's her first time drinking?" Ink asked, concerned. "Maybe we should take her to the hospital. She could have alcohol poisoning."

"I think she's allergic," Savage said. He glanced at his watch. He had club business tonight, but he couldn't leave her, not when she was so sick. There was nothing left for her to throw up, but she still hugged the toilet bowl, miserable and retching. He had gathered her hair, bunched it in his hand and held it out of the way. Finally, he loosely braided it to keep it away from her face. The moment she stopped vomiting, he was putting her in the shower, and then hoping she'd go to sleep.

Ink sat in an armchair. Preacher perched on the end of the bed. His two fellow Torpedo Ink brothers regarded him solemnly.

"You have to get out of here soon," Preacher reminded him. "Transporter said to tell you the same man who's been coming around the place, just walking by, did again tonight. This time he had a girl with him. He walked slow and kept his eyes on the cottage. Had his arm around the girl but not his attention on the girl."

Savage wrapped his arm around Seychelle's waist and lifted her off the floor. She groaned and turned her face away from him, or tried to. He had her braid bunched in his fist, and he didn't let up on her scalp, forcing her head toward the sink so he could rinse out her mouth and brush her teeth before taking her ass into the shower.

"What kind of shape was the girl in that he was with? Did Transporter say? I need to get Seychelle into the shower. In the top drawer she has some tanks. Can you get one out for me?"

"Savage?" Seychelle looked up at him, misery on her face. "I'm sorry. You don't have to stay. I think I'm done throwing up."

"Just brush your teeth, baby. I'm getting you cleaned up and then into bed. We'll talk about this later. When I'm not so pissed and you're not so screwed up."

"Guy with the chick wasn't the only one, Savage. Transporter said Seychelle went into town to help some older couple, and that wormy asshole Arnold was creeping around her house. He tried her doors, both front and back and even the garage. He even tried the windows. At one point he picked up a rock like he might throw it through a window, but Transporter started walking toward the cottage and the asshole jumped in his car and took off," Preacher said.

"Why the hell wasn't I told immediately?" Savage demanded.

Ink shrugged. "I went to the hotel. He'd already checked out and left for the Bay Area. Figured there was no real hurry and it could wait until this evening."

Holding Seychelle close to him as she brushed her teeth, Savage realized they were right. What could he have done? "Can you stay with her while I'm gone? Don't feel comfortable leaving her alone. And did Transporter say anything about the girl Campbell was with? I'm sure it was Campbell hanging around too."

"No, Transporter didn't say anything about the girl, but I'll text him and ask," Preacher said. He exchanged a long look with Ink. "You need us to stay, there's no problem."

"Just so we're clear on this woman, Savage," Ink said. "This is a permanent situation?"

"Guess you didn't hear what I said. Seychelle belongs to me. She's mine. I'm not ever turning her loose. I don't know

how to put it any fuckin' plainer than that. She's going to
live with me, and she's stayin' no matter how rough it gets.
So be her friend and watch out for her. She's never going to
have an easy life."

Seychelle spit into the sink and rinsed out her mouth
repeatedly. Savage reached around her and turned off the
faucet. He unbraided her hair and set her down on the bathroom floor, so he could turn on the shower and then strip.
She was next. Fuckin' devil in hell was trying to tempt him.

Bog, his woman. She had curves in abundance. Slender
legs, small waist and rib cage, but hips, tits and ass. It was
all there, but even better, her skin was porcelain white. Perfect skin. A fuckin' canvas. Her tits had perfect nipples, just
as he had suspected. Because her breasts were ample, her
nipples were tight buds that stood out perfectly for clamps,
a pretty, blushing pink. She'd been created for him, his perfect little angel he was going to corrupt and lead straight to
the fires of hell.

She kept winding herself around him, her hands straying
south, stroking when he didn't need her touching his
already-hard-as-a-rock cock. No matter how many times he
took her hands off him, they were back. She wound her leg
around him, the one with the scars, rubbing her sweet
pussy over his thigh, and she was hotter than hell.

He gave up trying to keep her hands from pumping his
cock, carried her into the shower and took advantage, licking at her nipples to see how sensitive they were. He used
the edge of his teeth, then bit down and pulled gently, listening to her gasp, listening to the way her breathing
changed. His hand moved between her legs to feel the
damp heat. His fingers found her slick, and each time he
tugged or bit down a little harder on her nipples, a fresh
flood of liquid coated his fingers. He couldn't stop the need
welling up like a volcano, but he could be disciplined. She
was drunk and sick. He needed to lay everything out in
front of her, let her know what his needs were. What kinds

of things were going to be expected of her. This wasn't fair to her.

"Okay, baby, we have to stop before this gets out of hand," he advised, although that was the last thing he wanted to do. "Put your hands on my chest and leave them there."

Her eyes closed, and she began to slump. He had to catch her around the waist and hold her up to wash her carefully, wash that waterfall of gold-and-platinum-colored hair, condition it and then pass her off to Preacher and Ink while he showered. They wrapped her hair in a towel and dried her off, pulled on her tank and then tucked her into bed. He dressed, found a blow-dryer and started on her hair.

Preacher took the dryer out of his hand. "You're already going to be late if you don't rocket. They aren't going to wait for you, Savage. Czar's meeting with Plank at three in the morning. It takes an hour to get there, and you're running out of time. You have to be on time."

Savage pulled on his jacket and gloves. "You keep her safe for me."

"You don't have to ask twice, brother," Ink said.

Preacher nodded. "She's safe."

Savage took one last look at his woman. Her lashes lifted, and she looked directly at him with those teal-blue eyes of hers. His gut twisted. Never in his life had he been reluctant to go to a meet that could very well result in blood and death. That brought him up short.

As he made the ride to Boonville, speeding on his Night Rod Special, he thought about what he was asking of Seychelle. He wanted her to take a leap of faith and give herself to him. Just surrender everything. She would have to in order to live with him.

He was so fucked up he needed strict rules in his life in order to survive—in order for those around him to survive. His brothers and sisters in Torpedo Ink recognized that he had to live a certain way, and they gave him that space. It would be very difficult for a woman to do so. To give him everything she was and more. He would demand so much more from her.

If he was asking that of her, to choose him over any other life, knowing what she was getting into—and it was only fair to warn her, to show her—then he had to give her something equal in return. Her life would be a sacrifice, most likely a continuous one. So what the hell was he going to give her back that was of equal value?

What did a man so fucked up, a man who actually lived up to his name of Savage, give to a woman whose life he planned to take over completely? Whatever it was, it had to be worth it to her. What would she value? What would make sacrificing her life for his worthwhile? Once she committed to him, there would be no going back. His fucked-up personality, as well as the lifestyle he would teach her, would never allow that. He needed her to want to stay—to choose him in spite of knowing just what she was getting herself into.

Loving someone, caring on any level, made a man—or a woman—vulnerable. Every member of Torpedo Ink knew that, knew what it was like to suffer, to do despicable things in order to save the life of a loved one. Even worse, you could allow yourself to be shaped into a monster in order to save those you loved.

He groaned aloud as he hurtled through the bends in the road, mostly straightening them out. He could outrun almost anything, and he knew every back road there was between Boonville and the coast. All of them did. They left nothing to chance. That was Czar's training. The president of Torpedo Ink had drilled it into them that every detail counted. From the moment they had arrived and chosen Caspar as their home, they had begun to study every escape route possible. He could outrun the cops, but he couldn't outrun Seychelle Dubois.

He was so in love with her, he could barely think straight. She had to know that. She had to know that he was giving her all of him. He'd sworn to himself, on the lives of his parents, his sisters, on Reaper's life, that he would never love another person so deeply that he would do anything to save them, no matter how vile. He did love her that much. More. She'd slipped inside him when he wasn't looking and was wrapped there so tight, and she had to know. He had to tell her what that meant. It was the only thing he had to offer her—himself.

Seychelle had to know his life. It didn't matter that no one else would ever have him or see that one tiny place inside him he had tried to hold sacred. She had to know that he took on the pain for his brothers and sisters and couldn't stop even now, and what that meant for her. For them. What and why he needed her the way he did. Libby Drake was right. He had to risk everything and give Seychelle the absolute truth.

His Harley was fast, but Transporter and Mechanic had worked their magic and it was even more of a road rocket, with a wealth of hidden compartments allowing him to carry the tools he needed when he was sent on a job. He kept the weight light enough to keep the speed he needed if he was forced to outrun an enemy—or the cops. They never engaged with law enforcement. That was part of the code they all abided by. Unless, of course, a particular individual was corrupt. Then all bets were off.

The members of his club were waiting, and they weren't happy. He was only a few minutes late, but those minutes counted. Those minutes were used to set up their escape routes and lay out their plan of action and the protection of their president. Savage had cut down their available time by being late.

"I'm sorry," he said immediately, because he was. Not for the reason that he was late, but because he was Torpedo Ink and his club always came first. He'd screwed up, but this was his screwup, not Seychelle's. "Had to retrieve Seychelle tonight. She came to the clubhouse and auditioned with the band, then got herself in a little trouble. Drank too much. Preacher and Ink are looking out for her."

Czar looked him over carefully, as did his birth brother, Reaper. "You got your head in the game tonight? Because

I need you here with us. If you're worried about her, that could be a problem," Czar said.

"Wouldn't be here if my head wasn't straight, Czar," Savage assured him.

Czar looked him over a second time and then nodded. "Let's get this done. I have a bad feeling about this meeting. Something's going down. Alena, you and Lana go in first. Get a feel for what's going on. Reaper is with me. Savage, you're our eyes on this one. You're in the shadows. Remember, if we have to kill one Diamondback, we may as well kill them all. That club will hunt us to the end of our days. They will never forget. Having said that, you can fuck one up royally if you have to. Let's try to get along, but if we have no choice, take them down hard but keep them alive. If you have to make a kill, that's a signal to take all of them. No one gets away to warn the others. That gives us time to get out and get our families away."

Savage studied Czar's hawklike features. He was worried. A club like the Diamondbacks asking for a meet at three in the morning, not in either of their clubhouses, signaled trouble. The Diamondbacks had chosen a bar on the outskirts of Boonville. Torpedo Ink scouted the place out numerous times. It was closed, but the lights were on. There were bikes parked in the front along with a couple of cars. The Diamondbacks brought a full contingent. Plank wasn't going to take any chances with Torpedo Ink. Technically, the Diamondbacks could call on them, and did, to go after enemies the club couldn't afford to have traced back to them. This looked more like a war council. The members of Torpedo Ink nodded, their expressions sober. Like Savage, they understood this meeting could change everything.

Alena took lead. She sometimes hooked up with one of the Diamondbacks' enforcers, a man who went by the name of Pierce. He was a former SEAL and had joined the Diamondback club years earlier, working his way through the ranks. The man could handle himself, there was no question of that. If the president of his chapter was there, he would be as well.

She rode with Lana by her side into the parking lot of the bar and, in true Alena fashion, was off her bike without seeming to pay attention to the small group of women just getting into a car, obviously to leave. The moment they saw Alena and Lana, the women thrust open the doors and got out again.

Alena turned to Lana and took a small compact from her and began to fix her lipstick. Four women, led by Tawny Farmer, a woman who had been banned from anything to do with Torpedo Ink, surrounded the two newcomers. Alena glanced up as if just noticing them.

Several Diamondbacks emerged from the bar, hearing the sound of the motorcycles. Their prospect, no doubt, had reported the arrival of two of the Torpedo Ink members, with others coming in right behind them.

"What the fuck are you doing here, Alena?" Tawny demanded. "If you think you're going to fuck Pierce, he's already been taken care of. He's with me now, not you, so keep your hands off him. I ride on the back of his bike and I fuck him until he can't see straight."

Alena looked her up and down coolly, one eyebrow up, but she said nothing. She glanced at Lana, who looked amused.

That only incited Tawny more. "You don't have to believe me, but that stupid little video of you, naked, your fingers busy, and your fake moans, everyone has that. He mailed it to all the members of the club and showed it to me while we lay in bed together laughing over it."

Alena didn't so much as blink. Her expression remained as bored as ever. Lana rolled her eyes as if to say who cared who had a video.

Tawny shrieked and threw herself at Alena, her long nails curved like claws going for Alena's face. At the last minute, Alena turned her head, but she didn't try to defend herself or even block the series of blows Tawny rained down on her. Lana held herself very still. The other three women shouted encouragements at Tawny and obscenities at Alena.

Pierce and four of the Diamondbacks pulled Tawny away from Alena. Czar, Reaper, Ice and Storm rushed the small group as Plank, the president of the Diamondbacks' chapter, hurried out with two more of their club members. Pierce reached for Alena, but she stepped back to stand with her Torpedo Ink members.

"What the fuck just happened?" Plank demanded. He'd obviously witnessed it but couldn't seem to believe his eyes.

"Seems that you can't control your women," Czar said, his tone low, furious. "My members know how to conduct themselves when we've been invited to an important meet. We don't have club trash attacking the invited club."

Tawny hissed an angry obscenity at him, but one of the other women tried to cover it by telling her to shut up. The man holding Tawny shook her like a rag doll.

Czar was so furious he simply looked up, whistled and did a low circle with his finger, indicating all of Torpedo Ink get on their bikes. Immediately, the club members complied with their president's order, all of them returning to their motorcycles with the exception of Reaper, Ice and Storm.

"This is bullshit, and *insulting*," Czar snapped, never once raising his voice, but his gaze flicked to Pierce briefly, then returned to center on Plank. "We gave you every respect, and to have a piece of trash like Tawny—and I don't particularly give a fuck if she is riding on the back of your enforcer's bike—attack one of my people is pure bullshit. He can't control that shit, he isn't where he should be. We're gone. You have a problem with that, you let me know."

He looked directly at Plank. "If this was a fuckin' setup, you hopin' my girls would fight so you'd have an excuse for a war, they're too good for that shit. And just so you know, you would have been the first to die. We fuckin' had you covered all the way, and you should have known that."

He turned on the heel of his boot and started for his bike. Reaper didn't move a muscle. Neither did Ice or Storm. They formed a line between Czar and the Diamondbacks. Each wore a grim face, one that said clearly that they were willing to die, but they'd take everyone with them.

"Pierce, that damn bitch is always causin' trouble. What the fuck was she doing here? None of them should have been here. She just lost us one of the best support clubs we've got." Plank hissed his displeasure, flicking his gaze at the group of women.

Tawny's face had gone from white to so pale she looked like a ghost. She made a move toward the car, but three of the Diamondbacks cut her off.

"I have no idea how they found out about the meet, Plank, but I'll get to the bottom of it. That's Judge's old lady." Pierce glanced over his shoulder at the Diamondback behind him. "Tawny's got a mouth on her. She's never been on the back of my bike. I let her blow me, but I never talked about this meet to her."

"You fuckin' couldn't keep it in your pants until we had this deal in the bag?" Plank turned away in disgust. "I want to know how she found out. And she's banned. The rest are disciplined hard. I don't care if they're someone's old lady, they had no fuckin' business being here. Find out who let them come and why. I want a report. This was club business. Bitches weren't welcome."

Plank stormed back into the bar. Reaper, Ice and Storm made their way back to their bikes, all three eyeing Pierce. Storm gestured toward him, giving him the finger. Ice stared at him for a long time. He'd promised the man if he hurt Alena in any way, he'd kill him, and he meant it. He saluted and backed all the way to his bike. The three took off.

Savage waited until they were all the way down the road before he secured his rifle and slipped it into his carrying bag. He'd been so tempted to end Pierce, but Czar would never give the go-ahead until a sufficient amount of time had passed. Only when no one would remember, when there would be no associating his death with Alena or Torpedo Ink, would he give them a green light.

Savage's bike was parked up the road from the bar, deep in the shadows of the trees. He was making his way toward the bar, sliding up onto the roof, when a smaller shadow joined him. He closed his eyes. "Not a smart move, babe."

Eavesdropping on the Diamondbacks was a risky business under any conditions. Alena listening in when she was highly emotional, even though she was a professional, might be courting disaster.

She gave him one emotion-laden look and, using toes and fingers, slid her body closer to the vent. The two of them entered the attic, which was open-beamed in several places, giving them both sight and audio to the small group gathered below.

Plank was still furious, pacing back and forth. "I want that bitch gone, Pierce. She's been trouble since the day she came. She's split up two families, and she's trying to get my wife to think I've been with her, which is never going to happen. After the run, I want you to take care of that permanently, Pierce. You have a problem with that?"

"None at all."

"What about you, Judge?" Plank spun around to confront his second-in-command. "I believe your old lady is her friend."

Judge held up both hands. "Not anymore. That bitch stepped way over the line, and Theresa knows it. She tried to stop her. She already knows she never should have been here tonight. Tawny has way too much influence over all the women. I'm good with getting rid of her."

"Wait until after the run. We can use the bitch to get information on the Venomous club. She likes to use her mouth. Let her actually be useful. You like that shit so much, Pierce, that you blew your one chance for us to have an in with Torpedo Ink."

"That's bullshit. You were the one who insisted I get that fucking video from Alena."

"You were getting too close to her. You're always immune to the ladies, and she had you wrapped around her little finger. I needed you to show me where your loyalties were."

"That's bullshit and you know it. My loyalties have always been to the club. You didn't expect Alena to have loyalty to her club. Frankly, neither did I, but that should have earned her respect, not this kind of crap. I gave you the video as proof of loyalty, and instead of deleting it like you said you would, you sent it out to everyone. You were the one who just lost us the one asset we had, so don't put that shit on me." Pierce sounded furious.

Plank sighed. "That might have been a mistake. Now we have to find another way to keep Torpedo Ink under our thumb. We don't have anything on them. You have Alena's fingerprints, right?"

"Yeah, I lifted a couple, like you told me."

"Plant them on the body somewhere to implicate her."

"You sure you want to do that?" Pierce asked. "We can't take a chance on losing that club. They're an asset no one else has, not even another chapter, Plank. You saw how they pulled off that job in Sac. They're smooth. Fast. We know they did everything we asked, and we couldn't catch them at it, even when we set them up. Anything you ask, they can do for you, but you take down one of their own, especially Alena or Lana, they'll never forgive us."

"If you kept your damn dick in your pants instead of in that bitch's mouth, we wouldn't have to go this route, but I doubt she's going to be taking you back." Plank turned and walked right up to Pierce. "You had it in the bag, and you blew it."

"You were the one who suggested I have her send me a video, and then you wanted to see it and immediately sent it to everyone," Pierce reiterated. "I don't want to give her up. She's different. I actually entertained keeping her. Making her my old lady."

"You can't keep it in your pants for five seconds," Plank scoffed.

Pierce shrugged. "She's better than anyone I've ever had. Doesn't mean I'm not going to keep sampling what's offered."

Plank shook his head, grinning. "Should have known you'd never change. During the run, you keep that bitch Tawny concentrating on the Venomous boys, tell her she can earn her way back into my good graces if she brings us good intel. That should keep her working hard. Then I want her gone. Plant Alena's prints on the bitch's body, Pierce, and make it good, somewhere between Caspar and Boonville. Once the cops pick up Alena, we can offer our help to Torpedo Ink, get them indebted to us, but you take care of Tawny permanently."

"Want that bitch to blow me again, and then I'll have the pleasure of telling her she doesn't come close to Alena, not even a little bit. She'll fuckin' hate that. She was always asking me if she was better. I'd tell her she was going to have to try a hell of a lot harder to beat Alena. That would make her crazy and she'd do anything. Not that it helped, but the guys thought it was great, because they benefited from her trying."

"Alena's really that good?"

"You have no idea," Pierce said. "Never going to have that again. This could backfire on us. If the cops take her in and she doesn't have an alibi . . ."

"She's always at that restaurant of hers, and we'll offer our lawyer."

"They have Absinthe."

Plank shrugged. "Small-time. We have a powerhouse. We'll make it look like Tawny's been hanging with the Venomous club. She goes from club to club; they'll believe it. The cops will too. Plant that trail as well. You're good at that."

"Consider it done. After the run, I'll have plenty of evidence to point them in both directions."

Plank downed a small glass of whiskey and turned away. "I'll offer an olive branch to Czar in a day or two and ask for another meet just before the run. Lay out to him my concerns about the Venomous club. I'll offer to meet on his turf. That should appease him." He walked to the door and turned back. "Find out which of those women talked about the meet. Judge, if it was your old lady, you're responsible. If not, she needs to be punished for being here."

Savage didn't look at Alena. He couldn't. The betrayal ran too deep. He slid out of the vent and back onto the roof, where they waited until the Diamondbacks disappeared down the road before they headed back to their own clubhouse. Because everything had gone to shit, he went with Alena rather than going back to Sea Haven and his woman. He wanted to find Pierce and extract Torpedo Ink justice for hurting one of their own, but he knew only Czar could make that call.

The moment they swept into the parking lot, Alena was off her bike and inside. Savage reported the conversation to his president and the rest of the club.

Czar immediately signaled to Lana. "I want you with her, you understand me? She leaves, I don't care if she doesn't want you to go, you do it. This was another violation. A huge break in trust again for her."

"I'm with her," Lana agreed readily.

"I'll follow in the distance," Storm said.

"I'll go too," Mechanic said.

Czar nodded. "Fuck the Diamondbacks. We'll get Pierce. Play it cool for now. Ice, you understand me? They'll be looking for retaliation. We're not giving it to them. Not yet."

Ice nodded. He was off the bar stool and heading inside to his sister. Alena was already walking out of the back room, a small bag hastily thrown together. He caught her arm. She stopped when the others filled the common room.

"I don't want any of you to touch him," she hissed. "This was my mistake. Mine. I trusted someone I shouldn't have. It wasn't like I couldn't see all the signs of trouble. I did this to myself."

"Alena," Czar said. "You weren't the only one he took in. We all liked him. Every single one of us. If I thought for one minute he was playing you, or playing all of us, I would have ordered you to stop. I didn't. That's on me. I didn't see it coming, and I should have. His loyalty is to his club."

"I've got to get out of here for a couple of days," Alena said. "I texted Delia and she said she'd look after the restaurant for me. Just promise me no one is going to hurt him." Delia Swanson had owned her own diner for years, was retired and often helped Alena when needed.

"You did great, letting that bitch come at you," Czar continued, as if she hadn't spoken. "I was proud of you. You could have killed her, and you let her put her fuckin' hands on you."

Alena's chin lifted. "I'm Torpedo Ink. We were there for a purpose. I wasn't about to blow the deal because some trashy bitch wanted to rub my face into the fact that I was stupid. Yes, a video exists, but I don't want any of you to act like it's a big deal, because there's probably a million videos of me— of all of us. You all know that. Let it go. He isn't worth it."

"However you want to play it, honey," Ice agreed immediately, lying through his teeth. "Where are you heading?"

"I don't know, up north, I think, the Rogue River. I've always wanted to see it."

"Lana's going with you," Czar said. He gestured with his chin toward the back room.

Lana immediately headed back to pack a few things. Storm and Mechanic did the same.

Alena shook her head. "No. I just need to be alone for a little while, Czar. I'm not going to do anything crazy because someone distributed a sex video I was stupid enough to make for him. I've got all of you and my dream restaurant. I just need a little time to get myself together."

"I fuckin' hate that I couldn't put a bullet in his head right there for you," Czar said. "His president was less than happy with him."

"He wasn't happy," Reaper confirmed. "At. All."

Savage remained silent, his gaze on Alena's face. He detested that someone had hurt her—worse, someone she'd given her trust to. He had to walk a fine line with his woman. He'd seen that look of devastation already on Seychelle's face twice now. Once when he'd carried her into her home and she'd shared the memory of what she considered his betrayal of her. And tonight, before she'd gotten drunk. In the bar, when she'd been so happy singing—all that changed in one brief moment. He never wanted to see it again.

Alena was good at masking, but she didn't bother, not with them. Pierce had stabbed her through the heart. He'd done that. It didn't take a man hitting a woman. It took breaking trust. Physical or emotional, it was all bad if you broke trust. Savage had learned that lesson.

Czar wasn't the only man in the room who wanted to put a bullet in Pierce's head. Savage wanted to take him apart, hurt him the way he could see the man had hurt Alena. He knew Ice and Reaper felt the same way. Maestro as well. Pierce was a dumb fuck for playing Alena and leaving her exposed to someone like Tawny. He should have known Torpedo Ink would come for him—and they would. They were patient and they would bide their time.

He looked at Destroyer, the newest member of their club. Yeah, he felt the same way Savage, Ice and Storm did. He could take apart Pierce just as easily. They exchanged long, knowing looks with Maestro and Keys.

Alena nodded. "I'm heading out. Lana, if you're coming with me?"

"I'm ready, baby," Lana said.

Alena looked at her brother. "Ice, you have a woman here at home. She's your responsibility. You don't need to shadow us."

"You're my responsibility," Ice corrected. "You belong to all of us, just as we belong to you. Storm and Mechanic will go with you. Those are the rules we set up, and you're Torpedo Ink. You'll follow them. I assume you've blocked Pierce on your phone?"

She nodded. "As soon as possible, I'll change phone

numbers. Don't worry, I've learned my lesson. I should have learned it a long time ago, but ever the fool, I guess."

"You're not that, Alena," Ice said, slinging his arm around her. He pulled her to him and dropped a kiss on top of her head. "He's the fuckin' fool. Tawny isn't worth the tip of your little finger. She'll go from man to man, and she'll never be a partner. She's a taker."

"They're going to kill her," she whispered. "Pierce is, and he's going to try to implicate me." She put her arms around her older brother and for one moment let herself sag against him for comfort.

Savage clenched his teeth. The pain Alena felt was almost agony, compounded by memories of childhood betrayal. He shouldered what he could, let it swirl through him until the rage was so strong, breaking close to the surface. He had to look away. So many times, everything they wanted or needed had been ripped away from them. When they were children, time and again they would be duped into trusting someone, an adult, another child, and they'd get their hearts torn out. That cycle had continued for years—until Czar had put a stop to it.

The code—they lived by it. They had woven their lives together and become whole. The few they allowed into their closed society had been tested, and they'd paid a high price for becoming part of Torpedo Ink. They might not be patched members, but they lived by the same rules and were held up to the same code.

Alena pulled back and gave him a small smile. She looked to her birth brother Storm, and Mechanic, her Torpedo Ink brother. "You both ready?"

"Let's go," Storm said and indicated the door.

Alena went out without looking back. The room was eerily silent for a long while.

It was Czar who broke that silence. "We're going to get that fucker. He won't get away with this. I want everything we can get on him. Code, you hear me? Find out everything about Pierce so we can bury that pissant. We just bide our time before we take him down. I mean it: no one goes near him. No one threatens him. Nothing at all. Let him sweat. He'll know it's coming. The longer he has to wait for it, the more his nerves are going to stretch to the breaking point. We're going to have to keep a lookout to make sure that he doesn't come for us."

They all nodded.

"Savage, I'd like to see you privately." Czar indicated their meeting room.

Savage shrugged. A part of him had known this was coming, especially after what Pierce had done to Alena. He walked ahead of Czar into the familiar room and sank down onto one of the very comfortable leather chairs that surrounded the long oval table. The table was very thick and made of gleaming, polished wood. The room was large, the walls formed of warm wood. A bank of windows looked out toward the pounding sea. He liked everything about their meeting place.

Reaper closed the door and leaned against it. His brother. He always took Savage's back, even when Czar was about to lay into him. They both had known it was coming sooner or later. In a way, Savage welcomed it. He had to know his brothers would watch out for Seychelle. If Savage ever tipped too far, went wrong, they'd take her back.

"We're going to protect your woman. There has to be a plan in place."

It was a demand, nothing less. No one else would dare, other than Reaper, tell Savage his business. Czar was more than their president. He was the man who had found a way for all of them to survive. Two hundred and eighty-seven children had entered that brutal, vile "school," and only nineteen had made it out alive. They survived because Czar had taught them how to survive.

They were in a school to learn how to kill, and they did. As children, some starting younger than five, they learned.

They absorbed every lesson, they practiced any gift they might find they were good at and they wove themselves together, forming a pack every bit as strong as the wolves they shaped themselves after.

"She has to know everything, Savage. That's the code. That's what we live by."

"I'm well aware, Czar." Savage sighed and rubbed his temples. "You think I want to be the way I am? I've tried everything to be different. Nothing works."

"I'm aware you've tried. I've done the research as well. There isn't a cure for any of us, but none of us can tolerate any member of this club abusing a woman. If you bring her into this club, she's ours to protect. You understand fully what I'm saying to you." Czar pinned him with his direct stare, the one that warned all of them not to fuck with him. "You hit that girl, you punch her, slap her, abuse her in any way, I'll put a bullet in your head."

Savage was more than happy to hear it. He'd put the bullet in his own fuckin' head. But he had to clarify. Czar had to know this wasn't going to be so black and white.

"I needed to hear that from you, Czar. I would never hit her like that. It's never been about that, and I think you know it. I won't tolerate her fuckin' with the rules, she'll be punished, but she'll agree ahead of time what that is."

Czar shrugged. "That's between the two of you, and I'm not talking about that."

"No, you're talking about when I lose it and need to fuckin' get off when my woman is carrying my shit. I've always been careful, you know that. Seychelle is mine. I would protect her with everything in me. What that means is, I'll have her consent and I'll always be careful never to go too far. If I fail, I'll be the first one to go for the gun."

He didn't look at his brother. Not one single time. He'd been there. He'd been forced to watch. Then it continued in order to keep Reaper alive. So long. So many girls, and all the while someone had been making certain that he'd been feeling great, that his cock was sucked or fucked and he was very happy. He hadn't had a chance to ever be normal. He didn't know how to be normal. He never would. Seychelle would pay the price and he would hate himself always. There was no way out for either of them now.

"I fuckin' hate what they did to you," Czar said. "There was no way to stop them, Savage. I didn't know. Reaper didn't know. Not at first, the first few years, and after, it was already too late. I'm sorry, brother. I'm fuckin' sorry."

Savage pressed his fingers tighter against his temples. "Wasn't anyone's fault. We all had it bad, but we got out. I'll deal with it. I've always dealt with it."

"She has to know ahead of time. Give me your word on that. I don't care how you bring her in, how you make her yours, but you have to get her consent. Once she gives it and she's in, we'll back you all the way."

"And you'll have her back," Savage clarified again. "Once I've claimed her and she's mine, every single member, including my brother, has to have her back." This time he looked at his brother. Reaper. His world before Torpedo Ink. His reason for becoming the way he was.

Reaper nodded and then abruptly turned and stalked out, slamming the door behind him.

Czar looked down at his hands. "You get into trouble anytime, day or night, you come to me. You understand, Savage? You've always carried this alone, but now you have a woman. If she's the right one, she's worth everything, including your pride. You come to me if it gets too bad and you get worried for her."

Savage pushed himself up and looked at his president, father, brother, all rolled into one. "I swear it on Torpedo Ink." It was all he had to give. His word. He knew they took that as gold. He gave it that way.

He took his time riding back to Sea Haven, needing the cool wind in his face, blowing out the memories that clung too close. Pierce's betrayal had brought them too close.

They all had liked the man, but they had to remember always, his entire loyalty was to his club and he had no room to be loyal to anyone outside of it. Neither did they. They were Torpedo Ink, and only those within their club could be trusted. It was a hard lesson for all of them.

He thanked Preacher and Ink and let them know he'd be riding the next day and he'd text them. He stood for a long time looking down at his woman. She looked small in the big bed. She wasn't curled up but looked as if she'd fallen asleep on her back, her arms flung out, her legs stretched out in front of her. Her hair had not been put back into a braid, and all that thick, silky hair was over her pillow and around her face.

Savage took his time removing his motorcycle boots and then his clothes, all the while looking down at the woman he was irrevocably tying to him. He sat beside her for a long time, his hand on her leg, his gaze on her face.

"I'm sorry for this, baby. You have no idea how sorry I am, but I'm not going to make it another day without you. I can only tell you no one else will ever love or treasure you more. It won't seem that way a lot of the time, but it's the truth. You've crawled inside me, and without you, I can't take this anymore. I just can't do it. So, baby, you're going to have to take it for me. It isn't fair. It isn't nice. In fact, it's fuckin' wrong, but I've got no choice, and that means you don't either."

He stretched out on the bed next to Seychelle, inhaling her scent, that special fragrance that clung to her skin and hair. The moment he turned on his side and laid his head on her belly, he wrapped his arm tightly around her hips. Holding her. Trying not to feel like he was a monster, but knowing he was. Knowing it was Seychelle who would take the terrible burden off of him long enough for him to breathe. To gather himself enough to let that terrible weight settle back on his shoulders.

He kissed her soft belly and then nuzzled her bare skin.

She wore a tank and nothing else. He ran his fingers through those soft blond curls that he was going to shave off. He wanted her completely bare, so he could see, and she could feel everything he did to her. Good things. Bad things. Dirty things. Things that would make her scream for him. Things that would made him so aroused and hard it wouldn't matter that his cock was scarred and too tight to stretch properly. And she would give him her tears freely. Just as he took on the pain for his brothers and sisters, proving his love for them over and over, she would do it for him. The only person in the world who would give him unconditional love, she would do that for him.

He pressed another kiss into her soft skin. His canvas. His woman. He found he liked that. He'd never thought in terms of having a woman, but that something in her that called to him had found its way deep. Lying there in the dark, his head on her belly, his arm around her hips, he let himself breathe her in. Love welled up, swallowing the rage like it did every time he laid his head on her. Closing his eyes, he inhaled all the beauty that was Seychelle Dubois.

ELEVEN

Seychelle woke with a fierce headache. Her mouth felt like cotton, dry and sour. She groaned and turned over, keeping her eyes shut tight in case the sun was blazing through the window. Silently, she sent up a prayer that there would be fog. Lots and lots of dense fog, so she could see if she dared open her eyes.

"Come on, baby, time to get up. You've slept the day away, when you weren't throwing up." There was amusement in the voice. "You could just possibly be the worst drinker on the planet."

She knew that voice. She didn't have to see him to know her worst nightmare was right there in her house. She vaguely remembered Savage putting her in the car and driving her home. She spread her fingers over her eyes and slowly opened them. He'd pulled the screens, thank heavens. Outside, the wind hit the windows and rattled them. Just the slight whistling noise reverberated through her head.

Even through her fingers, the room spun a little bit. Her

stomach lurched. Hastily, she closed her eyes. She remembered him holding her hair out of the way while she vomited. Worse, she remembered being on the floor of the bathroom. Why couldn't she just have blacked out completely and never recalled a single detail?

It was even worse than the worst, if that was possible. He'd put her in the shower. He'd been in the shower with her. She'd been naked. Was she still naked? She dared to look down at her body. She was, thankfully, wearing one of her racer-back tanks. Oh God, she'd been all over him, touching him, stroking him. She hoped she hadn't done more than that, but she might have.

"Come on, baby, you can't hide forever. It's time to face the music."

"Why not?" She tested her voice. "I'm pretty sure it wasn't good last night."

"I'm sure you're right. You can't drink worth shit."

She forced herself to look at him. The moment she did, her heart did a funny little flip. He looked so invincible. So strong. He had roped muscles and not an ounce of fat. He had horrendous scars and burns, terrible burns, but on him, those scars just made him more attractive, as well as giving him the illusion of being indestructible.

She had the grace to look ashamed. "I know. I should never drink. Never. One, and I'm going under fast."

"Was that your first time?"

"No. I tried another time and threw up like crazy on one drink."

"You spent most of the night throwing up. It wasn't pretty."

She pushed back her hair, trying not to remember anything else, but she couldn't stop herself from seeing another man's face. "There was someone named Bill. Please tell me I didn't do anything dumb."

He shook his head. "Baby, you were going home with that man."

"I wasn't." She was shocked. That couldn't be true. That was more than dumb. Worse than dumb. She thought she might have talked to him. Flirted. Used her voice shamelessly. But going home with him? She groaned and covered her face with her hands.

"You were. I would have had to track your ass down and haul you home. Don't know what I would have done to him, but it wouldn't have been pretty. Let's just not do that again. You understand me? You need to be with me on that one."

She pushed her forehead into her palm. "I'm with you all the way on that one. I need to get dressed."

"You need to let the aspirin do its work. I'm bringing you a little soup. Drink all the water. You're dehydrated. When you drink alcohol, Seychelle, you have to stay hydrated."

"I wasn't really going home with him, was I?" She was a little horrified that he was telling the truth. Images were crowding in. She was fairly certain she was never drinking alcohol again, so he didn't need to coach her on how it was done properly.

"Yeah, babe, you were. I didn't let you, so we'll call it a near miss."

"Thanks, Savage. I don't know what the hell got into me." She was sincerely grateful to him.

"You were scared. Running. You didn't want to face the inevitable, and I can't really blame you. You made a few mistakes, baby, and we're going to have to address them, but that's after you're not hungover."

"I slept all day—how can I be hungover?"

"First, I think you're allergic to alcohol, and second, you didn't sleep all day. It doesn't look sunny because it's so overcast, but it isn't that late. I'm going to take you for a ride this evening to get you out in the fresh air. You'll have to dress warm."

Her heart did that funny twist, and this time her stomach engaged, doing a full flip. There was a part of her that hoped he was right and she really was allergic to alcohol.

Still, she doubted that she could blame her bad behavior on that. She decided to focus on his offer. A ride on his bike. That could be just plain awesome.

"A ride? On your motorcycle?" She loved the idea.

"Yeah. That would be the ride, Seychelle. You have to learn to trust me, and there's no better way than on the back of my bike."

Now her heart was accelerating right into the danger zone. "Savage, I need you to tell me what we're doing here. Because you've never really shown a lot of interest in me . . . um . . . sexually. I thought you wanted a friendship. That was difficult enough for me to try to explain."

He sat on the edge of the bed, reached across her and snagged the bottle of water. "Drink this now. Who are you trying to explain our friendship to?"

"Me." She drank because he sat there watching her, very closely, those blue eyes like twin flames just burning into her. She'd never met anyone who could focus completely the way he did. He never once took his eyes off her.

"You have difficulty explaining our friendship to you?"

Put like that, with that little hint of male amusement, it made her head want to explode. She sounded like an idiot. Exasperated, she drank more water. "Yes. What's going on? It isn't like you're looking at me for . . ." She broke off, unsure what she wanted to say.

"I'm looking at you like you're my everything, which you are. You just don't know it yet, and you're scared to death of me."

She shook her head before she could stop herself. What was the use, anyway? There was something about him that made her want to give him the truth, even if it left her stripped bare. "I'm not so much afraid of you as what you'll do to me. There is no way I can be with you and not get hurt. Really hurt. That cut-to-the-bone kind of hurt. I don't want that. You already shredded my heart, and I can't go there again. I just can't. Knowing you're going to be with other women so you can satisfy some dark craving I can't . . ." She broke off, shaking her head.

She wanted to be the one to satisfy his darker cravings but was too terrified to do more than fantasize. She didn't even know exactly what he really wanted or needed, only that every time she caught glimpses, they made her body come alive in ways she hadn't known it could.

He was silent for a long time, those eyes of his drifting possessively over her face and down her body. She had one leg out from under the sheets. Her scarred leg. The pits went from her ankle all the way up the side of her leg to the top of her thigh, where gravel had dug deep. His gaze fell on that, and immediately he circled her ankle with his hand and began to move his palm up her leg. Even his touch was possessive. Every time he did that, rubbed with his palm, she felt he was claiming her.

She wanted him to deny that he would hurt her. She needed him to say it, although she wouldn't have believed him. The rage in him was violent and barely contained. It beat at her, and eventually, she had to open up and allow it in, allow her peace to surround him and slowly absorb the brutal needs in him.

"There aren't going to be other women," he said quietly. "And you'll learn to be what I need."

Her breath caught in her throat. "I don't understand."

"You will. I'll teach you."

"You aren't telling me I won't get hurt," she pointed out.

"I want to tell you that won't happen, Seychelle, but there always has to be truth between us. You have to learn that I'll always tell you the truth no matter what, no matter how much it might hurt or scare you, and I'll know that you'll do the same for me. We've got a lot to talk about. Hit the bathroom while I get you some soup."

She wanted the bathroom break, especially to brush her teeth, but her stomach lurched at the idea of eating. "I'll be right back, but nothing to eat yet."

She hurried, her heart racing. At least they were going to talk things out. She had no problems being straight with him, telling him how she felt, but he had to accept that she couldn't be with him, not when he needed to be with other women—and he did, no matter what he said now.

She even believed him when he said she was his everything. He came back to her over and over. He suffered just the way she had, all those nights outside her window. She'd felt it when they'd breathed together with a wall separating them.

Those women in the bar. The way they'd fixated on him. She couldn't take that, not knowing he would go back to them and give them what he would never give her. She wasn't the type of woman to share. She didn't know about the other women who were with the men in the Torpedo Ink club, but she knew, emotionally, she just wasn't built that way.

She sighed and looked at herself in the mirror. She'd tried being without him. That hadn't worked so well. She'd thought she could be with him. That hadn't worked either. She looked pale and strained. Her hair was a mess. She vaguely remembered Savage holding her braid to keep it off her face when she was puking nonstop. Great. Lovely. She sighed again. There was no use hiding. She might as well get it over with.

Seychelle went back into her bedroom, climbing up onto the bed, scooting up to her favorite place, back to the headboard, where she felt a little safer as she faced him. He looked . . . invincible. So tough. Scary even. Sexy as hell. Always her choice, and she didn't even know why, but she wasn't going to be that woman, pushed into something she knew wouldn't work because she was so in love. She had spent the last month acting like her life was over, moping over a man who preferred other women sexually, and her for what? Sleeping? She had to get her tough on and stand up for herself.

Savage sat on the edge of the bed, shaping her ankle with his palm the way he always did, as if he couldn't stop himself from touching her. His touch was gentle. The pads of his fingers moved over her skin in small strokes. Like caresses. Like sin. Like the promise of something she could never have with him.

"You've got your chin up, babe. I know what that means. You're spoiling for a fight." His eyes turned bluer than ever. "We're not fighting here. We're going to do this thing. You and me, Seychelle. There's going to be a you and me."

She shook her head, her heart beating too hard. Hoping. Afraid to hope. Afraid of being hurt again. "I don't see how. I just don't see how it can work. I want it to work more than anything, but how can it?" She kept her gaze fixed on his face. His eyes. The way they moved over her face. Her body. Taking her in. So much for her resolve. He melted it away just by the way he looked at her.

"You have to learn to trust me, and that trust has to be so strong that you know you can tell me anything. I'll listen to you, Seychelle. I'll hear you and we'll talk it out. The two of us. We'll work through the problems together and it will be all right."

"But it won't. I tried to tell you about those other women in the bar last night. How they couldn't keep their eyes off you. The way they made me feel. But you just dismissed my feelings as if they didn't count."

He was silent for a long time, his gaze moving over her face, his fingers moving on her calf. "I shouldn't have done that, Seychelle. In all honesty, I couldn't have identified those women to you. I don't know their names. They mean absolutely nothing to me. I know that makes me sound like a dick, but it's the truth, and we have to have truth between us. The only woman who matters to me is you. I didn't see anyone else last night. So yeah, I did dismiss what I considered unimportant. I shouldn't have. Just because they weren't important to me didn't mean they weren't important to you."

She didn't know what to say to that. She hadn't expected him to admit he was wrong. Savage didn't seem the type of man to ever say he was wrong. She liked that he had.

His palm slid up and down her leg. His touch was mesmerizing. The heat he generated slipped through her pores into her bloodstream. Even the sight of his hand on her bare leg was almost hypnotizing.

"You're the only woman who matters to me. I don't want another woman sexually, Seychelle. I want you. I wanted you when I left you this last time. The idea of another woman touching me was abhorrent to me. Quite frankly, it disgusted me."

She knew he was telling the truth. She'd shared that moment with him when he'd picked her up on Doris's porch and she felt his distaste of the woman. "I don't understand why you went to her, Savage. You knew I would have done anything for you."

His hand slid behind her knee, making her breath catch. "I couldn't get you ready in time, baby. I can get you there, but it takes time. That's something we have to talk about. Things I need. Things you have to go into our relationship knowing, with your eyes wide open. I want you to ask questions if you don't understand something. You need to know this isn't going to be easy, but I swear to you, I'll never let you down. Never."

Seychelle swallowed every question she had, her heart beating so loud it sounded like thunder booming in her ears.

"I want a full commitment from you, baby, but you have to know what being my woman means. There are rules, and those rules are always going to be there. More, you have to know what being with me is going to be like."

Her heart thudded. There it was. She knew it was coming. Her mouth went dry, and deliberately she took another sip of water. "Rules?" She'd never been good with rules. Never. She'd grown up without them. She went her own way. Did her own thing.

"I'm fucked up. Don't pretend you don't know, Seychelle. You knew it the moment you made the decision to save my life. You connected with me. I felt it. You felt it. You slipped inside me and you know what's there. It isn't pretty, and it scares the hell out of you."

She couldn't deny it, but at the same time, she was drawn to him. That was one side of him, not all of him. He couldn't hide the best part of him, that giving part, so selfless, looking out for his brethren, for her. She had seen the violence in him, but she'd also seen his tremendous need to protect those he loved. That determination to stop their pain when it was so strong they couldn't bear it, because he had the capacity to love that much.

"There has to be truth between us at all times, because this lifestyle demands it. My sexual practices are disturbing to others, but hot as hell and arousing for me. I have to have them in order to be in any way both aroused and satisfied."

His hand never stopped stroking those caresses up and down her leg. It felt good. It felt like possession. The things he said were terrifying, and yet at the same time, just the fact that he was willing to give that to her pulled her deeper into him.

"I went to a friend of mine, one of the brothers in my club, Absinthe. He's the smartest man I know. I wanted him to tell me I could learn to be different if I was with a woman who truly meant something to me. I'd done my research, and everything I read said no. I was already having too many fantasies about us, so I was worried."

His gaze touched on her breasts under her thin tank, and instantly her nipples hardened. Satisfaction gleamed in his eyes. The pads of his fingers brushed over the tops of her breasts, raising goose bumps over her skin. "I spent weeks imagining what your nipples were like. I even asked Ice to make me several different kinds of jewelry for you."

The idea intrigued her. More than that, she felt her body react, go damp. She'd looked up nipple clamps on an adult site several times and read about them and then been ashamed of herself for even thinking about such things. The idea that Savage had thought of it for her, even had his friend make jewelry for her, sent hot blood pooling wickedly low.

He slid his hand under her tank, first cupping her breast and then finding her nipple to pinch, at first gently, but then biting down with steady pressure as his other hand slid up her thigh, his fingers dancing close to her slick heat. She gasped, her nipple stinging, but before she could protest, his mouth was on her other breast, right through the material of her tank, and his fingers brushed her clit. She cried out, nearly exploding with a mini orgasm.

Her breathing turned ragged as he lifted his head and looked at her, his eyes turbulent, hot-burning flames of blue. His hands were once more back on her leg, but his expression was pure possession.

"I dreamt of your nipples, baby, and the things I could do with them to bring you pleasure. To bring us both pleasure. Things that would scare you at first, but I knew I could make you love in the end. Still, I didn't want this life for you. I went to Absinthe hoping he would tell me I could learn to be someone else for you. I already knew that answer, because there's no going back for me, Seychelle. If you're with me, if you're my woman, my partner, you have to live my lifestyle. That's the bottom line. You're with me, you live this lifestyle with me, because I can't get out of it."

She swallowed hard, because there was caution in his tone and caution in his mind, even if his eyes were alive with those bright, hot flames and his hand on her leg felt like pure possession. Her breasts ached for him. Her nipples were so hard now, pulsing with a dark desire she had no understanding of but he'd given her a sudden taste for.

Secretly, that forbidden need for a mixture of pain with pleasure had been there all along. She didn't know why, and it scared her, embarrassed her, humiliated her. She didn't understand why the nice men she had tried to date hadn't aroused her at all. Only Savage. When he had turned her around in the alley, lifted the hem of her dress and swatted the cheeks of her bottom, he'd done it hard. That heat and pain had spread, morphing into something altogether different and setting up a craving for more.

"I didn't think I had anything to give you back when I would be asking so much from you. But you need me just as much as I need you. You can't control your gift of healing. It's eating you alive. If you don't stop, Seychelle, you're not going to live long, and you know it. I can help you with that. While you were driving me insane deciding whether or not you could let me back into your life, I found a woman with a gift similar to yours and asked her how she manages it. She gave me a lot of tips."

Seychelle was shocked. Savage was not the kind of man to go outside his circle for advice.

"You won't always like me saying *enough*, but once we figure it out and we have our signals, you'll be able to sing with the band and go where you want as long as you look to me when you know you're in over your head. I'll trust you to give me the heads-up when you need me to step in, and you trust me to do it. When I say you're done, you are. That means, baby, I'm willing to carry your sweet little ass out of the bar, or away from one of your friends' houses, right at that moment. That's going to be the number one rule we have between us. Always, always when I say you're done, you have to agree that you are. That is what's going to keep you alive, and more than anything, Seychelle, you have to be alive and in this world."

He was being serious. Very serious. She did her best to

suppress a smile, but one slipped out before she could stop it. "Rules? Savage, I haven't lived with rules ever. You do get that my parents were ill, and I ran the household? At eight, no one was telling me what to do. I took over paying the bills around the time I turned twelve. I got part-time jobs to help out with money until my father hit it big with his software program. I was thirteen when I started contributing. I don't do rules very well."

"Then you're going to have a fuckin' hard few months until you do, baby." He was implacable. "I have to live with rules in order to keep sane. That means my woman does as well. You do have a choice whether or not you want to make that commitment to me, and it's a big decision. This right here, the first rule, that's to save your life. This is the easy one. It isn't about controlling you, Seychelle, this is the one that gives you freedom."

Seychelle pressed her lips together. Savage was doing his best to lay things out for her. His truth. Her needs. She knew he wanted to be very clear what she was facing before she made a commitment to him, but a part of her wanted to jump in blindfolded with both feet. Learn along the way. One tiny thing at a time, as long as he knew what she needed from him. Her needs weren't a long laundry list, but he was right. She did need help with her gift.

"You have to commit to that. Out loud. You tell me you're with me on that, and after we go through this we'll sit down and figure out what works for you. But I need to hear the words, babe. You have to give that to me."

Savage was a man who would demand she lean on him, not the other way around. She knew she wouldn't live long if she kept going the way she was. "Savage." She kept her voice low. "If we end up together, of course I'll commit to allowing you to say when I've had enough. Hopefully you're right, and we can come up with ways to control my inability to stop taking on too much sickness."

She meant it too. Nothing would make her happier. She

knew her inability to control her gift was slowly killing her. She hadn't realized Savage knew it, and it melted her heart that he'd gone to another healer to try to find a way to help her. She hadn't expected that. He'd surprised her twice.

"We're going to end up together, Seychelle. You have to have that in your mind when I'm laying this out for you, or every step of the way, you're going to be protesting. You already know it's going to be a shit deal for you. If it wasn't, I would have laid it out weeks ago, and we wouldn't have been in this mess."

That was so true. She wasn't a coward. She wanted this. She wanted him. She had no real idea of what to expect of his lifestyle. She might have caught frightening glimpses that had intrigued her, but at the same time, she knew she wasn't even close to knowing what he might ultimately demand from her. And then there were the women . . .

If she couldn't be what he needed, she was terrified she'd lose him to them. "You said it would just be the two of us, Savage. You and me. How do I know that's the truth?"

She leaned her head against the headboard. His touch was mesmerizing her. The way his eyes focused so completely on her sent hot blood rushing through her veins. Her stomach reacted with a slow roll, and no matter how hard she tried to prevent it, her sex clenched hard, needing him.

"Because as much as I fucking hate it, I tell you the truth about me. I give you my word. I give you the real man."

The pads of his fingers slid over her leg. He bent his head, and his lips were there, following the path of his fingers, a whisper of velvet, a touch of his tongue, as if he was tasting the sacrifice she'd made—her flawless skin for his life. He was blatantly seducing her into staying, and she was letting him when she should be thinking about self-preservation.

Savage ached for Seychelle. Her struggles touched him, a physical reaction, an actual heavy ache in his chest. So many weeks with her now, knowing her. Wanting her. Seeing who she was. "All those nights I lay right there on this bed next to you, wrapping my arms around your hips, laying my head on your belly and falling asleep. I don't do that, I don't *ever* lay in a bed with a woman. I don't fall asleep on her. You're . . ." He searched for the right word.

She needed to know what she meant to him. He could see she didn't have the confidence that she would be different to him than any other woman. "Extraordinary."

She blinked, her long lashes sweeping down and then back up. Her fingers plucked nervously at the sheet. He covered her hand gently.

"I lay there a long time, listening to your heartbeat. Thinking about what I would be asking of you. I realized I have to give you that same exact measure of surrender. If I want you all in, I have to make that same commitment to you—only to you." He wanted her to have that assurance.

"That was easy to do, Seychelle. I was already there, long before you. I was already so in love with you, just looking at you hurt sometimes. I wake up and breathe you in, happy you're on this earth."

All the while, his hand moved over her belly. His touch was very gentle, showing her he could be, he would be, gentle with her. "I know that's not much in the face of what I'm asking of you, but it's all I can give you. My promise that you have me one hundred percent. Everything I am is yours."

Tears glittered in her eyes. His heart jerked hard in his chest. He had her. She was still fighting for self-preservation, but he had her. He didn't make the mistake of saying any more. She had to think about it. Ask questions.

Her tongue touched her lip. "What I saw with that woman. That isn't all you need, is it? You weren't satisfied."

He didn't look away from her, looked right into her eyes, unflinching. "I wasn't at all satisfied. Not even close. She wasn't you, and by that time I needed just you. But no, my cravings are much, much darker than even what I did with her."

"The things you need scare me, Savage. You really scare me."

"That's understandable, Seychelle. The things I need during sex to be aroused are very frightening to most women. You don't just jump into them, but I can teach you to enjoy them with me. I can bring you so much pleasure it will be unbelievable, baby, but there will be pain involved. Only you can decide whether or not I'm worth what you would have to endure in order to learn to enjoy it."

Her gaze jumped to his face again. He tried not to grip her leg to keep her there, but it was a struggle. That was another brutally honest moment, and he knew he could easily lose her.

"What's involved?"

He gave a little shake of his head, but he didn't back off from telling her. "You already have a little idea. I like nipple play, so clamps. Ginger. Spankings. Strap. Cane. Flogger. Whips. I'll work you up to that." He continued to stroke her leg, draw his name on her. Write silent little pleas that she would have the courage to love him enough to overcome the fear of what he was asking of her.

Seychelle fell silent again, moistening her lips while she thought it over. "You can really get me to like all that? To find some kind of pleasure in it?"

His heart jumped. He had thought she might order him out. *Bog*, but she was courageous. He'd thought he couldn't love her more, but every minute that he was in her company just added to the way that emotion swamped him. "Yeah, baby, there's no doubt I can do that. I can give you my word that you'll have multiple orgasms and they'll be wild. You'll crave sex with me, just the way I do with you."

"How do you know I'll like it?"

"We tried our dirty, sinful sex lesson and you got off, remember? I got a little carried away when I was smacking your ass, because my handprints looked so perfect on you. You just about shattered, and we hadn't done anything.

When I get rough with your nipples, your body responds. In the shower, baby, you were very responsive to nipple play. That isn't the case with everyone. And you love me. You want to please me."

"And?" she prompted.

He sighed. "You've seen the words branded into my skin. They were put there for a reason. I'm damn good. I was a child learning that shit. I was forced to continue through my teens and early into my twenties and then was able to get out. Telling you that is for later, and you're the only one I'll ever give that to. The bottom line is, you're the only woman I want for myself. I used other women when my cycle got to the point that I needed to get rid of some of the rage inside me, but I never used my skills on them. Never."

"I don't understand what you mean. You say you used other women, but not your skills."

"Anyone can use a fuckin' whip, Seychelle. A few strikes, get the job done, shove your cock down their throat and get a little relief. That's what I mean by not using my skills on any other woman. With you, I would want to actually put my marks on you. Patterns. I would lay awake every damn night thinking about it, craving it, wishing for one woman, *my* woman. You. You're the only woman I crave to use my skills on. They're considerable. The minute I laid eyes on you, I started putting in real time making certain I would never make a mistake."

There was pride in his voice, and he couldn't keep it out. Maybe there should have been shame, but he was long past that. He had come to terms with who he was, what he was, and now that he had accepted that he was going to claim her, he wasn't going to apologize. He still expected her to tell him to go to hell and get out. What woman would stay after that confession? But she sat there in her favorite spot, just looking at him with her big blue eyes, making it impossible for him to tell what she was thinking.

"You've thought about this a lot."

"Just about every fucking minute of the day since I met you." He slid his palm up her thigh. "I look at your skin and know it's mine." He dropped his hand over his hard cock. "That's arousing, Seychelle, just the thought of what I can do. What you would let me do. The tears that you give to me. They're mine." He'd said that before to her, but she never asked him what he meant. He'd stolen those tears more than once from her, and she hadn't stopped him.

She took a deep breath. "I'm at my limit right now. I have to think about what you've said. I'd really like to take that ride with you."

She would like the bike. That was a plus on his side. He nodded and slid off the bed. "Dress warm, baby. It's cold on the highway at night."

He watched her slide off the bed. The way she moved was poetry. More than her looks, it was the brightness shining out of her that got to him. He felt it when he was with her. He was dark and ugly inside. She was light and so damned good he had no business pulling her down to his level, but it didn't matter. It really wasn't a choice anymore, not now that he knew she existed, not now that he'd been with her for so many weeks and he knew she needed him. He would be careful with her, but at the same time, it was necessary to prepare her for the bad times—and there were always going to be bad times with him.

She went into the bathroom, and he waited a couple of minutes and then opened the door and leaned against the doorjamb. She looked startled, outraged and then resigned.

"Do you understand about privacy?" She didn't even bother to get angry.

"I understand very little about it," he admitted, uncaring about anyone else and their privacy. This was about conditioning. This was about slowly drawing her into his world.

"Great. I'll explain it to you. Privacy is where a person is free from being observed by another person. In this case, me shutting the door means don't disturb me, I want to be alone."

"Thanks for that explanation. In this case, I don't really give a fuck. I wanted to tell you something."

"What was so important you thought you would disturb my privacy?"

Now there was amusement in her voice. He liked that about her. She had a great sense of humor, and she was going to need it.

"Not certain you deserve to know."

"Fine, don't tell me. Just remember the definition of privacy."

"I will, baby, if you promise to remember that you follow my rules."

Her gaze met his across the room. "Do your rules include me not going to the bathroom by myself? Because, seriously, if you have a fetish that includes anything to do with the bathroom, that's kind of a deal breaker for me right off the bat."

"No fetish, babe. Just don't like you closing doors on me."

She studied his expression for a long time, so long he felt his heart begin to accelerate. "Are you going to lay out your rules for me, or do I have to guess at them?"

"I'll lay them out, Seychelle. Because breaking them carries consequences, some pretty rough. It wouldn't be fair to you if you didn't know the rules ahead of time. I am Torpedo Ink, same as my brothers and Alena and Lana. There are rules to living in a club as well."

"What happened to freedom, Savage? I thought clubs were all about freedom."

"Just as society has bullshit rules, we have them too."

She blinked and then laughed as she washed her hands in the sink. "At least you're aware your rules are bullshit."

"Yeah, they're bullshit, but you still have to follow them. It's the only way to keep me sane." He waited until she pulled on jeans and a sweater, then held out his hand. "Let's go. You're going to get a real taste of what freedom is."

She took his hand with only the briefest of hesitations. He pulled her into him. She was small, soft and all curves. He loved fitting her close to him.

"Where are we going?"

"Up the coast." He swept his arm around her and walked her out to his bike. Just the sight of it settled him. The two things that mattered most in his world were coming together. He handed her gloves and then checked to make certain her jacket was very warm. He turned her so she was facing away from him, and he put his arms around her in order to zip the jacket all the way up.

"I'm going over the bike with you, babe, so don't be nervous. You're shaking."

"I am a little nervous," she admitted. "But mostly I'm excited."

He showed her the foot pegs, folding and unfolding them, and explained how to get on and off. He explained how hot the pipes could get and to keep clear. He took her patiently through everything there was about being on a bike with him. He was a little astonished when she repeated everything back to him verbatim.

"I want your arms around my waist, Seychelle, at all times. When I lean, you just go with me. Not any further. Just exactly what I do. Like we're making love. You got that, baby? You think you're ready for this?"

She nodded. "Absolutely."

Savage put Seychelle's helmet on her, making certain it was snug. He made a mental note to buy her motorcycle gear.

She got on like a pro, swinging up behind him and settling close. Her arms circled his waist and then her hands pressed into his belly. He fuckin' loved that. He hadn't known what it would feel like, but it felt natural. Like she belonged.

Then they were flying down the road. Highway 1 was a perfect road for motorcycles. The curves were sweet, banking first one way and then the other. Some were wide and sweeping, while others were tight. There were switchbacks and then stretches of open road, all with the ocean on one side and the mountains rising on the other.

Savage had never allowed a woman on the back of his bike. He would have taken Lana or Alena, had they needed it, but they were his sisters. He'd grown up with them and he had known both since they were toddlers, but they had their own motorcycles. He'd been apprehensive about how he would feel with Seychelle on his bike, his one sanctuary.

She moved with him. The slightest shift in his body, and her body followed his. She was a natural rider. A natural passenger. She didn't anticipate, she only moved when he did. To Savage, it felt as if they were one being, man, woman and machine. It was a little surreal and very sexy. He became aware of the heavy vibration of his ride. The pulsation moved through his body, taking him places he had never gone when she wasn't with him.

As they roared down the highway, he knew the connection between them continued to grow. He felt it. That woman in her, reaching for him, adjusting to the road with him, draining that hot rage inside of him away, the way the bike and the open highway did. He dropped his hand over hers and pressed her palms deep into his belly. Over his jacket. His colors.

Savage had plenty of practice living in the moment. He chose to do that right then. Live in that moment with Seychelle and his bike. He let the wind take him. He wrapped his hand around her thigh possessively and settled back to let the machine move through the turns with the ease of long practice. His Night Rod Special was smooth and took every curve as if it weren't there.

He heard the others coming up behind him long before they actually managed to catch up, although he'd been going slow, mostly for Seychelle's sake. He wanted her to get used to the way the bike reacted to every bend in the road. He wanted to get a feel for her moving with him. There was satisfaction in knowing she trusted him implicitly on the back of his bike. She would need that same trust in every aspect of their relationship.

He took her to his favorite place, where the bluff over-looked the ocean. It would give the others a chance to catch up before they hit the restaurant in Elk. He liked the food, as a rule. The place wasn't Alena's, but they had a good chef. He helped her dismount, knowing her legs would be shaky. She kept her hand on his shoulder for a few moments, steadying herself before she stepped away and carefully walked toward the edge.

"Don't get too close," he cautioned, coming up behind her and putting his arms around her waist. She leaned back against him, almost without thinking. "Love it when the sun goes down—you can see the water turning colors," he added.

The bikes came up behind them. Four of them. He glanced over his shoulder to see Reaper helping Anya off his Harley-Davidson Fat Boy Softail. The paint was a dark burgundy, like dried blood. Dark black leather seat, black trim, black chrome, and there was an image of a scythe with a heart wrapped around it. His brother and his old lady. Anya, in such a short time, had become a sister to Savage. She was very accepting of everyone. She waited patiently while Reaper situated the bike, and then he slung his arm around her and walked her up beside Savage and Seychelle.

Anya bumped his hip. "See you brought your girl to the best spot to watch the sunset." She gave Seychelle a cheer-ful smile. "I love evenings on the coast. The sun always looks like it's pouring gold into the sea."

"Or flames," Savage said, his mouth close to Seychelle's ear.

"It is beautiful," Seychelle agreed, giving Anya a quick, welcoming smile.

Her gaze went straight back to the sun. It appeared huge, a giant red-gold ball dropping fast from the sky, pouring colors into the water.

Preacher, Ink and Code had arrived with Reaper and Anya. They came up behind them, their gazes drawn to the colors streaking across the sky and turning the sea into a panorama of golds, reds and oranges, blazing as it sank into the water. It was a breathtaking sight, and Seychelle reacted, turning her face up to look at Savage over her shoulder.

"It's always different, isn't it?" she said to him.

Savage took advantage, one hand cupping Seychelle's face to keep her there as he bent to brush his lips gently over hers. Coaxing. Seducing. His heart lurched, and he pulled back abruptly, love for her swamping him.

"It *is* always different," Anya answered for him. "I love this coast. Sometimes it's wild and turbulent, so stormy it looks like something out of a gothic novel, and then it's like glass, smooth, brilliant and so calm it looks like you could walk on it."

"Kind of like you," Reaper said, his arm tightening around her neck.

She threw back her head and laughed. Seychelle laughed with her, and Savage found the sound spread out for him in the form of musical notes, floating out toward the sea and that amazing spinning ball of fire. The notes were golden, skipping through the air on the slight breeze. He often saw sounds as notes, and when he was young, he used to point them out to his brother and others, but no one else could see them. He'd learned to judge people by the colors of the notes. He hadn't seen them in years—not until Seychelle brought them back in the form of gold.

Code nudged Savage. "Message came in for Czar. Plank wants another meet."

Savage wanted time with Seychelle. As much as he could get. He sent Code a look that warned him to back off. He didn't want to have to explain anything to do with the club before he clarified what she would be getting into if she chose to stay with him. And, God help them both, he needed her to stay.

"The sea does look like you could walk on it," Preacher said. "Maybe we should toss Ink out there and see if he can."

"Yeah, and I can, so then what would you do? Worship me as you should. As all the ladies do."

Savage put his hands over Seychelle's ears. "Don't listen, babe, he's full of shit."

"I think all of you are," Seychelle said, laughing, those golden notes floating out to sea.

Savage was captivated by her sound. He couldn't help but laugh as well. It wasn't a big laugh, because he was very rusty, but it was there. That soft, underlying note in her voice seemed to reach inside him and find an answering note in him.

Never once had he seen his own musical notes floating in the air. Not as a child. Not as a teen. Not even when he rode his bike or wore his colors. Now he could see them, plain as day, traveling with hers, interlocking her gold to his deeper antique silver. They linked together, melted into each other, blending colors so that they gleamed like flames as the sun plunged into the sea.

His breath caught in his throat. His chest hurt, as if a huge weight pressed down on him. His lungs burned for air. He couldn't take his gaze from the spot where those notes sank with the blazing fire of the sun. Her notes were beautiful, like she was, inside and out. He had always thought, if he could see notes he created, they would be dark and ugly, but they hadn't been.

His notes were darker than hers, and they didn't skitter across the sky in the same joyful way hers had, but they were beautiful in their own way. And they overtook hers and merged so that, joined, they appeared different, even more brilliant, although the colors were deeper, and took on the fiery colors that were falling into the sea. When they disappeared beneath the water, he stood, arms around her, transfixed, unable to move or even think.

"That was amazing," Seychelle whispered, as in awe as he was, although he was certain it was the sunset and not the musical notes they shared.

He reached for her hand and brought her palm to his chest as they turned back toward the bikes. "You need to eat something. There's a great little restaurant a few more miles up the road in Elk, unless you're getting too cold or uncomfortable."

Seychelle looked up at him, started to reply but then hesitated.

"It's good food, Seychelle," Preacher said.

"We're not that far from it," Reaper pointed out.

"The chef is nearly as good as Alena," Ink added. "Okay, not nearly her caliber, but he's good. You'll like it."

"She's not used to riding on a motorcycle, and we still have to make it back home," Savage interjected, running interference, just in case.

"I'm good," Seychelle said, her free hand rubbing her backside with a rueful little grin. "It's just that you didn't get much sleep last night, Savage, and you have to be tired."

He kept himself from looking at the others, but his heart sank. She'd been more aware than any of them thought the night before. No one outside their club could know about that meeting with the Diamondbacks, especially since everything had gone to hell. They were all concerned that Plank might change his mind and retaliate against Tawny for blowing his deal immediately. It wouldn't be pretty, and it would be permanent. They had to have alibis that were not only plausible but tight if the Diamondbacks really went through with killing the bitch before the run and blaming her death on Alena.

"Babe. I woke up in your bed, my head in your lap."

She blushed and avoided looking at the others. "I got so drunk you were up half the night with me sick."

"I slept during the day with you. I'm good." Relief swept through him, along with another emotion he wasn't used to experiencing. She'd been concerned for him. She'd been sick. She had awakened dehydrated with a hell of a headache. She was in an uncertain situation, yet she was expressing concern for him. That was a new one for him. "Let's get something to eat."

She nodded and flashed a small smile. "Thank you for that sunset. It was beyond beautiful." She looked around her. "I've never been this far south on this road. I should explore more. I've got a good little car for it."

"Now you've got me," he corrected. He handed her the helmet and waited for her to put it on before he helped her onto the bike. "I love to ride these roads. We can go together."

"I'd like that." She smiled at him, one hand on his shoulder. "I didn't realize how much you could see from the back of a motorcycle."

Savage watched Seychelle through dinner. He'd purposely had her sit beside Anya so the two women could get to know each other better. The women of Torpedo Ink would become the female companionship she needed, her sisters, the ones she'd never had. He remained quiet. He wasn't much of a talker, although when they were alone, he seemed to have more to say. He enjoyed watching her have a good time. When she laughed, her entire face lit up. He dropped a hand onto her thigh, because he needed that connection with her. She put her hand over his as if she knew he needed that physical link right at that moment.

Anya, Preacher, Code and Ink carried most of the conversation, but Seychelle joined in, and he liked that she wasn't the least bit afraid of expressing her opinion, although she was very thoughtful about what she said. She definitely had no problems debating with any of them.

He rubbed his palm up and down her thigh, and then transferred her hand to his thigh. She glanced up at him and smiled. His heart nearly stopped. That smile was his alone. Reserved for him. It felt intimate in a way he'd never experienced before. He tucked stray strands of her thick, gold-and-platinum-colored hair behind her ear and reached for his coffee cup with his free hand.

Her palm burned a brand through his jeans. Marking him. He loved her so fucking much, and that was unexpected and took getting used to. She leaned in close and put her mouth against his ear. Now his heart reacted by pounding. Accelerating.

"I can make an excuse to leave if you need to get out of here." Her lips brushed against his earlobe with every word, a soft, velvety caress that sent fingers of desire dancing up his thighs and down his spine. "You have a headache."

He did. His head was pounding. He knew when they got home, he had to really explain everything. She would either commit or walk out on him. He'd never been so afraid of losing in his life.

Seychelle didn't hesitate. "I got a little crazy last night and drank way too much. I'm sorry, everyone, but I think I need to just call it a night and get back home. This has been so fun, though. I'm sorry to cut it short."

Savage immediately stood, throwing money on the table. "You all stay and finish your coffee. We'll head back."

More money was thrown on the table, and Reaper signaled the waiter. "We're finished. We'll ride with you."

His family, surrounding them. Taking his back. Taking her back. Showing Seychelle she wouldn't be alone living with the monster.

TWELVE

~~~~~

Savage waited until Seychelle had gotten ready for bed. There was something comforting about lying in bed with her. Holding her. And she was brave in that bed. She had the courage to be alone in the dark with him. Now more than ever, she knew what she was facing. Not the details, but that darkness in him that was never going away.

He sat on the edge of the bed, pulling off his boots, making it clear he was staying. She shot him several nervous glances, but she didn't protest, and so far she hadn't run screaming from him. He knew she had the kind of courage it would take to be with him. She'd run into the path of a truck when no one else had dared to move, to save his life.

"I had a wonderful time, Savage. I love being on the motorcycle with you."

"That's good, baby, because you're going to be spending quite a bit of time there." He didn't look at her as he hung his jacket on the back of the chair.

Seychelle moved past him, leaving a trail behind, that faint fragrance of wild strawberries. He had no idea, when he'd been in her shower and seen her products, how she could smell and taste like that, but she did. He turned to watch her crawl onto the bed from the end of it. She was graceful, on her hands and knees, her lace-covered ass swaying as she moved to the top of the bed.

Immediately, erotic images crowded into his mind. There was no stopping them. His handprints decorating those perfect pale globes. Red stripes across them, running from the top of the curve to her thighs. A plug pushed deep between those cheeks, preparing her for him. A vibe. Gingerroot carved in the shape of a thick penis. His cock responded all on its own, a fucking miracle when it never had before, because men residing in hell didn't get erections.

She settled with her back to the headboard, legs stretched out in that way she had. He turned off the lights but left the window shade open so the reflection of the moonlight spilling down onto the wide ocean surface would light the room enough for him to read her. The revolving base beneath the intertwined rose sculpture cast colors up on the ceiling. He stripped, leaving just his jeans, although they weren't staying on. He just wanted her to feel safe. He needed her to hear him out.

"We have to get everything worked out tonight, Seychelle." He sank down onto the bed and reached for her, sliding his hand onto her bare hip. That pale skin. It would show every mark for a long time. His cock stirred restlessly, pulsing like the monster inside of him, already seeing the results of the whip on her skin.

"It's a lot to take in, Savage."

"I know it is, baby, but we have to get it done. I want you to agree to be my old lady. My woman. My wife. Not just because I decreed it, saying if you came into the club that was what it meant. You have to make that choice knowing what you're facing. Knowing what I want and would expect from you. It isn't a surprise, but you're going to have to listen to me very carefully, Seychelle. If you agree to be with me, you're all in. You don't get to back out when the going gets tough—and it will. I'm letting you know up front, it won't be easy." Savage stroked her thigh. "And this life. I'm going to be honest. Once I teach you to like these things, there's no going back from that."

She liked sitting with her back to the headboard. He'd been with her enough to know she was comfortable there. Relaxed. He turned onto his side and laid his head on her belly, his arm around her hips. That was his favorite place. For some reason, when he held her like that, his demons calmed and he found a place of peace.

"I'm listening."

He heard the note in her voice—that small hitch of fear. This time, he knew it was because she wanted to be with him—she wanted to take his offer, and she feared that he was going to say something to make her back out. He shared her fear.

He was grateful that she had the courage and was willing to hear him out. If she did learn to crave pain with pleasure, she would need it, would always have to have it in order to be truly satisfied physically. That had been his hesitation all along. Taking her down this path with him meant she would be all in, no going back. He wanted her to know, no matter what, no matter how tough things got, once they were committed, he was just as committed, and he would work things out. Make it work between them.

"It's important you know that once you're in, you don't get out. We work things out. I'll stay, Seychelle. I'll be faithful. I'll be committed to making you happy. But we don't divorce. We make it work."

"That might be difficult, Savage, when I have no idea what any of this means. You tend to be a dictator when you want your way."

That was the truth, and it always would be. He traced his name on her hip. "It's always going to be my way, baby. You know that. You're going to do things the way I need them done. That's the only way I can stay sane. I'm being honest with you.

I need certain things in my life, and I have to have them. That means you give them to me. I need your obedience."

"Like a child?"

"No, not like a child." How could he explain? Make her understand? "When I say that, I mean you do what you enjoy doing, but you follow the rules when you're doing it. You have to trust me enough to know I'll always see to your happiness, but if you don't do what I say, there's going to be consequences."

"Like?"

"Like what you've already earned. You got drunk and you almost went off with another man. I told you to go home and you didn't do it."

"We weren't together." She waved her hand dismissively.

He wasn't buying it. "We were together. You came to the club. I laid it out for you. I was plain when I laid that out. You knew when you walked in the bar that you were stating you chose me. I had already told you I had chosen you. You were scared, and you ran. You didn't trust me. That earns you a punishment."

"I'm not five. Why in the world would you want to punish me?"

"Because I like it." His hand curled around her thigh, his fingers pressing deep while he confessed. She had to know what he was. She had to live with it—with him. With his darkest needs. "I even crave it. Right now, my cock is a fuckin' steel rod because I know I'm going to put my handprints on your ass. You're going to cry when I do. You'll beg me to stop, and I'm going to get even harder because I can't resist your tears or your pleas. I'll take your tears away, one by one, and make it all better by making you scream my name when you come."

There was a long silence. He didn't move. He didn't look up at her face. He couldn't. For a moment he couldn't even find air to breathe. His lungs burned. He went back to writing his name on her bare skin. Savage. Then her name. Seychelle. His heart pounded. He'd just laid it on the line.

Told her how fucked up he was. That wasn't even close to how fucked up he was. There was no getting around it. Not now. Not ever. He craved that shit. Needed it the way he needed to breathe air.

"You're going to hurt me?" Her voice was soft. Small. Afraid.

He took a breath. Found the strawberries. "Yes. Sometimes. When you fuck up."

"Hit me? You're going to beat me up?"

He turned his head, his jaw sliding across her soft belly. He stroked the curve of her hip. His eyes met hers. Her fear was visible in her eyes, in the expression on her face. Her lips trembled, and she twisted her fingers in the sheet beside her hips. But that wasn't the only thing in her eyes. There was a flicker of excitement. Desire. A cautious dark anticipation. He hated that his cock responded, throbbing with expectation. With urgent demand. It felt like fuckin' paradise and yet was hell at the same time. He knew absolutely, if he slid his hand up her thigh into her panties, he would find her slick with heat.

"I would never beat you, Seychelle. Or hit you in anger. I'm not talking about that kind of relationship, and I think you know that. I'm saying you fuck up by disobeying one of my rules, I'm going to put you across my knee and leave my handprints on your ass. I'm warning you ahead of time, I'll enjoy it. I'm also going to tell you, you will learn to enjoy it as well. Not all of it, but in the end, you'll be craving everything I give you."

"This is all part of what you talked about earlier."

"Yes, and it's the easiest part, easing you into the more demanding things I will expect. I will demand all kinds of sex with you, and yes, bondage and pain will be included, but we'll work up to that. I can teach you to like the things I need, baby." He turned his head back to her belly, pressing kisses into her soft flesh. His teeth scraped and then nipped, his tongue easing the ache. "Like that, baby. You liked that."

"You aren't talking about that, Savage."

"No, but no one runs before they walk. I'll make you love most of what I do to you."

"Most of what you do?"

He nodded. He had to be honest, no matter what. She had to come into the relationship knowing what she was getting. "I told you straight up, I wasn't satisfied with what I'd done to that woman. I'll teach you to like most of what we do, but there will be times when that shit gets very real, Seychelle, when I need to put stripes on your body. It will hurt. I can turn pain into pleasure, and I can take care of you after, but you will suffer for me. You have to know that going into this." His hand moved on her leg. On the scars there.

She was silent for a long time while his heart pounded and his mind screamed at him that he was a monster no one could ever accept or love.

"What if I can't take it, Savage? What if the pain is too much?"

"Then you call a stop. You say *red.*"

"And you stop?"

"I would hope you would know when we get to that point that I would never initiate that kind of sex unless I was desperate. At the same time, I would know you would never say *red* unless you truly couldn't take any more. That's what trust is. That's what we would need to have between us, so yes, I would stop instantly."

He studied her face for a long moment. "Seychelle, we would need to be a partnership. I can never be out of control. When I'm at my worst, at that point, you need to be in total control, and it won't be easy for you. I don't want to ever break your skin. That's going too far. If I were to do that, you'd have to stop us. There can't ever be permanent marks on you. Not ever. I don't do that shit to you. Everything between us is consensual at all times. You agree, I agree. That's the way it has to be."

"How do you know you won't cross the line, Savage,

outside of sex? What if you're so angry with me you beat me? That could happen."

"You're not understanding me, baby. I swear on my life, I could never beat you in anger. I'm not that man. When I start getting bad, and it's a cycle I can't prevent, and I know I'm going to need certain things during sex, I fight it. I go to the club in San Francisco and beat the hell out of anyone challenging me to a fight. That sometimes helps. You help me already. I feel peace when I'm with you. It's the only time."

"How do you know I'll be enough for you when those other women weren't?"

"Someone I don't give a shit about can help a little, but you . . . you're different, Seychelle. When I'm with you, it's like you have the potential of taking it all away for a very long time. You can't know what a rare gift you give to me."

That was such bullshit. She was so much more than that to him. She had found her way inside of him. They'd been together now for months. They had the *R* word. Relationship. He wanted to laugh when he thought about it. That was so not him, but he knew he wanted to wake up every morning for the rest of his life with her lying next to him. He wanted to go to bed with her in his arms. Yeah, she gave him peace, but this thing between them was so much more than he was conveying to her.

"How do you know I can do that for you?"

He pressed a kiss to her belly. "I know. I know you're mine. That for the first time in my life I want a woman to belong to me. I want to see my marks on her skin. I want to see her tears for me on her face and know she's willing to give them to me. I know you can do that for me. My body responds to you by itself without me ordering it to respond, just at the thought of my marks on you. I have to order my cock to work any other time." That was all true. He *needed* to use his whips on her. He never thought he'd be able to have someone who would love him enough to take on his pain the way he took on the pain for those he loved. He hadn't believed there was a woman alive who would think he was worth it.

"That rage inside you. What happened to you? You weren't born that way. I can feel the other side of you. Gentle. Sweet. Even kind. Tell me what happened to you."

That was the last thing he wanted to do, but he knew he had no choice. Not if he was going to keep her. He'd promised himself he'd go in a hundred percent if she did. He was being honest, and he knew he was giving her the worst possible side of him, but he had to if he was going to lay out the bad and hope his good could make her want to stay.

"You feel the demon just as strong as you feel that other side of me. I need you to have the kind of courage it will take to face that monster when he emerges, and he will. There are times I can't stop him. The small stuff, the consequences, they hold him at bay. The fight club. The rides late at night. The sex will help. All of it. But he'll come out eventually, and you're going to have to face him. You're going to have to trust me, especially when he's out."

"You said you crave those things. All the time?"

This was another one of those telling moments. Having to admit out loud to the woman he wanted to spend his life with that he was so fucked up he liked to see his marks on her before he fucked her, all the time. Every time. He rested his head on her belly again, needing to feel her peace. The way she soothed him.

"Savage?"

She dropped her hand to his head, her fingers doing the slow massage that sent peace easing the knots in his belly. He didn't want her to stop. He didn't want her to ask any more questions. He just wanted her to say she would hand herself over to him. It wasn't fair. It wasn't even logical.

"Answer me, honey," she said softly. "You've gone this far. I need to know."

"When I have sex, yes. It arouses me. But finding you, knowing you would give yourself to me willingly, let me mark your skin, take a strap to you or cane you, do that for me, really participate and get off with me because you actually can love me . . ." He stopped himself. "That's the ultimate, Seychelle. That's the fucking dream."

Seychelle remained silent, her fingers moving on his scalp in that relaxing way she had that made him feel as if he mattered to her.

"The truth is, Seychelle, we need each other. If you're honest with yourself, you need me as much as I need you. You can't say no when all those people start taking pieces of you. You need someone strong to step in and put a stop to it. I'm that man. I can take care of you when you need it."

Savage rubbed her hip gently, moved his fingers inside her thigh to stroke along those nerve endings. He wrote his name there in bold letters, down the inside of her thigh and then back up, the pads of his fingers stroking along the lacy strip of cloth that barely covered her sweet little pussy. His thumb slid along her pussy lips. He would shave her bare tonight.

"I think if you're honest, angel, you have to admit, the thought of this type of sex arouses you." He said it gently, knowing it was a gamble.

"Fantasizing about something and doing it are two different things, Savage. The actual idea is terrifying. I don't know if I'm that brave."

His Seychelle. She was that brave. That courageous. He was seducing her gently. Bringing her into his world with infinite care. Loving a woman could be overwhelming at times. "You're that brave," he murmured against her hip bone, and then licked along the top of it.

"Tell me how you got this way."

Savage pressed kisses along her hip bone, taking his time, building something good when he was about to give her something bad. He went back to using the pads of his fingers to stroke her inner thigh, moving higher to slide over her sex, feeling her heat. Her slickness. Her need for him. He rubbed his shadowed jaw over her belly, leaving red whisker burn. He kissed his way from her belly button to the very edge of her sweet, nearly nonexistent panties.

His teeth continued nipping, this time a little harder, pinching, and then immediately he used his tongue to soothe away the shocking ache. Each time he did, her breath hitched. She never once pulled away from him. He ran his finger under the edge of that strip of lace, rubbing gently, barely there. Her breathing left her lungs in a little explosion and then turned ragged.

This woman. He knew her and her courage. She could do what no one else could. She could love him. He saw that clearly in her. She would give him everything he ever asked of her. More, even. And she would stand strong when the worst happened—and it would. She would love him through it.

He knew what he was capable of. He could give her the world. He could and would make her scream with pleasure over and over, a thousand different ways. He could love her with everything in him, even the monster—especially the monster—and it would never add up to what he was asking her to give to him. Every single day he would see to it that she was happy and well loved, so when those dark days came, she would have something to hang on to.

He closed his eyes for a moment and then rolled over to sit on the edge of the bed, his heart suddenly pounding in his chest. Not accelerating, just hitting so hard he felt the blows like punches.

"I'm from Russia," he said unnecessarily, certain she already knew that. "I told you that my parents opposed a man who wanted to be president. His second-in-command, a man by the name of Sorbacov, quietly began to purge those who were against his candidate. Our family was wealthy and had influence, so they had to go. Sorbacov came in the dead of night with his soldiers, murdered my parents and took my two older sisters, Reaper and me to one of his 'schools,' supposedly to make us into assets for our country. I've told you this before, but I didn't tell you the rest. The truth about those schools."

He put his head in his hands, breathing deep, trying to still the screams, trying to drive out the voices of the monsters running through his head. He pressed his thumbs against his temples, the pressure on his chest increasing.

"There were four schools, each progressively harsher. The fourth school, the one he took us to, was a special school. Very special. Sorbacov looked normal to the outside world. He was married with children of his own and always acted the perfect husband and father, but he was a pedophile. He liked little boys. He liked to see children tortured and raped. It aroused him, and he had many like-minded friends. Criminals and pedophiles ran the school and were given carte blanche to do whatever they wanted. He laughingly referred to it as his great experiment."

He reached back and circled her ankle with his hand because he needed their very strong connection in order to get through the memories, the ones he tried so hard never to think about. That door he locked and barricaded in his mind, but no matter what he did, it always cracked open and he went a little berserk.

"I was very young, and I really thought I shouldn't remember the things that happened. The first time they took me, kicking and screaming from Reaper and my sisters. That first time when they hurt me so bad, I didn't think I could survive. My sisters tried to stop them from taking us, and they beat them in front of us. Then they took them and did horrible things to them and threw them down into the freezing-cold basement, where we had to watch them die."

Little beads of sweat trickled down his face. He tightened his fingers around her ankle as the doors in his mind widened, spilling those memories out along with blood and death. So many. He pressed his fingers deeper into his eyes, deeper into her ankle.

"I had no real idea of sex. What it should or shouldn't be. I was too young. I just knew I didn't want to hurt like that, and I fought them every chance I could get. Apparently, there was a group that really enjoyed hurting their partners, and they thought it would be great fun to teach me that was how to get aroused."

He shook his head. "I'm not telling you this very well, but it's the best I can do, Seychelle. I watched them whipping girls and boys. The first time it was done to me, I went after them, ripping the whip out of their hands and trying to flog them. I was just a little kid, and they found it amusing. I was considered really good-looking, and they liked to take turns whipping me. By that, I mean forcing me to go down on one of them while another whipped me. The more I fought, the more they kept at me. This went on for years. The rapes, the whips, the floggings. It was brutal."

He couldn't look at her, his past merging with his present so that he could smell the sex, the blood. Feel the combination surrounding him. "They were training some boy, about fifteen, and I was probably eight when I took the whip from the fifteen-year-old and turned it on him. After that, I was the one learning to wield that whip. There was no way I was going to let them tear me up like that if I could help it."

He had no idea those little droplets of sweat were tears until the room turned blurry. He used his arm to swipe across his face because he couldn't let go of her. She was sanity. His only sanity in that moment when his past was so close.

"When I would lay perfect stripes on someone, they would reward me, sucking my dick, making me come. I swear I didn't know the difference, only that it was better to feel good than to hurt like hell. I was very good at training others to like pain. Erotic pain. Pain and pleasure are so close, so intertwined, and it isn't that difficult to confuse the two sensations. I was so good at it. I could turn pain into pleasure every time. Every way. I did that shit for years, Seychelle, and they called me the Master of Pain, the Whip Master, so many other titles. And I earned every one of them."

He closed his eyes against the memories, of thin red streaks and tears, of his body moving in others. The trouble was, those memories were behind his eyelids. Carved into his soul. There was no getting rid of them.

"I liked training them. I liked seeing my mark on them. Each year I got better. The better I got, the harder it was for anyone to assault me. I learned to fight. I learned to hurt others. I learned so many really ugly things without knowing they weren't right. It was the only sex I knew. I didn't even know it was done any other way."

He had been shaped into a monster without any realization that was what was happening. He was twisted into something unrecognizable. Something vile.

"I hurt others so I wouldn't get hurt, at first. Then because it kept my brother from getting hurt—at least, that was what I believed. Then my body was so confused it didn't know how to have an erection unless I was marking someone. While I trained my partners to like pain, I didn't realize I was being trained to need to give it. To see those marks. It's been impossible to have any kind of an erection without it."

It was a confession, straight up. He left out the terrible, brutal details. The things that had put those scars all over his body. The children he'd watched die. The girls he'd trained given away when his handlers got tired of them and wanted newer playthings so they could start all over again. Watching those first girls being cruelly tortured and eventually killed. He didn't give her those things, but they were all there inside of him, swimming in that red-hot pool of rage.

"There's no way to reverse years of damage. Over twenty years, Seychelle. I've tried to fight it. I've read everything I could get my hands on in the hopes of being different, but it isn't going to happen. I know that. And I know that these things trapped inside of me, the voices of the dead wailing for justice, I know I'll never be rid of them. I need to avenge them just the way I need to mark my partner and then make it all better."

He took a breath. Needing it. He had to face her. Had to look at her and see the truth of what she thought. Seychelle couldn't hide from him any more than he could hide from her. She either would order him away from her, sickened by what she'd heard, or she would have the courage in her to face the monster with him.

He slowly turned his head until his eyes met hers. Those blue eyes swam with tears. There was no condemnation on her face. She had too much empathy in her, too much compassion. She saw the things he'd told her in vivid detail. The little boy beaten, brutalized, raped. The cigarettes put out on his body. The blowtorch they'd used on him. The branding iron. The terrible scars left from the deep lashes of the bullwhips and slashes of the knives. She could see a lot more evidence than that, but now those images were in her mind. Trapped there, both a gift and a curse. A gift to pull out when she needed a reminder of how he got the way he was. A curse because the images would haunt her, give her nightmares.

"Savage." She whispered his name. "I'm so sorry. I don't understand how anyone could do those things to a child."

Neither could he. She wouldn't understand his need for justice. His need to show those fuckers what it was like to be brutalized. To be tortured. He hadn't told her the things he'd seen. The children who had died because he wasn't strong enough to save them. He didn't tell her how he and the others had escaped, but he knew one day she'd ask.

"I don't know if I'm strong enough," Seychelle admitted in a small voice. "I've never considered doing anything like this."

"You're strong enough. You're the strongest woman I've ever come across. It's a commitment for both of us. We both have to choose. Here. Tonight. You have to be certain I'm trustworthy. The things I'll demand of you, the things I'll do to you, will take trust. You have to give that to me the way you did when you got on the back of my bike. You have to know I would never harm you. Never. You're mine to take care of. I want to give you every reason to stay in love with me, to want to turn over control to me when we're in that situation because you trust that you're safe with me at all times, no matter what is happening. I want you to marry me, Seychelle. To know I'm in love with you and committed to this relationship and to you one hundred percent."

"You're that certain that you want marriage?"

"Once you're mine, baby, I'd never be stupid enough to let you go. But you have to make that choice. I have to know you want me the same way I want you."

"I don't know the first thing about what you need or how I would provide that for you."

"I know more than enough for both of us. I'll always take care of you, Seychelle. There won't be other women. There won't be anyone I put higher than you. I'll always know what I've asked of you."

"And you're going to do that to me? Whip me? Put red marks on my body?"

He nodded, his heart pounding until he was afraid he couldn't catch his breath, but he wasn't going to lie to her or pretend he wouldn't do the things he craved. "I'll do more than use a whip. It will hurt, but it will also give you the most pleasure you'll ever know. I'll make certain of that. You already know you respond. I showed you. A small preview, just to see if you would like what we did, and your body was extremely responsive."

She was silent for a long time. He rubbed his hand down his face, trying to give her space. Trying not to touch her. To add seduction to his sins, but it was impossible. This was the most important battle of his life, and he had to use every weapon in his arsenal. It was for both of them. Her life. His. He stretched out on the bed again, his head on her belly, his arm around her hip, so he could use the pads of his fingers shamelessly, stroking caresses along that thin strip of lace. So he could breathe on her bare skin, rub the sandpaper bristles over her soft belly, leaving his mark.

"Tell me the rules. I don't know if I can be someone you really need, Savage. I'm not going to say I can if I think it's impossible." Her voice shook. Her body trembled. In her eyes there was that hint of speculation, of desire. Of hope.

She wanted to be able to be his partner, to find his brand of sex as erotic in reality as it was in her fantasy. He knew it was frightening. She would be insane not to be scared. He used his hand to soothe her. Pressed little kisses along her hip bone.

"We already talked about you singing in the bar. When I say you're done, that's it. You're finished. My brothers will know the signal, and they'll be cool with it. You and I will work that out, and we'll get good at it."

"I think that's a good rule."

"Same thing goes when you're visiting your friends or anywhere else, baby. You get in trouble, and you see someone's ill, you need to give me the sign we'll work out so I can step in and help you."

She nodded. "I can live with that."

"We talked about me needing to know where you are. I've got enemies. So does the club. I'll have to know you're safe, Seychelle. Most of the time, I'll want to be with you. If you want to make plans with the other women, you consult me before you agree to anything. That's what the phone is for. You can get good at texting. In our home, you can have any damn thing you want. Decorate it. Buy furniture. You don't want to cook, you tell me, we'll go out if I don't want to cook. That will never be a big deal."

"I'll want to know you're safe as well, Savage. If you're imposing rules like that on me, I would hope they go both ways."

"Naturally. The only thing we don't share is club business. Sometimes I have to go out on business, and I can't talk about that."

"And I won't know where you are?"

"If there's trouble, you'll be at the clubhouse, or you can stay with Blythe if Czar thinks you'll be safer there. I'll have someone watching out for you."

"That isn't what I asked you." Seychelle's gaze was steady on his face. Unflinching.

He wanted to smile. She could never say she lacked courage. The woman would stand up to him, and that was a good thing. He respected that in her. He wanted a partner. "No, babe, you won't know where I am, but you can text me and I'll answer as soon as I can. If you're worried, you can text Czar. He'll know where I am and if I'm safe. Because I have enemies, it's best we always have a bag ready to go at a moment's notice. Your travel papers, money, although that isn't necessary—Code will fix up papers, and I have enough money. But anything important to you should be ready to go at a moment's notice. If we do ever have to leave fast, we travel light."

"That's easy, Savage. My mother's hairbrush and the rose sculpture. My parents were cremated. That was what they wanted. Neither could travel much, so they asked if their ashes could be scattered at sea. I took care of that, but I kept enough to have a glassblower make that sculpture for me. My mother loved roses, and I do too. Their ashes are in the sculpture. That's why it's so bright when it's lit up. So, if we ever have to go fast, grab those two things for me if I'm not with you."

She'd be with him. She hadn't even flinched at the idea of having to make a fast getaway. She hadn't inquired why they might have to make a run for it. *Bog*, every minute, he was falling more in love with her.

Savage rubbed his chin on her soft belly. "I think about sex all the time. Since I laid eyes on you, it's been every minute, night and day. When I want you, however I want you, I expect to have you. No other man is ever going to touch you. I don't share. They may see us, because at the parties we'll go to, sex is everywhere. We prefer the others around because we've always been safer . . ."

She shook her head, drawing back from him, and when he looked up at her, he could see the utter rejection, the absolute abhorrence. "No. Absolutely not. If you're going to do things to me that are scary and painful and then turn them into something I get off on, I'm not having anyone watch. That's either private between the two of us, or it is never going to happen between us. I mean that, Savage. I'm terrified and out of my element as it is. The things you know and want, I can't conceive of. I would be humiliated to have anyone else know I not only let you do those things to me, but I want them, if I ever get to that place."

He turned his head so he could rest his chin on her belly, just above her mound. That scent of wild strawberries clinging to her was driving him mad. "That's your bottom line? Sex is okay at parties as long as I don't cross that line?"

He knew that line would begin to blur for both of them, but she had a point. There would be added intimacy if they kept their proclivities solely between the two of them. He wasn't an exhibitionist. He didn't care if others watched or not. It was about Seychelle and her body, his canvas, his private playground. He would worship her forever.

"I just couldn't do that."

"What are we talking here? At the events, the runs and parties, I can keep us in the shadows, where no one else can really see, but you know I'm going to have to have some of the easier things we'll do. Nipple clamps? My hand? A switch? A crop? Something simple like that? I want to have your fuckin' body, baby, and I have to be aroused. I'm not just using you to get off."

"Those things are simple?"

"Yeah, baby, very simple—you'll be loving them by the end of the week." His body was already hard and aching with the images of teaching her. "We'll have to figure out what we can do at parties that you find acceptable, so we don't cross any lines."

"I want to try things first before we make any rules. Right now, I don't even know if I can do any of this."

That was reasonable. More than reasonable. "Tell me you'll stay with me. Always, Seychelle. Tell me you can live with me just the way I am. No one in your life will ever need you more. You can make me happy."

"Only you can make yourself happy, Savage," she corrected.

"That's what I'm doing. I found you. I laid it all out for you. I'm doing everything in my power to ensure you'll give me your word that you're mine. That you want to be mine and that you're willing to live your life my way."

"If I say yes, I want to try, right now, if I give you that, what's going to happen?"

Triumph burst through him, but he didn't let it show. He sat up slowly, turning toward her so she could see his expression clearly. "First, we're going to take care of unfinished business."

She touched her tongue to her lips, drawing his attention. He wanted to fuck her every single way he could. Her mouth. Her pussy. Her ass. Even her tits. He wanted to mark every inch of her body, cover her with him. He would have all the time in the world to do those things. She needed time to learn. He would enjoy teaching her.

She rubbed her hand anxiously down her thigh. "Take care of unfinished business?"

"I told you, baby, you got drunk and nearly went off with another man. I fuckin' would have killed the bastard if he had taken you home and put his hands on you. It's just a lesson, and you know how it made you feel when I showed you sinful, dirty sex. You're going to get so slick and hot for me. It will hurt, but you're going to like it at the same time."

She pressed her hand into her thigh, and he took it, pried her fingers open and pushed a kiss into the center of her palm.

"Say yes, Seychelle. Be that brave for me. Choose me, baby. Choose a life with me and trust me that much."

She swallowed hard and inclined her head. "I want to be with you, Savage. I'm going to tell you up front, I've never been so scared in my life, but I'm willing to try."

He shook his head. "You have to go all in, baby. There's

no way we can survive if you aren't all in, if you can't look at me and say you want my happiness before your own. You have to want to give me everything I need. I have to make that same commitment to you, and I do. I'm one hundred percent in."

"But if my body doesn't respond the way you expect it to, and I can't go that far into what you need, Savage, you can't stop yourself—you would have to seek what you need from other women."

He didn't want to bring up his past again. Absolutely, he didn't want to remind her of what he'd done for all those years, but there was no way around it if he wasn't going to give her reassurance. "Baby." He kept his voice as gentle as possible. "Don't you think, after training girls to love that shit for over fifteen years—girls who really didn't have any proclivity toward it, to crave it—that I could guide you down that path when you want to go on it with me? I've craved this since before I knew what sex really was."

He needed to be very cautious saying much more. Seychelle wasn't quite ready to accept that she had darker cravings. She was embarrassed and didn't quite understand them in herself. "Don't you think I can read when a woman is going to be more accepting of my rougher sexual practices?"

"I think I'm afraid because I don't really know what to expect."

It was difficult to look away from Savage's eyes. They were mesmerizing. *He* was mesmerizing. Seychelle was very aware he had gifts, talents, psychic talents. She did too. Seychelle also knew this was the most important decision of her life. She had more than one psychic talent, and they were both gifts and curses. She had been drawn to Savage because of those talents, and she continued to be.

She kept contact, her fingers moving on his scalp, her hand pressed to his thigh. He was strong in the places she was weak. She was strong where he needed someone. And he did need someone. He certainly didn't show that on the outside. He was just plain scary. A dark, dangerous man with violence swirling inside him like a deep volcanic well.

She'd touched on that well more than once. She saw it when she knew it was successfully hidden from others. Savage lived in isolation, even from his brothers in the club. They knew about him. They probably even knew what had shaped him into being the way he was, and he'd sugarcoated it for her. She'd caught glimpses of images in his mind. With those images came that rage. Dark and ugly and filled with such terrifying memories, her mind could barely comprehend them. Not only his, but his brothers' and sisters' as well. He took it all on.

She only knew that the risks were enormous. He was capable of things she knew she couldn't live with. That didn't mean he'd do them. Without her, she knew he'd eventually go under. His hand was moving up her leg with those slow, mesmerizing circles that sent heat waves rushing through her veins, a seduction that would clearly work if she wasn't going over every detail in her head.

She couldn't blame him. He knew he was fighting for his life—and for hers. She would go under as well. She was slowly dying, unable to control her gift of healing. She'd never been happier than when she was with Savage. He wasn't going to find another woman who would see into him, see what he had to battle every single day, and be willing to face that and join with him.

Savage was well aware she was his one shot and she saw more than that swirling pool of rage. She saw that other side of him. He had a strong need to protect. To have someone of his own. He was intensely loyal. He wasn't at all a selfish man. He was capable of loving deeply.

Right now, when he knew she was weighing judgment, he might be using the pads of his fingers shamelessly, but he didn't push for an answer. He didn't say anything at all. He gave her the space—and the time she needed—to make a decision. *You need us to stay, there's no problem.* If this was for the rest of her life, she had to believe she could do it. Both of them had to have faith she could do it. That's what they would be going on. Faith, because neither could really know until she was in that position. She knew she wanted to do it for both of them, and that was half the battle.

He made it clear it wouldn't be easy, and looking at the violence in him, she knew it wouldn't be. Hearing him state the things he needed, she was more than scared: she was terrified. Even being terrified, she had to acknowledge to herself that deep inside, in a secret part of herself, she was more than excited at the prospect of what he would be asking of her. When he talked about his sexual needs, instead of flinching as she should have done, her body had grown hotter than she thought possible. Her blood pounded through her veins so hard she could barely hear him through the thunder in her ears. Was it terror or secret exhilaration?

Savage was a good man. She saw that clearly. He was losing his battle. He no longer believed he was worth saving, but she did, and he clung to that in her. Still, it wasn't her job to save him. She knew that. She couldn't make him happy; that wasn't her responsibility. If she was going to be with him, she had to do it because she wanted to.

She wasn't going to lie to herself. She needed him. She was drowning. She couldn't keep the continual assault from her day and night when she was in any public situation. She didn't want to hide in her house. She wanted to work. She loved to sing. She didn't know how to stop giving herself away, and having Savage standing in front of her—and he would whether she liked it or not—would allow her freedom she didn't have now.

She needed to be needed. That was who she was. If there was one person on the face of the earth who needed her, it was Savage. The relationship was dangerous and scary to just jump into, but he saw her when no one else did or could. Just as she saw into him, he saw into her. They were connected by their talents.

She wanted that scary, dangerous sex. She'd always craved it but was too afraid to seek it out. There were too many pitfalls if one went in that direction. She was intelligent enough to know that, but here he was, offering her a chance. It was a gamble. Nothing less.

She looked at him then. His gaze had never left her face. Her heart clenched in her chest. She knew she had already fallen hard. She was well on her way to loving him with everything in her. She could do this if she gave herself into his keeping, surrendered completely, but that was terrifying—living for someone else. Trusting that they lived for you.

Was he capable of loving her that completely? Giving her everything, as he promised he would? Could he really do that? The way he was looking at her, as if she was already his everything, was as addicting as the feeling of his fingers on her skin. He swore to her he was already there. She closed her eyes, knowing she was going to give him everything he wanted and more. She was going to take that leap, because it was impossible not to want to be with a man like Savage when he was offering it to her.

Savage hadn't taken his gaze from Seychelle the entire time she weighed his fate. Every second that went by felt like hours, but she needed to work things out her own way. He wanted to kiss her, to use every one of the considerable sexual tools in his arsenal to persuade her, but if she was going to make that commitment to him, it had to be real.

It was there on her face first. Resolve. Terror. She took a deep breath. His heart went crazy. His stomach did a slow somersault. It was his cock that reacted the most, knowing what was coming. It hurt, pulsing and throbbing, even jerking with dark lust and a depraved carnal need that was bone deep in him. She was going to sacrifice her life for him all over again. She was going to give him everything. Life. She was giving him life.

"Yes, then, Savage. I want to belong to you, but I can

only promise to try. I hope you're as good as you say you are, and my body does what you say it will."

He leaned into her, framing her face with his hands. That beautiful, innocent face that he knew would always turn men's heads. She didn't see it, but he did. He took her mouth. Gentle at first, because she was his everything. He would always cherish her. The moment he tasted that wild strawberry, his heart seemed to melt inside his body. It was such a dichotomy. His heart at war with his cock. His kisses were the same. Gentle, caressing strokes of his tongue. Then his mouth went completely dominant. Hard. Rough. Demanding. Forcing her compliance when he had coaxed before.

His teeth tugged at her lower lip and then bit down. She gasped, and he soothed the bite with his tongue, slipped it into her mouth and stroked caresses, wanting to eat her up, devour her completely. Her taste was wild, exotic and addicting. There was a hint of a smoldering fire that suddenly flared to life and threatened to consume him. He wanted that burn.

He deepened the kiss, added more command, needing rougher. Needing to hear her gasp. Needing her to surrender everything to him. And she did. She kissed him back, melting into him even as he bit down on her lower lip a second time in exactly the same place. This time he slipped two fingers along the lacy edge of her panties, and then farther to test her reaction as he increased the pressure on her lip. She gasped, but her body went hot and liquid. He instantly released her lower lip and swept his tongue into her mouth.

He felt her taste taking him over just as he was taking her over. A coup with her kisses. Those flames rushed straight to his belly, where the monster crouched, swirling with dark threads, waiting to leap out. Orange and red consumed black, taking it all, leaving behind ash. Leaving him with a burning steel cock and a mind filled with images of his woman in graphic positions, waiting for him to put his stripes on her, frightened and exhilarated just as she was now.

He broke the kiss. "I need you to come lay across my

lap, Seychelle. Let's get the punishment over fast so I can be in you, where I belong."

Her breath caught in her lungs and her gaze moved over his face, judging how serious he was. Did he mean it? If he did, what would he do to her?

He was so fucking proud of her, that internal struggle warring on her face. Her eyes, two bright sapphires, so filled with trepidation. With surrender. She didn't know it yet, but she was giving herself to him—inch by slow inch.

Savage kept looking at her, his gaze holding her captive. "It's only going to get worse if you fight me on this, Seychelle. This is something important. Just get up and stand right there." He pointed to the spot just beside him. "Remove your panties, hand them to me and lay over my lap."

He knew her heart was pounding. She looked so frightened, he was torn between pulling her to him to help her make the decision or pulling her into his arms and comforting her. He did neither. She had to do this herself. This first crucial step. There would be so many, and he would enjoy every single one, their journey through life together.

He kept staring at her, slowly asserting his will on her. It was subtle. She was ready to capitulate on her own, but he needed to see how much influence he had on her when it was needed—and it would be in the coming weeks. He would train her as slowly as possible, but he knew himself. The cycle was there, and she had to be prepared for the monster when he escaped. She'd been right about the woman he'd used weeks earlier—she hadn't been in the least satisfying, and he was already getting edgy.

Seychelle turned on the bed, putting both feet on the floor. His cock grew so thick he wanted to unzip his jeans to give himself a little room. He never took his eyes off of her, and he knew the exact moment when she really became his. She made up her mind, her chin going up, and she stood and walked right over to the side of the bed in front of him, slipped off her panties and tossed them at him. He had to stifle a grin as he caught them. She was going to get one extra-hard smack on the ass for that, but he kept his mouth shut, still watching her.

He took his time, staring up at her, waiting for her to lay across his lap, pushing her panties into his back pocket. His eyes holding hers captive, he reached out and stroked his fingers up the inside of her thigh—close to all that heat—so hot it felt like a furnace. Her nipples peaked beneath the thin tank she wore. He would have commanded her to take it off, but he wanted to do that himself. She had a narrow waist and a soft belly he was very, very fond of.

He slid his fingers down her left thigh and then brushed the tiny damp curls, his thumb sliding intimately over her clit. She shuddered, but she didn't back off. She had so much courage. He had known all along she did. She'd need that courage and a lot more.

"I'm going to shave you myself. You're so beautiful, baby, and I want to see and feel every inch of you. Lay across my lap, Seychelle."

Her breath hitched. Her blue eyes swam with liquid, and he was forever damned, because seeing that sent his cock into a frenzy of urgent demand.

"Savage." His name came out a plea.

Her tongue touched her lower lip right over his mark. Her lip was slightly swollen, the small mark dark. Satisfaction slid through him like a dark shadow.

"I've read enough about the lifestyle to know you should have gone over limits with me and given me a safe word." Her hands rubbed up and down her belly nervously. "I'm pretty sure I have like a million limits."

He resisted smiling. This was all about surrender and demand. She had to be a willing participant. She had to want to give him everything he needed. That had to come from her.

"We're not living that kind of lifestyle, Seychelle. I laid it out for you. I need control in order to keep from letting loose a monster that could destroy so many people. People I love. I've learned what I need in my life in order to survive intact. My woman, and that's you, has to live within those rules. I need certain things in the bedroom from you, and I'm going to get them. You'll get whatever you want or need, but there's no doubt that at times, it will be frightening for you. You'll have to trust me enough that you know I'd never harm you and I'll rock your world every single time I touch you. When we're doing something with whips, baby, you'll use your safe word, *red*. Punishments, like this, you don't have a safe word. You'll just have to trust me that I know when to stop."

She pushed at her hair anxiously. This time he could see her hand shaking. He stroked the pads of his fingers down her belly to her mound, made little circles and then wrote his name across her pussy lips. His. Seychelle belonged to him. Few women would ever be able to live with a fucked-up, broken, damaged-beyond-all-repair man like him, but he knew not only could she live with him, but she would love him with every breath she took.

"I think I'd feel better about everything if you just gave me a safe word and agreed to stop when I say it."

He suppressed a smile. There it was: that little snippy voice that told him she wasn't submissive. She would give him every gift of her own free will. She might want to soothe the monster, but she would speak her mind. A lot. His cock leaked with need. She would not only soothe the monster, she'd feed him. Pet him. She'd give him every single one of her tears as a gift of love. She would suffer willingly for him because she loved him. She would give him the thing of his dreams.

"I think you'd feel lots better laying across my lap like you were told so that I don't add on to the punishment you've already earned."

THIRTEEN

Savage reached around Seychelle's hip to touch her left ass cheek softly, fingers kneading and then rubbing in a soothing circle before he slid his thumb between her pussy lips to find moisture. "I love the way you look right now, Seychelle. I'm so proud of you. I know this isn't easy." His hands cupped both cheeks, rubbing circles gently.

He'd dreamt of her ass, the perfection of her firm globes. He'd dreamt of this moment when she gave him her body. He wanted everything. He would claim every inch of her, make her irrevocably his. He'd been trained in the art of seduction. He knew more about sex than anything else, other than how to kill or extract information from an unwilling prisoner. He was extremely proficient in all three subjects. He would make certain her body responded only to his command. But that wasn't enough for him. He wanted her heart and soul.

"Lay across my lap, Seychelle." He gave the order in a firm voice, all the while rubbing her perfect ass cheeks. "Don't be afraid, baby. I've got you."

She touched her tongue to his mark on her lip as if that tiny spot gave her courage. And then she leaned toward him and he immediately helped her to lie over his lap. Her beautiful bottom gleamed like two pale globes. He pressed his hand to her back between her shoulder blades.

"Wrap your fingers around the legs of the chair and hold on," he instructed. "I'm not going to let you fall." He gentled his voice but kept his tone a velvet command.

Seychelle complied, her fists so tight on the legs of the chair that her knuckles turned white. She was trembling, her body almost vibrating with fear. He rubbed soothingly between her shoulder blades, pressing her to him while he devoured the sight of her. She was beautiful. The pale cheeks of her bottom gleamed with the silvery light shining across them. He'd positioned himself perfectly in front of the window.

He ran his fingers from the backs of her knees up the backs of her thighs, first right and then left, all the way to the seam of her buttocks. So many nerve endings waiting for him to ignite. He used the tips of his fingers, tracing the seam while the back of his knuckles rubbed along the underside of her sweet little ass.

Taking his time and building the anticipation was crucial. He ran his fingers along her bare hip and then under her tank to skim very gently along her spine to her neck. He massaged some of the tension from her before pulling his hand from the racer-back, grasping the back of the flimsy tank and ripping it straight down.

She gasped and started to rise. His hand held her in place. "Shh, baby, you're fine. Let the material fall to the floor. I love your skin. It's like porcelain. Silky. It will hold the marks of my possession so beautifully."

He slid his hand down her back and over her perfect bottom, to glide his fingers across her little pussy. She was damp with anticipation. Hot. He wanted to taste her. He'd been waiting an eternity and he couldn't resist sliding his fingers deeper to catch at the slick, hot honey. He brought his fingers to his mouth and sucked. She tasted like her skin. Wild strawberries. An exotic mix of honey and strawberries.

The addiction was never going to end for him. He realized, as he smoothed his hand over her bottom, that he was breathing hard, almost as ragged as she was. This woman belonged to him. She'd given herself to him, had the courage to face the monster with him. *Adoration* was a mild word for the way he was feeling, but it was crucial that he stay in control.

He rubbed her bottom gently and then reached down, caught the long messy knot on top of her head and forced her head around so she was looking at him. His cock ached. Was so painful he knew he was going to have to end this soon, not for her, but for him. He'd never been so hard in his life.

"I'm so proud of you, Seychelle. Your courage astounds me." He stared into her blue eyes as he rubbed small circles all over her bottom and then kneaded the firm muscles. Her body tensed. "Trust me, baby. Remember? We're building something special here. A bond that's so intimate, so close, nothing will ever get between us. I'm not going to chance ruining that. You put yourself in my hands, and you have to know I'll only take you as far as you're capable of going. I'll always have you."

Her eyes searched his, looking for reassurance, and he gave it to her. If she fucked up again, that wouldn't be there. The punishment would be real, not a learning experience. "Tell me why you're laying across my lap."

"Because you like this."

"No, baby, I love this. Do you feel what you're doing to me? My cock is fuckin' steel because I love this. That's all yours, but you need to answer me." He moved one palm across her left cheek and then trailed his fingertips to that seam where her ass cheek met her thigh. He felt her shiver.

Saw the goose bumps rise on her skin. Endorphins already rising. She was highly sensitive there. She was so responsive, so perfect for him. She wanted this, even if she was afraid.

"I got drunk and nearly went home with someone."

He loved her for that alone. She remembered exactly what the infraction was, which meant she would always remember.

"Exactly. And you were smoking again. Let's not forget that. Now lie still. Don't try to cover your bottom, just accept the burn." Deliberately, he ran his finger along that moist, hot entrance, for both of them. He wanted her body to feel pleasure. To mix the two sensations, so that eventually she would crave the things he needed. He also wanted another taste of her. He needed to prolong this time with her, surveying her perfect offering. More, he needed to savor the fact that she was really giving her body to him for his needs, for his pleasure, as well as surrendering to the possibility of finding her own pleasure in what they would do.

His palm fell lightly on her left cheek. She jumped, but his other hand was firm between her shoulders, preventing movement, and she settled immediately. He smacked her right cheek just as lightly and then set a rhythm. Two smacks and then he rubbed away the sting, spread the heat over her pink cheeks and then slipped his finger into her hot little pussy.

His heart pounded. He felt that rhythm through his entire body as he warmed her up—as he brought that same pounding beat to her sheath. He could feel that silken fist squeezing on his finger when he penetrated her. Abruptly, he smacked her harder on her left cheek, leaving a perfect pink handprint. She nearly jumped out of his lap, but he held her in place.

"Don't move." He hissed the command, pouring displeasure into his voice.

She settled instantly while he rubbed the sting away. Again, without warning, he rained fire on her ass, turning both cheeks from a glowing pink to a bright red. This time he didn't stop when she tried to wiggle off of him. He held her tighter and kept going until she began to cry.

When he heard her sob, he rubbed caresses over her, spreading the heat along the nerve endings, and then he trailed the pads of his fingers through the enticing crack between her cheeks down to her wet pussy. He cupped his hand there and then pushed a finger inside to feel her clamp down on him like a vise.

"You can cry, baby—teardrops are mine, remember? But no sound. You stay quiet for me. You give that to me."

She took a deep breath and went silent. Immediately, he circled her clit with his thumb, stroking and caressing, flicking occasionally until she was riding his finger. His cock felt like a fucking steel pole, pressing tight against her. The heat radiating from her red ass enveloped him, along with her fragrance of sex and strawberries. He never wanted to stop. He traced that crease between her thighs and buttocks and added handprints to her upper thighs before working her pussy again. She was close to an orgasm. So close. He could tip her over the edge. He took a breath and let it out, knowing this had to be the last round.

Nothing had ever felt like this before. A kind of euphoria settled over him. His woman, her gift to him. She was scared. She had no idea what to expect, but she still gave herself to him. He hadn't realized how much he needed this. His woman naked, squirming, her sweet ass covered in his handprints, her tears dripping down her face for him. Her pussy saturated, hot and melting. Needing.

All along he'd thought it was only about his physical reaction, his arousal, but it wasn't true. Every one of his senses was engaged, but even more than that, it was his emotions. He was completely wrapped up in her. Completely focused on her. Overwhelmed with the need of her, with wanting her. With near adoration for her. He'd never experienced anything like it.

He took his time, making each swat count, placing them carefully so that one or two overlapped, building the intensity. Her sobs turned ragged, but they were silent, all in her body. He rubbed with one hand and slowly pushed his finger deep into that tight, hot, pulsing pussy. He found her sweet spot and stroked. She went over the edge instantly, her body nearly convulsing, the orgasm taking her hard in a series of powerful ripples. He felt each potent wave moving through her stomach and sheath to her thighs because she was lying across his legs.

Savage lifted her and turned with her to put her on the bed. He followed her down, coming on top of her, pinning her under him so he could frame her face with his hands and look into her liquid-filled eyes. Her tears had turned the blue to a vibrant undersea color. The tears on her face resembled diamonds, and he instantly visualized diamonds dripping from clamps on her nipples.

He sipped at the tears on her left cheek, tasting them, removing them one by one. He took his time, savoring the taste. There was a hint of salt, as if she'd been swimming in the sea, his little naked mermaid. He kissed her face after each tear until he got to her eye, and then he removed the tears from her lashes before switching to her right side.

"Baby, put your arms around me," he coached gently and licked at her tears, removing them as they slipped down her face.

It took a moment before she complied, her arms sliding around his neck.

"Why are you crying?"

"It hurt. I didn't think it would really hurt like that."

"Did it really hurt?" He kissed the corner of her mouth and then her throat. He slipped lower down her body so that his mouth was over the temptation of her breasts. His hips were wedged between her legs, keeping them spread apart for him. He cupped her mound and then dipped his thumb inside her. "Your sweet little pussy is telling me you felt good, not bad, baby. I think you liked what I did to you."

He nuzzled the side of her breast with the bristles on his jaw and then pulled her nipple into the heat of his mouth. She was perfect. Responsive. Gasping, arching into him, her hips bucking. He sucked and used his tongue to tease and stroke, and then he bit down, just a flash of pain, but his thumb stroked that sweet spot in her pussy, sending more powerful ripples through her body.

He kissed her again, over and over, worshipping her mouth, pouring flames down her throat to spread through her body. All the while his hands were at her luscious tits, feasting greedily the way his mouth was at her lips. He tugged and rolled, pinched and stroked. Gentle, then aggressive, back to gentle, and then harsh, then back up to claim every inch of her face. Her mouth. Her throat. Her neck. His mouth swept down her collarbone, his tongue seeking that elusive wild strawberry taste.

She kissed him, her hands sliding down his back, exploring, so receptive, her soft skin taking his every mark, from his mouth, his teeth, his hands, so beautiful he could barely breathe. Her moans sent those golden notes dancing in the air all around them. Her body just melted under his, radiating heat, surrounding them with the sultry scent of sex and her fragrance.

He kissed his way over her tits again and down her belly, nipping, his teeth leaving marks, his tongue soothing every ache, and then he closed his eyes and forced himself to regain control. He was breathing too deep. He was far too lost in her. He couldn't make mistakes and trigger any kind of aggression in himself.

For a moment he pressed his forehead against her mound, those gold-and-platinum curls that had to go. They were so sweet. They even looked and felt innocent, like her.

He didn't want them gone, but they could be a trigger—he had so many—and there was no use in taking chances. He breathed her in, letting her natural scent soothe him. Letting her notes sink into his skin right over the whip marks on his back.

"Baby, give me a minute. I want you to just lay right here, the way you are—don't move at all. Will you do that for me?"

Her hand found his head, fingers moving on his scalp in that way she had of making him feel like he was worthwhile. Worth everything. "Of course."

It only took a few minutes to get the things he needed: the hot water, the wet cloth, the razor and foaming shaving cream. He returned to his woman, pushing her legs apart and standing between them.

Seychelle pushed up on her elbows. "What are you doing?"

"I'm shaving you, so hold still. I'll tell you why I have to do this another time. You've heard enough crap about me to last you a lifetime, and this story isn't much better. Just let me do this, babe."

She lay back, her hands behind her head, which made her tits jut upward toward the ceiling. He had a lot of fantasies about her tits and those perfect erect nipples he had so many plans for. He smeared shaving cream on those gorgeous golden curls, swirled his name there.

"I love that you belong to me, Seychelle. I forgot to tell you about the house." He wanted to distract her from what he was doing. It was very personal. She would find that anything personal belonged to him. He pushed her legs farther apart, positioning her knee high and to one side, exposing more of her pussy.

"The house?"

He had the feeling she knew what he was doing, but she went along with it anyway. "Yeah. The house. I own a house. It's a damn cool house, at least I think you'll love it.

It's ours. Well, it's mine right now, but we'll get your name on it as soon as possible. Absinthe does all that."

"Savage, don't move so fast. We're working into this," she cautioned. "I just let you spank me, hard, as punishment. And I had an orgasm. Do you have any idea how confusing and humiliating that is?"

"Why would you find it humiliating?" He was genuinely curious. Women didn't always make sense to him. "You gave me something I needed. If anyone should be humiliated because they need to spank their woman, that would be me." He shrugged his shoulders. "I accepted who I was a long time ago."

"But grown women don't allow themselves to be spanked. And they don't enjoy it."

"Who makes that fuckin' rule? You gave me a gift. Isn't seeing to your partner's needs part of being with someone? You didn't particularly want to do it, but you did it anyway. For me. Because I needed it. We both made a commitment. You know what I need because I laid that shit out there for you. If you're willing to give me what I need, I'm going to make certain you feel pleasure when you're giving that to me."

She blinked at him, her long lashes sweeping down and then back up. "I never thought of it that way."

"You should. You're the one giving me the gift. I'm the one taking. It's our relationship; nobody else has the right to stick their nose in and judge us. Or at least judge you." He was adamant about that. He didn't want a single person passing judgment on her. She was a miracle, a woman of such courage that she chose to stay with him when he'd told her point-blank what he had to have in his life.

She smiled up at the ceiling, shaking her head. "You're so strange, Savage. One minute you're spanking me, the next you're giving me an orgasm that rocks my world and then you're kissing me senseless. Now you're saying the nicest things possible. I'm not certain what to think."

He stroked the razor very carefully over those beautiful little curls he hated to see go. His fingertips slipped inside her thigh, fondling that soft skin there. It was such an intimate thing to do—shave his woman's cute little pussy.

"I'm still confused that I could feel so afraid, pained and have such an amazing, shocking and fantastic orgasm all at the same time."

He straightened and waited until her eyes met his. He grinned at her, gesturing with the razor. "You're going to have a lot of those, babe, so be prepared." He loved that she was so honest with him. She'd need to be.

Her eyes searched his. "That was all you."

"You're not going to suffer for me and then not get anything back," he said. "I told you that. I'm a bastard, and I can be a monster, but I will always, always take care of you. You're the most important person in my life, and I'm going to make certain you never regret your decision to stick with me."

"Savage, really? When I was hanging upside down over your lap, scared and feeling humiliated, I was totally regretting that decision."

Again, she spoke the truth, and he could have kissed her all over again for it. She made him happy. He knew she would. Those moments might be brief and fleeting, but he experienced them. And the longer they were together, the more he believed she would stay, the more those moments would last.

"But you didn't tell me to get out," Savage said. "You didn't go back on your word. You let me do what I needed to do."

"I'm not going to get drunk again or go off with some strange man." Her voice rang with humor, and those little golden musical notes slipped into the room and danced toward the ceiling.

"Good plan. Tell me five things you love doing." He lovingly ran the razor over her bare skin, making certain to get every last hair before once again wiping away the cream. Her skin was so pale it would show his every mark. Just looking at her bare lips and pretty sloping mound where his stripes would lay so perfectly had his cock back to a steel spike. It amazed him that she could do that. His reaction to her was astonishing.

"I'll tell you five things I love doing if you match me every time."

"That's fair," he agreed, rinsing the razor and drying her off.

"Singing. I *have* to sing. Sometimes there's a buildup inside of me that won't let up, and I know if I don't go somewhere and sing, I'm going to explode. It sounds crazy, but if anyone can understand, it's you."

Savage liked that. He liked that they shared a bond, even if her needs were far healthier than his. He needed to see his marks all over his woman to get aroused, or the images in his mind, at least with this woman. He wasn't certain that counted.

"Riding my motorcycle, especially with the brothers, fast down a highway like Highway 1. The wind in my face, blowing me clean. Your turn." He carried the supplies back into the bathroom, leaving the door open as he washed his hands.

"I totally love gardening. I have a thing about plants. I like all flowers and potted plants, and the ones I can put in the ground to grow, I love. Someday I'm going to have the most wonderful gardens, and I'm going to design them myself. I've got so many ideas."

She turned onto her side, propping up her head on her hand. "Your turn."

"Old movies. B movies, or classics like *Creature from the Black Lagoon*. I like the modern-day B movies as well, although I'm pickier. You go." He leaned his hip against the doorjamb, enjoying their silly game because she was. He could see it on her face. She liked the exchange between them.

"Baths. Deep tubs and bath oils. Really long, luxurious baths. I like them better than a hot tub. I can read in the bathtub or listen to music. Sometimes I just fall asleep. Baths are the best. All you now."

She was going to like the tubs at the house he'd purchased. "What kinds of books do you read?" He knew the answer, but he had to ask.

"Romance," she said without hesitation or embarrassment.

"Where you learned a little about bondage."

She nodded. "A very little. It's your turn."

"My family. My club. Now you. This."

"That may be cheating, but I like it." She twisted her fingers in the covers, hesitating. "Isn't that five?"

He immediately was on alert. "Baby, you know it isn't. Tell me whatever you don't want to say. If you do, I'll tell you what I enjoy that I'd rather not say."

"I'm certain yours is far more interesting. It's just personal." She shrugged. "I like to write songs. I have an entire journal filled with them. Just things I need to get out, you know. Nothing that's going to move the world, but the words are mine, and sometimes I have to go back and just sing them to the empty sky so they're out there. I can't always say things I want to tell people, so I write my truth in songs."

"I think that's beautiful, Seychelle."

She was so damn beautiful. Not just her body, but that soul of hers. He liked her. He liked everything about her, especially the fact that she was comfortable talking to him about anything. Part of that was the connection between them, but part of that was just her. She was honest. She just came out and said whatever was on her mind to him. They needed that between them, and that meant he had to give her the same.

"Your skin. I saw your skin and I knew what it would look like with my marks covering you. I couldn't get that image out of my mind. I enjoy that, Seychelle. Thinking about putting those marks of my possession on you. Thinking about each one of them and where I'd put it. How I'd do it. Wondering how many days I'd have to enjoy seeing them there, knowing you belong to me, and every fucking time I see them, or you see them, we both know it." He straightened. "And then knowing, the moment they faded, I was going to be able to do it all over again."

He kept his eyes on her face. Watching her. He was as honest with her as she was with him, and he wanted to see her reaction. Her gaze moved over him, dropping to the front of his jeans and the bulge he didn't try to hide from her, and then climbed back to his face. A slow little enigmatic smile curved her lips briefly and she rubbed her bottom, but there was excitement in her eyes.

"I can see I'm going to have to get tougher."

"I'm never going to apologize for who or what I am, Seychelle. I came to terms with it a long time ago. I don't have to like it, but I'm no longer ashamed. I don't want to be with a woman who's ashamed of me either. Or embarrassed by what we do." He knew her body was excited, but her mind was definitely very much not.

She sat up slowly, pulled her legs up to her chest and wrapped her arms around them. Putting her chin on top of her knees, she regarded him steadily. "I'm going to be embarrassed and maybe even humiliated until I can think the way you do. You have to give me that and the time I need to adjust to what you need in a relationship, Savage. You can't push to have everything your way and expect me to think and feel the way you want me to."

She was right, and he liked that she defended herself. He sat on the edge of the bed and circled the ankle that belonged to him. His thumb slid over the scars there, soothing him. "I don't want you embarrassed because you choose to give yourself to me, Seychelle. I never want that for you. What you do for me is between us, but there are other women I've been with, other women who are aware of what

I demand. They talk. Our world can be rough, and the men and women in it can be deliberately cruel. I'm not talking about Torpedo Ink—they're your club, they'll have your back—but others will come to the bar and say things. You keep your head up. You're mine."

She reached out, shocking him, cupping the side of his face, her expression soft. "I gave you my word, my commitment, and I intend to keep it. I just need a little time to understand your needs. Letting you spank me was very difficult because that's something I associate with a child's punishment, although it didn't feel like something you would do to a child."

"How did it feel?"

"Erotic," she admitted, her color rising. "Just the way I always fantasized it would be."

The blush was sweet, moving up her body, turning her breasts a soft rose, going up her throat to her face. Her nipples drew his attention. He leaned down and pulled the left one into his mouth. She could have been made for him. A gift. Her body was as perfect for his needs as it could be, but it wasn't even that that got to him anymore, it was her. Seychelle. Who she was.

"But you made it that way for me; you know you did. It hurt at times, and then you took that sting away and turned it into something erotic and sinful and beautiful. I needed to know you would do that for me, and you did."

He brushed kisses over her nipples and then more back up her throat to her mouth. He spent time there, indulging himself, letting the taste of her transport him to a place where he just felt. Her. His body. She did that for him.

When he lifted his head, she was once more lying under him, and he needed to get his jeans off before his cock was permanently injured. He rolled over, yanked them down and tossed them aside. When he turned his head, she was looking at him, her eyes wide, her expression a little intimidated.

"I've got you," he whispered, framing her face with his hands. "I've always got you. Just keep believing that. No matter what I ask. Or tell you to do. Remember I've got you. Some things are going to scare you, but just like that spanking, you're going to end up experiencing more pleasure than you could possibly imagine."

Her eyes searched his for a long time. Those beautiful vivid blue eyes that made him think of rare gems. Her lashes fluttered, swept down and then back up. She nodded. He kissed her because he had to. Her mouth was too tempting. She was his now, all of her. Her body. She'd given herself to him and promised she wouldn't go back on her word. He saw into her enough to know she wouldn't, no matter how hard things got. Or how difficult each step into his world was. He intended to make them as easy and as pleasurable as possible for her.

Kissing Seychelle was a new experience for him. She might be inexperienced, and he might have kissed hundreds, but with her, kissing became something different, something fresh and perfect. Smoldering heat slid into his veins, spreading like slow embers throughout his body. Blood pooled low and wicked. Flames raced up his thighs, engulfed his balls, consumed his cock, that steel pole that had never been so hard, or so needy.

She moaned softly, those musical notes of gold fanning the flames into a hot fire that rushed through his veins like a storm, mixing with emotion—something that had *never* happened before. The firestorm rushing through him, mingled with the unfamiliar feelings, added to the sensations roaring through him, heightening his pleasure and his passion for her.

He would never be the poet, the bring-her-flowers-and-candy man. He wasn't even a gentle man. For her, he wanted to be. He'd started out that way with her, but it hadn't lasted. His kisses had turned to devouring her. Commanding her. Taking her over. He loved her mouth. The fire there. Her taste. The way she surrendered to him. The way she gave him everything he demanded. He was more the rip-her-clothes-off-anywhere-anytime kind of man. That was him showing her she was desired. Beautiful. Wanted. She hadn't experienced that yet, but she would. He hoped she would always understand what he was telling her.

His teeth tugged at her lower lip and then bit down. That same spot. Right on his mark. He pulled her lip back gently with his teeth. He loved her mouth. Loved the shape of it. The look of it. The feel of it. "I could kiss you forever. There are so many things I want to teach you," he whispered against the silk of her lower lip, right over the little mark his teeth had made.

"There are so many things I want to learn," she whispered back. "I catch images from your mind and they're so erotic, Savage."

She was killing him. Slowly killing him. Once she'd made up her mind to give herself to him, she did it all the way. He kissed her again, slow. Taking his time. Breathing for both of them. Exchanging fire. Passion. Giving her the promise of his absolute loyalty—even more. When he lifted his head, her blue eyes were wide with shock.

"You have perfect tits, Seychelle, perfect nipples." He kissed his way down to them, sucking her left one deep into his mouth, using his tongue to flatten her nipple while his fingers tugged and pinched her right one. He created a wave of sensations, flooding her body with so many different new needs, feeding her passion. She was exceptionally responsive to nipple play. He switched sides, his mouth on her right breast, his hand at her left. She moaned and pushed herself into his mouth, a desperate needy sound escaping her.

His tongue lapped at her. He found himself getting lost in her breasts, the symmetry, the rounded curves that jutted so perfectly out and thrust into his palm, begging him for attention. He couldn't stop himself from taking things further. He'd thought of her body so many times, the way it would feel to have her breasts just like this, his mouth on her, his hands. Belonging to him.

His teeth caught at her right nipple, closed like a light clamp and tugged, while his fingers pinched, doing the same to her left. She gasped, her eyes going wide, looking down at the sight, just as he flicked a glance up, trying to take in the beauty of her nipples pinched and elongated, waiting for his art, waiting to learn what would make her body come apart for him.

"That's too hard, too much, Savage. It hurts," she whispered, arching her back, pushing her breasts deeper into his mouth, trying to get away from his teeth and fingers.

"Does it, baby?" He licked at her nipple, soothing the sting. His voice turned to a velvet lure. "Does it hurt bad or good? Like the spanking? Is your sweet little pussy on fire?"

His hand slid between her legs, his thumb massaging her clit, his finger sliding into that tight, slick tunnel. It was so hot. So moist. Her muscles clamped down on him. "I think you like it, Seychelle." He kissed her nipple and deliberately used his teeth again, this time biting gently and tugging, feeling the hot liquid coating his finger. "Yeah, baby, you like that, don't you? You like it a little rough. Your tits were made just for me, and I'm so in love with your nipples. Do you have any idea the things I can do to make you wild?"

He lifted his head and looked down at her, knowing his gaze was possessive, filled with a dark lust he couldn't hide and didn't want to. He wanted her to see she was the only woman he truly wanted. He really needed. She had been worried he wasn't physically attracted. "Baby, I know you feel what I'm feeling. You see inside of me. I can't fake this kind of need for you. Or this kind of emotion. It's been growing ever since I first laid eyes on you."

She blinked, her lashes wet, spiky and turned up so that

he couldn't resist leaning down to lick at her stinging nipple, swirling his tongue around her areola and then pressing kisses over that perfect rounded globe before lifting his head.

"Tell me what your body is feeling." He whispered the enticement.

She took a breath, but her gaze stayed melded to his. "Hot. A little out of control. I can't keep still because I'm feeling a burning sensation that's getting worse, and a coiling tightness that's becoming a terrible pressure."

"And when I bite down on your nipple? When pain mixes with pleasure?" He pushed her for the answer. He'd been mostly gentle, but a couple of times he'd tested her to see how her body would respond to what he needed. How fast or slow he would have to go with her. He wanted to go slow, but that wasn't going to happen, not as slow as he'd like.

"At first I thought it hurt too bad and I wanted to cry, but then it felt amazing, like this heat wave rushing through my body and centering low, as if all my blood pooled there. I thought for a moment I might even climax."

His heart jumped. She was perfect for him. That honesty he would always be able to count on. The way her body reacted to his needs. He'd known it the moment she'd touched him and forged that connection between them. He'd seen it in her eyes, the curiosity. The need. The start of a dark desire. He just had to bring her into his world carefully. Lovingly. Make certain every single time the pleasure outweighed everything else. He nuzzled her breasts with the bristles along his jaw. "I can't wait to clamp you, baby. You're going to love how it makes you feel."

He continued to move down her body, kissing his way along her ribs and then her belly, his teeth nipping occasionally, not always gently, leaving little marks, until he came to her smooth, bare mound. Circling her thighs with his hands, he pulled her legs wide apart and settled between them, lapping at that sweet little bare spot he'd created and then her pussy lips.

"Love this so much, Seychelle. I thought I'd never have this. You taste like honey and wild strawberries. Your skin. Your mouth and your sweet, sweet pussy." He ran his tongue up her inner thigh.

Her fingers went to his shoulders, digging deep. Her hips squirming. Her breath came in ragged little explosions. She didn't once pull away from him, not even when he nipped her, or when his teeth caught her bare lip and tugged and then his tongue flicked her clit. She gasped and gave him more liquid to lap up, but she didn't pull away.

"Savage." His name was a plea.

"Tell me what you want, baby." Before she could answer, he circled, lapped and then flattened his tongue and used broad strokes on her clit until she was writhing against his mouth.

She strained against him, pushing her needy pussy against him. He breathed warm air over her while she moaned and then thrashed when he worked one finger into her tight, saturated folds. He couldn't stop himself from devouring her. He'd promised himself he'd go slow, but she tasted so damn good and he'd waited so long. Her body's response was beyond anything he'd hoped.

She sobbed his name and he heard the edge of fear. Instantly, he lifted his head and looked at her. Her eyes were closed as tight as her fists.

"Baby, look at me. I want you to look at me and breathe. Relax for me. Open your eyes. Nothing is happening here that you aren't going to like." He poured a mixture of command and velvet into his voice. In between his words he stroked his tongue and kisses along her thighs.

At first Seychelle shook her head, but she couldn't resist his voice. Eyelashes fluttering, she finally focused on him.

"Talk to me, Seychelle. What are you so afraid of?" He rubbed his bristles along her inner thighs and flicked his tongue over her clit. She squirmed in response, liquid drops spilling out for him to taste.

"I don't know what to do." Her voice came out in a thin, frantic wail. "I read that women never really orgasm the first time. I just feel this tremendous pressure. A buildup coiling tighter and tighter, and it feels like I'm going to go insane, Savage. I don't know what I'm supposed to do." Her gaze clung to his.

He smoothed his palm down her leg. He should have known. Should have reassured her. "It doesn't matter what you read, Seychelle. This is us. You. Me. I know what I'm doing. You're going to have multiple orgasms. Powerful ones. You just relax for me, and when I tell you to let go, you just let go. Trust me. I've got you. I'll be there every time." He poured reassurance into his voice.

All the while he circled and flicked her clit. Leaned down to lick or stab her swollen, saturated pussy with his tongue. She was so ready for him. It wouldn't take much, and she was going to fall apart big-time for him. "You understand, baby? You trust me, not some book you read."

She nodded, her gaze clinging to his. Eyes still on hers, he dipped his head to her very sensitive slit and indulged himself, strumming her clit at the same time. She cried out and jerked in his arms. He took her up slow, feeling the tension in her body build, the miracle that was his woman, then he settled his mouth on her clit, using his tongue as his greatest gift while his finger made a foray into those hot, tight folds.

Her channel felt like a silken fist wrapping tightly around his finger. His cock reacted, pulsing and jerking with need. He felt her body's automatic response, those delicate muscles racing toward an orgasm as he curled his finger, stroking her sweet spot while his mouth commanded her clit.

"Now, baby, relax into it. Give yourself to me. Let me have you. Just let go." He flicked her clit hard with his finger, stroked caresses with his thumb. Her eyes were on his as the first powerful wave took her.

It washed over her, a long series of ripples that shook her and gave him more wild strawberry honey he couldn't resist. "Again, Seychelle. You have to be ready for me."

He used the edge of his teeth, raking her clit, and she cried out his name, her hips bucking, body thrashing. He simply caught her cheeks in his hands and lifted her to his mouth so he could eat her like the starving man he was. More than anything, he wanted to show her that every time with him, no matter what they were doing, she was going to feel intense pleasure, that he could rock her world and he'd take care of her. This time he took her up fast, her body coiling tighter and tighter, while he ate that delicious brand of wild that was his alone. She was close. So close.

He loved the sounds she made. The little mewling cries. The way his name sounded like music. Like worship. Like love. He lifted his head. "Now, baby. Let go for me. Again." He used his tongue and fingers ruthlessly, sending her over the edge, letting the powerful orgasm take her over. He held her hips down while she nearly convulsed with pleasure, sobbing his name, her nails in his back, in his shoulders. His wild woman. His.

"Again, baby. We're going again."

"I can't. It will kill me." She could barely get the words out.

Her breathing sounded ragged. Her tits rose and fell rapidly. Her head thrashed on the pillow, her eyes shocked but dark with desire and wide with lust.

"So good, it feels so good, doesn't it?" He said. "I need you slick and hot, baby, when I'm inside you."

He didn't wait. He slid her legs over his shoulders, standing so her bottom was off the bed. Swatting her ass until her cheeks were hot added to his arousal, and evidently hers as well. More hot cream leaked out of her pussy. He brought her pussy to his mouth so he could devour her the way he wanted.

Seychelle writhed and cried out, her nails raking him as he paid more attention to her inflamed clit. Dipping his fingers in her honey, he began to paint between her cheeks, claiming every inch of her body for his own. He stroked that little star and pushed in to his knuckle, lapping at the fresh flood of liquid that came in response as he made his demands on her body.

He couldn't take it another minute. Not one more fucking second. Pulling back, he wiped his face on her thighs and yanked her to the very edge of the bed. He was already standing, his cock in his hand, skin stretched so tight, tighter than it had ever been, just from the few faint marks of his possession. He looked down at her, those perfect tits, her nipples that stood out so beautifully for him, that tucked-in waist that led to her bare mound. He knew when he laid his patterns, when his stripes decorated her body, his cock would roar.

He lodged the sensitive head between the pulsing fire of her pussy lips. She was saturated, and yet so tight. "Look at me, Seychelle. I'm going to take you hard, baby. Bury myself deep inside you. You're going to feel me all the way in your throat. So fucking deep."

"Yes. I want you so much. Hurry, Savage." She whispered it, trying to push herself onto him.

He waited until he had her eyes fully focused on him and then he slammed home. Drove right through those tight folds. He met resistance all the way, but there was no stopping him—or her. Her channel was slick and scorching hot. Gripping him like a thousand fingers made of silk. He threw back his head and roared with pure ecstasy.

She was so tight, milking his cock each time he withdrew and plunged back. The friction was incredible, dragging over the terrible scars, scars he'd thought would make it so he couldn't feel, but instead he felt so much more. He was that much more sensitive to her—to the grip of her silken muscles constricting him like a vise—massaging his cock again and again in that tight, hot clasp.

He tried to stay in control. He wanted her first time to be beautiful and amazing, but he could barely think straight. A red haze was in his mind. Thunder clapped in his ears. His balls drew up tight, burning, a sensation he'd never experienced before. Fire raced down his spine.

He angled Seychelle's body so he could put more pressure on her clit, on her sweet spot. She had to be close. Her breathing was ragged. Her moaning was constant. Her body shuddered around his—clamped down like a vise as if he was an invader and she wasn't about to let him get away. He felt that long, silken tunnel like a fist of tongues stroking his cock, squeezing and milking him, sucking him dry.

"Now, Seychelle. Give me everything." He could barely manage to give her the command. His throat closed off. He already felt the volcano erupting. Powerful ripples started through her body from breasts to groin, swamping her, swamping him, clamping down viciously on his cock, a silken fist pumping and jerking at him in wild strokes that were merciless, endless, so strong she was sobbing his name and driving her nails into his back.

Seychelle's body was dragging the hot, fiery magma right out of him. Jet after jet, rope after rope, he emptied himself into her. There was no thinking, only feeling, that explosive release he'd never experienced before. It was violent and brutal, the constriction of her hot channel around his cock almost vicious. He wasn't sure if it was heaven or hell, but it was mind-blowing perfection.

Savage collapsed over the top of her, his legs so shaky there was no way to stay upright. His lungs burned for air and his mind refused to work. For the longest time there was just the sound of the two of them fighting for air, their minds floating somewhere else, their bodies feeling every ripple of every aftershock. He rode out every one with her, his lips on her belly, kissing her there. Bringing up a strawberry. Marking her in the way he had her inner thighs, her breasts and her bare pussy lips.

Those weren't the marks that would normally set him off. Not the ones that he dreamt of putting on her, but he was more than excited to see them on her skin. He found the strength to kiss the ones he could get to.

"Are you all right, baby? Did I hurt you? I think we got carried away."

"I think we were perfect," Seychelle corrected.

Her hand found his head and she did a slow massage, one that he hated to miss when he stood up, but he had to take care of her. Very slowly, he slid out of her. There was blood mixed with seed and sex. He had no idea why, but the sight of that mixture gave him satisfaction. Even as he pulled out of her, that hot, slick tunnel dragged over his sensitive cock, sending waves of sensation through him where before he'd felt half-alive. He had no idea what she did to him, but it felt like a miracle.

"Stay there, baby. Let me take care of you." He managed to find his way to the bathroom to clean up and get a warm cloth for her. He'd given her several orgasms, powerful ones, and each time he'd managed to send her over the edge at his command. That would come to be very important. He wanted her to always associate pleasure with him. Always.

Savage took his time, was meticulous in washing her before stretching out beside her on his belly, his hands framing her face. "I will love you, Seychelle, more than any other man in this world can possibly love you. I swear that to you. At the end of our days, you'll never be sorry you took a chance with me."

He meant every single word of that promise. Her smile was slow in coming, but it lit her face and then her eyes, taking his heart. She traced the lines cut deep in his face.

"I love you, Savage. I'll stick with you. Just take your time with me."

He wished they had all the time in the world and he didn't have to worry about how his mind was so fucked up, but she already knew. "I'll do my best, baby." He rolled over, slid down in the bed and laid his head on her belly. His favorite place to sleep.

"Just so you know, I'm throwing those books in the garbage," Seychelle declared, her hand on Savage's head, fingers massaging his scalp. "They are no help at all. If they have one huge lie, maybe everything is a lie."

He tilted his head to look up at her. "What kind of books have you been reading?"

Her blue eyes shifted away from his, long lashes sweeping down. "This and that. Self-help. That kind of thing."

He turned onto his stomach so he could look up at her easily. "What are you trying to learn, babe?" It was a demand.

She started laughing. Little golden notes rose in a musical symphony all around, forcing him to turn back so he could watch them dance their way to the ceiling. He loved that. She could make his life like those musical notes. Floating. Drifting. Happy.

"I don't know that much about sex, Savage. I went to the bar with the idea that we'd get together, and I didn't want to disappoint you, so I read as much as I could. I was already on birth control, which, by the way, you should have asked me before we did anything."

"I already knew you were. I've been here for a few months now. It's not exactly a huge bathroom. You keep it in the top drawer. Why the hell are you on birth control when you weren't sleeping with anyone?"

"I intended to sleep with tons of men. *Tons* of them. I didn't think I had long to live, and I wanted to experience everything. I was going to be a wild woman. But then I started meeting them and I didn't exactly like them enough to get all sinful and dirty with them."

It was his turn to laugh. He was shocked when silver notes rose to the ceiling, floating up in a glittering musical display. A lump rose in his throat, and he turned back over and tightened his arm around her hips. "I don't know whether to turn you over my knee or just kiss you until you can't think straight and won't ever consider that again."

"After what we did together, I don't think I'll be considering other men, Savage."

He rolled, caught her waist, flipped her over him to bring her onto his lap and swatted her hard on her bottom, then put her back into the same position so he could pillow his head on her belly. She let out a squeal of protest when he smacked her hard, but only glared at him.

"That's not a proper answer, Seychelle. The proper answer would be, 'I will never, ever, under any circumstances consider going off with other men, Savage. The possibility won't enter my mind.'"

"Is that what I should have said?"

Laughter spilled sassy little notes toward the ceiling to catch up with his silver ones, wrapping around them, intertwining like the rose sculpture she loved so much. Someday he was going to have Lissa make some kind of sculpture representing the two of them. Something beautiful she would treasure.

"That's what you should have said. Go to sleep, you little demon. You aren't going to be getting much sleep tonight, so be warned."

FOURTEEN

"I don't really understand what a run is," Seychelle said to Lana. "Would you explain it to me? Savage is so sweet, and he's kind of spoiled me rotten the last two weeks. Some things he explains very succinctly, and for other things I think he expects I can just read his mind. He brought up the run and said we'd be going in a few weeks, that it was important, but he didn't really say what it was."

She looked around the clubhouse curiously. She didn't know what she'd expected, but not this very neat, comfortable, *large* space. This was the common room they all shared and mostly congregated in. The chairs were the most relaxing furniture she'd ever sat in. She wouldn't mind trying to fit a couple of them in her Mini Cooper and making a getaway for her cottage.

"That's our boy. Well, I don't know about the sweet part." Lana gave her a smile, but her vivid green eyes examined Seychelle's face carefully. "You do make him happy." She turned her head to look at Savage, who was behind the bar, no expression on his hard features, talking to his birth brother, Reaper, and club brother Destroyer.

Seychelle didn't think he looked happy. She thought he looked as if he was discussing murder. If that was what the three men were doing, they were keeping their heads down and doing so in low tones. Everyone seemed to be talking about the "run," but no one really seemed to be excited about going on it.

"Seychelle, he's really in love with you."

Instantly, Lana had her full attention. Lana didn't sound ecstatic. If anything, she sounded leery. In fact, the look Seychelle caught being exchanged between Alena and Lana was worrisome.

She sighed. "What's wrong with that? Isn't he supposed to fall in love? Isn't that a good thing?"

"Of course," Alena said hastily, all the while watching Savage. "Don't get upset. He'll know, and believe me, honey, he won't be happy with us for getting his chicklet upset. It's just that Savage doesn't just love you. He's mad, crazy, all-in, you're-his-world in love with you."

"That's the way I feel about him."

"It's all right if you feel that way about him, Seychelle," Lana said. "You really are sweet. Savage didn't get that name because he's a nice guy. Someone looks at you wrong and he could end up in prison."

"At this run? That's what you're mostly worried about, isn't it?" Seychelle guessed shrewdly. She tapped her fingers on her thigh. "He did mention several times that a lot of different clubs would be there, and he wanted me to stick very close to him and to the other members of Torpedo Ink."

Lana nodded. "Runs can be fun, but they can be dangerous. You're a beautiful woman, and you've got the kind of body men are going to be looking at. You have a voice that draws men in. Also . . ." She glanced at Alena.

Alena shrugged. "It's no big deal. She's Savage's old

lady—that makes her Torpedo Ink. She can hear. I hooked up with one of the Diamondbacks. Pierce. It was stupid of me. I was lonely and he was intriguing. And hot. I kept missing our dates when I was opening the restaurant. Standing him up. He came around one night and was really upset. He talked me into making a sex video for him. I knew better, but I felt guilty and I did it. He shared it with his club, and he hooked up with a woman who used to party with all the boys here and in various other clubs. He did that while he was with me. Apparently, that's his thing, and, you know, lesson learned. It hurt, but I'm getting over it. My brothers, not so much. They're pretending they're over it, but they aren't. It's like a powder keg ready to blow up in our faces. The least little provocation between the two clubs, and we could be on the run for the rest of our lives."

Seychelle heard the very real worry in her voice. It was easy to see the uneasiness on their faces. She had felt the heightened tension since she'd come with Savage to the clubhouse. She thought it was because he'd brought a newcomer there.

She glanced at her watch. She was supposed to be at the bar at ten o'clock to sing with the band. She'd promised Keys and Master. Savage had been adamant that she signal to him if anyone in the crowd was really ill. He said it was important she sing tonight, and if anyone in the crowd was sick, they needed to practice their signals, and he would remove the person. There was still a little time left before she had to go.

"Savage mentioned that several of the Diamondbacks would be showing up tonight, that they had a meeting with Czar."

Alena nodded. "That's true. They'll be meeting with him in the back room. Everyone else will carry on as usual. As if nothing is happening. A normal crowd will be there, just dancing and having a good time, listening to the music."

Seychelle was suddenly very uneasy. "What would be

happening? Maybe you should just tell me what's going on tonight. Am I some kind of distraction?" She didn't know if she was upset by the idea or if it excited her. Seychelle, the wild girl, providing the diversion while her man and his club carried out some nefarious deed. Except she had no idea what the wicked, reprehensible deed was, and what was the fun in that?

"No one knows exactly," Lana said. "We went to a meet recently and it didn't pan out so well. Pierce's new girl-friend attacked Alena."

"We can change the subject," Alena suggested. "What do you think of Savage's house?"

Seychelle tried to control the color rushing up her neck to cover her face. "I haven't seen it yet." They'd started out the door several times, but they'd never made it. She blamed Savage. He was insatiable. Totally.

They had run out of food, though, and desperately needed groceries. Savage told her they could have them delivered, and they had, several times. Now, she knew time was getting away from them and they had to get back to the real world. He had a big meeting he had to attend. She could sing with the band, and she hadn't visited her older friends and made certain they had all the things they needed. She felt a little guilty about that. Some of them counted on her.

"You haven't seen his house yet?" Lana repeated, a small grin on her face.

"No." Seychelle looked at her watch again, a little desperate for time to keep marching forward now that they were discussing things she didn't want to get into. "I'm sure it's quite nice."

"I'm sure it is," Alena said and burst out laughing. "Don't look so apprehensive. They all have nice houses. They like ocean views, forest and privacy. That adds up to nice. You're going to have to come to my restaurant."

"I didn't thank you for all the times you brought me

meals when I wasn't doing so well," Seychelle said. "I really appreciated it. It made me feel that someone cared. For a good part of my life I felt very alone. Even when my parents were alive, and they were very loving, they just didn't have the energy to put out toward a child."

"You gave your energy to them," Lana guessed.

Seychelle shrugged. "They were my parents. I wanted them to live forever. It was hard to let them go. I didn't have anyone else in my life. It was the three of us. Mom was so worn out, though, sometimes she couldn't talk, so I'd just sit on the bed with her and sing to her for hours. Dad would come into the room and climb on her bed on the other side of her and snuggle too. It was a strange childhood by normal standards."

"What's normal?" Alena shrugged. "None of us know. We all just get by, I suppose. Here comes your man. You'll do fine tonight, Seychelle. Just do whatever Savage tells you to do, and if anything goes wrong, stick with the band until he gets to you."

Seychelle nodded, her mouth suddenly dry. She'd been happy, feeling like she had it all, maybe a little nervous to come to the exalted clubhouse, but still, Savage made her feel like she was extraordinary. She felt as long as they were together, they could face anything. With the dire warnings the two women had passed on to her, she suddenly felt as if she shouldn't go on the run with Savage after all—and she'd been looking forward to it. And now, after wanting to sing with the club's band again, she wanted to go back home and be safe in her cottage.

Savage wrapped his arm around her, pulling her under his shoulder and up tight against his side, his all-too-seeing gaze sweeping over her face. "What's wrong, babe?" He glanced at Alena and Lana as they walked away, heading toward the back rooms. "They say something to upset you?"

His tone was low, even, but there was a small underlying

note that warned Seychelle Alena and Lana were right: Savage wasn't going to tolerate anyone—not even his brothers and sisters in the club—making his woman uncomfortable. She tried a tentative smile but kept her eyes veiled with her lashes, knowing the man could read her like a book.

"I don't exactly know what's going on tonight, and the atmosphere is pretty tense. This is definitely a club thing. None of the women are here other than Alena and Lana. Are they going to be in the bar?"

"Some will be. I didn't want to bring you, babe." Savage walked her to the door and caught up the jacket hanging there to hand to her. "We need your voice tonight. This is important, Seychelle. I can't stress it enough. When you first go in and look around, I want you to signal to me if there is anyone in the bar who is extremely ill or has something that is going to distract you in any way. If so, I need to know. We'll take care of it. The club will politely get them to leave. After that, I need you to focus on the Diamondbacks. Just on them, especially the ones who will be in the back room with Czar and a few Torpedo Ink members. You can do that, right? You can feel everyone in the building, even at that distance?"

Savage held out the jacket, so she turned and put her arms into it. He always had her turn her back to him so he could slide his arms around her and zip it up. He nuzzled her neck, first with his chin, and then he trailed kisses from her neck to her ear. He tugged on her earlobe with his teeth until she had goose bumps.

There was no doubt in her mind he was as worried as Alena and Lana had been. "Did it occur to you that you should have discussed this with me before you brought me into the situation, Savage?" She turned around and tilted her chin at him, her gaze meeting his directly.

Savage didn't look away from her. She knew he wouldn't. His piercing blue eyes were back to glacier cold—that dense blue that was icy and could chill to the bone. She refused to back down.

"Yeah, baby, I thought about it for a long time, but I thought it would just make you more nervous. And I don't know what this meet with the Diamondbacks is about. Not even Czar knows. We don't have any idea what to expect. They called a meet recently in the middle of the night, so no witnesses. That didn't go well. This time they wanted it in the full bar, with civilians, and on a night when the band was playing." Savage stroked caresses in her hair. "We gotta get there, Seychelle."

"Maybe we do, honey, but I need to know what you're going to be doing while I'm singing, and where you are, so I'm not terrified something's going to happen to you." She refused to budge in spite of the hand he put on her back, urging her to move out the door.

His eyes went flat. They were already cold. "Baby, you worry about the other guy, not me. Now get your ass on my bike—we've got to go now. I want to know you can feel us in the back room. We have to set up."

Seychelle went with him, her stomach churning. Their "honeymoon" period was coming to an abrupt end. She didn't say a word as she took her place behind him on the bike. The night was foggy, as it often was on the coast, but just barely. She thought of it as a gray cloud enveloping them as they made their way to the bar. What had been something she'd been looking forward to was now a little frightening—and her temper was stirring.

The bar was up the road, just below Highway 1. Above the bar were the two apartments the club owned and rented out to Bannister and Delia. There was a large parking lot in front of the terraced landscaping that wrapped around the building. A narrow path led up to the highway through overgrown grass to one side of the property. The other side was by parts parking and landscaped.

Savage had known he was taking her into a dicey situation, and he had waited until the last minute to tell her. She was someone who had to process information. He knew that about her. Lana and Alena had cast doubts on her going on the run; in fact, she'd decided she'd just stay home while he went on it. She wasn't going to take any chances of being the cause of Savage going to prison. And now this . . . Yeah, her temper was quite close to the surface.

By the time Savage parked the bike, Seychelle was seething. She smacked him in the back of the head as she got off, all but tossed the helmet to him and started walking toward the bar without him.

"Woman. You wait for me."

That was a direct order. There was no doubt about it. That was Savage being the enforcer. She stopped in her tracks but didn't turn around. Maybe it hadn't been the best idea to smack the back of his head, but if she was going to be in trouble for it, she wished she'd put a little more effort into it.

She felt the heat of his body before he reached her. He was always so silent in the way he moved, like some great jungle cat stalking his prey. Her body gave a little shiver all on its own, responding to his aggression in spite of her own anger at him. He slung his arm possessively around her neck and pulled her in to the shelter of his body. He was solid muscle, a wall of sheer strength. When he locked her against him, she wasn't going anywhere. She stood very still, waiting, trembling, but not with fear, more with a mixture of anger and anticipation.

"You have every right to have your nasty temper exploding right now, Seychelle. I fucked up. I should have listened to my instincts regarding you. I know your personality. You like to hear about things, even a little bit at a time, and then think it over. I was happy in that cottage with you and I didn't want to leave. We were laughing every day. All night. The last thing I wanted to do was bring this mess up, especially when I didn't know what we were walking into, but I should have."

She turned to face him and he pulled her in close again, sliding one hand down her back to the curve of her bottom. "You've gotten so you like my hand or even occasionally the leather decorating your ass. And you've let me clamp your nipples a couple of times, and you enjoyed it. I was so wrapped up in you and me that I didn't want anything else to interfere. I didn't want to bring the outside into our world. What I did was wrong, and I'm fully aware of it."

Seychelle pressed her forehead against his chest. When he did that, just simply and succinctly owned his mistakes, it turned her heart over. Savage never beat around the bush, he just simply told her outright what he thought was his part in what went wrong.

"Not the leather. I'm not sure about that leather strap thing yet. Clamps I love. Your hand too. Leather, um . . . not so much."

"Your body always tells me something else."

"I know, but I think I'm going to have a serious talk with my body. Okay. I'm not angry anymore, but please, when something big is up, let me know ahead of time. I really do have to think things through. I'm not good at this caught-off-guard thing."

He tipped her chin up so he could look into her eyes. His eyes had gone from ice-cold blue to flames, ones that licked over her body and turned her to pure fire. "You're good at everything, Seychelle. I love you. Just remember that and you'll be fine. Stay with the band. Don't step into the crowd for any reason. When we go in, you search that crowd for anyone with illnesses who could distract you or force you to help them. That's the first thing."

He framed her face with his hands and brushed kisses over her lips. "You can do this, baby. More than anything, you stay safe for me. Tell me you understand that's the most important thing. You'll sweep that room, and we'll clear it of anyone with an illness."

She nodded. "I can do that."

That earned her a kiss. His kisses robbed her of all ability to think. If he wanted a thinking person in the bar, he couldn't kiss her. Not only did her brain turn to mush, but her body went into meltdown. One hand slipped into her hair, crushing it into his fist at the nape of her neck, holding her head in place while fire flared between them.

He lifted his head when she gripped his jacket hard and fought for control. "We've got this, baby. You and me. We can do this. You'll be safe as long as you do just what I tell you."

Seychelle realized he *really* didn't want her there. Whatever this was, for some reason, the club felt they needed her. That settled her when nothing else could have. She wanted to be important to him—a partner, not a burden. She wasn't just a distraction. The club was counting on her.

"What do you want me to do when I'm singing, Savage?" She searched his eyes. The blue flames had quickly faded back to that flat, cold, deadly look he sometimes got that made her shiver. His features had settled into his expressionless mask.

"I'll go into the back room. Czar and some of the others will already be in there. I want you to sit at the bar and talk to Anya right before you take the stage. I'll step out of the room, and you give me a sign whether or not you can read us and how tense we are, the mood in the room. I think you'll be able to. If you can't, we'll try to find a way to make it work so you will. When the Diamondbacks come in, zero in on the ones coming into the back. Keep tuned to them. This is very important, Seychelle. If they start to get upset, try to counter it. Signal the band and let them know. Work out something to play ahead of time, various songs to counter whatever emotions you might meet."

She nodded.

"There will be Diamondbacks scattered around the bar as well. You'll have to keep a read on them. I know it's a lot to ask, baby, but it's damned important."

"I can do it. I do it all the time," she assured him.

He brushed her lips with his again and wrapped his arm around her waist possessively, walking her across the parking lot. Savage stopped at the bottom of the stairs leading to the bar to introduce her to a club member.

"Seychelle, this is Fatei. He's a good man, a good brother. If there's trouble, he'll get to you. He'll be inside the bar as well, looking out for you."

Seychelle smiled at him. "Good to know. I'll be the one singing with the band."

Fatei sent her a faint answering grin that didn't quite light up his face. He didn't seem quite as intimidating to her as the other club members, but he looked like a man who could handle himself.

Music poured out of the building, as if it were impossible for the walls to contain the sound. Already, Seychelle was caught by the rhythm and perfect notes as the instruments welded together into a musical phenomenon that sent her spirits soaring. She loved this band and the way they played. Fatei opened the door and Savage walked her in, keeping her body clamped to his side. Fatei took her other side, so that when they moved through the crowd—and there was a huge, packed crowd—no one so much as brushed up against her.

Anya worked one side of the bar and Preacher worked the other. Seychelle did her best to block out everything but the crowd and the way each person felt to her. It was diffi- cult with the way her body responded to the music and the level of excitement emanating from the various occupants who had come to have a good time.

There were several parties of women. She recognized the two women fixated on Savage. Clearly, they hadn't given up. They were with three other women, one of whom looked a little older, and the moment Savage had entered the room, all of them had riveted their attention on him. Shari's eyes were hot with greed and her emotions were by turns lustful, filled with hatred toward Seychelle, and needy and determined. She danced and swayed seductively on the edge of the dance floor, making a path to intercept Savage so she could brush against his body.

"How the fuck did she get in here? I had her banned," Savage snarled in a low voice to Fatei.

"I'll look into it, Savage," Fatei promised. "Do you want me to throw her out?"

"Don't," Seychelle said. "Just let it go tonight, Savage." She knew there were too many other things riding on her singing tonight. Savage couldn't be distracted because of past issues she'd had. She didn't have them so much anymore.

"You sure, baby?"

"Absolutely."

Seychelle did her best to ignore Shari while sliding her healing gift over the other women with her, trying to find any actual illnesses that would suddenly pull her attention from her assignment. The women were emotionally fixated on Savage or the bikers, but other than one of them having a UTI, they seemed fine.

"Your harem is back, and it keeps expanding." She tried to tease him to get him to smile. When he didn't, she turned her attention to the rest of the crowd.

Savage bit her earlobe and then licked at it to take away the sting. "You're going to pay for that." He whispered it against her ear, his lips brushing against her skin with every word so that little goose bumps rose all over her body.

"Don't distract me." She pushed at him with one hand, although half-heartedly, as they neared the band and the end of the bar, where Bannister, one of the regulars, had been sitting, holding the bar stool for her.

Shari slid her body up against Savage's, or tried to, but at the last second, as she tried to make contact, he suddenly stepped sideways, taking Seychelle with him, his mouth on her neck, moving her back into the crowd and swinging them around so Fatei was between the woman and them. Shari glared at Seychelle as if she were to blame.

The band swung into another song and immediately the crowd was dancing to the beat. That made it easier for Seychelle to get a clearer take on those in the room. Most everyone was healthy. There were a few with unhealthy livers who insisted on drinking, but she knew she couldn't help them.

"Nothing big in here. We're good so far, Savage. You can head to the back room."

He escorted her to the bar stool. "Don't forget to give Fatei or the band the signal if you're in trouble. You need to be clear with them what that is ahead of time." He pushed her hair out of her face and tipped up her chin. "You understand? It gets too much and you have to bail, that's all right."

She cupped the side of his face. "I'm going to be fine. Go to your meeting. I've got this." Out of the corner of her eye, she saw the door to the club open and, to her dismay, Brandon Campbell sauntered in. He didn't have his girlfriend with him, the one now living in the house Sahara had vacated, but that didn't surprise Seychelle. The girl was underage.

Why in the world would Brandon come to a biker bar? It wasn't his scene. That was a definite red flag. With everything going on, she hoped that Savage wouldn't notice, but she should have known better. He leaned down and kissed her. "Stay close to the band and Fatei at all times. You need me, text or send Fatei. If that fails, look straight at the camera and say my name."

"I'm going to be fine. Go, so we can test the distance." She already knew she could read those in the back room. She knew Reaper was back there with Code, Czar, Ice, Storm and Mechanic. This meeting was big. Really big. Savage was joining them in the back room. Transporter was on the monitors, watching everything happening via cameras.

Savage leaned over and spoke in Fatei's ear. Her bodyguard for the night nodded once and glanced across the crowd at Brandon. It was just a quick sweep of his eyes, but Seychelle shivered. Why she thought Fatei seemed so much sweeter and less lethal than the others was anyone's guess. In that moment, he seemed just as likely as Savage to take Brandon outside and cut his throat.

Joseph Arnold slipped in so fast, not approaching the bar or her, but Seychelle's radar went off, so she caught sight of him before he managed to disappear into the crowd. She caught Fatei looking at her face and then doing another slow sweep of the bar as if looking for what or who had caught her attention.

"Hey, girl." Anya handed her a water bottle. "Big night tonight with you singing. The band's excited. Maestro's been bragging for days. He was annoyed when Savage was keeping you all to himself." She deftly served drinks to three customers leaning against the bar in between the stools.

Seychelle was grateful for the distraction. "I thought none of the other women were coming tonight, but I was wrong. Quite a few are here besides the two of us. I haven't met everyone, but I recognize them from Savage's descriptions. At least I think I do. The woman sitting at the table up close to the band with Alena—that's Scarlet, Absinthe's wife, right? She's got that red, red hair. And the table just inside the door, that's Lana, but is that Lissa? The famous glassblower? She's married to Casimir, Czar's birth brother, right? I've seen pictures of her. She's gorgeous. It's funny that she's got red hair as well, although not that same red as Scarlet's," Seychelle continued.

She knew she was chattering because she was nervous. It was silly. Now that the others were in place, the tension had eased in them. In fact, it was so low, she wouldn't have realized they expected trouble at all. She spotted Ink moving through the crowd, asking a girl to dance, taking her to the dance floor, but his attention wasn't really on her, no matter how hard the woman tried to rub her body all over his.

The number ended, and Seychelle slid from the bar stool to make her way to the platform where the band was. It was really only a couple of feet from where she'd been sitting, but Shari and her friend Melinda were obviously waiting to ambush her. Fatei stepped easily between them, and somehow, that smoothly, Alena and Scarlet were there as well, creating a wall, blocking the two women before they could reach her.

Seychelle expected to feel Shari's emotion at her loss of Savage, but instead, it was an intense hatred for Seychelle. The emotion was raw and passionate. Seychelle glanced down to see the woman's hands curled into claws, her long nails like talons, ready to rip at her eyes. That was how visceral her feelings were against Seychelle.

No one had ever hated Seychelle before, and it shook her to think this woman, a total stranger, did so now. She kept her head up, ignoring the woman, smiling at Alena and Scarlet, murmuring hello to Scarlet as Alena introduced her.

"You okay?" Alena whispered. "I don't know why she won't leave him alone. I can throw her out."

"She's no threat to me. I actually feel sorry for her," Seychelle said. "I'm good." She was. Savage loved her, and she was secure in that knowledge. She nodded to Fatei, not wanting him to think she hadn't noticed that he'd put his face on the line. Shari was capable of ripping his eyes out if she got angry enough. Seychelle did think the anger at her was strange. Especially as it was so strong. It didn't make sense. Seychelle was all about puzzles, and she wanted a little time to figure out why Shari was so focused on her, even more so than she was on Savage.

Maestro and Player greeted her. Keys and Master flashed grins at her. She took the microphone and faced them for a brief moment. Maestro indicated she had better signal them if anything went wrong. She nodded and they immediately swung into a fast, upbeat song that had the crowd going instantly.

She poured her magic into it, sending golden notes climbing up the walls and building webs across the ceiling. She spread those golden notes throughout the bar, beyond Preacher and Anya, so they moved along the ceiling down the long hallway behind the bar as well as the one beside it. It didn't matter that the door was closed; the notes found their way inside, climbing the walls and moving up the ceiling, an invisible golden net that was everywhere throughout the entire building by the time the last note of the song faded away.

The second song was slower, dreamier, but still with a dance beat, one that allowed her to sync with the crowd. It was so much easier to get a feeling for the emotions of individuals in the bar when she sang. If someone was very ill, that interfered, and then her ability to feel emotions would fade, but she'd already gone through the crowd, and no one had come in with an overwhelming disease that called to the healer in her. As she sang, she could touch on an individual and subtly change their mood.

Arnold had come to the bar, eyes on her, a mixture of feelings, possession, lust, arrogance, depression, determination. He signaled to Anya and was instantly annoyed when she didn't immediately serve him. Brandon was on the dance floor, close to Shari and the women, dancing with them, a smug smirk on his handsome face each time he looked at Seychelle.

Seychelle had a pulse on everyone in the building and was aware when the Diamondbacks arrived. There was the continual sound of Harleys, trucks or cars in the parking lot or on the road, but the heightened awareness of the members of Torpedo Ink tipped her off that the Diamondback club had arrived.

Steele, the vice president of Torpedo Ink, escorted several men inside, all wearing Diamondback colors. Destroyer was with them. The moment they entered the bar,

Seychelle felt a new strain introduced. Pain. Emotional pain. It was sharp and raw. Visceral. The pain of betrayal. That pain emanated from Alena.

Another thread twisted into Seychelle's golden web. Regret. Guilt. Determination. Sadness. That came from the man that had to be Pierce. He walked beside the one in the vest with a patch declaring he was the president. That man too felt guilt, but also worry. He had a heavy burden resting on him.

With Pierce and the president of the chapter of Diamondbacks were five others Steele escorted down the hall toward the back room. Those men were leery. Destroyer took up the rear. Five other Diamondback club members stayed behind in the bar. Three sat at a table close to Lana and Lissa and the exit.

The other two Diamondbacks moved through the crowd to get to the front where the tables were. The one beside Alena and Scarlet was occupied by a couple, but they rose immediately, allowing the two Diamondbacks to sit down. One took out his phone and brought up a video, turning up the sound and leaning in to show his companion what he was playing. His companion glanced at Alena, his gaze moving over her body in an open leer.

Alena and Scarlet ignored the two men, but Seychelle could feel that pain of betrayal coming off Alena in waves. With it mixed anger. Seychelle's expression didn't change, but her level of pain increased until it was difficult for her to sing. The golden threads vibrated with a wealth of silver, sliding along the string straight to the small table, swirling like tiny crystals of shiny glitter.

The music changed to another upbeat rock song, clearly meant for pulling the crowd to their feet for dancing. Her voice joined those notes, wrapping around them, pushing a gentle urge, a need to rise up and have fun, to be happy, to want to dance. All the while as the music did so, she watched the silver glitter swirl around Alena, absorbing the twisted pain and anger, each little crystal filling up, draining off some of the pain, little by little, until the crystals were full.

Seychelle was fascinated. Shocked. While she was singing with an entire crowd around her, she was seeing how Savage's gift worked. The silver crystals moved along her golden threads, finding their way back to him. The terrible emotional pain Alena had felt, that betrayal that went so deep, was still there, but Savage had siphoned the worst of it from her, taking the old pain and rage that mixed with the new, twisting it together until Alena didn't know the difference. Until she felt she couldn't bear the weight of one more betrayal. He'd lifted most of that from her and left her burden so much lighter.

Savage's gift was such a thing of beauty, Seychelle couldn't help but react to him with pride and respect, with joy at his abilities and sacrifice. The others didn't know. They hadn't seen. Alena still hurt, and the cut was deep, but she didn't know Savage had saved her, allowing her to present her cool, aloof demeanor.

Seychelle loved Savage all the more for his sacrifice. He would take on Alena's emotional pain. Shoulder it for her. Feel the deep wound cut right to his soul and allow it to build the rage in him until he had to find a way to rid himself of it. That was what he did for his brothers and sisters. For his club.

Because she had followed that chord back to him, she was even more aware of what he was doing than he was. He wasn't giving his complete attention to Alena; he was giving it to the meeting taking place in the back room between the two clubs. He was doing his job, and she needed to keep her mind on doing hers.

As the band swung from one song to the next, she kept her focus tuned to the men in the back room with Czar and the others. Twice, the tension seemed to rise sharply, and both times she sent notes of peace and harmony drifting along the main radial threads leading to the back room. She directed the golden notes to those in the back room with the most anxiety and the building anger suddenly coiling deep.

At the same time, she monitored those in the bar. Shari danced with her group of women and Brandon, at times grinding against Brandon while he whispered in her ear. Other times she nearly threw herself in a frenzied simulated sexual dance at the members of Torpedo Ink playing music. Sometimes Shari would try to get Fatei's attention or Ink's. Several times she nearly sat in the laps of the two Diamondbacks seated at the table close to Alena and Scarlet. Her desperation was difficult for Seychelle to take, but no matter what she tried, Shari didn't respond to any kind of persuasion by Seychelle's voice.

Brandon watched Seychelle so intently, she had to work to keep her attention focused on her job. She knew he was evaluating her voice. Her pitch. He had a talent similar to hers, and it was dangerous to give him any opening that might allow him to find his way into her mind. He clearly was trying to decide if she was influencing those in the audience as a whole intentionally, or simply singing and her voice was that persuasive.

The two Diamondbacks had switched their attention from Alena and Scarlet to Seychelle, and she realized her voice had enthralled them, just as it had several other men in the room. Arnold continued to sit at the bar, drinking and brooding. The bar was so crowded now with bikers, she could barely stay focused on those in the back room, and she was thirsty. Usually, she sang in sets. By now, she would have had a break, and she needed one desperately.

There was one member of the Diamondbacks in the back room who seemed as if he was so weighed down with his burden, he felt as if he was being pressed to the wall and had no way out but to fight. The man Seychelle had identified as Pierce had become more and more morose and miserable, as well as determined. In contrast, the members of Torpedo Ink seemed calm on the surface, but like Alena, their anger and pain ran deep. Something about this meeting brought back too many memories. She couldn't read their memories, but she could feel the terrible emotional toll the meeting was taking on each of the members.

She did her best to send peace and harmony to them, and when she felt Savage taking more and more of his brothers' and sisters' pain and anger onto his shoulders, she finally turned her head slightly and signaled to Maestro to play a ballad. She could control that rising tide of emotion and bring the level of despair down, but she couldn't absorb the pain the way her man was doing.

She sang about love. The power of it. The importance of it. The incredible journey. The way one sacrificed. She knew the road would be rough at times. That they would falter and sometimes even be angry and fail, but if they kept trying together, they would forge something so strong, nothing—no one—could ever break them apart. She poured her heart and soul into the lyrics. The pitch was perfection, going out onto the frame and those radial lines and sending the notes dancing up the walls and across the ceiling, down the hall and under the door to the meeting room.

In the bar, the notes found each spiral thread running to the crowd of various people and found specific ones, those needing solace or needing to simply relax into the music. She spun her golden net, ensnaring the crowd with her voice and lyrics, blending and weaving her notes with the incredible music the band played. The web vibrated with the power of her gift, resonating with each person individually, becoming what they needed, in that moment giving them the incentive and determination to get through every crisis with grace and strength and fairness.

When the last notes of the song faded, the band picked up the beat, swinging into a dance number, one the crowd would recognize instantly and not only dance to but sing along to. Maestro took up the vocals to give her a much-needed break. She felt as if her throat had been torn out. Nodding to him, she stepped off the stage, mindful of Savage's decree not to go too far from the band. There was no third chair to join Alena and Scarlet at their table, and Brandon was at the bar with Joseph Arnold. She didn't want to talk to either of them. Mostly, she wanted fresh air.

She signaled to Fatei, and he came right away as she stepped off the platform. "Is there a way I can go outside and still be close to the back room? They feel as if they're leaving, but just in case."

"Yeah, they're all going," Fatei agreed. "Czar sent the message just now."

Relief swept over Seychelle. "Is Savage coming to get me?"

"Not yet. He's got a little more club business. You'll have to stick with me for a little bit longer."

"Can you signal Anya for a water and we'll head outside? I saw Preacher use another door leading out. We could maybe go that way?" She made it a question and all but crossed her fingers, trying not to be upset that Savage had texted Fatei with his plans but not her. She'd glanced at her phone and there was nothing from him.

"Babe, Savage would prefer that you stay inside."

"I just want to step outside for a minute. I can't breathe. I've never sung that long without a break." Seychelle made it a statement. "I really have to go outside and get some fresh air."

Fatei took a long time to scan the bar, and then he nodded. "We'll head toward the bar. I'll grab your water and we'll head out. Just give me a minute to make sure it's clear. I'm texting Anya and Preacher that I'm bringing you out." He stood directly in front of her while he did so.

Seychelle took a deep breath and allowed herself to listen to the music and relax a little now that the Diamondbacks in the back room were leaving. The five in the bar were still seated, although the two near Alena's table had pushed back their chairs and drained their beers as if they were about to go. She felt eyes on her and saw Shari and her friend Melinda watching. Deliberately, she turned her back. In another minute, Fatei gestured toward the hallway that led to the exit she could take.

It was a huge relief to get out of the crowded bar and into the fresh air. Seychelle felt as if the night air enfolded her like a dark cloak as she went down the three cement stairs leading to the area behind the bar. The grounds opened up wide in several places, allowing for a few scattered picnic tables, but she walked to the narrow section, where she could sit in the deeper shadows along a cement railing where flowers and shrubs were planted.

"Ow. That hurts." The female voice came out of the darkness to her left.

Seychelle recognized a young woman named Sabelia, who worked in Sea Haven at a shop called the Floating Hat where she bought her lotions and teas.

"Stop being a baby. If you hadn't come out here with the scum of the earth, you wouldn't have a black eye already swelling closed. Hold still." Preacher's usual easygoing tone shook with repressed anger and frustration. "This is the last time you come to my place and do this, Sabelia. I mean it. I've had it with you getting drunk, going off with the worst asshole in the bar and getting beat up. Find another bar."

"You can't kick me out of the bar."

"I can. Sit still. I don't know what the hell is wrong with you. You have more talent in your little finger than most people, and more chances handed to you, but you throw them all away. You're like some little child constantly throwing tantrums, and it's getting damn old. If you were my sister, I'd do something about it, but you're not, so the only thing I can do is kick your ass out."

"You don't know anything about me or my life. You don't have a clue what my life has been like."

"No, I don't, Sabelia, and it doesn't matter, does it? We can't change what anyone did to us in the past, but we are responsible for what we choose to do with our lives in the future. I would give anything to have your talent."

"Oh, right, that's why you already know so much more than I do, and I've been working with Hannah longer than you have," Sabelia said. She sounded sulky.

"Hannah Drake Harrington took you under her wing because she saw your talent," Preacher snapped, his voice low, furious.

Seychelle wished she could gracefully exit, but it was too late. She just had to sit there and hope neither of them noticed her.

Preacher didn't stop there. "I study hard. You don't. You drink. You do anything but work at learning. I even offered to study with you, but you were too good to do anything like that. I was too far beneath you. The truth is, talent-wise, I am. Discipline-wise, you don't stand a chance. You want to feel sorry for yourself and blame everyone but you. You might have a shit past, baby, but I guarantee you I can match that past any day of the week. The difference is no one is going to fuck with my future. So you want to get drunk and get beat up, do it in someone else's bar. I'm taking your ass home tonight. My advice: sober up and take what Hannah's offering you. You're not going to find a better woman to follow. I've got a few things to do before I can leave, so come inside, stay in the back and drink coffee and don't piss me off any more than you already have."

Seychelle expected Sabelia to protest, to say something back, but she didn't say anything at all. She kept her head down as Preacher escorted her back into the bar. He towered over the woman. He still looked furious, and Sabelia looked very subdued. Seychelle caught a glimpse of her face as they walked past her. She definitely had bruises and swelling. Seychelle could see why Preacher was so angry.

That part of her that needed to heal others had her on her

feet and trailing slowly after them. She knew Savage wouldn't be happy if she followed Preacher and Sabelia back into the bar and took on some of Sabelia's injuries, but it was difficult to resist.

"There you are." Shari's strident voice jarred her nerves.

Seychelle turned to face her, aware of Fatei gliding close to her. Shari wasn't alone. Seychelle hadn't expected her to be. Melinda was with her, but also the two Diamondbacks who had been seated close at the table. At least, they rounded the corner of the building a few feet behind them. Behind the two Diamondbacks came Brandon, but he stayed right at the corner.

Seychelle glanced toward the bar, but Preacher and Sabelia had already disappeared inside the building. Seychelle wondered if Brandon had anything to do with Shari's hatred of her.

"Shit," Fatei hissed under his breath. "Come on, Seychelle. Let's go."

"Were you looking for me?" Seychelle asked, trying to get a feel for Shari's voice.

"Yes," Shari snapped. "You don't stand a chance in hell of keeping him. You know that, don't you? A prissy little thing like you can't begin to know what he likes."

"Do I know you?" Seychelle asked, her gaze moving over Shari's expression. Her eyes looked glassy. Drunk? Was she hypnotized? Did she really hate Seychelle that much? And what was she saying about Savage?

"Seychelle." Fatei indicated the back door. "You need to get inside."

"Run away," Shari sneered.

"What exactly do you want?" Seychelle challenged, ignoring Fatei. He put a restraining hand on her arm, and she shook it off, her chin up, her eyes cool as she regarded Shari.

FIFTEEN

What the fuck? He'd made himself very clear. Stick with the band. Stay right with them. Did she do it? No. There she was. Seychelle. She looked . . . gorgeous. A little wild. A sinful temptation to any biker. He should have made himself very clear to Fatei, not to her. She was completely oblivious to the way the men looked at her. He'd noticed that before. She looked at them through the eyes of the healer, not the woman.

She had that voice. That body—tits and ass. All that thick, wild hair. Those eyes and that mouth. Now she was absolutely challenging Shari and her friend right in front of the two Diamondbacks, who were already a little obsessed with her. Not to mention Brandon lurking around the corner like a creep. She was ignoring Fatei's instructions to get her ass back in the bar; in fact, she shook his hand off her arm.

Savage was going to *kill* that woman after he punished her and then fucked her brains out. He had a job to do, and it wasn't looking after her. Or even watching her. He was lying up on a rooftop with his rifle, eye to his scope, backing up his sister. Pierce had made his request to speak with

Alena formally, and Czar had had little choice but to agree to it.

Pierce had maneuvered them into a corner, and he knew it. They'd listened to Plank laying out his concerns about the Venomous club. It hadn't come as a huge surprise to them that the club continued to try to chop away at Diamondback territory. They moved into a small section without permission, without respect, and acted as if they were just a weekend club, doing nothing but getting together to have a good time. If the Diamondbacks made a move against them, to law enforcement and civilians, the Diamondbacks would look like an outlaw club bullying a group of nice weekend dads getting together to ride. In truth, Venomous was anything but.

Torpedo Ink had seen the tactic used over and over. The moment the larger club defended their territory, they were in the wrong to the outside world, but if they didn't defend it, inevitably they were perceived as weak, and they lost it. Venomous was coming at them from all directions, hitting chapter after chapter. Plank wanted Torpedo Ink to quietly take care of the problem before, during or after the run. Just make it go away but make it look like an accident, or if they got into a fight, anything that would distance itself from the Diamondbacks.

Plank had information that the Venomous club intended to take over the Mendocino territory first. It had already begun chipping away at the borders, swallowing the outside edges of the county and moving to take smaller pieces a little at a time. The county was rural and hard to patrol. Venomous frequented the Torpedo Ink bar and were often seen in Fort Bragg and Sea Haven as well as Caspar, all Diamondback territory. The Venomous club members were wearing their colors openly when riding, a major sign of disrespect when they'd never gone to the Diamondbacks to ask permission to be in their territory.

Plank had been very specific about the targets. He had

rumors of a conspiracy to kill him. He even had somewhat of a vague timeline. Supposedly, he and a few of his inner circle were to be assassinated on the run that was coming up. When questioned, he'd admitted to using a couple of the patch chasers to get information. Whether it was good data or not still had to be confirmed, but Savage suspected it was. The Venomous club members were all too cocky when they showed up wearing their colors in the bar and at local events. They believed they were in control.

Then Pierce had made his request to talk to Alena, and he'd made it through Plank, his president. It was impossible to deny him, the way Plank presented his case. Plank claimed they hadn't known Tawny would be at the last meet. She'd lied to hurt Alena. Pierce wanted a chance to explain things. Plank felt he'd had a hand in making things worse between the two and would appreciate a few minutes of Alena's time.

There was nothing for it, although all of Torpedo Ink were seething, knowing that Plank had ordered Pierce to kill Tawny and throw the blame on Alena. Savage had Pierce in his sights and settled on the roof, wire in his ear, listening to the conversation, as several of the other Torpedo Ink members were doing as well.

Alena looked sexy as hell. She always did. There was something about her that just screamed sensual with every step she took. She looked cool and calm on the outside, but Savage could feel the inner turmoil raging in her. She had agreed to meet with Pierce the moment Czar asked her. She would never shirk club duties, no matter how tough they were, but it cost her to even look at him. Savage took the brunt of that rage and pain for her so she could face Pierce just like she was, with her cool demeanor, as if the Diamondback enforcer counted for nothing.

Unfortunately, that pain transferred to a deep well of rage that just kept adding to that force, building and building until the volcano in Savage would have no choice but to erupt. And that meant his woman would have to be ready. The time he had to prepare her was getting shorter and shorter. The need to put a bullet in Pierce's head was stronger than he would have liked.

"Alena, I want you to just hear me out. That entire thing with Tawny, that was fucked up. I didn't have a chance to talk to you. To explain," Pierce said.

Alena shrugged, waved her hand as if dismissing him very casually. "It's all right, Pierce, it was a misunderstanding. I thought our relationship was exclusive, and you didn't. Had you been up front with me that you wanted something different, I would have known from the beginning what we were all about. But the video . . . That's something else altogether."

Alena shook her head, gave him a faint smile, but didn't change her mild tone. "That makes you a fucking bastard. I didn't want to give that to you, but you insisted. That was a pretty big deal, and you knew it. You played me, and I have to think about the why of that. Your ego?"

She shrugged. "Maybe you get off on playing women. I do hope you and Tawny had a good laugh together in bed the way she said. That one did hurt, I'll admit, but then I let myself care about you, and that's on me."

"Damn it, Alena. You know I never took that bitch to my bed. Never. She was lying to you. She might have been in someone else's bed watching the video, but it wasn't mine." There was a short silence while Pierce thought about what he'd just said.

He cursed while Savage thought about putting a bullet in the betrayer's head. He wanted to pull the trigger more than he wanted to take his next breath. To keep from doing it, he forced air through his lungs and wiped his forehead on his sleeve, all the while keeping the scope aimed dead center between Pierce's eyes.

Alena's pain was visceral. One could take only so many betrayals. Alena and her entire club had already had their share. She'd let Pierce in. She'd known better, but somehow, she'd let him in. He didn't deserve it, and the Diamondback enforcer knew it. He knew what he'd lost just looking at her. Savage could see it on his face. He drained off more of Alena's pain, a little at a time, just enough to allow her to keep functioning with that same cool demeanor.

"That didn't come out right, honey." Pierce shoved both hands through his hair. "Marry me. Before the run. I want you to marry me, Alena. We can fix this."

Alena stared at him for nearly thirty seconds without speaking while Savage resisted a second time, not pulling the trigger.

"I think you've really lost your mind. You want me to marry you? Before the run? How would that work, exactly? I'm Torpedo Ink. You're Diamondback. Nothing has changed, Pierce. You want me riding with you on the run?"

"Yes." He nodded. Frowned. Shook his head. "No. Not on the run. You'd stay home. Work at your restaurant. There's no need for you to be at that run."

She regarded him for another full thirty seconds in silence. "How would our marriage work, Pierce? You're not the faithful kind. You go on runs and have fun with other women? I go and have fun with other men? Or I stay home, and you think I'm going to be the good little old lady? We have an open marriage? How do you envision this?"

He shoved his hands through his hair again. "I don't know, Alena. I never thought about marrying anyone before. I can protect you."

She put her hand on her hip. "Do I need protection? From what?"

He shook his head. "I don't understand why you're making this difficult. I'm trying to do the right thing. Work this out."

"Like you did the right thing, setting me up when you asked for the video? You kept asking and I kept saying no. You guilt-tripped me the night you came to my restaurant and pointed out I kept missing our dates. You did that on purpose. Answer me why you would do that to me, Pierce."

"Damn it, Alena. I didn't distribute that to everyone."

"It just jumped off your phone."

"Will you at least think about it? Marrying me? I'm serious."

"I'm going on the run, Pierce. We can talk more then. Right now, I don't know what to think. Betrayal is really ugly. It feels ugly. Two of your boys sat next to me in the bar and made a show of playing that video. Being your old lady and having to put up with that crap would be very hard for me after the respect I'm used to having in my club. Even my old man wouldn't be giving me the same level of respect I'm used to getting here. Trading respect for what? Having my man getting blow jobs and whatever else when he's away from me doesn't sound like a great trade-off, but I'll give it thought. Thank you for the offer. I know it came from a well-meaning place."

Pierce stared at her for a long time and then he shook his head. "Damn it, Alena. I don't feel so easily. It just doesn't happen. You coming along was unexpected. I don't want anything to happen to you."

She studied his face. Savage studied it as well. He was fairly certain Lana and Scarlet were doing so from their positions on rooftops as well, each trying to figure out Pierce's real motives. Had Plank put him up to something else? Why have Alena stay away from the run? Insist she marry Pierce when he wasn't the kind of man to be faithful? Nothing about what Pierce was saying or doing made any sense.

"Maybe if you told me why you think I'm in some kind of danger it would help, Pierce," Alena said, her voice very quiet.

Pierce took a deep breath as a loud whistle cut through the night. "I've got to go. Unblock me. Talk to me on the phone."

Alena shook her head. "I don't think I'm quite ready to forgive the video thing yet, Pierce. Until you explain that to me, there isn't a way to talk."

"I can't explain it if you won't let me talk to you."

They stared at each other for a long time. Pierce sighed. "If you're going on the run, will you at least think about what I said? We can talk there."

"I'm going on the run with Torpedo Ink," Alena affirmed. "But I'm not making any promises about revisiting this very bizarre conversation. We'll see what transpires."

He stepped toward her, and she stepped back. "Don't. Don't even think about touching me. I have standards, Pierce. Tawny's leftovers leave me with a very bad taste in my mouth." She turned and sauntered off, hips swaying suggestively, Pierce cursing inventively.

Savage was proud of her. Alena never once showed the devastation Pierce had left behind. She looked classy, regal even. She walked right past the two Diamondbacks standing behind Shari and Melinda and went straight to Seychelle to wrap her arm around Seychelle's waist. Savage could have kissed her for that alone.

"You sing like an angel, girlfriend," Alena greeted as if she didn't notice the tension.

The two Diamondbacks reluctantly responded to the second whistle calling them back to their bikes. One of them he recognized as a man going by the name of Trade. He was a good friend of Pierce's. Code had done a little background work on him just because he seemed to be Pierce's closest friend. They'd been in the service together. Both had been on a SEAL team before they got out and eventually joined the Diamondbacks together. It was Trade who turned back to look at Seychelle before he reluctantly went around the corner to join the rest of his friends leaving the premises with their president.

Savage knew it wasn't just Seychelle's body. Her looks could definitely attract dozens of men, but she had a siren's

voice, one that could tempt the devil. She'd clearly drawn
Brandon Campbell to her. And Joseph Arnold. Now was he
going to have to contend with Trade from the Diamondbacks as well? That was always going to be the downside to
her singing. When she used that voice of hers to sing her
love songs, she could cast a spell without trying.

"She's no angel," Shari snapped.

The smile faded from Alena's face. "Excuse me? Just
who are you? I don't think I was talking to you. How did
you even get into the conversation?"

Shari jutted her hip out and stuck her hand on it. "I believe
you interrupted me first. Little Miss Not-So-Innocent Man
Stealer was talking to me when you rudely interrupted."

Alena's eyebrow shot up, and she turned to Seychelle.
"You're a man stealer? Whose man did you poach? Does
Savage know?"

Seychelle laughed. Savage's gut clenched. He was going
to use a crop on her body for his enjoyment. Teach her to
love it. His cock reacted. Hell. He was like some out-of-
control teenager around the woman. When she laughed,
those little golden notes floated in the air, light and airy,
touching him in places he'd thought long dead, giving him
a gift every time.

He forced his attention onto the departure of the Diamondbacks, making certain all of them really left, minus Brandon,
who was still on the premises. He counted them and then
handed them off to Mechanic and Transporter. The two were
already in positions to make certain no one backtracked.
Once the Diamondbacks were off the property and their Harleys were thundering down Highway 1, he broke the rifle
down, put it in the case and started to descend from the roof.

Joseph Arnold was standing on the cement planter
tucked back in the shrubbery with his cell out, obviously
trying to get photographs of Seychelle. He clearly had the
type of cell phone capable of taking night photos. He hadn't

approached Seychelle, but he wouldn't stop with his obsessive need to connect with her in some way.

Savage slipped off the roof and into the back meeting room to secrete the case with his rifle where it was easy for him to get to if needed. The door was open to the outside, leaving just the screen when he walked down the hall. He caught sight of Sabelia in one room, curled up in a chair, an ice pack on her face, Preacher's jacket over her. He kept walking. The sight of a woman's bruised face sickened him. Triggered him. He was the kind of man who could easily hunt down and kill someone over that shit. And the man wouldn't die easily. Better to stay out of it. Preacher was handling it.

"You have no idea what you're getting yourself into with a man like Savage," Shari's voice cut through the night, making Savage wince. "Look at you." She sounded sneering. Full of contempt. "He keeps coming back to me. He likes my mouth. Does he like yours?"

Savage cursed under his breath and slammed the flat of his hand against the screen, opening it. He'd lost Seychelle once because of this bitch; he wasn't losing her a second time. She had total confidence in herself in most areas. In fact, she had no problem going her own way when she wanted to—she just smiled and nodded when he said no, and she did it anyway. But not when it came to him and their relationship. She was very hesitant and unsure of herself. They hadn't gotten to lessons on oral sex. He knew her. She would be very self-conscious about that.

He walked up behind Alena and Seychelle, slung his arm around Seychelle's neck and dropped a kiss on top of her head. "Let's get out of here, babe. I'm wiped." He felt her stiffen. Resisting. He bent his head, his teeth nipping her earlobe. "This is one of those times we talked about when you just come with me without arguing." He whispered it, his lips against her ear.

Seychelle didn't answer him, but she didn't stop him when he slid his hand down her arm to shackle her wrist.

"You coming, Alena? You look tired, honey."

"I think I'll call it a night too," Alena conceded.

"Run away, baby," Shari hissed under her breath.

Savage had turned Seychelle around and they'd taken several steps toward the back door. She stiffened and started to turn back. He locked his arm around her.

"Keep walking." He made it an order. "She's done here. You won't be seeing her again. I don't know how she got in. I told them to keep her out."

"She probably blew the doorman," Alena said, laughing.

Seychelle ducked her head. "Yeah. She brags about how she's really good at that. Savage might be able to tell you. Just how good is she?"

"Let it go, Seychelle." He sounded harsher than he intended.

He could catch the emotions of every member of his club, even Destroyer, but Seychelle could close herself off to him when she wanted to. She was doing it right now. He glanced at Alena. She looked up at him and shook her head, warning him he was in trouble. He already knew he was. Seychelle was tired. Most likely exhausted after using her gift for so long. She hadn't had a single break once the Diamondbacks had arrived. The meeting took longer than expected.

He caught up her jacket and was extremely gentle as he helped her into it, wrapping his arms around her as he zipped it up, pulling her body into his, her back to his front. "I'm sorry this took so long. You were amazing, Seychelle. You held everything together for us. Things could have gone to hell fast a couple of times, but you kept everyone calm with your voice." He brushed kisses on her temple, over her ear, to her neck. "I was so fucking proud of you."

Her gaze shifted back to him, but she didn't smile. She just nodded to Alena and started toward the door. Savage caught her hand, holding on to her, letting her know that no matter what, they were a couple, and she wasn't leaving him again over Shari. He detested that he'd made such a mistake, allowing his needs to overcome his usual careful planning that ensured he didn't make mistakes with his choice of partners. He'd banned Shari, but she'd managed to get in. Seychelle had said it was fine, but clearly it wasn't.

His intention was never to hurt Seychelle emotionally. Already he could see he was failing her. She paused at the door of the bar and turned back.

"Fatei, thank you so much for looking out for me. I really appreciate it." She gave him her high-wattage smile.

Savage noted that the smile didn't light her eyes. He wanted to wrap his arms around her and just hold her, but there were too many interested eyes on them. Too many people looking at his woman with speculation. He didn't make the mistake of hurrying her. He waited until she was ready to leave. Her fingers tightened around his, and she straightened her shoulders before she once again started for the door.

"You going to stay mad at me all night?" He paced beside her down the stairs, keeping her body right up against his.

"Yes." She didn't look at him.

They walked in silence to his Harley. She put her helmet and gloves on while he straddled the bike and started it up. Hand on his shoulder, Seychelle took a careful look around. Savage knew that not only were Shari and her friend watching them, but Arnold was concealed in the bushes and Brandon Campbell had come out of the bar to follow at a distance. She got on as if she'd been doing it for years, fitting perfectly behind him, wrapping him up as if he were her Christmas present. She laid her body against his.

He took the shorter route to Highway 1 and circled away from Sea Haven. She tightened her arms around him, her palm pushing into his belly in protest. She wanted to go home. He was taking her there, just not to the one she expected. He dropped his gloved hand over hers to try to comfort her. Loving her was easy. Keeping her safe was proving to be something else altogether.

Savage had always thought that because it was easy for anyone to see he was the kind of man no one ever fucked with, he would never have a problem with anyone threatening his woman—not unless his club went to war. It had never occurred to him that if he did find a woman who would put up with his proclivities, she would have the kind of voice that would compel men to be obsessed. When he agreed to her singing with the band, the only thing he'd worried about was her gift of healing. Never once had he worried that those hearing her voice might hear the lure of a siren's call.

He turned off the highway to once more take a road that led toward the ocean and the very back side of Caspar. Slowing the motorcycle as he drove along the thick stone wall that surrounded part of the estate, he pressed the button on his key chain to open the gate so that when he approached, they could just ride through.

The estate was behind iron gates set between thick stone pillars. At the end of a long drive, the house had the luxury of an ocean view on two sides, as well as landscaping and woods on the other two sides. Savage felt protected and away from everyone. There was plenty of space between the house and the trees, so no one could just creep up on him, not to mention he had put in a state-of-the-art security system.

The house was elegant and built solid. It was an A-frame house, with forty-inch beams in the south section and thirty-five-inch beams in the north part. Savage liked the height of the ceilings. He liked space, and the house gave the feeling of that with twenty-five-foot ceilings.

He rode up the long drive to a carport that was in front of the garage. Again, he opened the door to the garage from his key chain so he could ride straight in and park. Seychelle sat there in silence for so long he didn't think she'd get off. He waited. Not saying a word. Letting her think about it. Finally, she put one hand on his shoulder and swung off, removing her helmet. She stood there waiting while he joined her.

Savage put his arm around her and walked her out of the four-car garage so she could look at the house. The estate was eight and a half acres. Complete privacy, something he needed at all times. Something they both would need. They were surrounded by beauty and serenity. It really was an exceptional piece of property.

"I bought the place recently. Czar wanted all of us to put down roots here. I wasn't sure it was worth me buying a house, but I liked this one for a lot of reasons. When I met you, I called the agent up and asked him if it was still on the market. You don't like it, you just say so, Seychelle. We'll sell it and find one you do like."

He walked her around to the impressive front. The entire façade was made of cobblestone. The front door wasn't just any front door. It was huge. Custom-made. Thick wood, twice the normal size and arched. She stood silently staring at it and then looked back at him. Her eyes were wide. Very blue. She looked a little shocked.

"You really bought this house, Savage?"

"Yes." He reached around her to unlock the door using a series of numbers on the keypad. "I knew it would be perfect for us. But, like I said, you don't like it, we'll get something else. It's three bedrooms, four bathrooms. The master bedroom is just about everything we could want. I love the decks and the views." He found himself smiling. "I sound a little like the real estate agent."

"Maybe a little," she admitted.

Savage took her hand as he opened the door. She was trembling. He really wanted her to like the house. It was nearly five thousand square feet of space if you didn't count the outside decks, just the inside living quarters. He liked space. He even needed it.

The door opened to reveal the living room with the teak

plank floors from Indonesia. The fireplace was impressive, massive, made of stone, and went from hearth to ceiling. Three enormous arched windows provided the tranquility of the ocean from one long panoramic view and one side observation. Like most of the high-end houses in the area with a lot of glass, the windows were self-cleaning, a must for a man like him. He didn't want a lot of people around, even housekeepers. The furniture Lana had chosen for him included two low-slung leather couches, wide and slouchy, very comfortable, inviting, in a dark charcoal to go with the stone on the fireplace. There were two matching armchairs as well.

The living room opened onto a deck, as did several of the other rooms. The master bedroom had its own private deck and courtyard. The decks were wide and covered, with ornate posts rising every four feet to the roof from the railing. They were solid just like the house. There were no neighbors, and he could bring Seychelle outside with him when the mood struck him. When the sea was as turbulent as he felt.

The rooms inside were all warm wood or thick carpet, with high ceilings and gas fireplaces. The bathrooms were spacious and had heated tiles along with deep tubs and very large showers. The kitchen was large and boasted top-of-the-line appliances and marble countertops. There was a long island in the center of the enormous space. The kitchen opened into the breakfast nook and dining room but also out onto the deck.

She stood in the center of the dining room, looking around her without speaking.

He threaded his fingers through hers, his thumb sliding over the back of her hand as he led her out to the deck. "You don't like the house."

She tilted her head up to his immediately. "I *love* the house. I love the location. It's beautiful here, Savage. How could I not love it?"

He brought her knuckles to his mouth and kissed her

gently. "Tell me what's wrong, then. I brought you here because I thought you would want to see something special. I bought the house for you because to me, you're this special. Gorgeous. Like this spot. This house. If I could have found something more spectacular for you, I would have." It was true. He'd give her the moon if he could—if that was what she wanted.

She gave him a little half smile. "When I'm nervous, I fall back on the things that are familiar to me. My house. My bed. Where I like to sit, where my crystals line up."

"Why are you nervous, baby? I know you're upset over Shari, but I'm not sure why. I thought we put that bitch to bed." He did his best not to growl. That would come later, when he was enumerating her sins. Right now, this was her turn. He was listening to any concerns she had.

She tugged at her hand until he reluctantly let go. "I feel more in control in my own home," she admitted. "I can talk to you about anything."

He didn't take his eyes from hers. "It shouldn't matter where we are, Seychelle. You should feel as if you can talk to me about anything anyplace. What did I do to make you feel as if you couldn't?"

She bit at her lower lip and then frowned. "I'm just more comfortable talking about difficult subjects in my bed with you." She sat on the wide railing, one hand on the column. The wind caught at her hair, blowing it around her face. "Shari had a few interesting things to say to me tonight."

Savage forced himself to stay silent. Shari was a huge thorn that didn't seem as if it was ever going to go away.

"She said I wouldn't be able to satisfy you because I had no idea what I was doing. And actually, she's right. I don't know what I'm doing, and that sucks." Her lashes fluttered.

Those long feathery lashes that got him in his cock every time. She looked so utterly vulnerable when her lashes swept down like that. He wished they were on her bed as well, where he could stroke his hand down her bare leg.

"I could feel you taking on Alena's pain when Pierce came in. You somehow bled the worst of it away so she could function. I doubt she's aware of it."

Savage wanted to shut that topic of conversation down fast. There was pain in her voice. Real awareness. She knew without a single doubt that he took on Alena's pain. Alena's righteous anger and rage at the childhood traumas were too much for her at times, so he took it on. It was impossible to continue to handle betrayal after betrayal after the childhood Alena had suffered. Savage was aware Alena was so very fragile deep inside, where no one could see beneath that thin shell she presented to the world. The cool, beautiful woman always in control. That woman wasn't real.

He didn't want Seychelle to resent Alena, or to ever tell Seychelle that she would suffer physical pain because he took on Alena's emotional pain. That would break Alena's heart. That would totally break Alena. Damage her beyond repair. He had never wanted to put his fellow members of Torpedo Ink, his brothers and sisters, into anyone else's hands—yet he had.

Seychelle was aware of one of his psychic talents—the one that made him feel worthwhile, worthy of living, when he was such a monster. He had spent so many years working on perfecting his ability, making his talent strong so he could help the others without their knowledge, the only real contribution he felt he could make that kept him human and showed them he loved them. They wouldn't ever know—but he would.

"I thought it was so beautiful what you gave her. What you did for her, Savage." She turned her head away from him, but not before he caught the sheen of tears. She blinked several times. "That's real love. I felt it on the notes. I can feel emotion on the notes I sing. I know that sounds insane, but I can. You love her so much. And you took all that pain for her, and it came through with such love." Her voice trembled, and she dashed at the tears on her face.

Savage wanted to gather her in his arms. He stepped closer to her, forcing her knees apart so he could wedge his hips between her legs, but he merely rested his palms on her thighs. Seychelle had something to say, and she took her time getting things out. He had to learn to let her say her piece.

"I loved you so much in that moment. I loved you so much it hurt, and I knew then, just knowing what you do, that I would have the courage to face that same thing for you, because I love you that much." She turned her head and looked at him, her gaze perfectly steady. "It isn't that I'm just physically attracted to you. I love who you are inside. I can see you. Sometimes I see you when you can't. But I know I don't know how to do the things that you're going to need. Just feeling what you were doing, I realized there really is a time frame, and what if I'm not ready? Just like last time?" There was a little sob in her voice. "I couldn't bear it if you went to someone else because I didn't know what I was doing, Savage."

He captured her face between his hands. "Baby, we've had this conversation. I told you, there will never be another woman for me. Never. It isn't going to happen. You're going to be all I ever need, and I'll be the same for you. We'll do this together." He poured absolute conviction into his voice. Deliberately, he used his dominant tone, velvet over steel, low and certain. His thumb moved gently over her lips. "I don't like that you don't have confidence in me. Or yourself. Or us."

"It's the time frame. I don't know how to learn the things you need faster, Savage. I've never even . . ." She broke off, her gaze dropping to his cock.

"You're doing just fine, Seychelle. You let me worry about what you need to learn and when. As far as you taking my cock down your throat, if that's what that bitch was taunting you with, the truth is, baby, I never took them any other way. I never used my own whips on them. It was too intimate. I never kissed them. I never put my marks, my patterns, on their backs or their fronts. I put stripes on them, and I fucked their mouths. I got my release and got them off with my hand and I got the hell out. I told you I wasn't a nice man."

Savage bent his head and brushed kisses over her eyes and then her lips. Tender. Soft little kisses. He straightened and pushed back her hair. "You're my woman. You're the one I'm intimate with. To everyone else it might be a fucked-up kind of intimacy, but it's ours. And every time I touch you, I'm saying I love you. No other woman can ever say that. I hope you feel it when I touch you, whether it's with my hand or with my whip."

He felt the little shiver that went through her body. He trailed one hand from her throat down the curves of her generous breasts to her nipples. "When I clamp you, or have my mouth or teeth on you, I hope you feel how much I love you, because I'm showing you."

She nodded her head, but her fingers were plucking nervously at the hem of her shirt. He stilled them.

"Baby, you have to stop worrying that we aren't going to be ready. I have you. Since the first day I met you I started getting you ready." He caught her restless hand and pulled her fingers to his mouth, biting down until her eyes went wide. He sucked at the stinging flesh until her eyes went dark and her lips parted.

"You have?"

He nodded. "It's always been you. *Always*. Ask any of the others in the club. I've never looked at another woman and wanted to claim her for my own. I don't necessarily think that makes you lucky, baby, but when I say I'm in a hundred percent, I mean it. I don't cheat. I don't lie. I'm loyal to you. I don't want you to let someone like Shari shake your confidence."

She leaned toward him and rested her forehead against his chest. "Alena's pain was visceral. There was so much. I could feel the others and the rage they felt because this man was causing her pain. They couldn't even feel how deep her emotion went, not like you. They couldn't tell what you were doing. I knew then that we were going to be on a very short timetable and it was going to be me slowing us down, causing you to carry that load much longer than necessary."

His heart stuttered in his chest. *Bog*, every time he thought it was impossible to love her any more, she said or did something like that and he was overwhelmed with emotion for her. Swamped with it. So much he could barely breathe. He knew rage. He knew pain. He hadn't known anything could be so good.

He caught the hair at the nape of her neck in his fist and pulled her head back so she was forced to meet his eyes. "We're on exactly the right timetable, Seychelle. You let me worry about what you need to know. I'm the one teaching you. Understand?"

Those long lashes fluttered, putting resolution in his heart and knots in his gut. She did him in so easily.

"Yes. I just want you to know I'm with you, Savage. I think I could do better at home. I'm not so nervous."

"Nervous is good. You should be nervous," he pointed out. "Are you finished? Did we cover everything you needed to say to me? Everything you were worried about?" Reluctantly, he released her hair.

"I should be nervous?" she echoed.

"Answer me first. I want to know we took care of everything you were concerned with."

Her eyes went wide. "Yes." She slid off the railing and leaned against it.

He paced away from her, taking a breath. "Baby, I think I explained the rules to you, right? We went over them very carefully, and why they were in place. I'm the kind of man who needs to be in control at all times. It's dangerous for me to be out of control. I have to be calm in every situation. I've never had problems with that before. My brothers say I have ice flowing in my veins." He turned to face her and gave her a faint smile, one that didn't reach his eyes. "The thought of you in danger throws me into a nightmare situation."

Her brows drew together as if she had no idea where he was going with what he was saying, which only took him up a notch higher. He took a deep breath and let it out.

"Tell me, babe, what exactly were you doing when Doris and Campbell went to visit you? Mechanic sent me a video. You were playing both of them, using your voice on Doris to counteract his. And you were deliberately egging that bastard on, letting him see you weren't falling for his shit." Instead of looking at her as if her answer meant something, Savage stared at the turbulent waves crashing against the boulders and sea stacks.

"Brandon Campbell keeps visiting Doris, and he's doing it on purpose as a threat to me." Seychelle leaned over the railing, her body close to his. Her hair blew around her face, the thick strands of platinum-and-gold-colored hair covering her expression. "He's telling me he can control Doris the way he did Sahara. I made certain to take Doris back and clear her mind so his stupid, pitiful voice doesn't work on her."

A surge of fear welled up like an eruption of a volcano, hot and massive, spewing adrenaline through his body, laced with a rage. Savage fought it down, although he had the urge to take one of her wrists and tie it to that column she was holding on to and then stretch her other arm to the other column. She needed a good lesson in making herself a target without her man to protect her.

"Did it occur to you that all he had to do was talk to Doris again when you weren't around and make suggestions for her to harm herself?"

Seychelle turned around to face him, her back to the railing, that particular stance causing her breasts to thrust right at him. She looked inviting. Too inviting. She gave him a little smug smile. "He can try, but it won't work. His little parlor trick of a voice doesn't hold a candle to mine. Once I found his exact sequence of notes, I was able to counter it easily. He won't be able to make suggestions to Doris or in any way influence her against me or anyone else."

Savage couldn't resist drawing a line with his fingertip from her chin down her throat between the valley of her breasts. She shivered, and her nipples grew into hard little pebbles for him. Her eyes went dark and remained steady on his.

"You wanted him to see that you took Sahara from him, didn't you?"

"I wish I could have taken Sahara completely from him. I tried. If I'd had more time with her, I could have. But she is safe, as long as her parents can keep her away, and then time will do the rest. He had so much time to ruin her. To get in her head. He's evil, Savage."

"Exactly, Seychelle." He held out his hand to her. She took it immediately. No hesitation. "He was in the bar. Watching you."

"I saw him. I suspect he's influencing Shari. I was trying to figure that out when she was talking to me outside."

Savage's gut knotted even more. "Did it occur to you that he's a vindictive little shit and that he's likely to come after you?" He stepped inside the house and took her with him.

"I'm not susceptible to his voice, and other than that, he's a coward, Savage. He doesn't really have any other weapons."

"He's a vindictive shit," he repeated and took her straight to the master bedroom.

SIXTEEN

The master suite was everything Savage could possibly want. He would have bought the house for that alone. He had wanted a room with a lot of space, one where he could see the ocean from nearly every angle. If not the wild sea, then the woods surrounding the privacy of the courtyard off the master suite. The bedroom, sitting room and master bath had everything he could possibly want and more.

The bedroom was enormous, the walls a textured seaweed in a muted sage color. The ceilings were high, with those same beams running throughout the house. The wood floor gleamed, but he had thick rugs in various places, including in front of the long in-wall gas fireplace. A padded bench was placed near the bed, carved from a dark cherrywood, the cover a deep royal-blue leather.

Three long curved stairs led down to the sitting area, another huge space where the walls of glass gave such a view of the sea. A royal-blue leather divan was placed facing inward, the head toward the window, foot toward the center of the room. A post rose from the floor at the head of the divan with several metal rings attached. There were two shorter posts on either side with rings at the end. A wide railing made of the same cherrywood as the spanking bench was curved around one bank of windows, the same thick royal-blue leather over the top of it.

There were so many little touches for him, so many discoveries for his woman. He couldn't wait to show them all to Seychelle. She was exhausted, and they had to get certain things out of the way before she could go to bed.

"We talked about the things that upset you, baby. I listened to every word. It's very important that you pay close attention to me now."

Her head went up alertly, sensing she was on dangerous ground.

"I told you not to leave the bar and the safety of the club members, Seychelle. Do you recall me saying that to you?" He kept his voice very low. A whisper of command. He saw the shiver go through her.

She bit her lower lip and nodded, avoiding his eyes.

"I require an answer, and look at me when you do." He poured steel into that. When he did, his cock responded. His body knew what was coming. He was already getting aroused just by being in the room with his woman and his personal toys.

"Yes."

"You had to have realized I would have come to you immediately if I wasn't still working. By going outside, where two obsessed Diamondbacks followed you—as well as Brandon Campbell and Joseph Arnold, who was in the bushes taking pictures of you—you divided my attention. Instead of doing the job I was supposed to do, I found myself worrying about my woman. If for some reason Alena was targeted and I had to protect her, I might have been too slow, and she could have gotten killed."

Her breath caught in her throat. "I'm sorry, Savage. I just

stepped outside for the fresh air. I've never gone that long without a break."

"You could have stepped into one of the back rooms. Fatei wasn't happy, and he must have expressed that to you." He could tell by her face that the man had. "You don't get to ignore or override whoever I put on you to look after you like that, Seychelle. They're there to protect you while I'm working." He kept his voice controlled.

Seychelle didn't pull away from him or slow down at all when he took her to the side of the bed. She had to know what was coming. They'd been there before. He'd warned her that the next time, he wasn't going to be quite so nice about it. His cock throbbed and ached with the strain of anticipation. Outside, the roar of the pounding sea added to the fierce, hot blood rushing through his veins.

"It wasn't fair to ignore Fatei when he was just following my orders. You put him in a bad situation. If the Diamondbacks had insisted on coming after you, he would have had to defend you, and what do you think would have happened then?"

"I'm sorry, Savage. I didn't think about any of that. I'll apologize to him."

"Then there's Shari. You continually put yourself in a position of having to deal with her. I told you we would get rid of her, but you said it wasn't a problem. You could have gone back into the bar, but you didn't. You deliberately decided to confront her. Again, Fatei tried, very gently, to get you to go into the bar . . ."

Her chin went up and her eyes flashed fire at him. "I refuse to retreat in front of that woman. She would gloat and think I was afraid of her."

He caught her chin, deliberately clamping down hard between his finger and thumb. "Perhaps you do need to be a little more afraid of me than I thought. Better that than put every member of our club in danger. Shari is nothing at all, and you know it. That isn't the real reason you decided to confront her. This was about Brandon Campbell. Once again, you were putting yourself in harm's way. You stay away from Campbell. You ignore Shari. Do you understand me? She won't be welcome in our bar, but if she comes around you again, you walk away without even looking at her."

His eyes refused to allow hers to look away. He held her gaze until her defiance melted and she nodded.

"Good." He leaned down and took her mouth. Gently. Tenderly. Loving her. *Bog*, love swamped him, wrapped him up until he felt as if he were drowning in it. She rained fire on him. In him. The flames rushed through his veins. His palms shaped her face when he lifted his head.

"I really did find this house some time ago but passed on it. What was the point, when I didn't have anyone that I could share it with? I was so damn sure I would never have anyone. I thought the house would just mock me if I kept it empty. When you came back from your trip that scared the shit out of me, I ended up calling the agent, took one look, imagined you here with me and had to have it."

One hand slid from her cheek to her throat, just lying across it to feel her heartbeat to see if it was going as crazy as his. "You're going to strip and put your clothes on the end table and then stand right there and wait for me. I'm going to give you another lesson in sinful, dirty sex. Tomorrow, when you're not so tired, maybe I'll teach you to crave the fire, baby."

She pressed her lips together and a shiver went through her body, but she didn't hesitate. She unbuttoned the little shells on her blouse and let the garment slip from her shoulders, folding it carefully and placing it on the end table before reaching behind her and unhooking her bra, spilling her tits out. They were firm and round with those perfect nipples, drawing his instant attention. She was tormenting him almost beyond his control.

His breath caught in his lungs and just stayed there at the erotic sight of her. "Keep stripping, baby."

Seychelle's hands dropped to the waistband of her jeans, and she slowly opened them and began peeling them off her hips, taking her panties with them.

His hands moved up her ribs, fingers tracing each one, finding the path to the undersides of her breasts. "Love the shape of you. I can wrap leather around your tit so nicely. One stroke. One easy curl. Do you have any idea what that would feel like? Or on your gorgeous ass? I can write my name. Lay the sun on your back."

Seychelle reacted with goose bumps forming on her body. Her legs moved restlessly.

He swept his hand over her bare mound. "Right here, I would mark you with my initials." His fingers traveled lower to feather over her clit and her entrance, already slick with heat and her golden liquid cream. Yeah, she wanted what he did. He took her hand and pressed it over the thick bulge stretching the material of his jeans. "Just the thought of it makes me harder than hell."

She moistened her lips with the tip of her tongue, her eyes on his, never looking away. "How do you do that, Savage?" Her voice was low, intrigued, already husky with need. "Make me want you so much I can barely think."

"I can teach you to love the feel of fire. Do you want to try tomorrow? It's early. Advanced. We can go easy, try something else. Something with just a different type of leather." He almost couldn't breathe waiting for her answer. He *needed* now. That fast, she'd seduced him into needing the whip. Made him want. Lust. Fuck, he couldn't lie to himself. He was desperate to have his partner fully in his world, but she had to consent, she had to want it. "With the crop. Keep building you up to it."

He bent his head and took her left tit into his mouth, pulling strong, loving the weight of it, the softness, the way she instantly cradled his head. His tongue slid over her nipple and teased and rolled with expert care. He lifted his gaze to hers and then let go. "Anything I do to you, I'm worshipping you. Not just your body, Seychelle. You. I want you to feel it. Do you?"

She nodded. "Last night when you woke me a million times, each time, each way, fast, slow, it didn't matter, it felt like worshipping."

He had been worshipping her. He kissed her chin. That little chin she liked to stick out at him sometimes. "I'm glad you felt it, baby. I do worship you. That's not ever going to be a secret, not to anyone who knows me. That's why it's so important that you stick close to me. I've got enemies, Seychelle. Torpedo Ink has enemies, but I personally have them too."

"You told me. I understand. I'm not going to go back on my word. You'll know where I am, and if you say I need to stick close, I will."

"You gotta learn that lesson, baby. Not just pay lip service to it. I tell you to stay put, you have to do it."

Savage cupped her breasts, his thumbs strumming her nipples. He loved them. The color, the way they stood out. The way she shivered for him and pushed into his hand. He tugged. Rolled. Pinched and then bit down just a little harder with his fingers and thumbs, watching her eyes darken. Watching the way the breath rushed from her lungs. He let go and leaned his head down to soothe the sting with his tongue.

"If something ever happens to me, Seychelle, you stick with Torpedo Ink. You have to let them watch over you. What you're learning. This thing we're doing together. It won't go away. You understand that, right?" He lapped at her right breast while he kneaded her left one, then took it into his mouth, still gently. Tenderly.

"You told me."

He lifted his head. "Telling you isn't you understanding." She was right. They were going to run out of time if he didn't get down to business and work her body up to accepting what she could handle. There was so much. So many things. Depending on how bad it was, the level he got to when the monster emerged, he needed her body to get used to mixing pain and pleasure, because when that time came, she would need the training desperately.

"You're absolutely certain, Seychelle?" He needed for her to give her consent. She had to be a willing participant. That was what made it all the more exciting to him—that Seychelle *wanted* to give herself to him, to allow him to whip her when she knew it would cause her pain and yet bring her multiple orgasms. Her dilemma. How long would she hold on for him? How long would she wait before she said *enough*? She'd never once stopped the hard spankings with his hands. Or the leather belt. The strap. Or the clamps. But he'd been relatively gentle.

"I'm certain."

"I have a little surprise for you. I know how much you love clamps." He tugged on her nipples. "You have the perfect nipples for them. I love your tits so damn much. They're perfect for jewelry. You were made for me. For everything I love and need. Stay right here. Don't move."

He waited until she complied before he went to the dresser and removed a pair of black drawstring pants. Shedding his clothes, he donned just the black pants. They gave him more room and were far more comfortable. There was a tall wooden cabinet built into the wall against the window. He pulled open the top drawer and selected a long black box. He carried it back to her.

"Ice is a jeweler—a rather famous one. When I said he was making a ring for you, I wasn't kidding around. He made these clamps at my request as well. I have several different ones for you, but these are beautiful, and I think they go with my mood right now." He lifted them out of the box to show her.

Seychelle's eyes went wide and then dark with arousal. She definitely had a thing with clamps, although he didn't think she would fall in love with this set right away. They were beautiful. The clips were heavy pieces of teardrop black metal, ornate and inlaid with sparkling teardrop gems.

"These are clover clamps. These aren't adjustable, baby, they just pinch down on your nipples the way I pinch them or bite them, a steady, relentless pressure." As he talked to her, he stroked her left breast, his cock going so hot he thought it might burst into flames. "The pressure is steady at all times, or increases when the chain is pulled or there are weights on the clip. See, I can add weights in the form of these beautiful gems Ice created."

He lifted the various chains of diamonds and sapphires and emeralds out of the box so he could hold them up. They swung invitingly. "You'll look so beautiful with jewelry on. And when it comes off, it will be such a rush. You'll want to scream for me to fuck you. But we have one rule, don't we? You never scream. You can give me your tears. Those are mine and I want them, but you don't scream, not unless you're coming, and you don't do that until I tell you it's the right time."

She ducked her head. "I'm not very good at controlling that, Savage. My body takes over and I can't stop."

"You're learning. I'll help you more." He kept stroking her breast as he replaced the chains of gems in the box. Those were for later. "Right now, we'll be fine with just a chain between the clamps. Later, one will go to your clit. You'll love that sensation as well."

The thought of what was to come was giving him such a rush it was incredible. He realized the combination of love and lust was intensifying the feelings he had. He let them take him as he put his mouth on her, pulling strongly, his tongue working her nipple, preparing her for the wicked bite of the clover clamp. There were so many sensitive nerve endings just waiting to be stimulated. He used his teeth to bite down and then pulled back so he could apply the clamp. He watched her expression closely as the two ends of the clamp tried to meet.

Her breath hissed out in a soft protest. "That's painful."

"Is it?" His voice was that same sinful tone, a soft inquiry. He kept one hand on her other breast, stroking. His other hand was on her hip. He slid it around until his fingers found her bare pussy lips and the moisture gathering there. "I think you like them, baby. You're hot and slick for me." He poured approval and heat into his voice.

Deliberately, as he put his mouth around her nipple, he pushed one finger into her, deep, curling it as he stroked and then brushed her clit with his thumb. Helplessly, she began to ride his hand, trying to get ahead of the fiery sensations generated by the clamp on her breast. It wasn't long before the two sensations mixed together and her breathing was ragged, her body flushed. He bit down and pulled back, clamping the other breast. Her eyes went liquid, and she rode his hand frantically before she realized movement could cause the clamps to pinch tighter.

"Do you remember your first lesson in dirty, sinful sex? I bought a toy just like yours. I want you to lie across the padded bench." He indicated the spanking bench with the thick leather cover. "Your breasts will hang down, the gold chain dangling. That will make things very interesting for you. I want you to keep that toy positioned right over your clit. You keep the power on low unless I tell you to turn it up. Do you understand? The first infraction, baiting Brandon Campbell, gets my hand. The second one is a huge infraction. Leaving the bar when I was working deserves the strap. If we were further along in our relationship, Seychelle, you would be getting more than that. Walk over to the bench and bend over it. Take the toy and do what I told you."

He made it a command, and she didn't hesitate. His Seychelle. Shoulders straight back, her eyes giving him a sweeping look of liquid blue, she walked to the bench, the toy in her hand. Her body was pure poetry. Her hips swayed. Her breasts bounced with every step. The chain rocked. The clamps had to pinch tighter. That was how they worked. Her ass beckoned, a siren's call. His temptress.

When she bent over, he could see her pretty little pussy

gleaming at him. All that moisture taunting him, that blank canvas calling to him to decorate it. He smacked her hard, sending the first jolt through her body with his bare palm. He liked skin on skin. It felt personal. Intimate. She didn't make a sound, but she started to pull away from the bench. He didn't have to correct her; she stayed down. He worked her buttocks and the backs of her thighs, turning them a dark red. Then he reached for the thick leather strap he'd put to the side.

He rubbed her bottom, dipping into her cream and pressing into the forbidden star between her cheeks. He kept rubbing to spread the heat over her bottom and into the bundles of nerves, so it would be impossible for her to know if she was feeling pain or pleasure. The two sensations would mix together so easily, heightening the erotic feeling.

"You're so beautiful, baby," he murmured, meaning it. "I don't know why the universe gave you to me, but I swear I'm going to do everything in my power to keep you."

He pressed kisses over her very red bottom, his heart beating hard as he picked up the strap and moved around her. His cock ached. Hurt. Was becoming a problem. He fucking loved that after years of having to command his cock to work, it was suddenly working all by itself just fine. *She* had done that for him. She'd fixed his broken cock.

Barefoot, he walked around the bench until he was directly in front of her. Grasping her hair in one hand, he pulled her head back. There were tears streaming down her face like a path of jewels. Diamonds. He took her mouth hungrily. There it was. She kissed like she fucked. Pure fire. Giving him everything. Pure sin.

"*Bog*, baby." He licked up her right cheek, collecting her tears even as he tugged on the chain gently. "I'm so fuckin' proud of you. You should see yourself. So gorgeous." He took every tear from her left side. "You aren't going to disobey me when I tell you to stay put again, are you?" Deliberately, he kept her chin up with the heavy leather strap, waiting for her eyes to meet his.

"No." Her voice came out a small sob.

"Do you want to stop?"

With the flat strap of leather, he massaged the curves of her breasts, patting gently. Twice he hit the chain where it swung free between her breasts, tugging at it. Her breath hissed out, but her eyes continued to meet his.

"No. I don't want to stop."

"You can turn your toy up to medium, but don't you dare come. If you get too close, you stop, turn it off, do you understand me?"

"Yes."

He took his time, walking silently around behind her, admiring her body. She really was beautiful, physically and in every other way. He loved that she was his. That she wanted to be his. That she gave herself freely to him. He was training her body to enjoy the things he was doing to her, mixing pain with pleasure, and she was aware of it, giving that to him as well.

The shape of her ass was perfection to him, her bare cheeks presented, darkened with his handprints. His hand slipped over her cheeks, rubbing and massaging gently, sliding to her slick entrance to dip his fingers into her heat and draw out her moisture.

"You're so wet, baby. You love this, don't you? It feels so good." He pumped his fingers into her, let her ride them while her toy worked her clit. He pulled his fingers free slowly and painted the crease between her cheeks with the thick moisture, pushing it over and over into her forbidden little star. "Remember I told you we were going for sinful and dirty, baby?"

Savage began to push the vibrating plug, the one he'd coated with cinnamon gel, into her tight little hole. She moaned softly, started to writhe, but the clamps tightened and she stopped abruptly. When the plug was fully seated, he stepped back and used his foot to widen her stance. He studied her for a moment, just drinking in the sight of her. He took his foot and widened her stance even more, needing to see her hot little pussy, now so wet she was almost dripping.

He struck with the strap without warning and didn't let up, putting a little muscle into it, decorating the backs of her thighs, the seam where her buttocks and thighs met, and then striping her buttocks, first horizontally and then vertically. He didn't put a single mark on her spine or back. Her sobs increased, her body shuddering.

"Let go, Seychelle, ride the pain. Let it take you."

He kept the steady rhythm going, using the strap on her skin, watching the heat blossom, the red turn to purple. She didn't make a sound, but her body jolted with each movement, and he knew what the mixture of pleasure and pain was doing to her, jumbling the brain, confusing her ideas of what felt good or bad until they were mixed together beyond her comprehension.

He tossed the strap aside, took the toy from her hand and threw it onto the bed. She remained bent over the bench, breathing hard, crying quietly. Savage shed his pants, his cock raging at him. He caught her arms and very gently helped her into a standing position.

"You did so good, baby. I'm so proud of you. What do you need? Tell me. Say it. Say it, Seychelle."

"I need you to fuck me, Savage. I hurt."

"You hurt so good," he replied, his tone sheer velvet. A sin. Teaching her. Training her. He walked her backward until she was against the wall. He circled his cock, so hard and thick, desperate to be in her, but holding it out to her in temptation. "You need my cock, don't you, baby?"

She reached up and circled her arms around his neck, one leg sliding around his waist, pressing her swollen, inflamed, very needy pussy against him. "I do." Her tears continued to track down her face. "Savage."

"You have to say it, Seychelle."

"I need your cock." She whispered it to him, a confession of truth.

He picked her up without preamble. "Wrap your legs around my waist, baby." He didn't wait. His cock was a monster and she was slick and hot. He drove into her, all but slamming her into the wall. She was tight, a scorching furnace wrapping him in a silken fist, and he began pounding into her. Her hands clutched his shoulders, fingernails biting deep into his skin, then tearing down his back as she tried for purchase so she could use him for leverage to impale herself as deep as she could get him.

"Harder. More," she whispered. "I'm so close. Make me go over."

"Not yet," he denied her. "You wait until I say. It's going to be so intense, a rush like you won't believe, baby. I promised you sinful. You're getting nothing less than spectacular. You deserve it, Seychelle, and I can give it to you." He pounded into her, over and over, his cock a hot friction, a piston, sawing over the bundle of inflamed nerves. He kept thrusting, watching her face, feeling her body coil tighter and tighter.

Reaching down, he suddenly tugged off the clamp on her right breast fast. As the blood rushed to her nipple, he shifted position just enough to ensure his cock hit the perfect spot inside her, and he kicked up the remote on the plug in her forbidden star while his finger thumped her clit hard. Her eyes went wide in shock.

"Now, baby. Come for me now."

Her mouth opened in a scream as a powerful orgasm swept through her, taking her over, ripping through her entire body in a merciless, seemingly endless series of tidal waves.

He kept pounding into her right through the tsunami, then gentled as the sensations lessened after a time. He leaned down to lick at her red, hot, sore nipple. "Intense, and such a rush, right, baby? You fucking loved that. I could tell. You're so perfect. You were born for me, but even more importantly, I was born for you."

Savage began to move in her again, watching not just the

chain on her breast swing; now the clamp he had released was swinging as well. The remaining clamp would tighten unless Seychelle could hold herself still. She became aware of the problem and tried to stay motionless, letting him do the work, but his cock was a monster, thick and long, invading her tight tunnel, the friction merciless.

Her body responded in spite of the wild, out-of-control orgasm she'd just experienced, already coiling hotter and tighter. He could feel her tight muscles gripping him like a fist, trying to milk him, desperate for his seed. He had left the vibrator on between her cheeks, keeping those forbidden nerve endings fired up. He slapped her bottom hard and then raked his fingernails across her cheeks.

Her breath hissed out. Ragged. Rushed. The liquid in her eyes put even more steel in his cock. He thought he might explode between the love and lust rising in him, threatening to overwhelm him. She'd wrapped herself around his heart so fast he hadn't known what hit him. She gave him everything. He hadn't yet earned that, but she gave it to him anyway.

His hips surged into hers, a ruthless machine, pounding out his love, his need of her total surrender, of her gift to him. The feeling was indescribable, moving through his body like an incomparable drug, rushing through his veins, a fire that built and built in intensity. Her body reacted, that silken fist tightening, twisting, tonguing and gripping his cock greedily. Her hips began to frantically reach for his, catching his rhythm, pulling back to come in just as hard so they came together in a mad rush of heated, frenzied fucking.

Seychelle's generous breasts jolted wildly with every frantic thrust, the jewelry swinging in a tangled symphony, causing a fresh flood of liquid to track down her face even as she begged him for more. She chanted his name, pleading mindlessly.

"What do you want, baby?" he murmured, watching her

closely again. That face. So close to ecstasy. He could send her flying, give her body and her mind the need for his cock, for him, for what he could do for her anytime she hurt. She would turn to him automatically and know he would be there for her.

"You, Savage. I need you."

"You want me to send you flying again, baby? You want that intense rush? So good, only I can give it to you? You ready for that?" He increased his pace. Hard. Sawing deliberately over that sweet spot. Again and again. Watching her face. The need building in her. The desperation.

He yanked the clamp from her left nipple, letting the jewelry fall away as he hit the remote, increasing the vibrator even as he thumped her clit hard. Simultaneously, he gave her the order. The command she always had to associate with him. The pleasure *he* gave her. "Now, Seychelle. Let go."

He slammed his swelling cock into her, over and over, hard and fast, pushing her over the edge as the blood rushed back into her nipple. Her body clamped down on his like a vise, strangling him, pumping. Milking. Squeezing. Even as the tears ran down her face. The sensation was somewhere between heaven and hell. There was nothing like loving her. No experience he'd ever had rivaled it.

Her orgasm should have waned, but it seemed to intensify as his hot seed coated the walls of her channel. The scorching fist pumped, while a million hot mouths sucked greedily in unison, determined to squeeze every last drop from him. His entire body seemed to go up in flames. She screamed, the sound definitely one of pleasure, a ragged calling of his name. For a moment they were locked together so tight, Savage knew they belonged. It wasn't just their bodies. It was something far deeper.

She sagged against him, her head dropping on his shoulder, her body shaking uncontrollably, hot tears flowing into his skin. Her legs wrapped around him as tightly as her arms, as if she was afraid that if she let him go, she'd be lost. Savage turned his head and brushed kisses along her temple.

His legs had turned to rubber, but he held her carefully, murmuring softly to her. "I've got you, baby. You're safe. I've got you." He kissed the side of her face. Sipped at her tears. His breath came in raw, ragged rushes, but he forced himself to pull in air. To take care of her. She was the most important thing in his world.

Seychelle had done every single thing he'd asked. Given him everything. Her complete surrender. She'd taken his hand and the strap, and he hadn't been gentle. She'd learned her orgasms came from him. She was beyond any partner he had ever imagined. Savage hadn't known he was capable of feeling tenderness, but she definitely brought that emotion out in him.

Seychelle was shaking almost uncontrollably. Certain she couldn't stand on her own, he eased her back against the wall and bent his head to her sore nipple, licking at it with exquisite tenderness. "I'm right here, baby. I've got you. You're flying too high. Come back to me." He kept his voice low, a velvet enticement, as he kissed his way back up her throat to her face to collect her tears. "I've got you. I'll always have you."

"Don't let go of me, Savage." There was real fear in her voice. She circled her arms around his shoulders, linking her fingers behind his neck, shaking so hard he was afraid she might go to pieces against him.

"Angel, I'm not going anywhere. I'm right here with you. Let me get you to a chair. I've got to take that plug out and wrap you up, then I'll hold you close." He kissed his way up her neck and behind her ear, talking softly to her, reassuring her with the sound of his voice, bringing her down gently.

With one hand, he reached around her and managed to find the plug nestled between her cheeks. "I'm going to pull this out, baby." He had no idea where he'd tossed the remote, and the damn thing was still vibrating. He tugged. She shuddered in his arms, then gasped when her breasts slid over his chest, her nipples pressing tightly against him. "Shh, I've got you," he murmured over and over in reassurance.

Once he knew he had his legs under him, he shifted her in his arms, allowing his cock to slide out of her. The movement triggered a series of aftershocks to ripple through her body. She moaned, her mouth against him, teeth biting into his shoulder as he lifted her, cradling her against him.

Savage carried her to the wide chair in front of the large window overlooking the view of the ocean. Waves rushed toward the bluffs, a turbulent wall of dark blue water, pounding them. White spray rose into the night sky like diamond drops—or crystal tears. He had a warm throw on the back of the chair, and he wrapped it around both of them and settled into the chair, Seychelle on his lap, cuddling her protectively.

He smoothed his hand over her hair and rocked her gently until the storm of tears passed. All the while he dropped little kisses on top of her head and along her temples. For a long time, he kept his eyes closed, his heart aching. She was his angel, giving him a miracle he never thought he'd have. He'd come to terms with what he was and what he needed, but he hadn't thought how he'd feel when he actually loved someone. Really loved them.

"I'm so fucking proud of you, Seychelle," he murmured. "I love you. Those words can't even convey to you how much I feel for you. I know what gift you're giving me, and I can only tell you how much I'll always treasure you." There was no real way to say what was in his heart. The ache that was there. The regret. The deep need that he knew would only grow.

He wasn't a fucking poet, although he wrote in a secret journal for her, and he hoped someday he'd have the courage to give it to her. Maybe. Because she had such courage, and she deserved anything he could give her. Her sobs faded to soft little hiccups, and he caught up the bottle of water he'd put next to the chair earlier, in preparation.

"You need to hydrate, Seychelle. Drink just a little for

me." He coaxed her; he didn't command her. He kept nuzzling her neck, alternating between kissing her soft skin and tasting with his tongue while her hair tumbled wildly around his face, the silken strands reminding him how fragile she was.

She took the bottle, her hand trembling. He sat her straighter on his lap and helped her, making certain not a drop spilled on her but that she drank quite a bit before he put the bottle back on the end table. He pushed her hair back so he could tip her face up to his.

"Look at me, baby. I need to know you're back with me." He kept possession of her chin, his thumb sliding along her cheek gently while his palm framed her jaw. Her bone structure felt delicate in his hand. "That's it. Look right at me." Her pupils were dilated, and she still looked a little dazed, but her eyelashes fluttered a few times and she focused on him.

"I'm okay, Savage. That was . . . intense. I didn't expect it to be like that." She laid her head back on his shoulder.

He bunched her hair in his fist. "We have to talk about it, Seychelle. Now, and again when you've rested. I need to know if at any time you were going to tell me to stop. You have to be honest with me."

She was silent, and then she nodded. "Just once, after you took off the first clamp and we started to move again. The chain on the second one was swinging. The clamp tightened and it felt like it pulled so much. It was painful. Too painful." Her voice was muffled by his shoulder.

Savage couldn't tell if she was beginning to cry again. He tugged on her hair until she tilted her head up, her blue eyes meeting his. There was that liquid in them that made his cock stir. "Why didn't you tell me to stop?"

She frowned. "There was so much pain, and it radiated out and down to my . . . sex, and then the pain turned scorching hot, and you were moving so hard and fast. The vibrator was going crazy. My bottom was on fire. Everything came together, and I couldn't tell what was happening to my body, only that I was hot and needed you desperately."

"Did you like it?"

Her frown deepened. Her fingers on his arm dug into his muscle. "I don't think *like* is the word I'd use. I think it's addicting. This time I came so much harder than last time."

He let his breath out. She had recognized that her body wanted the things he had been slowly introducing to her. Each time he made love to her or fucked her hard, he had to have some level of this kind of interaction, and he'd done different things to coax her body into accepting them.

"It's also a little terrifying, Savage. I was so scared of why my body responds to this kind of sex when I never really responded to other men. Why, when I bent over that bench, was I already getting hot and slick at what you were going to do, and what you would do after? I think about you teaching me to take you in my mouth. You haven't done that yet. I don't know why, but I know it's going to be a lesson that might be scary and yet my body reacts the same way. I think about the ultimate end, what you're going to need, and that's the most terrifying of all, and yet I'm so hot I can't sleep sometimes. What's wrong with me, Savage?"

A fresh flood of tears accompanied her question. She wrapped her arms around his neck and pressed her forehead to his chest.

"You fell in love with me, Seychelle," he said gently. "That's the only thing wrong with you. The only way you know how to love is wholly. Completely. With everything in you. You gave yourself to me knowing I was a fucked-up mess. I don't know another woman who could have done that. You came into this with your eyes wide open, but more importantly, baby, so was your heart. You turned your body over to me to be trained in the things I need."

He brushed kisses down her temple to her ear. "I love you so much, Seychelle." He whispered it to her. "I can't be any different. I want to be. I was trained to be this way from the time I was a little kid. It was every day. Weeks. Months. Years. I trained girls for them. Boys. I did things to keep my brother alive. To keep the others alive. I don't know when I crossed the line into needing this shit, but somewhere I did, and there was no going back. I never knew any other way of having sex. I didn't know there was another way."

Savage stroked her hair and then nuzzled the top of her head with his chin. "I can't lose you, Seychelle, I can't, but I'm never going to be different. I thought, when I realized how much I loved you and that it was growing every day, that maybe I could overcome those needs for your sake, but instead of them lessening, I needed them more."

He pushed his forehead against hers as he made the confession. "The idea of putting my marks on you, of you allowing it, of *wanting* them there." His lungs burned as the rush took him. "It won't go away, baby. And with it, there's going to be other things I thought I could give you, that you asked me for, but that we might need to talk about again."

"I'm so scared for both of us," Seychelle whispered. "Going down this path with you, and then if something goes wrong and I lose you . . ." She trailed off. "What if I can't be what you need after all? What if I'm not that woman? I almost stopped you."

"Baby, we would have stopped. You say *stop*, we stop. You're so far ahead of where I thought we'd be, it's insane. Clover clamps are for very advanced users, not beginners. I expected you to put the brakes on. I wanted you to see it would be perfectly all right and you could trust me to stop."

He tipped her face up to his again and captured her tears. "Don't get me wrong, it was the best fucking turn-on ever, but I would have stopped if you told me to. I've got to get you in a bath. Drink more water while I get that ready. I'll cut up fruit and clean up in here while you're soaking, and we can talk more before you go to sleep."

SEVENTEEN

———◆———

Seychelle was shocked when she saw the master bathtub. The master bathroom was enormous, with a long double sink that looked as if it was made from abalone shells. The countertop was thick and covered in a pearlescent, shimmery granite. The shower was a huge tiled room with more golden jets and a complicated overhead rack of long showerheads. She only caught glimpses of both, because he carried her down a short hallway that looked almost like they were entering a grotto.

The wide cavern was arched and made of stones, grays and blues that were soothing, but set in the stones were floating jellyfish of various colors, all lit, tentacles floating behind them. In the darkness they looked beautiful and serene. Forests of kelp seemed to float along the bottom of the stone wall, swaying slightly in rhythm with the tentacles of the jellyfish.

The tub itself was huge, the water blue and steamy. Savage lowered her gently, seating her carefully almost all the way up to her neck in the water, which clearly had some kind of bath salts in it. She felt the effects on her bottom, thighs and nipples immediately.

"There's a cushion for your neck. Just lean back and rest. You have a bottle of water right next to your hand. I'll get us some fruit."

She didn't want him to leave her, but the water was soothing, even the seat her sore bottom rested on was cushioned. She felt the padding with her neck. Part of her didn't want to close her eyes. The bath looked like an underwater cave. It truly was beautiful. Another part of her wanted to relive the experience with Savage. It should have been terrible. She was sore. Her bottom, for certain. Not terribly sore yet, but she would be. She thought about that a lot. She'd been right on the edge, so close, the entire time he was administering his reminder to her. What did that mean?

Just thinking about how he made her feel, the sound of his voice, the shock of the strap as it laid across her skin and the heat spreading straight to her sex. Rushing like a freight train. She kept him in her mind the entire time. Savage. What he needed. What he wanted. That look on his face when he clamped her nipples. When he took her tears. So much heat. All that heat and fire belonged to her.

In a million years she had never imagined the absolute pleasure he could give her when he slammed his cock into her. She hadn't been able to think. Only feel. Only want. She would have done anything for him. She would do anything for him. She knew she would. It wasn't just the intensity of the orgasms he gave her; it was the look of utter love on his face after. She knew she loved him already with every breath she drew. She hadn't been as certain of what he felt for her until that moment.

That knowledge was what she needed to give her the courage to go forward, no matter where their strange sexual relationship took them. He was honest with her. He said he would have to talk about things she'd asked him for that he might not be able to give her. She was concerned what they might be. She'd been with him quite a while—not always in a sexual way, but with him—for months now, and he'd given her everything she'd ever wanted.

"Why are you frowning? Are you hurting?"

She lifted her lashes and looked up at him as he stepped into the deep blue tub, which looked more like a lagoon. He set a plate of fresh cut-up fruit on the wide ledge beside the water bottle. The fruit looked refreshing and tempting. She sat up straight and immediately took a piece of mango.

"I was trying to think what you might not be able to give me that I asked you for. You've given me everything so far." The fruit was so delicious, just what she needed.

"Drink the water too, baby." He sat close to her, his hand on her leg, sliding his fingers along her scars the way he often did.

He was silent for so long she was afraid he might not answer her. She didn't ask him again. Shadows from the floating jellyfish and kelp seemed to move on the wall, and she looked at the cave surrounding her. There were octopi hidden, and a few other sea creatures, when one really studied the clever design.

"You wanted to keep what we did only between us, and I agreed. It's intimate. A gift you give me. I hope you feel love every time I touch you, the way I feel and see it when you surrender to me."

Her heart began to pound. She had loved surrendering to him. It was terrifying, but at the same time, it was her gift to him. She wanted to submit to his desires. To give herself time, she drank some of the water before she asked.

"We did say we would always keep this part of our relationship between only us." She kept her voice strictly neutral.

"I did tell you that our club members have no problem with nudity or having sex in front of one another. It's no big deal, right? I would never let another man touch you. Not ever. But if you were nude or I was in front of others, I wouldn't think twice. I was raised without clothes, and so were they. We don't think about it."

"I wasn't raised that way." Again, she kept her voice nonjudgmental.

"I'm aware of that, baby, but you're also adventurous. I don't think if we're at a party, and it's late and dark and the music is playing, and women are dancing nude and some of the others are fucking their brains out, you would care all that much."

She wouldn't, if she was going to be honest. She'd probably look too and find it interesting. Maybe even hot. She found it hot thinking about it, but she had been hot thinking about the way Savage had taken her after he'd pulled the last clamp off, and her orgasm had roared through her over and over until she thought she'd go insane from sheer pleasure.

"All right, maybe not," she conceded, because he was waiting for an answer and she was determined to always be honest with him. Especially about sex.

"We talked about going on runs and going to parties. I go to them, Seychelle. As my wife, or my partner—and let's be honest, I prefer you to marry me as quickly as possible with as little fuss as possible—you go with me."

"What does that mean? Little fuss as possible?"

"Don't change the subject. One thing at a time. You accompany me to these events."

She sighed and looked down at the mango. She'd eaten quite a lot of it without even knowing she was eating it. "About the run, Savage. I was thinking maybe it wasn't such a good idea for me to go this time. Before you get upset, I don't know the rules. I could do something wrong and get you killed or get the entire club in trouble with the Diamondbacks. I could stay with Blythe and you wouldn't have to worry."

She was determined not to go. She'd made up her mind about it, and she did her best to look him directly in the eyes so he could see she meant business, even though she couched it in terms of hesitancy.

His blue eyes moved over her face, a moody, ice-cold glacier. He had his death mask on, the one that could look right into a person, and he was looking right into her. "Those damn sisters of mine. They scared the crap out of you at the clubhouse. I knew they were talking shit to you.

I could see it on your face. You're not going to start a war with the Diamondbacks, because you're going to follow the rules, Seychelle. You'll do fine. You always do, and you have a few weapons of your own. You have that voice that can calm any storm if you have to use it."

His hand moved over her scars. She felt him write something. His name.

"And I want you there with me. I need you with me."

The way he said it. That voice. His eyes, when they looked into hers. Her heart clenched and so did her sex, totally betraying her. There was no staying strong, not when she was looking at him—or listening to him. Or he was naked. Or dressed. There was just no denying him anything. She sighed and took another piece of mango. It was the only sane thing to do.

"Fine, but if I do anything wrong, it's totally on you, Savage. I'm not going home with a sore butt."

"Yes, you will, if you break a rule on a run." He leaned over and bit her earlobe, then sucked it into his mouth before she could yelp. "But I'll guarantee you'll like it."

Seychelle glared at him, but there was no denying her sex clenched. She really was becoming needy around him. "Tell me what has changed about our talk, Savage."

"I can't have sex with you without some kind of pain included. It won't work for me. I thought it would, baby, but it won't. The more we're together, the greater that need is. To treat you like every other woman I've been with since I was a kid, forcing my cock to work by telling it to cooperate because I marked skin and then fucked a mouth, is repugnant to me. I'm not sure I could do it to you, and I don't fuckin' want to."

Seychelle pressed her lips together, going over what he said. She didn't want him to have to tell his cock to work, and she sure didn't want to be lumped in with his other women—hundreds, maybe thousands. He'd said that so casually and contemptuously. She didn't want to be one of that number. She wanted to be . . . his.

"Do you have to go to these parties and runs?"

"Not every time, and we won't when I don't have to, but I hold a position in the club that means I'm needed right now. It's important I go."

She studied his face. "You protect everyone."

He didn't answer her, but she knew. His expression was unreadable. She took a deep breath and guessed again. "And Alena will have to see Pierce there again, won't she? He'll most likely be with another woman. Alena's going to hurt like hell. You're going to take that on as well. You're going to take on a lot while you're there, aren't you?"

Again, he remained silent, just watching her. Seychelle finished the slice of mango and then took a drink of water. "What would I have to do?"

He rubbed his hand over her scars. Little circles. Massaging her. Soothing her. "I wouldn't do anything obvious, and I'd take you where no one else could see you—outside club members, who would make certain no one else would come near us."

Seychelle was already shaking her head, hunching her shoulders. "I don't know if I could do that, Savage."

"Seychelle, stop. You're thinking too much, in your head too much. Just listen to me. First of all, you don't really give a damn if you're naked in front of anyone else, as long as I'm with you. You're gorgeous and you know it. Right? If the other women are naked, you wouldn't be uncomfortable. Say it. Tell the truth."

"Probably not."

"You wouldn't. It makes you hot thinking about it. If you're with me, and I'm sitting on a fucking picnic table drinking a beer, and I want to see your gorgeous tits and I tell you to take your shirt off, you know you'd do it for me. And if I want to suck on your tit or clamp your nipples, you'd do that too. You wouldn't give a damn who was around. You would give me whatever I asked."

She would. She *so* would. It did make her hot thinking about it. She nodded.

"So we know clamps are okay to bring with us. I can use them, and we make sure we have somewhere dark and to ourselves. Nothing obvious like a flogger or strap, but I can find something to mark you mine. I'll think of something unique and different, something special you'll love but that won't be obvious to anyone. Are you okay changing our rules a little?"

His blue eyes stared straight into hers, refusing to allow her to look away. Refusing to allow her to hide from him. She sighed. She wished she could tell him she didn't want to change them. A part of her didn't.

"What is it, baby? We promised each other we'd talk about everything. Talk it through. I didn't expect to have to change the rules. We made them in good faith. I made you a promise. You have every right to decide that's a hard no for you. We would have to go back to me makin' my cock cooperate, which I would hate, but I would do it. That's me being honest. You have every right to hate it as well, but if you can't make yourself do this, it's what we both have to do."

"I want to get out of here," Seychelle said. "It's beautiful, and I appreciate you putting this all together for me, but I want to go to bed. I'll talk in bed." She could tell there were things about the run he wasn't telling her. Club business. Things he had to do that she couldn't know, but it was going to be important for him that she was there—like the Alena and Pierce thing, but more.

She stood up, water pouring off of her. Savage did as well. He snagged two warm towels from a towel warmer and wrapped her in one before removing two plugs to allow the water to swirl out. Seychelle tried not to allow the towel to brush over her very sensitive nipples as she walked down the hall to the bathroom. Savage had provided a brand-new electric toothbrush and water flosser exactly like the ones she had at her house. She used both and dried off gingerly.

"I've got lotion that will help your ass and nipples, Seychelle. Once you're ready, go on into the bedroom and I'll apply it for you."

"I can do my nipples."

Savage raised his eyebrow at her. Seychelle sighed and walked into the bedroom. It was immaculate. He'd cleaned everything. Her clothes, the toys, his strap, all of it was gone. There was water on the end table. He really believed in hydration. She sat carefully on the bed, waiting for him, hands folded for some reason, her heart pounding.

Savage looked larger than life when he walked into the bedroom, totally naked. Her breath caught in her throat. He had more muscles than she'd imagined a man could have. He was bigger than she thought, even when he wasn't as hard as a steel pole. She couldn't imagine how he fit inside of her, or how a woman took him in her mouth. She was going to have to keep practicing, something she'd been doing behind his back with cucumbers, because that hideous woman wasn't going to be able to do something for her man that she couldn't do a thousand times better. But she might have to find a bigger cucumber. He seemed to be growing as she stared at him.

"Babe." He kind of groaned his endearment. "Stop looking at my dick. You're already sore and we're not going for another round. You need to rest. Eyes on mine."

It took effort to raise her gaze to his. Now he knew she was thinking about that portion of his anatomy. She'd been thinking about *all* of his anatomy, but now she was concentrating. A girl had to have her priorities.

"Seychelle. Your ass is already sore. If I put you over my knee, you're not going to be able to sit down for a few days." There was distinct warning in his tone.

"Fine. You're *such* a killjoy. I was just looking. Admiring. Maybe planning."

"Planning?"

That caught his attention, just like she knew it would. Men were so easy when it came to their cocks.

"Yes, but you stopped me mid-plan, so I'm not sharing. You don't deserve it." She was rather smug about her punishment. She knew he'd think about that for a long while.

He poured lotion into his palm. "Your nipples are going to be sore for a few days. We aren't going to use clamps for a little while, and I'll have to be careful. We'll use this lotion several times a day. That will help with the soreness. You tell me if you get worse."

He was exquisitely gentle as he applied the lotion to both nipples. Whatever was in the lotion definitely soothed away the soreness. The skin on her breasts felt silky soft as well.

"Lay on your belly, Seychelle, so I can apply the lotion to your ass and the backs of your thighs. You shouldn't have any lasting marks, not even from the strap. I was very careful."

Seychelle stretched out. Her body was already humming from the lotion he'd applied to her breasts and nipples. He rubbed it into her shoulders and back and then began to gently massage it into her buttocks. He was careful as he applied, never putting too much pressure on her bottom but using a gentle circular motion to cover every inch of both cheeks before moving down to the backs of her thighs.

"Talk to me about why you're hesitant to have sex with me on the run or at parties, the way we both need it."

Seychelle closed her eyes. His voice got her right in the heart. Maybe the soul. He took her over. "It's private. For us. It's the way we show love for one another. If we give that to them, it isn't special between us anymore. What we do together feels so intimate. If we have others around us, it might feel sexy in that moment, but it takes away from our intimacy."

He was silent, and she liked that he listened and was thinking about what she said. Savage never just dismissed her concerns. That was one of the things she loved most about him. He had said he would listen to her, and he did.

"Shit," he finally said softly. "You're right, baby." He finished rubbing the lotion into her legs and then put it on the end table before sliding into bed beside her.

She was used to the feel of his body, but for some reason, this time when he wound his body around hers, he felt like a shield. A hard covering that totally surrounded her.

Pure protection. She'd never had that before in her entire life. She'd been the one to protect her parents when they were too weak to do much more than walk around their home. He wrapped his arm around her waist and put his chin on her shoulder, his warm breath in her ear.

"We can both live without sex at the parties, Seychelle. It's worth it in order to keep what we have."

The sincerity in his voice turned her heart over. Could she love him any more? Each time she thought she couldn't, he proved her wrong. She also heard something else. A note of caution. He was worried. It had nothing to do with the parties. He could live without sex for a night or two, or even come up with something fun for the two of them to do that would work. She knew he could. It was the run he was concerned about.

"Bad things are going to happen on the run, aren't they, Savage?"

He shrugged. "It's entirely possible, angel. Probable."

She closed her eyes and took a deep breath. That was why he needed to change the rules. He expected to need to have sex with her on the run to drain off some of the rage that would build up in him.

"How are we going to cope with your needs, Savage?"

"We'll figure it out, baby," he answered. "We're both intelligent, and we have time." He nuzzled her neck and then kissed her. "Tomorrow we can move all your things in. Put your house up for sale."

She stiffened. She couldn't help it, even knowing he would feel it. Half turning toward him, she shook her head decisively. "Absolutely not. I'm not selling my house. I'm not."

"You don't like this one?"

"I love this house, Savage, but I'm not there yet. I can't give up my house. You can run away to the clubhouse. To the bar. Wherever it is you go on your motorcycle. I need my house. When you get how you get, I need a place to run away to. That's my house."

"Absolutely not. You have the clubhouse now as well.

You can run to Czar's house. You don't run to your house, where fucking Arnold or Campbell are lurking around ready to pounce, especially if you're pissed at me."

"I won't be pissed. Well, I might be. You're scary and overwhelming sometimes. I need my house. I love my house. I love this one too, but I'm not ready to sell my house." She turned back over, her shoulder in his face. "You can argue all you want, Savage, but as far as I'm concerned, this discussion is over. I'm not selling it."

"You have a stubborn streak in you a mile wide." His teeth scraped back and forth gently over the nape of her neck, spreading goose bumps all over her body. He kissed the same spot. "I love you, angel. Stubborn streak and all."

She smiled. "I love you too. Bossy streak and all."

Seychelle woke to an empty bed. She lifted her head and looked around. She had gotten used to Savage being with her. He liked to wake her up with his mouth on her. Usually between her legs. She wanted to try waking him up the same way, but he was very strict on her lessons and what direction they would take. Maybe she should have suggested that for their parties. Learning to give him a blow job while at a party. That might be fun—or not. For both of them.

Savage had been in the shower; the glass doors were still wet. She liked that the tiles were warm under her feet when she stepped out and that the towels were warm. That felt very decadent. She knew absolutely that Savage wouldn't care about those things—but he did care that she had them. He was surprising in so many ways. He was rough on the outside, but with her, so incredibly soft on the inside—most of the time.

She found clothes in a far-too-large closet. There was a faded pair of blue jeans that fit like a glove, and a tank top that maybe showed a little bit too much of her generous breasts. Savage insisted she had the perfect figure. He didn't seem to notice that because she was on the short side, one or two extra pounds really showed, always in her butt or her boobs or, most times, both. He didn't seem to mind, but when it came to clothes . . .

She tugged at the tank top. It was tighter than anything she'd ever worn. The bra barely covered her breasts. They tended to sit high, and so the tops of the curves showed, and she could see the marks from Savage's mouth, the strawberries he'd left behind. Just looking at them sent flutters to her sex. Her nipples had been a little sore when she woke up, but she had rubbed the lotion into them and tried to do the same on her bottom and thighs. That had been a little more difficult.

She kept staring at herself in the mirror, wondering how Savage had managed to make her feel sexy. He made her feel like she looked sexy. Her hair was a little wild, like it always was. Instead of being annoyed and thinking she looked awful, she thought the honey-colored out-of-control volume suited her face. Seeing the way her breasts stretched the tank top, instead of agonizing over being too heavy, she knew Savage would have a difficult time keeping his hands—and mouth—off of her. She liked that her bottom was cupped by the jeans, and that with every step she took, she felt just a little ache.

Seychelle strapped on a pair of sandals she found in the closet and went to the sliding glass door off the bedroom leading to the private courtyard. She could see the ocean from one view and, turning slightly, the woods from another. Stepping outside, she immediately felt the cool salt air and the flutter of the sea breeze.

A strange whistle and then a crack made her jump. The sound came from around the corner. It wasn't particularly loud, but it was distinct and raised goose bumps on her skin. Instinctively, she stood very still. She knew immediately that Savage was using one of his whips. The compulsion to see him in action was extremely strong. Just the sound of the whip cracking in the air sent heat rushing through her veins. At the same time, there was trepidation, her heart accelerating.

She wanted to be everything for Savage. She really did.

She didn't know why she responded the way she did to the pain and pleasure he mixed together. She was ashamed of the way she seemed to need his hand on her bottom or the clamps on her nipples in order to become excited, but she wanted to be more like he was and own her sexuality. She just wasn't certain how to do it yet, or if she could follow him as far down the dark path as he needed her to go.

She took a deep breath and forced herself to walk around the corner to view the courtyard that was hidden from everyone. It was right off their bedroom, if one chose to access it from the sliding glass door and the porch there.

Savage stood in the middle of the yard. He was dressed in only a pair of soft vintage blue jeans. When he moved, his muscles rippled beneath the skin, bringing his tattoos alive and showing every scar and burn on his back.

Mannequin figures were set at various distances from him, some with their backs to him, some facing him. Thin paper covered their material skin. She could see through the paper to the white material that covered the wire bones of the cage that was the bodice of each mannequin. It seemed as if the entire courtyard had various visitors, all posed in different positions, some facing slightly away from the bedroom, some with their backs fully to it. Others had their fronts fully exposed, and others were turned slightly to the side.

Savage didn't even appear as if he was looking directly at the mannequins. He noticed her immediately, which didn't surprise her. He was always aware of his surroundings. He spun around, his body a blur as the whip became an extension of his arm, singing through the air, landing in perfect symmetry, producing a line to add to the obvious tree he was creating on the back of the model he was using.

The lines were beautiful. *He* was beautiful. She could see the various patterns he'd created with the whip as well as others. He was so casual, so on target, even as he was smiling at her. She was so caught up in his artistry that it took a moment to realize how her body reacted to the whip.

The crack of it. The way it flew through the air and landed with such perfect precision. Her entire body flooded with endorphins. Hot blood rushed through her veins and pooled low. Her clit throbbed and her sex clenched. Her head went up and her hand fluttered to her throat protectively. Even the sound of the whip was thrilling, but watching Savage wield it was more of a thrill than anything else. Her breath caught in her lungs and just burned there.

"Good morning," he said as he casually coiled the whip. "I expected you to sleep the day away." He came right to her and bent his head to kiss her.

His kisses were never fast, not little pecks. He took his time. All heat. All fire. Taking her over. Pulling her to him, one hand spanning her throat and the other fisting in her hair and holding her head absolutely still for him. She gave herself to him. Surrendering. Sliding her arms around his neck and pressing her body as close to his as she could get, still a little shocked that he could actually be hers.

When he lifted his head, she turned to gesture toward the mannequins. "That's the coolest thing I've ever seen, Savage." She indicated the various patterns. "It's really beautiful. I didn't realize art could be done with a whip."

He nuzzled her neck. "Thank you, angel. That's exactly how I see it. My art. I need to see your nipples, baby, just to make certain we didn't get too crazy last night." He set the whip on the railing and caught the hem of her tank top, pulling it over her head. "I can do quite a lot of things with whips. Did you remember to use the lotion?"

She nodded, shivering a little at the darkness in his eyes. "What are you doing out here?"

"Practicing. I practice every day. Now that I've got you, I'll step that up even more. I want to make certain I don't make any mistakes. I never want to cut into your skin too deep and leave a scar."

She shivered. "Cut into my skin?"

He nodded, watching her closely as he unhooked her

bra, letting her breasts free. "The air is good for your nipples. While you're home, you should just go without a top and bra. You'll heal faster."

His finger slid over the top curve of her breast and then traced one of the many strawberries. "The strap, the various floggers I'll use, none of those would make a real mark on you like this whip would. This would make a slice into your skin. I could make it just a slight one, or deep. I have to have absolute control." All the while, his eyes never left hers. "I can do all kinds of things with different whips, baby. The point of all this practice is not to cut your skin. If you look at the mannequins, the paper is cut, but not the material under it. Hopefully, I stay in control and raise welts, striping you with my art, but not actually breaking your skin."

She couldn't look away, mesmerized by him, mesmerized by the whip he had somehow coiled in his hand again. It seemed an extension of him.

"What kinds of things?"

"You'll find out, baby. Some you'll love, some not so much, but in the end, you're going to be screaming for more. Just like last night."

"Are you finished practicing? I want to watch you." She touched her tongue to her lips, trying not to breathe too deep, but her breasts rose and fell in time to her rapid pulse.

He hooked his palm around the nape of her neck and slid first the handle and then the leather tails over her mounds. "It's arousing, isn't it?" His voice was a soft, mesmerizing velvet whisper that played over her skin like a touch. "Do you wonder what it will feel like when I wrap your tit in pure fire? When it spreads straight to your pussy? When I put my name into your skin?" Each word was a sin. A temptation. His lips moved against her jaw. Small little kisses. His teeth nipped her throat. "I can do that, you know. Burn my name into your skin with my whip. Right there on your bare little mound." He sounded like pure sensual enticement, taking her down a dark path without using much more than his voice.

He scraped the shadowy bristles on his jaw across her breasts, a slow burn, sending darts of fire, little spears of lightning, straight to her sex. The handle of his whip was suddenly between her legs, moving, sawing back and forth in a steady assault on her senses.

"Answer me, Seychelle. Are you wondering right now what it would feel like to have me strip you naked and tie your arms up, legs wide, your body at my mercy? What would I decide to put on your skin? What would you do for me, baby? Would you take every single thing I wanted to give you? Would you say *no*? *Enough?* Would you want it all? What no other woman has ever had from me?"

She shivered, that velvet whisper slipping inside her, wrapping her up, until she knew she wanted to hear his voice asking those questions to her over and over. He was waiting. His eyes those twin blue flames she couldn't resist. "Yes. I can't help but wonder. It's both alluring and terrifying."

He cupped her cheek gently, his thumb sliding softly over her lips. "You're not nearly there, baby. I love that you want to go there with me. Thank you for that. Been working on a new pattern for about three years now. Nowhere near satisfied yet, certainly not enough to try on you. Stay up here on the deck. You tend to be distracting. This takes concentration."

She stuck her chin out at him. "You didn't look like you were concentrating all that much before when I came out here. You turned and hit that mannequin precisely where you wanted to without looking."

His gaze burned through her like two hot flames. She refused to look away, staring right back at him. A slow smile finally touched his hard mouth, nearly melting her resolve, but she wasn't going to let him charm her. She didn't want to stay on the porch. She wanted to watch his every move. It was sexy. It was all Savage. This was the real man. She could see inside him when he used that whip, and he knew it.

"I knew where my mark was. That's the point of practicing like this. I always have to know exactly what I'm doing in order to be absolutely certain I will never permanently mark you—unless, of course, we both agree to putting my name on your skin." He threw the last out there casually.

She drew in her breath as he stepped off the porch and walked toward the mannequins, shaking out the whip as he did so. He was extraordinary. He moved with that sexy, silent, predatory gait, muscles rippling like a jungle cat's. The way he said *permanently mark you*, as if he could do it whenever he wanted to, put his name into her skin for eternity with his whip.

His hand moved. The whip cracked, a glorious sound that moved through her like a lightning bolt, searing and cleansing. The flick of the lash was flawless, coiling around the mannequin's breast for a long moment and then slithering off to come back to Savage at his command. Her breath caught in her lungs. Burned in her core like a hot pool of molten lava. Savage turned his head, those blue eyes, flames burning over her as if he knew what just the sound of the whip had done to her.

Seychelle touched her tongue to her lips. "That was amazing. I can't believe you can do that, Savage. Can I look closer?" She was already moving toward the mannequin, needing to see that precise cut he'd made in the paper. Had it pierced the material beneath?

Savage wrapped his arm around her waist. "I want you to look. These are my creations, my artistry. No one else is ever going to see them. Only you."

A little shiver went down her spine as she stood in front of one of the mannequins that faced forward. The pattern was exquisite. The whip had coiled around the mannequin's breast, adding to the pattern he was already making. It was a beautiful top of fringe. She could barely believe he could make such a thing with a whip.

Seychelle turned away, almost running back to the porch to snatch up her bra and tank. Her body was on fire. Weep-ing for his. Almost desperate. There was something really, really wrong with her to even think of going to such a dark place. If she did stay with Savage as she promised, she knew she would let him lead her straight to that whip. Fantasy was one thing, but reality was something altogether different.

She was terrified of those dark corners whispering to her in her own mind. She couldn't let him lead her there. She fled into the house, only to find herself in the master bedroom. She looked around. It was beautiful, but again, she saw the metal rings in the posts. The drawers holding his toys. His lotions. Even the grotto had been built for a reason. This was a place for kink, for a way of life, and she was committing to living it with him.

She needed to go somewhere and really think about what she was doing before she took that next step. It wasn't that she was afraid of Savage. She was more afraid of herself. Did she really want those things in her to come to light?

"Baby, stop." Savage put a hand on her shoulder as she hurried down the hall toward the living room. "You're running again. That seems to be your standard method of operation when you get scared."

"I just need to think. Lana is picking me up. We're meeting Doris and a couple of others for tea at the Floating Hat."

"Think about what?" he prompted.

She wished she were in her own home. She felt trapped in his. He was everywhere. Savage. Her man. She wanted him so much, and he could sway her so easily. With his kisses. With his need of her. With the way she loved him. How could she think clearly?

"I just have to think. This is all so scary, Savage. I love you. It isn't about that. It's about me and whether or not I can still be me at the end of the day."

"You're not making any sense, baby."

"I know I'm not." Because she was panicking.

Savage put his arms around her. "Don't run from us, Seychelle. We both knew it was going to get hard at some point, but we're going to take it slow. We'll only go as far as you want to go."

That was the trouble. What if she wanted to go further than she should? She buried her face against his chest, conversely the only place she felt safe.

"Who else is meeting you at the Floating Hat?"

She knew he was changing the subject in order to give her space. "Eden Ravard is having tea with us as well. You remember her, right? I play cards at her home with Inez and a couple of the others when someone can't make it. She had a seizure once."

"Right, she's a sweet woman."

"I'm talking to Sabelia about teaching a few of us how to conjure up toads," she added, just to make him smile.

"Great." He raised his head and looked toward the door. "Lana's here. You stay out of trouble, and think good thoughts about us, baby." Cupping her chin in his palm, he took her mouth. His kiss was gentle. Loving. So tender he stole her heart and refused to give it back to her. She felt more lost than ever. More terrified.

EIGHTEEN

Seychelle loved the Floating Hat. It was difficult to feel sad or upset when you were there. First, the little bells welcoming anyone to the tearoom were all in the shape of hats, which seemed funny since it was a tea shop. One display window held delicious-looking pastries, all tempting people to enter and choose various exotic teas to go along with the decadent desserts. The other display window on the opposite side of the door held lotions and specialty bath items in various beautifully shaped bottles and jars.

The shop smelled wonderful. Every time she inhaled, she drew fresh air into her lungs, and with it a subtle fragrance she couldn't quite identify, but it seemed to clear her mind and make her feel so much better. One side of the shop was dedicated to the tearoom. The other was a shop where people could buy the bath or specialty items Hannah Drake Harrington, the owner, or Sabelia, her assistant, made up for them.

Seychelle had discovered the Floating Hat the very first day she'd moved into her new house. She'd walked all over Sea Haven. The sign and name of the shop had intrigued her, and she couldn't help going in to see what it was all about. Once she'd entered, she knew she'd always go back. She especially loved the hair and bath products.

"Seychelle," Doris called, waving merrily. She sat at the largest table, by two windows, which gave it the illusion of being very spacious. "Lana. I'm so glad you're joining us. Inez said you might come. Eden texted and said she was running late, but she'll definitely join us in time for lunch. Her monthly hair appointment, you know. The hairdresser is always getting behind."

"I was happy you invited me," Lana returned. "This is one of my favorite places for tea. Alena usually comes in with me, but she was too busy today. That girl is always working."

Seychelle nodded. "Her food is so delicious." It was too, although it was almost a sacrilege to say so when everything served at the Floating Hat was so wonderful as well.

Her phone vibrated in the pocket of her jeans, and she took it out, her heart accelerating. She knew exactly who it was. **Know you're upset, baby, but we're a couple. We don't walk out on each other. You made that commitment to me.**

She'd already reassured him, but she didn't know if she could keep that commitment, not when she was so confused about who she was anymore. She was willing to go so far out of her comfort zone for him to meet his needs. So far. She loved him enough to convince herself that their relationship would be worth it. It would be stronger for it, more intimate. She knew what Savage gave to his club, and she knew as he took on their pain that she would take it on for him. He loved the club members enough to do that for them. She loved him enough to take on that pain physically for him. She knew she would be strong enough.

That part was all good. She was fine with making sacrifices. That felt good. She'd done that for her parents. She did that for others when she healed them. It was the *liking* it she wasn't so certain about. Losing herself in the pleasure-pain of it, she wasn't okay with. Bringing those dark corners to the forefront and owning them. Taking that responsibility. A little shiver crept down her spine. She didn't know if she could be like Savage, respecting herself, looking at herself in the mirror and being okay with who she was.

Seychelle slipped the phone back into her pocket without answering the text. Savage was just as exciting and sexy to her when texting as he was in person. She had a tendency to give in to him—to give him whatever he wanted. Right now, she needed desperately to sort herself out.

"Seychelle, sit right here, honey. You look like you're a hundred miles away." Inez was already at the table. She knew everyone in Sea Haven almost from the moment they arrived. She owned the local grocery store and could ferret out information on anyone very quickly. With her was Rebecca Jetspun, a widow Seychelle often visited. Seychelle was happy to see Rebecca getting out. She tended to stay isolated in her home, although Eden had managed to coax her into playing cards and introduced her to Inez and Doris. Doris had actually gotten her to go to bingo once or twice.

"She's been off with her fiancé," Doris supplied.

"*Fake* fiancé," Seychelle corrected, deliberately sounding snippy. "You know very well he's my fake fiancé." She held up her naked hand. "No ring on this finger."

"It isn't always necessary to have a ring, dear," Rebecca said.

"That's the truth." Lana backed her immediately.

Lana was particularly gracious to Rebecca, as if she could sense that the woman needed a little extra drawing out. Seychelle could see that everyone tended to relax in Lana's company. She had an extraordinary gift of making each person feel very special, as if when she spoke, she focused solely on them—and that she was truly interested in everything they had to say.

Seychelle's phone vibrated again. She tried to resist looking at it. No one needed to look at their phone just because someone sent a text. She already knew who it was from. There was no denying who had sent it. And he was going to start sending one after another if she didn't answer. It was just that she didn't know exactly what to say. With a little sigh, she pulled the offending phone from her pocket and glared down at the screen.

Baby. I'm lonely without you. You could at least text me and tell me if you're thinking of me, because I'm thinking of you.

She tried not to smile. **I'm busy. Having tea. Go away.**

Right there: that was the problem. He could twist her around his little finger with his sweet text messages. She stopped thinking about the future and started thinking about how much she loved him.

Around her, the others laughed and talked, discussing which teas were their favorites and whether they wanted to try something new and different. As a rule, each person at the table could order a pot of tea and share with the others so they could try it if they wanted. Seychelle looked up to see Lana watching her speculatively. She sent her a small smile, knowing Lana wouldn't ask her anything in front of the others.

Inhaling to try to bring the scent of the shop into her lungs, Seychelle did her best to focus on the conversation. Doris and Inez had a lively discussion going about a new couple who had moved to Sea Haven and were doing their best to fit in. Doris thought they were "pushy" and Inez thought they were "lovely."

"Who are they?" Seychelle asked. She felt as if she should have met the newcomers.

"They retired from the city, dear," Inez said.

"You can't say 'city,' Inez," Doris corrected. "She'll think you mean the Bay. They came from LA. They're bigwigs, in movies or television. Think they're powerful, and that when they go to a restaurant they should get a table first, whether they have a reservation or not. They're very entitled, is what I'm trying to say."

"I'm afraid Doris might be right, Inez," Rebecca agreed, her voice a little timid, portraying her reluctance. "Seychelle,

Lana, their names are Logan and Ava Chutney. They bought the old Tubbs estate. I think it sold for eight million. In any case, they sent their 'man' in to get some items in Donna's gift shop that Ava saw in the window. I was purchasing one of the items Ava wanted, and the man became very upset. He offered me all kinds of money for it. It was a hand-painted one-of-a-kind scarf. I was sending it to a dear friend in Seattle for her birthday. I truly didn't want to part with it."

Seychelle's phone vibrated again. She pulled it out of her pocket, tempted to dunk it in the glass of water in front of her. The water was in a beautiful, hand-blown, very classy tall cylinder, with what looked like lilies floating in between the two sheets of glass, condensation making it all the more appealing. She wasn't about to drop her cell phone into it just because Savage was being annoying.

Well, okay, Savage wasn't annoying. It was just that he was far more tempting than the conversation. She was trying to distance herself from him so she could be normal. Feel normal. Be around normal. Live it again. She pushed at the hair tumbling around her face, wishing she were sitting on his lap and he was holding her while her head was in such a state of absolute chaos.

Baby, I can feel that you need me. My Seychelle radar is going off right in the middle of a very important meeting with Czar.

Your radar is so completely off track. U need one of those techies to work on it. I'm not thinking about U at all. I'm having the time of my life.

Liar, liar, panties are on fire, or they will be when I get you over my knees for lying.

He could text so fast. She put the phone in her pocket without replying. She was not touching that, not when her sex clenched and her panties went damp just reading his silly text. That was the problem. Right there. That was the problem. That wasn't normal. How was anything about that normal? She'd just come from his house. In the courtyard were mannequins with whip patterns all over them, front and back, and she'd thought it was the sexiest thing she'd ever seen. When she'd heard the sound of the whip, instead of running for her life like any intelligent human being, she'd wanted Savage to slam her up against a wall and take her right then and there. That was definitely *not* a normal reaction.

Savage was still texting. She knew because her phone vibrated several times with alarming determination. She groaned and dropped her head into her hands, trying hard to resist his pull on her. Taking a deep breath, she looked up, determined to join the conversation swirling around her. As she did, she looked out the window. Joseph Arnold was directly across the street, staring right at her.

She groaned again. Technically, she should tell Savage that Arnold was back in Sea Haven. He had no real reason for being there that she could think of, other than to stalk her. Once she was engaged to Savage, that would give him every reason to continue to drive her crazy. She needed to go to her house, shut the door and close out the world, just for a little while.

"What is it, Seychelle?" Lana asked and turned her head to look toward the street.

Fortunately, Joseph had his back to them, already walking away. Seychelle shook her head. "Nothing, really. Savage is texting me like a madman."

Lana laughed. "Really? He's in a meeting with Czar and Steele. It's a big deal too. Reaper's there as well. If they catch him . . ." She broke off as if he could get in trouble, as if anyone could make Sávage do anything he didn't want to do.

"Nonstop," Seychelle reported, suddenly happy that Savage would put himself on the line during an important meeting just to reassure her.

Lana laughed again and shook her head. "That man has it bad for you."

Seychelle knew he did. She loved him the same way. Love wasn't the problem. The lifestyle was.

Sabelia took their orders for the various teas to go along

with the pastries and sandwiches being served. Her face still had very faint bruising, but the swelling was gone, and there was little evidence that she had been beaten by the man she'd picked up at the bar. She smiled at them with her usual welcoming greeting and waited patiently while the older women pored over the menu, which they'd seen countless times.

"Your voice is beautiful," Sabelia offered a little shyly, shocking Seychelle. She'd been in the tea shop many times. Sabelia had always been unfailingly polite, but she never invited private conversation, and she didn't make personal comments.

Seychelle gave her a genuine smile, feeling the vibrations going off steadily in her pocket. She rubbed her hand over her phone, unable to keep from touching it. She loved that Savage would keep reaching out to her even when she didn't respond.

"Thank you, Sabelia. It's nice to have someone appreciate my efforts. Most of the women don't hear me. They just see those men up there playing. I'm not certain they hear them either, and they're the best band I've heard in a long time."

Sabelia laughed, and her laughter was soft and gorgeous to hear, the notes like little sparks of ruby-red glitter dancing in the air. "The band was good, but your voice is incredible. You certainly give people something to think about."

"Thank you. Seriously. Thank you. Sometimes I need to hear that. Right now is one of those times."

Sabelia's smile faded as she studied Seychelle's face. Seychelle did her best to put a happy mask on, but she had never been particularly good at hiding her true feelings. In any case, she had the feeling that Sabelia could see more than most people.

The waitress leaned down. "I'm going to bring you a very special tea, Seychelle," Sabelia whispered. "I'll make the blend myself. It's very soothing. And no, I didn't put in a toad or anything like that, if Preacher asks. And he will if you tell him." She straightened and narrowed her eyes at Lana.

"I wouldn't tell him just because I'm his sister," Lana said, holding up her hands. "Don't you remember I told you I'd help you fill his truck with toads?"

"Fill whose truck with toads?" Doris demanded.

Rebecca gave a delicate little shudder. "You wouldn't really do that, would you?"

"Hannah did it to Jonas more than once," Inez said, referring to the owner of the shop and her husband, who just happened to be the sheriff.

"She filled his truck with toads?" Rebecca was horrified. Everyone else at the table looked amused. Sabelia walked away laughing.

"She certainly did," Inez confirmed. "And when he was a teenager and snuck a girl into his bedroom, there is a rumor that toads leapt into his room and filled that as well."

"How did Hannah do that?" Rebecca asked. "Not that I'd do it, but you have to admit, filling cars and trucks with toads could come in handy."

Inez looked at her sharply. "Whose car would you fill with toads, Rebecca? I always considered you so sweet."

Doris burst out laughing. "We all change spending time with you, Inez. I'm not always certain it's for the better, but we have way more fun."

Seychelle joined in the laughter, but she thought controlling toads might be a good idea. She'd have a bunch of them jump right on Savage's thick skull and do a little froggy dance. "I'm all for Hannah teaching us. I already asked Sabelia to teach a class. I haven't quite convinced her, but at the time she wasn't talking as much as she is now."

Lana smirked. "I'm reading your mind."

"The question is, are you willing to take the class?" Seychelle asked.

"Absolutely. I'm all for petitioning Hannah right now. Alena would be in as well," Lana said solemnly. "Blythe is too nice, Soleil would never do anything like that to Ice, but Anya might need to know how to have a trick or two on her side around Reaper. Breezy is just as sweet as they come, and Zyah is capable, but Player's too nice, so she doesn't have the need. I think Anya and Alena are the only others for the class." Lana went through the list of potentials from the women of Torpedo Ink.

"You left out Lissa and Lexi," Inez pointed out. "Technically, they're women of Torpedo Ink as well."

Lissa was married to Casimir Prakenskii and Lexi to Gavriil Prakenskii, both men fully patched members of Torpedo Ink.

"Lissa comes to a few events, and she'd be all in. I'll invite her too, if we can get Hannah and Sabelia to agree," Lana conceded. "But Gavriil has brought Lexi only once. He's extremely protective of her. I honestly don't know her at all."

"I don't think you young girls should have all the fun," Rebecca said daringly.

The door to the shop swung open, the bells tinkling merrily, announcing more customers. Seychelle turned her head, expecting to see Eden Ravard. Brandon Campbell walked in with a very young woman under his arm. Head down, she looked extremely pale as she stared at the floor with no expression on her face. She wore dark jeans and a wrinkled T-shirt with a very thin, light sweater over it.

Brandon whispered to her, and her body jerked as if he'd struck her. She tilted her head up like a puppet, looking toward their table but staring past them, not at them, with vacant eyes. Brandon came right up to the table. He looked anxious as he gave them a little half smile in greeting.

"Hello, Doris, Inez. Everyone. This is Tessa Deering, my friend. Tessa, honey, can you say hello? Please?"

Tessa swallowed and looked up at him, nodding several times. "Hello." She murmured the greeting to the window behind them. Her voice sounded hollow and far off.

Brandon sighed and shook his head, looking very discouraged. "We're on a little outing. I thought it might bring her out of her shell. Tessa's very . . ." He broke off as if searching for the right word. "Come here, honey. Sit right at this table." His fingers bit into her arm as he all but forcibly put her into the chair at the little intimate table straight across from the one where the women were sitting. "She won't even move on her own anymore. I'm running out of ideas."

"Oh, Brandon, that's such a shame," Rebecca said. "Have you tried a counselor?"

"She refuses to go. She won't leave me long enough to go. It's a good thing I work from home. I'm getting worried about her dependency." He talked as if Tessa weren't even there.

Seychelle caught Lana's gaze. Brandon was using his "voice." Just a note here and there, but it was enough to ensnare everyone. Doris wouldn't fall under his spell because Seychelle had built a shield for her. Lana clearly was aware that something was off about Brandon, and she knew Tessa was in trouble. She was fighting the effects of that tone.

"We were just discussing the silliest thing, Brandon," Seychelle said cheerfully. "We were going to ask Hannah and Sabelia to teach us classes in some of the craziest arts." Deliberately, she used counterpoints to his voice, almost like stabbing through his tones with little pinpoints, but so sweetly he wouldn't notice.

She rested her chin in her palm and looked at him with wide blue eyes. "Let me try with her. I hate that you're so upset. Women can sometimes do things men can't." Before he could object, she turned her attention to Tessa.

Around her, the women were all nodding their heads in agreement and murmuring, "Yes." "Try, Seychelle."

"Tessa, honey, look at me." Seychelle used a tone with absolute command, one impossible to ignore, notes tuned specifically to the girl. It had been difficult to find them since Tessa had only spoken the one brief word, but Seychelle was very motivated to get her away from her abuser.

Tessa blinked several times and then focused, as if surfacing from far away. Her gaze settled on Seychelle's eyes. Seychelle smiled at her.

"That's right. Keep looking at me. You're perfectly safe here. Brandon, can you go to the car and get her a proper jacket? She's cold. That sweater isn't warm enough."

"I don't think . . ." Brandon started.

"That would be such a good thing," Lana said. "I'll go with you." Lana shot him her beautiful smile. She was an exceptionally gorgeous woman. Very sensual. When she stood up, her body was purely feminine. It was impossible to resist her.

Brandon rose immediately. Lana tucked her hand in the crook of his arm, and they walked out of the shop together. Lana's voice drifted back to them. She sounded so admiring as she told him how wonderful he was to take care of a girl who clearly needed help.

For the first time, Seychelle felt as if she really did have a family. She knew what it felt like to work smoothly with Lana, completely in sync, not having to look at her and yet knowing instantly what she was doing and that she was on board to help get this young girl to safety.

Brandon Campbell was a predator, and somehow Seychelle was going to find a way to deal with him. It wasn't going to be that day, but it would be soon. She was grateful she wasn't alone, and Lana was so ready and willing to help. Now that she had the predator out of the way, and her voice had compelled the older women at the table to hear only truth, she could concentrate on Tessa and do her best to undo the damage in the short time Lana was buying her.

"All right, Tessa, keep looking at me. Tell me the truth so I can help you."

"No one can help me. I'm not worth anything. He reminds me of that all the time. I'm lucky he bothers with me," Tessa whispered in a low voice.

A collective gasp went up from the table, but Seychelle waved them to silence. She already knew Brandon's methods. He made certain he took away all self-esteem from his victims.

"That isn't *your* truth. I know I can help you. If I can get you away, would you go? What would you like to do? What was your dream?"

For one moment, Tessa's eyes lit up and her face was animated. "I wanted to be a fashion designer and make clothes. I was really good at it in school. But he said . . ."

"We don't really care what he said, do we?" Seychelle said. "We only care what you want and what we can do for you. Do you want to go home? To your parents?"

Tessa shuddered and wrapped her arms around her middle, shaking her head. "No, I'll stay with him. I'll stay with Brandon. My father gets drunk and he . . ." She broke off and shuddered again. "No. I'm never going back there."

"You don't have to. Not ever. And you don't have to stay with Brandon," Seychelle soothed. The door to the shop opened and her stomach knotted. She kept her voice calm. "Honey, how old are you?"

"Eighteen."

"When is your birthday?" Because, honestly, the girl looked like a baby to her. Seychelle knew she looked young. But Tessa looked like she was fifteen. Maybe sixteen at most.

"It was two days ago." That was said in a whisper.

Another gasp went around the table. That meant Brandon Campbell had been with an underage girl. He had to have known.

Seychelle was getting serious vibes, a warning tingle sliding down her spine. The hairs on the back of her neck standing up. A flutter in her sex. *He* had walked in. Savage. He was in the Floating Hat. Another thing about Savage she loved: as stubborn as he could be, he was also sensitive, and he could see her hold on Tessa was very fragile and could be broken with the slightest distraction. Sabelia hadn't come to the table with their tea either. That didn't surprise her. Sabelia clearly had psychic gifts.

"All right, honey, we're going to get you some help. What do you think about leaving with Lana? Have you met her before? She's seriously wonderful. She's coming back now."

Those little bells in the shape of hats announced the door to the shop had once again opened, allowing Brandon and Lana back inside. Lana's soft voice kept Brandon enthralled as they walked toward the table.

"No one can hurt you when Lana's around. And you know what she does?" Seychelle poured enthusiasm into her voice. "Lana designs clothes. She owns Label 287. Have you heard of that boutique?"

Again, there was a flare of interest in Tessa's eyes.

"She's right here, Tessa. She'll walk you right out and take you to a place no one can hurt you. She'll give you a job."

Brandon sank into his chair and Lana took her seat at the table. Brandon barely glanced at Tessa, seemingly completely taken with Lana.

"Brandon." Seychelle leaned toward him and waited until his gaze jumped to her face. She had used the merest hint of compulsion in her voice. The thinnest note, just enough that it covered his heavier copper-colored ones without penetrating into them. The gold slid against the copper and very gently settled over the top of those notes. "We discovered a huge problem while you were gone."

The older women nodded solemnly, all three backing Seychelle up, looking at Brandon as if he was in terrible trouble.

"Don't be alarmed, we're going to fix it. There's no way we'll let this affect your reputation or work," Seychelle continued, her voice pitched in that same low, almost intimate tone. The golden notes continued to slip out. "Tessa only turned eighteen two days ago." She dropped her voice and looked around the tearoom before continuing. "That means the *entire* time she's been with you, she's been underage."

"What?" Brandon feigned horror.

The three older women continued to nod. Lana put her hand over her mouth, her eyes going wide in shock.

"I'm afraid it's true. If this gets out, it will ruin you," Seychelle said. "We think we can minimize the damage to your reputation if we move fast. Lana can take Tessa now to a safe place. You can get her things to Inez at the store, and it will simply look as if you were rescuing her from a bad situation."

Tessa shook her head. "Brandon said no one else will want me."

The older women looked horrified again. It was impossible not to be aware of it. Lana made a move to stand, but Seychelle signaled her to wait.

"You misunderstood him, didn't she, Brandon? He would never mean that," Seychelle said. Brandon had to give Tessa his permission or Tessa wouldn't go. She was still too far under his spell.

Brandon felt those golden notes weighing on him, pushing on his need to cooperate. At the same time, he always counted on the goodwill of the older women in Sea Haven, and they were looking to him to do the right thing as well. He gave Tessa his best smile. "Honey, everyone would want you. You're a wonderful girl and you're going to go far in this world." He pushed his most persuasive tone into his voice. "Go with Lana like a good girl and cooperate with her. She wants you to do well. All of us do."

Tessa nearly leapt out of her seat. Lana rose smoothly and took the girl's hand. Seychelle didn't allow triumph to show on her face as the two left the Floating Hat together. She was certain Tessa was going to end up at Blythe and Czar's home. It didn't matter as long as she was safe.

She turned her attention back to Brandon, giving him a smile. "We were all so worried when we found out her age."

Brandon leaned toward her, all charm. "I appreciate you caring enough to be concerned."

"It was very disconcerting," Inez said. "Really, Brandon, how could you not realize her age when she lived with you for months?"

Doris frowned. "She looks so young too. I thought Seychelle looked young, but that girl looks like a baby. You need to be far more careful in the future, Brandon."

He scowled and got up, shoving back his chair, but his eyes were on Seychelle. Steady. Refusing to look away. "I'll get her things and bring them to the store, Inez. I'm glad to be done with her. She was difficult."

"She was a child," Rebecca pointed out.

Brandon's eyes narrowed on Seychelle. Grew dark and stormy. "This is twice now you've chosen to interfere. Do you think I'm going to let you get away with it?" He hissed the question at her, low and mean. This time his tone was heavy with pure copper, pushing the notes down so they dropped into her mind like weights.

She maintained eye contact. "You do what you have to do, Brandon." Her notes were pure gold, sliding into his mind, pouring over it and surrounding it, coating it and covering it completely until the notes were lifted and carried away, drifting toward the ceiling.

He swore at her, crouching down so he could stare directly into her eyes. "This isn't over."

"I think it is," Savage said. "Back off now." He stepped between Seychelle and Brandon, breaking the eye contact between them, his crotch practically wedged in Brandon's face, his motorcycle boots inches from his legs. His voice was low, barely heard, but it carried enough menace to send shivers down Seychelle's spine.

Brandon nearly fell over trying to get on his feet. Swearing, he stormed out.

Savage took Lana's chair, his thigh brushing Seychelle's. "Hi, ladies, I thought I'd join my fiancée for tea this afternoon. As always, when she's away from me, she gets herself in a little bit of trouble."

"Fake fiancée," Seychelle corrected. Her phone vibrated in her pocket and she took it out automatically, glancing down at it. **You are in such trouble.**

That's a shocker. It took a hot minute to type that reply back when she really wanted to laugh. He looked so relaxed and at ease sitting there with the women around him. He was dressed in his jeans and boots, his tight tee and vest with his colors, looking hotter than hell. How did he do that? So sexy. And he'd left his meeting to come see her. To reassure her. He also hadn't left her alone the way she needed. Maybe she should just kick him under the table.

"Ah yes, you did forget something this morning when you left so fast with Lana, didn't you, baby?" Savage said. He picked up her left hand and displayed her bare finger to the women at the table. "Looks a little naked to me. What do you think, Inez?"

"Definitely naked," Inez agreed.

Seychelle tried to pull her hand away. "Don't encourage him." He was up to something. She wasn't going to like it, she could tell. This was retaliation. Big-time.

Savage pushed a ring onto her finger. It glided on as if made for her. As if it had been on her finger a thousand times and fit perfectly. She tried not to look at it, but she couldn't help it. She didn't know a lot about jewelry or diamonds, but she did know when something was incredibly beautiful. The center stone was a fancy oval-shaped vivid teal-blue diamond. It nearly took her breath away, it was so beautiful. Small petals made of sparkling diamonds wrapped around the center stone like a flower, so they would lay on her finger perfectly.

A collective gasp went up around the table. Seychelle just stared at the ring, almost uncomprehending. She lifted her lashes and looked up at Savage, unable to think what to say. She couldn't embarrass him in front of everyone and say no, she wouldn't marry him, but she didn't know how to feel. What to feel. She loved him more than she loved anyone. Herself.

She knew why he'd put the ring on her finger. It was so beautiful. It sat there, weighing on her, making her feel as if she was his, just the way he wanted her to feel, although she didn't need the ring. Just being in his company did that. Breathing him in made her feel as if she belonged with Savage. It wasn't the ring, no matter how much she wanted to blame it on the ring.

"You left home without your engagement ring?" Rebecca asked. Her voice trembled and her fingers shook as she placed them protectively over her wedding rings and rolled them back and forth soothingly. "You took it off?" She made it sound as if that would be a sacrilege.

Savage put his hand over Seychelle's. "I like to tease her, but no, she didn't leave home without it. Seychelle would never do that. This is the first time she's ever seen it. I asked her to marry me some time ago, but the ring wasn't made, so she called me her fake fiancé. That's been a running joke between us. Ice finished it and gave it to me, so I brought it right away. I thought you ladies might enjoy seeing it as well."

"Seychelle." Doris whispered her name. "Let me see it, child. Ice made it. He's so famous too." She looked up as Sabelia came up to the table, carrying a tray with several teapots on it. "Sabelia, look. Savage and Seychelle are official. He isn't her fake fiancé anymore."

"Congratulations, Savage, you actually pulled it off," Sabelia said as she put the teapots on the table. "The ring is beautiful, Seychelle." She admired it for a long moment, then flashed Savage a grin. "You do have good taste. That was very intense, the scene with Campbell. He's brought that girl in here more than once. He's got a dark aura surrounding him."

Savage sighed as the women began to pour tea into their cups. "Sabelia, do you think I could get a cup of coffee?"

"Your aura is as dark as they come," Sabelia volunteered. "With a great deal of red swirling around in it. Wouldn't want to try to figure you out. I'll be right back with the pastries."

"And my coffee," Savage added.

Doris laughed. "I forgot you think tea is poison, Savage. He believes we're trying to do him in with tea, ladies."

Savage glanced at his watch. "Don't think it, Doris, I know it. Blythe looks like an angel, same as this one right here." He brought up Seychelle's hand and kissed it. "But both are little hellions. They disagree with me on just about everything and then sweetly ask if I want a cup of tea. Don't you think that's just a little suspicious?"

Seychelle couldn't help the way her heart stuttered around him. Her big, bad biker sitting with the older women, making them laugh the way he did. He looked so wicked, his low, clipped voice so sexy she could barely stand it. A tearoom was the last place a man like Savage would ever go. He would never sit at a table with a group of older women, chatting, making them laugh. She knew he was there for one reason. For her. He was there for her.

He had his fingers threaded through hers, their joined hands on his thigh, rubbing seductively back and forth while he conversed. Sabelia brought his coffee and the pastries and sandwiches, which he ate with one hand so he could keep hers captive. It was impossible not to be in love with him, to slide deeper and deeper under his spell, when she knew she was only going to suffer more heartache if she didn't save herself.

As if he knew what she was thinking, Savage suddenly pressed her hand tighter against his thigh and leaned close, his lips whispering against her ear. A touch only. The lightest of kisses, if it was even really that, but the caress sent little darts of fire racing down her spine, straight to her sex. He was addicting. It was scary how much he could wrap her up emotionally as well as physically.

The bells tinkled merrily and Eden Ravard hurried in. She waved to them, smiling widely. "I didn't think my hair was ever going to get finished. It isn't even long, and it took forever to get blown out."

"Well worth the wait," Savage said.

Eden giggled like a schoolgirl. Savage had gone to her house twice with Seychelle, helping out in emergencies in spite of the fact that she had four sons and a stepson, none of whom were ever around. The ladies fanned themselves and Seychelle shook her head. "Don't fall for his charm. He's a bad-boy biker."

Sometimes Seychelle didn't know who Savage was. He

rarely spoke, even when they went together to visit her older friends' homes. He would prowl around looking to do repairs, and she would do all the actual visiting. Other times, he'd turn into Mr. Charm, like now.

"Best kind," Eden said. "What did I miss?"

Doris nodded in agreement. "Look at Seychelle's ring, Eden. You missed that."

Savage brought her hand out over the table, securely trapped in his, for Eden to admire the ring. When she'd done enough complimenting, he kissed the stone and stood up, tugging Seychelle with him. She couldn't help the way her stomach did little somersaults and her heart accelerated.

"I really have to get back to the clubhouse, ladies. I left a meeting to come here and see my woman. I'd like to borrow her for a few minutes if you don't mind."

She shouldn't go with him. She didn't need to be alone with him, not for one moment. She had to finish her lunch with the ladies, ask for a ride to her house—or just walk now that Lana was gone—and be alone just for a little while to think things over. The last thing she needed to do was be alone with Savage. Even knowing that it was the worst possible idea, Seychelle followed him right out of the Floating Hat.

"Savage." She tried a half-hearted protest when he tucked her under his arm once they were on the sidewalk, heading toward his Harley.

Jackson Deveau, the deputy sheriff, was standing next to the motorcycle in full uniform, looking as if he was inspecting it. Savage didn't even hesitate. He walked her right up to the motorcycle, ignoring the cop.

"Stopped by to tell you congratulations," Jackson said.

Savage glanced at him, no expression on his face. "News travels fast. Thanks. Just gave her the ring a little while ago."

Jackson frowned and then turned his attention to Seychelle as Savage swung his leg over the bike and settled onto the seat with a creak of the leather.

"Ma'am. Didn't realize. I was talking about your man

and his little prank he pulled. It was a nice one, and I want him to know the full extent so he can gloat about it."

"Don't have a clue what you're going on about, Deveau, so spit it out. Got a meeting to get to." Savage's tone, his voice, were as expressionless as the mask on his face. "Was just going to say good-bye to my woman."

He was lying. Nothing gave him away, but he knew exactly what Jackson was talking about, and Seychelle wanted to know what it was.

"Those ladies you got all excited about buying a present for me for my birthday went right to Clyde Darden and asked him to name one of his fuckin' flowers after me. Not just any flower either. They wanted one he could show all up and down the state. Wanted it to be named something heroic. Notice I'm givin' you the details, Savage, so you can spend a lot of time thinking about how you got me good. Those ladies needed to raise a lot of money so Darden could grow this flower in his greenhouse and then travel to those shows and enter it. So they went to the Red Hat Society, two chapters, and asked if anyone wanted to help them out with their birthday funds so Darden could keep entering those damned contests. Red Hat ladies not only got behind the idea, but they decided to do fund-raisers for Darden in my name. And the fuckin' flower's name."

Seychelle had no choice. She had to bury her face against Savage's shoulder. Bite her lip. Count in her head. Press her hands tight in a fist into his abs. How he could sit there straight-faced she had no idea. Savage was definitely behind that prank, but how? She was *so* going to ask him.

"There's a reason I'm giving you all the gruesome details, Savage. I believe in revenge. I bide my time, and I go for total revenge. You are going to know it's coming, and you deserve it. It will be far worse than what you did to me. So enjoy this while you can—you got me good, but know I'll be planning the payback." Jackson smiled at Seychelle. "I'd say congratulations, ma'am, but I think you're a little crazy to be hooking up with this one. Think about what I just told you he did. That's one of his jokes. He gets serious, and Lord only knows what he might plan." He turned and walked away.

"You totally did that, didn't you?" Seychelle demanded. "How?"

Savage shrugged. "The ladies were worried about what to give him for his birthday. Said he didn't like birthday presents. I just mentioned how Darden names his flowers, and the conversation went from there. I don't see how that could be construed as my fault."

"You're not telling me the entire truth, are you?" Because he wasn't. She was certain of it.

He laughed, his gloved hand over hers. "No, babe. I'm not." His smile faded, his blue eyes looking into hers. "I came here to talk about us. I only have so much time, and you left this morning really upset."

Seychelle wasn't going to lie to him. "I'm in love with you, Savage, but I don't know if I can be what you need."

"You're exactly what I need, baby. We'll work things out. What you saw this morning scared you. I shouldn't have . . ." His eyes went even colder, and he cursed in his native language. "I'm not trying to be impatient. We've got time, Seychelle. You never have to get there. Never."

She shook her head. "Don't. You know that isn't the truth. You need that, and I want you to have everything you need. I just have to think whether or not I can be that person."

"I told you I would know. You respond to the things we do."

Her stomach knotted. "I know I do, and I don't know if I like that in myself. I don't know how far I'm willing to let myself go. I have to really think about it, Savage. Living that reality isn't the same as fantasizing over it. You have a reason for being the way you are. If I was only going down that path because I love you and wanted to sacrifice for you, then I would be able to say yes in a heartbeat. But there's a part of me that wants it for me. I don't have any excuse. None."

"Why do you think you need an excuse?" His fingers found her ring.

"Shouldn't I have a reason for craving something like that? You don't like yourself at times, and you were shaped into who you are. It doesn't make sense to me. It isn't normal."

"What the fuck is normal, Seychelle? Because my normal is mixing pain and pleasure. That's normal. That's hot as hell. Arousing. And I'm as pleased as fuck it's arousing to you. I know it's difficult to think you enjoy that kind of thing when everyone around you has a different sexual practice, but what they do is their business and what we do is ours. You think about how much I love you. Think on that, baby. Think how much I take care of you and always will."

Savage hooked his palm around the nape of her neck and dragged her to him for one of his long, claiming kisses that stole her sanity, then indicated for her to go back into the tea shop. He waited until she was safe inside before he took off on his bike. She listened to the pipes fade away before she joined the others.

NINETEEN

Seychelle walked to her cottage. She needed to feel the fresh sea air on her skin and listen to the roar of the waves as they raced to the bluffs and crashed against them. She had purchased the house on the narrow road across from the headlands because she liked the privacy and the close proximity to the ocean.

She detoured and took a path through the tall grass leading to the bluffs. The grass rippled with the wind, bending and swaying as if dancing to the sound of the waves as they rushed the rocks. The wildness of this coast appealed to her. The Southern California coast was warmer and so much more predictable, but here there were rip currents and undertows, and the water was cold and crazy rough.

She wrapped her arms around herself and walked slowly along the path she'd taken hundreds of times. It was narrow and all sandy dirt. Gulls screamed and dove at the water or circled the sea stacks before settling and folding their wings. Some of the birds squabbled in the air, making her want to laugh.

She loved Sea Haven and her little home here. She'd come here at her lowest, when she knew she was going to die. She'd been so exhausted, barely able to stand most of the time. Walking to the bluffs had become her first goal, and then to the town of Sea Haven. She couldn't believe how far she'd come, how much stronger she'd gotten. How much happier she was.

She lifted her gaze to the sky and the seagulls again. Savage made her happy. There was no doubt about that. He made her feel as if she wasn't alone when she'd been so terribly lonely even in the middle of a crowd. Truthfully, when she'd tried to date and hadn't reacted at all to any man kissing her or touching her, she'd felt as if she wasn't normal. So why was she upset that she was reacting to him and his brand of sex? Why did she have to question everything good that came her way?

She turned back toward her house and began to walk slowly. She still could die very young. Just because she was feeling stronger and she was with Savage didn't mean her heart was suddenly better. She hadn't gone to a doctor. They hadn't actually been successful at stopping her from taking on an illness, because they hadn't tried yet. She still wanted to live life to the fullest, experience everything she could. She didn't want to miss anything. Why was she suddenly thinking about retreating from Savage? It made no sense. She was panicking, just the way she always did.

She put her hand over the ring he'd had made for her. She was looking up the diamond when she got home. She'd never seen one like that. She knew Ice was a famous jeweler, although few knew he was a biker, just that his pieces were sought-after. She was certain that if anyone knew he was a biker, it would make the demand for his jewelry skyrocket.

Savage and she had just moved so fast, she felt like she couldn't catch her breath. She was a processor. She liked to think about things. She wasn't impulsive, as a rule. She liked the way they'd been at the beginning of their relationship, when she could lie on the bed with him and not worry about what was coming next and how fast she'd have to get there. At least, that was what she told herself, because it was so much easier than facing the truth.

Seychelle didn't want to have to figure out why she'd been born the way she was. Or if not born with those little dark corners, why she'd developed them. How deep did they go? Could she stop before she got into territory that was beyond what she thought was too much? How much was too much? How did she even answer those questions? She needed to go into her haven of safety, sit in her favorite spot on the bed and just let herself meditate. Maybe the answer would come.

The house was cool and shadowy when she unlocked the front door and stepped inside. All the shades were drawn over the windows. She frowned, wondering if Savage had pulled them down so people couldn't see in while they were at the other house. She'd never done that. She had live plants in the house, and they thrived on light. She went to the window closest to the door and raised that shade.

It wasn't like her cottage was large. The rooms flowed into one another, and when she turned and looked straight from the cozy living room to her kitchen, her breath caught in her throat. Facing her, seated at the table as if he belonged there, was Joseph Arnold. There was a gun in front of him, just lying there on the kitchen table, right within his reach.

"You're home." He sounded strange, like a lover welcoming her back after a long absence.

Seychelle's mouth went dry, and she glanced at the door. She was only a few feet from it. Could she make it out? She had no idea why, but she knew with absolute certainty he had come there to kill her. "What are you doing here?"

"Waiting for you. I didn't think you'd ever get back. Those old ladies take up far too much of your time, Seychelle. You're always helping them when you should be paying attention to your duties here at home," Joseph scolded.

A million things ran through her mind at top speed. She'd read about stalkers when Joseph Arnold had first begun turning up at every venue she'd sung at. Then small things disappeared from her home. She'd talked to a police officer in San Francisco. The officer had been kind but explained that Arnold hadn't really done anything that could be construed as threatening at that point. Once he identified himself as a music scout, he appeared to be trying to help her. The cop believed her, but still said with regret that there was nothing they could do. They couldn't catch him at anything.

Seychelle had tried to be very clear with each encounter she'd had with Joseph that she wasn't interested, but it never seemed to faze him. He kept following her everywhere she went. She'd thought after Savage's rather violent reaction, he would stop, but he didn't. There he sat, right at her kitchen table, as if he owned the place—and her. He acted as if he thought they were in a relationship.

She walked farther into the room, going to the next window and raising the shade. "You know something? You're right. I do spend way too much time with all of them. I feel so bad for them. Most of them are completely alone in the world. I sort their medications out for them and make certain they have groceries, but I do stay too long. It tires me out."

Deliberately, she walked past him to enter the bedroom. It was easy to see into the room, and again she went straight to the window and raised the shade. "I thought I'd change my clothes really quick. I like to get comfortable in the evenings. Are you hungry? I was going to make myself a salad."

She went to the dresser, pulled off the engagement ring and placed it in the top drawer. Right there, she exchanged the top she wore for a long sweater. The sweater went almost to her knees. Sitting on the edge of the bed, she removed her shoes and then went back over to the dresser to shimmy out of her jeans. As she did, she grabbed her phone and hit the contact number of the last person she'd called—Savage.

"Joseph. Did you want a salad?" She pulled on leggings and slipped the phone into the pocket as she called to the intruder loudly.

When she looked in at him, he had the refrigerator open and was staring at the contents. Very slowly he turned back to her, his face flushed, eyes narrowed. "Why do you have a steak marinating in here? You're a vegetarian."

"Doris was coming over. She wasn't feeling very good—one of her migraines coming on—so she gave me a rain check. Why?" She walked straight over to the table where he'd been sitting and stared in feigned horror at the gun. "Oh my God, Joseph, you brought a gun into my house. Is it loaded? Why did you bring that here? You know I hate guns. Get it out of my sight right now." She started to cry, backing away from the table, hands in the air. "Why did you bring that in here? Just go. That was so mean of you. You know guns freak me out. Go, get out of the house and take that horrid thing with you."

Seychelle turned and ran into the bedroom and flung herself on the bed, crawling up it to the headboard, pulling the sheet over her so she could hide the cell phone. Hopefully, Savage was hearing every single dramatic word. She put her face in her hands and sobbed. It wasn't that hard to do. She really was scared. She just didn't cry in loud, heaving wails that could wake the dead, as a rule.

Joseph came into the room a few minutes later, looking around and then dropping into the chair in the corner of the room. "It's all right now, Seychelle. Stop crying. It's gone. I've put it away."

"It's still in the house. I know it is. I didn't hear the door open. Go put it in your car, or on the porch. I don't want it inside my house." She hiccupped and sobbed in between each word.

"That's unreasonable. If you can't see it . . ."

She cried harder and shook her head. "Why are you here? You ruined everything. I thought we could eat together and just have a nice time, but you had to bring that horrid thing into my house for no reason. I mean it, Joseph, get it out of here."

She kept her head down, face in one hand, but with the other she mopped the tears with the hem of the sheet. She really wanted Joseph to take the gun outside. If Savage and his brothers from Torpedo Ink showed up, she didn't want bullets flying.

Why hadn't she thought to call 911? It hadn't even occurred to her. She had automatically turned to Savage for help.

"Seychelle." Joseph's tone was sharp. Nasally. His temper was beginning to fray. "Stop crying. You can't see the gun. I put it in a drawer, out of sight."

She didn't want to take a chance on making him angry with her. As slowly as she thought she could get away with it, she lowered the sheet from her face and dashed at the tears with her palm. With the other hand she made certain to turn the phone over, so the speaker was facing upward. Savage was her lifeline, and she knew he would come. She *knew* it. That told her everything she needed to know about her relationship with him.

She might have uncertainties about herself, but she wasn't unsure of Savage. He was never going to let her down. He came to her visits with her elderly friends and went out of his way to make sure their homes were safe for them. He didn't like talking but went out of his comfort zone to be charming. He told her ahead of time what to expect and made everything her choice. He gave her adventures she would never have on her own, and she loved them even if sometimes she was scared. Savage would come because she could count on him. That was an absolute certainty.

"Are you certain I won't come across it when I'm making our salads? I have to get out utensils." She was careful to keep a wobble in her voice. She risked a quick look at his face, not wanting to take things too far but needing to stall. How long did it take to get from Caspar to Sea Haven on the Harleys? Ten minutes? Less? Five? She had to think in terms of longer. The longest. What if they had gone out of town? The club did that sometimes, and when it was club business, Savage didn't tell her.

"Make the salad for us, Seychelle. You won't find it, but if you get close, I'll warn you and get whatever you need out of the drawer for you."

She wiped her face again and nodded. "Thank you." She forced herself to slip off the bed and walk on bare feet right past him.

Joseph turned to follow her. He was so close she could smell him. His drug of choice was cocaine, and that, mingled with his natural body odor, sickened her. She coughed delicately into her elbow and kept walking. In the kitchen he toed a chair around, straddled it and stared at her with a little smirk on his face.

"Tell me what those old ladies had to say that was so exciting you were late getting home. I saw Inez; she's such a busybody."

Seychelle retrieved the items she would need to make a salad from the refrigerator. She took her time, still stalling. Still hoping. "Why do you say that? Has she said something to you?"

Joseph glared at her. "Said she noticed I was always watching you."

"She never said a word to me." Inez hadn't, and she should have. "I hope you told her you worked in the music industry and were just trying to find a way to help me be successful."

He watched her wash all the vegetables before spinning the lettuce to get it dry. "You don't want to be successful; that's why you always quit."

She sighed and half turned to face him, as if in resignation. "I don't like to admit it, even to myself, but my health isn't very good, and after a while, singing in bars is exhausting. I went to a doctor, and he told me if I kept it up, I wouldn't live very long."

Joseph's face darkened into a scowl. His eyes narrowed to twin points of blazing anger. "If that's true, why would you sing in that biker bar?"

Where the hell were her rescuers? How long had it been? It felt like a million years had gone by. She took a deep breath and let it out, striving for a normal voice. "You know I love to sing. Did you hear that band? I've never, not once in my life, had the opportunity to sing with a band like that. It was amazing. The good thing is that they don't play on a regular basis. I wouldn't have to commit to singing every weekend. I could pick and choose when I felt up to it. They're kind of laid-back that way." She poured enthusiasm into her voice.

"Are you fucking them?" He spat the words at her.

She let the silence stretch between them for a long time. "That's just insulting. I'm not going to talk to you, Joseph, if you're going to be ugly like that."

He stood up, kicked the chair out of the way and caught her by the arm, fingers biting into flesh. She smashed the salad bowl right into the bridge of his nose as hard as she could and slammed the ball of her foot into his upper thigh, hoping to give him a dead leg. The moment he let go, she drove her foot into his groin and turned and ran to the front door.

Joseph dropped to the floor with a roar of rage and pain. Seychelle hesitated for a moment, thinking to go back and look for his gun, but decided she'd be crazy to waste what little time she'd bought herself. She flung the door open and ran outside. Her car was in the garage. The door was closed, and sometimes it took a few minutes to warm her baby up. She knew she wouldn't have that kind of time, so she just ran straight down the road toward Sea Haven.

Already, she could hear the sound of vehicles coming toward her. Not the reassuring roar of pipes. Torpedo Ink hadn't wanted Joseph to hear them coming. Then Savage had her in his arms, holding her close. Tight. Very tight.

"Did he hurt you, baby?"

There was something very deadly in his voice—in his eyes when she looked up at him. "He's got a gun," she whispered. "Savage, don't do anything crazy. We should just call the cops. He isn't worth it."

"We don't call the cops, Seychelle."

He handed her off to Ice and turned toward the house with a dark menace in every step. Behind him, Maestro and Keys prowled, looking every bit as grim. Mechanic drove a truck with dark, forbidding windows.

"Ice." She started to follow the others.

"Sorry, honey, you're not going with them. You're going to stay out of the way and let your man handle this the way he has to."

"You don't understand, Joseph has a gun. He put it in one of the drawers in my house. I should have stayed inside and looked for it." She was all but wringing her hands together.

Ice guided her off the main road. Once off the road and facing the house, she saw two other Torpedo Ink members, Destroyer and Storm, at the back door.

"It's locked," she whispered.

"We put in the locks," he reminded her. "There are all kinds of stalkers, Seychelle. His kind don't stop. He fantasizes he's in a relationship with you, and that makes him dangerous. You aren't on the same page with him. One misstep and he will kill you. They would lock him up for a short while and then he'd be right back."

Seychelle was well aware Ice was telling the truth. Joseph had been following her around for a long time. He kept approaching her in different guises, trying to get her to go out with him. He seemed to have dropped the music scout this time and believed himself in a relationship with her. He had sunk into a delusion she wanted no part of.

His car was parked to the right of her house. She recognized the nice little sport coupe he was very proud of. He had talked about his car in San Francisco and how nice it was. What a luxury car, yet sporty. It was a pretty color, she would hand him that, but she wasn't a car person. She wouldn't know the make and model of any car, if the truth was told. One of the Torpedo Ink members, Transporter, slid inside and drove the car off, headed south.

There was a sharp whistle, and Storm and Destroyer disappeared inside. Then Savage, Maestro and Keys went in through the front door. A muffled gunshot made her jump, but Ice was unfazed. He just stood there, watching the cottage, keeping her in the brush several yards from the house.

Her heart began to thud hard as the front door banged open, and from her vantage point, she could see Savage emerging, dragging Joseph by his arms. Joseph was trying to struggle, but it was a half-hearted attempt. Destroyer came through the door, let Joseph's legs drag for a minute, then reached down and picked them up by the ankles. The two men carried him to the truck, where Mechanic waited patiently behind the wheel, apparently listening to music.

Savage opened a door to the back passenger seat, easily flung Joseph inside and then bent in after him. Destroyer was at the other door and also leaned in.

"What are they doing to him?" Seychelle asked.

"Just restraining him so he can't move while Mechanic takes him to the clubhouse. We're going to have a little talk with him. Savage has a lot to say and some questions to ask him. Then he's going away. We don't want anyone seeing him. You didn't see him today. Fortunately, he didn't tell anyone he was coming to see you, mostly because he came here to kill you today."

"Why would he want to kill me?" Seychelle turned her gaze up to Ice's. But she knew it was true. She'd known it the moment she saw the gun.

"Because his delusional fantasy isn't working for him anymore, and when it doesn't work, he kills his victim and moves on," Ice explained. "He's been clever enough to make certain there's not enough evidence to point to him. We've had Code looking into him."

"What's Savage going to do?" she whispered, dread filling her.

"What he should have done the first time he found that man in your house, stealing your things. You asked him not to and he spared him," Ice explained. "That was a big fucking mistake, Seychelle. You could be dead right now, and he knows it. That would have been on him."

She shook her head. "No, it would have been on me, not him. Joseph is sick. He needs help. Savage was showing compassion."

Ice snorted his derision. "Savage was showing you he loves you and giving you something he shouldn't have. He doesn't have an ounce of compassion for someone like Joseph Arnold. Once they cross the line and kill an innocent, there's no going back."

She shook her head. "He can't live with that kind of thing on his conscience day in and day out, Ice. You all expect too much of him."

She watched as both doors slammed shut and Mechanic took off with his prisoner. Savage and Destroyer walked back toward her with Maestro and Keys. Savage looked grim. The lines in his face were cut deep. His eyes were colder than she'd ever seen them as he strode back to her.

"Babe, there's some things you have to know about your man. For things like this, when it comes to vermin like that, he doesn't have a conscience," Ice said.

Savage came right up to her, grasped her by the shoulders and started her toward her cottage. "Get what you need, Seychelle, to bring to the other house. I have some work to do tonight, and I don't know how long it's going to take. The other house is more secure, and I'll leave you there with a guard."

"Now that you have Joseph, don't you think it's safe for me here?" Something told her not to push him, but she didn't want to go back to his place yet. He might feel as if his home was far safer for her, but she didn't necessarily feel that way about it.

His grip tightened on her and he continued to walk her toward her home. "Babe, just please do as I ask. Scared the holy fuck out of me when I heard your voice on the phone and then you said the word *gun*. We just sounded the alarm and raced out of there as fast as we could. Gotta get you home, where I know you're safe."

Her house looked the same. Felt the same. Like home. It didn't feel as if a madman had taken it over. Lettuce was all over the kitchen floor, and she bent to pick up the bowl. Savage took it from her.

"I'll clean this up. You put a few things together for a couple of nights. We'll stay at my place and talk things out. Come back here after."

Seychelle didn't bother to argue with him, especially since he was wearing that implacable look on his face and his eyes were not only glacier cold but flat and dead inside. She knew no matter what she said, she wasn't going to get her way. This was one of those times he'd warned her about.

She pulled out clothes and pushed them into a small overnight bag. Her ring was in the top drawer under her leggings, where she'd shoved it. She slipped it back on her finger, needing the reassurance of it and not understanding why. Savage seemed distant from her, even though he was right there, dictating to her. The weight of the ring on her finger made her feel instantly closer to him, and she needed that when she already was so uncertain.

In her small bathroom, she collected a few personal items, but she actually had most things already duplicated. Savage had thought of just about anything she could need or want at the other house. She mostly took things she wanted for familiarity. She nearly took the rose sculpture with her parents' ashes, but this was her home, and she wanted it there. She did bring her mother's hairbrush.

Savage stood by the door with the other Torpedo Ink members, and it took a little courage to walk up to him. The men were intimidating, and she really didn't know them all that well yet.

"I'm ready. I can drive my car. Do you want to ride with me, or do you have your bike with you?"

He reached down and caught her left hand, bringing it up so he could see the ring. His thumb slid over it. Of course he would have noticed that it was missing. He looked at her, clearly waiting for an explanation.

"I took it off so he wouldn't notice it. He was acting so weird, and I thought it best to just go along with whatever he said and stall as long as possible."

"Smart woman," Ice said. "Too fuckin' smart for you, Savage. Knew it the minute I laid eyes on her."

Savage kissed her knuckles, then the ring. "I'll drive you home and then head to the clubhouse. Ice and Soleil will stay with you until I come home. It will be late, baby, so they'll probably stay in one of the guest rooms. Alena's going to send over dinner."

Seychelle lifted her chin. "I'm capable of cooking for a guest." She was capable of driving her own car as well, but she wasn't telling him that, not in front of his "brothers."

He reached around her, caught up her overnight bag and left it to Ice to lock up her cottage as Savage led the way to the garage. "Babe, I'm sticking you with guests for the night and asking you to stay at a house you don't want to stay in." He opened the back door of her car and tossed her overnight bag in with a little more force than necessary. "I'm trying to make things easier on you. I didn't want you to have to go grocery shopping on top of everything else."

She yanked her seat belt around her and waited for him to adjust the driver's seat in order to be able to get behind the wheel. "You didn't want me to go grocery shopping," she clarified.

He sent her a chilling look as he started the car. "You're right, I would prefer that you not go anywhere until I know there aren't any other threats to you. At the same time, I don't want you to have to cook for unexpected guests."

She stared out the window as he easily handled the car, taking it along the highway toward Caspar. "I'm just out of sorts. I have been all day. Crazy person with gun trying to kill me in my house might have put me in a bad mood on top of everything else. Just saying. I'm a processor. I just need a little time to get a handle on all this." She did her best not to burst into tears.

Savage ran his finger down her cheek. "I know this is hard for you, Seychelle. I'll come home the minute I can, and I know it's important you have some alone time. Ice and Soleil will go to the guest room long before I'll make it home tonight. They're used to being alone. She could use a friend, though. She doesn't come to the clubhouse very often with the other women."

"I'll be happy to visit with her," she assured him, not really meaning it but knowing she would do it. She pushed back her hair and then reached out her hand, needing the physical connection with him.

Savage immediately engulfed her smaller hand in his and pressed it to the heavy muscle of his thigh. "We're going to be fine, Seychelle. We're new, and I get that can be scary."

Seychelle nodded. There was little doubt in her mind that any new relationship could be frightening at the time, but hers was more than that if she thought too much about it. On the other hand, did she really want to be without Savage? She looked up at him. She had been alone without him. Lonely. She hadn't felt alive. Or beautiful. She certainly didn't know what it was like to be loved so intensely. Savage made her feel as if she belonged with him. She just didn't know how to fit into his world. There were so many things she questioned, and she didn't have anyone she could talk things over with.

Savage pulled the Mini Cooper into the garage and parked it. "Babe, for me, just leave everything for tonight. I'll be home in the morning, and we can talk then. I promise you, I can make things better." He turned her hand up to the warmth of his mouth, kissing her fingers.

Seychelle nodded. "I can do that, Savage." She wasn't leaving him, she knew that much. She wanted to work things out, but it wasn't with him, it was in her own mind. She had to find some kind of balance she could live with. "About Joseph . . ."

Savage shook his head. "We aren't going to talk about him. Arnold is no longer your business. He's mine. Go into the house, babe. Try to forget everything bothering you and just enjoy Soleil. She's very sweet, and she hasn't had the best life." He leaned into her and then brushed a kiss onto her forehead before sliding out of the car, one hand retrieving her overnight bag. Once he rounded the hood, he handed her the bag and indicated the door leading to the house from the huge garage.

Seychelle didn't look back. Savage was already somewhere else in his head. He was at the clubhouse, or wherever they'd taken Joseph Arnold.

She put her overnight case against the wall in the hall leading to the master bedroom and went to meet with her guests. Ice was in the great room with his wife, Soleil, his arm around her, looking protective. Ice was a gorgeous man, with the same platinum hair Alena had and startling crystal-blue eyes. He had three tears dripping down from his left eye tattooed on his face. Soleil was a beautiful woman, and every time she tilted her chin up to look at her husband, her face lit up.

"Soleil, this is Seychelle, Savage's old lady. She's new to the club and could use a friend. I thought the two of you could get to know one another. I can get some drinks together if you'd like."

Soleil smiled at her. "It's nice to meet you. Ice has talked about you so much." She indicated the ring on Seychelle's finger. "I really loved watching him make the ring for you. Getting that stone was difficult, but Savage had his heart set on it, and fortunately, Ice has amazing connections."

Seychelle held up her hand to look at the ring. It really was unique and beautiful. She had never seen a stone like the one in her ring. "It's so beautiful. He surprised me with it. I always called him my fake fiancé, and now I can't. The Red Hat ladies loved it when I did that."

Seychelle indicated the chairs by the stone fireplace that went from the floor to the ceiling. The glass wall gave them an incredible view of the ocean. She really did love the house. And her ring. Everything Savage gave her seemed to have been chosen so it would fit for her.

"Do you make the jewelry with Ice?"

"I draw pieces sometimes, but he really does the work. He's amazing. I paint. That's always been my big dream, and Ice is really encouraging me to pursue it. Until he came along, I'd never had a family, and I was very lonely. Now the club is my family and Ice is my everything."

Soleil looked in the direction Ice had disappeared. She lowered her voice. "I still can't believe it's true sometimes. I can't believe he loves me. I never had that growing up, and I keep expecting him to throw me away, but he doesn't. He wouldn't be too happy hearing I still get doubts about us."

Seychelle sank back in the chair, grateful for the soothing properties Savage had told her Lana somehow put into furniture she chose for them. "Isn't it funny how we all have insecurities? I look at you and think you're so beautiful. Ice thinks you're incredibly talented. Savage told me you're sweet and kind. But somehow you expect to be thrown away because you're conditioned to think that."

"What is your insecurity, Seychelle?" Soleil asked softly.

Seychelle regarded her in silence for a long time, but Soleil didn't push. Outside, the waves rushed toward the bluff and crashed against them, spraying white foam and mist high into the air. She felt a little like that water, worn out and tossed into the sky to fly apart.

"That I'll fail him. And I'll fail myself." She looked at Soleil, shocked that she'd told a perfect stranger something she hadn't even told herself. "I think about running away all the time. There are so many reasons for running."

Soleil nodded. "I know that feeling. I was going to run. I was so afraid he was going to break my heart. I just couldn't let that happen. The silly thing was, if I left, my heart would break anyway. I love Ice. I know that I love him. I just couldn't convince myself that he could really love me."

"No one stays, Soleil. They don't. No matter what you do or how hard you try, what you give of yourself, they die. They get sick and die. Or they do really dangerous things and die. Or they leave." She pushed back her hair and tried a smile. "I don't even know what I'm saying or thinking anymore. I don't know where this is coming from. I've been out of sorts lately, and I can't seem to get back on track. It didn't help that a madman was out at my house with a gun today to kill me, and Savage and the others just went right in as if it was nothing." She apparently was upset about a lot of things. It was lucky she hadn't blurted out she liked to have her sex with pain and pleasure mixed together and had no idea why. She was very confused.

Soleil nodded. "I get what you're saying. When I was

young, the only aunt I had who wanted me died. Then my life was pretty awful. The only constant I had was a lawyer who I didn't really see in person, but I still loved him because he was the only person who seemed to care. He was murdered. So yeah, I get that. And when Ice goes off with the club to do something dark and mysterious I'm not allowed to know about, I sit on our upstairs bedroom balcony in this rocking chair I have, and I wait for him there. Sometimes he's gone for days. I can't eat or sleep. I just sit there. The only time I get up is to use the bathroom. I feel sick and afraid and alone. It's like living in hell. I can't paint. I can barely breathe."

Seychelle drew in a deep breath and sat up straight, her fingers closing in a tight fist, pressing over her thudding heart. "He doesn't know you do that, does he?"

Soleil shook her head. "I would never tell him. What would be the use? He can't change who he is or what he does. He's Torpedo Ink, and I love him, so I love Torpedo Ink. He's worth those terrible days that I have to wait in fear. It took me time to come to terms with that. Those fears are real because I know I could lose him. The fears I manufacture are silly, and I work to overcome them all the time."

"Savage does dangerous things all the time and he won't talk about them to me." Seychelle couldn't tell Soleil that she sometimes caught glimpses of things she wasn't meant to see. If Savage ever did those things and came near her too soon, she would see everything, just as she had when he'd been with Shari.

"Does the danger bother you, or the fact that he won't discuss it with you?" Soleil asked.

Seychelle considered that. "Both. I like to know what I'm getting into. I want to hear about it and take time to think it through."

"If it's their business and not yours, then why should you know about it? If you had a business, would you want Savage to insist you tell him every detail?"

Seychelle thought that over. "I would hope he would be interested in everything I did and would want to talk about it with me. I wouldn't want him to interfere or tell me how to run my business, but I would definitely want him to be interested enough to talk about it with me." She tilted her head and studied Soleil. "You're interested in Ice's jewelry business. He's interested in your paintings. Do you both talk about each other's work together?"

Soleil smiled at her. "We do. I see your point, but neither of those things are club business." She drummed her fingers on her thigh and then indicated Seychelle's engagement ring. "Savage chose that stone himself. It was a huge deal to him. He spent hours going over stones with Ice, talking to him about your eyes and how he wanted the exact color, and the stone had to be unique and special. He didn't care about the money. Apparently, he rarely spends money. This house, because all of them were told they needed to have a home. He chose this place because he thought you would love it. But the stone, for him, was important, because he wanted you to know that he sees you. The heart of you. That's what he said to Ice. He said you were his angel and you have a pure heart. He sees all of you. That's a fancy teal-blue flawless diamond. Very hard to come by. The diamonds surrounding it are unique as well. And of course, Ice's design gives the ring added flair. What I'm telling you is, that man loves you, Seychelle, and he's trying, in the only way he knows how, to tell you."

TWENTY

Savage sat in the chair across from the bed in the master bedroom and watched Seychelle sleep. He'd lowered the privacy
screens on the windows to black out the morning light, leaving
just enough for him to see his woman as she lay curled up in
the middle of the giant bed. Ice and Soleil had gone home after
breakfast, but Seychelle had slept through their departure. It
was clear she'd sat up most of the night. She had one of her
notebooks by the bed with a page listing her pros and cons.

The notebook had dropped to the floor and he'd picked it
up and read it. It wasn't meant for him, but then he had been
very up-front with her about the fact that he had never learned
much about privacy and didn't intend to when it came to his
woman. He loved her, and he could soften his personality
only so much for her, but he was always going to be who he
was. She would have to understand that and accept him.

He knew she was struggling; not only to accept him, the
club, his lifestyle, but also to come to terms with aspects
she hadn't realized about herself. It was a lot to expect of
anyone. He looked down at the list in his hand. It wasn't about

him. He wished it were all about him. His little angel didn't understand that she was perfect for him just the way she was. *Angel* to him didn't mean the same thing it did to her.

She listed cons about herself. He read every single one of them. Afraid of failing him? That one got to him the most. How in the world could she fail him? That was impossible. He knew he would be the one in their relationship to fail over and over. What he had going for them was absolute determination. He never stopped. Never. He would continue to try no matter what, and he wasn't above apologizing for his fuckups and learning from them.

He read the list again and shook his head before he stood up and went to the bank of drawers where he kept his favorite whips. She would never touch the drawers that held his whips. He knew that about her. Those were his and sacred to him, so they were sacred to her. He carefully tore the list from the notebook so it wasn't frayed on the edges and placed it in the bottom of the drawer under his favorite whip. He stared at the page a long time. He was keeping that list. Someday it was going under glass and he'd hang it on the wall for one thing, one line. At the bottom she had written, *I will never leave him. I love him. It's that simple. I'll find a way to make it work.*

There it was. His everything. She felt the same way he did. They would find a way. They had things to work through, but the commitment was there, and they'd do it. He closed the drawer softly and crossed the room to the bed. He was tired. He'd showered twice thoroughly at the clubhouse to make certain there was no blood on him. His interrogation clothes had been burned, and he'd returned in fresh clothes. Still, after meeting with Ice and Soleil, he showered again in the master bath and stayed in their bedroom in only his soft drawstring pants.

Each move had been calculated. He had wanted to ensure that Seychelle didn't catch glimpses into his night's activities. There could be no hint of the smell of blood. The clothing he wore couldn't be the clothing he'd had on when he was around

Joseph Arnold. He'd created memories at the clubhouse of meeting with other members in the community room and then at breakfast with Ice and Soleil. After taking a shower and donning the soft pants she equated with their games in the bedroom, he had let time go by so the memories wouldn't be so sharp.

He stood beside the bed, looking at the wealth of thick gold-and-platinum hair spilling everywhere over his pillow and sheets. She was on her belly, and the shape of her under the twisted sheet was enough to make a man sweat. So much woman. All feminine. All his. Love welled up and hit him hard. It always did, because he never expected to have it. Because of that, because he knew what a true gift it was, he intended to guard it carefully.

He slid off the soft drawstring pants, folded them, and put them on the end table before pulling up the covers, straightening them and then sliding his body in beside hers. He claimed his space easily by simply putting his arms around Seychelle and moving her where he wanted her. He curled his body around hers, claiming her the way he had his space.

Her lashes fluttered and she tilted her head back to look at him over her shoulders. A soft smile that got him right in the gut lit her face. "Savage. You're home. Do you need anything? I can make you something to eat if you're hungry." She made the offer without hesitation, clearly having no idea of the time.

She sounded drowsy. Sexy. She looked sexy. His body reacted the way it always did around her, but he was wiped, and he wanted more time to pass before anything intense happened between them. It was just safer. He curved his arm possessively around her waist and pulled her in tight against his body. "I need sleep, babe, but thanks for the offer." He nuzzled her neck, inhaling her scent. He loved the way she smelled. "A couple of hours from now you can feed me. Go back to sleep, Seychelle."

"Mmmkay, if you're sure." Her blue eyes drifted over his face as if checking to make certain he was all right, and then her head settled on the pillow again, her lashes falling.

His heart settled and he realized his beat had accelerated. Not once when he was interrogating Arnold, questioning him on the disappearance of the other women he'd stalked, had his heart rate risen. Just looking at his woman, just knowing he had fallen so hard, so fast, put that anxious beat in him. It had to stop. It made him too dangerous. Too out of control. He'd tried to give her everything she wanted, even knowing it wasn't a good idea. He'd promised himself he would give her who he was. He hadn't been doing that. He was already taking her down such a dark path, he was afraid of losing her.

His club, the problems Torpedo Ink faced, all of it was taking them down so fast, he didn't have the time to work her in slowly. It had little to do with the sex. He had no doubt he could get her there. Restrictions, constraints, living with the man that was Savage, his role in the club, that was something altogether different, and he knew she would have to be told. She would see it in him. The enforcer. The protector. The killer. She would know. Whether she could live with him or not, he didn't know. He needed more time with her. He did know he had to give her the real man. All of him. It wasn't fair to her not to.

"I love you, Seychelle Dubois," he whispered. "More than anything in the world. I love you." He waited. Hearing the rush of the ocean waves the way his blood moved in his body. She really was his everything, because without her, he didn't have much to anchor him when the demons came knocking. He hadn't known he was capable of real love, not with a woman, a partner, not until Seychelle.

Her body moved slightly, slid along his, melted into his. Her hand found his, the one around her waist, where he trapped her so close to him. She threaded her fingers through his. "I love you, Savin 'Savage' Pajari. You're my everything."

Savage closed his eyes and breathed evenly, tasting love, knowing it was real, knowing he had it. They both had made the commitment; now they just, like all couples, had to find a way to keep love at the forefront, above all the obstacles.

They could face together whatever dangers Campbell was throwing Sea Haven's way. Seychelle wouldn't be alone guarding the elderly or the women there. She'd have the club to help protect them. Whatever was going on with the various clubs, Savage was used to dealing with. They'd get through it together.

RESOURCES

Advocates for Youth

1325 G Street NW, Suite 980
Washington, D.C. 20005
1-202-419-3420
advocatesforyouth.org

Against Child Abuse Hong Kong

Wai Yuen House
107-108 G/F
Chuk Yuen North Estate
Wong Tai Sin, Kowloon
Phone: 2351 6060
Hotline: 2755 1122
aca.org.hk

American Academy of Child & Adolescent Psychiatry

3615 Wisconsin Avenue NW
Washington, D.C. 20016-3007
1-202-966-7300
aacap.org

American Academy of Pediatrics

345 Park Boulevard
Itasca, IL 60143
1-800-433-9016
aap.org

American Counseling Association

6101 Stevenson Avenue Suite 600
Alexandria, VA 22304-3300
1-800-347-6647
counseling.org

American Psychological Association

750 First Street NE
Washington, D.C. 20002-4242
1-202-336-5500
Toll-free: 1-800-374-2721
apa.org

Bikers Against Child Abuse (BACA)

bacaworld.org

Casa Alianza

Moctezuma #68 Col. Guerero
Alcaldía Cuauhtémoc CDMX. CP. 06300
Mexico
casa-alianzamexico.org

Center for Healthier Children, Families & Communities

10960 Wilshire Boulevard, Suite 960
Los Angeles, CA 90024-3913

1-310-794-0967
healthychild.ucla.edu

Child Exploitation and Obscenity Section

Criminal Division
U.S. Department of Justice
1-202-514-5780
usdoj.gov/criminal/ceos

The ChildTrauma Academy

5161 San Felipe, Suite 320
Houston, TX 77056
Toll-free: 1-866-943-9779
childtrauma.org

Child Welfare Information Gateway

330 C Street SW
Washington, D.C. 20201
Toll-free: 1-800-394-3366
childwelfare.gov

Child Welfare League of America

727 15th Street NW, Suite 1200
Washington, D.C. 20005
1-202-688-4200
cwla.org

Dunkelziffer e.V.

Albert-Einstein-Ring 15
22761 Hamburg
Phone: 040 42107000
dunkelziffer.de

ECPAT International

328/1 Phaya Thai Road Ratchathewi
Bangkok 10400 Thailand
thecode.org

ECPAT-USA

ECPAT-USA
86 Wyckoff Avenue, #609
Brooklyn, NY 11237
1-718-935-9192
ecpatusa.org

European Children's Network (EURONET)

europeanchildrensnetwork.org

Frauenberatung Sexuelle Gewalt

Phone: 044 291 46 46
frauenberatung.ch

Institute on Violence, Abuse and Trauma at Alliant International University

10065 Old Grove Road, Suite 101
San Diego, CA 92131
1-858-527-1860
ivatcenters.org

International List of Sexual & Domestic Violence Agencies

hotpeachpages.net

Justice for Children

justiceforchildren.org

KIDSPEACE

5300 KidsPeace Drive
Orefield, PA 18069
1-800-25-PEACE
kidspeace.org

Male Survivor

350 Central Park West, Suite 1H
New York, NY 10025
1-800-738-4181
malesurvivor.org

Mental Health America

500 Montgomery Street, Suite 820
Alexandria, VA 22314
1-703-684-7722
Toll-free: 1-800-969-6642
nmha.org

National Association for Prevention of Child Abuse and Neglect

9/162 Goulburn Street
Surry Hills NSW 2010
Phone: 02 8073 3300
napcan.org.au

National Association of School Psychologists

4340 East West Highway, Suite 402
Bethesda, MD 20814
1-301-657-0270
Toll-free: 1-866-331-NASP
nasponline.org

National Center for Children in Poverty

475 Riverside Drive, Suite 1400
New York, NY 10115
nccp.org

National Children's Alliance

516 C Street NE
Washington, D.C. 20002
1-202-548-0090
nca-online.org

National Data Archive on Child Abuse and Neglect

Surge 1—FLDC
Cornell University
Ithaca, NY 14853
1-607-255-7799
ndacan.cornell.edu

National Domestic Violence Hotline (Canada)

All provinces; bilingual (English & French)
Toll-free: 1-800-363-9010

National Indian Child Welfare Association

5100 S. Macadam Avenue, Suite 300
Portland, OR 97239

1-503-222-4044
nicwa.org

National Organization of Battered Women's Shelters (Sweden)

Roks, Hornsgatan 66
118 21 Stockholm, Sweden
Phone: 08-422 99 30
roks.se

Provincial Association of Transition Houses and Services of Saskatchewan (PATHS)

abusehelplines.org

Rape, Abuse, and Incest National Network (RAINN)

1-800-656-HOPE

Reporting Crimes Against Children

Federal Bureau of Investigation
fbi.gov/report-threats-and-crime

Scottish Women's Aid

132 Rose Street, 2nd floor
Edinburgh EH2 3JD
United Kingdom
Phone: 0131 475 2372
24-hour help line: 0800 027 1234
womensaid.scot

S.E.S.A.M.E. (Stop Educator Sexual Abuse Misconduct & Exploitation)

10863 Florence Hills Street
Las Vegas, NV 89141
1-702-371-1290
sesamenet.org

Silent Edge

108 Terrace Drive
Syracuse, NY 13219
silent-edge.org

The United Nations Convention on the Rights of the Child

unicef.org/crc

U.S. Department of Justice

Project Safe Childhood
810 Seventh Street NW
Washington, D.C. 20531
AskDOJ@usdoj.gov
justice.gov/psc/index.html

U.S. ICE (Immigration and Customs Enforcement) Cyber Crimes Center, Child Exploitation Investigations Unit

1-866-DHS-2-ICE
ice.gov/features/cyber

Women Against Violence Europe (WAVE)

Bacherplatz 10/6

1050 Vienna
Austria
Phone: 01-5482720
wave-network.org

Women's Aid Federation of England

PO Box 3245
Bristol BS2 2EH, England
womensaid.org.uk

CONTINUE READING FOR A SNEAK PEEK OF

SAVAGE ROAD

THE NEXT NOVEL IN THE TORPEDO INK SERIES
AVAILABLE JANUARY 2022 FROM PIATKUS

Seychelle Dubois sat on the bathroom floor staring at the toilet for the second morning in a row. She felt like an idiot. "No, Savage, I'm not pregnant. And I'm not a secret drinker either."

"What the hell is wrong? Should I call Steele? I want you to go see him."

She pushed herself up, glaring at him. "I do not need to see a doctor. Do you remember the talk we had on privacy?" Stumbling over to the sink, Seychelle washed her face with cold water, rinsed out her mouth and then started the process of brushing her teeth.

Savin "Savage" Pajari continued to watch her in the mirror. He leaned one hip against the doorjamb, arms crossed over his chest. His eyes were arctic blue, so cold they made her shiver. It didn't help that he wore a thin pair of drawstring pants, indicating he was going out to practice with his whip. She had been avoiding watching him the last couple of days because for some unexplained reason, just the sight and sound of it turned her on like nothing else in the world possibly could. That was the last thing she needed to know right now on top of everything else—that she was truly messed up in the head, or body, however one wanted to look at it.

"Seychelle, we did have a talk about privacy, and I told you how I felt about it when it came to my woman. Now fuckin' tell me what's going on."

She took her time finishing with her teeth, rinsed her mouth multiple times and then turned to face him, leaning her butt against the sink, arms crossed to match his. "I'm having hideous nightmares. Really vivid nightmares. They make me sick." She did her best not to make it an accusation, but she knew it came out like one. What was she accusing him of? He wasn't in her nightmares.

Savage studied her face for a long time without speaking, those blue eyes burning like ice over her. He was gorgeous. That was half her problem. She could stare at him endlessly—forever. He had a body on him, all man, more muscles than was good for him, tattoos over scars and burns. He had the words *Whip Master* burned into his skin on his chest and *Master of Pain* burned into his back. The tats didn't cover either burns, although she knew Ink, a brother in his club, had done his best with the beautiful artwork on him.

"You gonna stop there and make me ask or you goin' tell me what these nightmares are about, angel? If they're making you sick, they're fucked the hell up."

There was a warning in his voice, but no expression on his face, just those blue, blue eyes, cold as a glacier, telling her he wasn't going to let it go.

They had agreed to have truth between them, but that really meant *she* told him the truth and he withheld things he didn't want to talk about. They'd been together for months, and she loved him far too much. It wasn't a good thing by any means.

"Last chance, Seychelle, start talking."

"It was a nightmare, Savage. People have them."

"Two fuckin' nights in a row. The same nightmare. Bad enough that you puke in the toilet and you don't want to tell me about it."

That was a straight-up accusation. Worse, he was right. She didn't want to tell him. That stance. Arms across his chest. Those eyes that wouldn't let her look away no matter how much she wanted to. He'd given her space the day before because she'd asked him to. She'd been upset. Joseph Arnold, a stalker, had been sitting in her cottage waiting for her with a gun, and Savage thought she was upset about that. She had been, of course, but that wasn't the only reason. There was a multitude of reasons she was questioning her sanity. Mostly, it had to do with herself, the things she was discovering she needed in her own sexual relationship, and that truly frightened her. She needed to come to terms with it.

There were just so many things coming at her so fast. She wasn't a person who took things in fast. She just wanted everything to slow down so she could take a breath and assimilate everything at a much different pace than they were going.

"It isn't me that is going to have the sore ass. I'm not asking again."

She detested the little flare of dark excitement that sent heat to her sex. It didn't matter how annoying she found it that he just stood there so casually. He was unmoving, those eyes of his holding her in place, probably seeing that flicker of reaction she couldn't control, knowing blood pounded in her clit and her sex fluttered just at the thought of what he intended in spite of her absolute abhorrence of his intentions.

"I shouldn't be punished because I choose not to talk to you about a nightmare I have, Savage. If I ask you about nightmares, you wouldn't tell me if you didn't want to."

"I have them all the time, angel, or I used to until you came into my life. You want to know about them, you ask me. I'll lay that shit out for you."

Of course he'd say that now. Her fingers formed two tight fists in frustrations. Why couldn't she just lie to him? Make something up? People did that all the time. She wasn't a liar. She'd never been, but maybe this one time it would be okay.

She shrugged. Tried to look away. She couldn't lie looking at him, for heaven's sake.

"Damn good thing you're just wearing that little robe, angel, and nothing else. Take it off, hang it on the hook inside the bathroom right by the shower and come on out here. I'll be waiting for you, and the longer you make me wait, the more punishment I'm going to add on."

He turned and walked away. Out of sight. He didn't go sit on the end of their bed, where she might see him. He walked out of sight, which meant he might have gone over to the chair close to the spanking bench. She nearly groaned aloud. She could close and lock the bathroom door—except there were no locks on the bathroom door. Why? Because her man had a thing about privacy.

She didn't have to go out there. She didn't have to do what he said. She was a grown woman. She made her own choices. That was the bottom line, and Savage always made that very, very clear. Everything they did together was ultimately her choice. She walked over to the mirror and stared at herself. Her eyes were dilated. Her face flushed. Already she was breathing too fast.

Why was she like this? Why did she respond sexually to something painful? Her body craved whatever Savage did to her, even when her brain refused to want it. She knew he would never stop until she told him what he wanted to know. She didn't want to tell him because what if she was right? What if the man in her nightmares was really Savage, and it was one more thing she was going to have to sort out? She was already at a breaking point.

Seychelle rinsed her face again with cold water, hoping to clear her mind. Savage was her choice. She had to sort through her problems fast. She was committed to him—to their life together. She wasn't so committed to his club. To that life. She didn't really understand it, and that was part of who he was. She needed that piece of him. He pulled her into it, then pushed her back out, and she resented it.

She took a deep breath, her lashes lifting so she found herself staring at herself in the mirror, realizing she'd just had a revelation. She didn't resent the fact that Savage had a psychic gift that allowed him to take on the anger, the very real rage his brothers and sisters of Torpedo Ink felt which made him the way he was. She was actually proud of him for that. She resented that all of them shared deep secrets and he shut her out. At the same time, he expected her to use her gifts to aid them and him when the club needed those gifts. Where was the fairness in that?

Ordinarily, Seychelle would gladly help anyone in need. Especially Savage. Anyone of Savage's friends. But not like this, not when she was shut out and she was supposed to be his partner. He demanded 100 percent from her. He told her he was giving her 100 percent of him, but he wasn't.

She pushed at the hair tumbling around her face. When she did, she noticed the ring on her left hand. How could she not? It was gorgeous. A rare fancy teal-blue diamond surrounded by diamonds that appeared to be petals hugging her finger. The entire thing glittered every time she moved. It should have been ostentatious, but it wasn't. It was simply beautiful. Savage had a way of knowing exactly what she would love.

He was trained to read body language. Every facial expression. Every single subtle hint, from elevated breathing to the parting of her lips. He knew her. And she was an open book anyway, even when she tried not to be. He had been trained from childhood in the arts of sex: giving, receiving, training one to do what he commanded, and he was very, very good at what he did. He had too many weapons to use against her, and she had fallen too fast to get her armor in place.

It wasn't that she didn't want to be where she was—she did. She had come on board with her eyes open—sort of. Living in reality was always a far cry from being dreamily in love. "Let that be a lesson to you, Seychelle," she whispered.

She couldn't blame all of it on Savage or all the frightening things he brought to their relationship. She hadn't realized the extent of the lure of mixing pain and pleasure. She'd been so attracted to him, to that darkness in him. The first time he'd spun her around in an alley, lifted the hem of her dress and smacked her bottom, she'd gotten so damp, reacting to him when no one had ever made her body come alive before. That had been a revelation—a bit confusing, actually.

She went home and immediately delved deeper into spankings and even floggers, but she didn't really understand it. She had no idea why her body would respond to such a thing when no matter what she'd tried, she'd thought she was absolutely frigid. The deeper into his world Savage took her—and granted, it wasn't very far, but she saw where they were going—the more alarmed she got. She was intrigued. Terrified, but intrigued. That wasn't a good thing in her opinion.

In her mind, when she'd gotten together with Savage, she believed she would give herself to him and there would be that moment when she would have to "suffer" for him. He suffered for those he loved, and she would do it for him. She was very confused with the way she felt about pain and the effects on her body. She didn't want to crave pain. Did she? Or did she crave Savage? She didn't even know anymore what was right or wrong. She only knew that she loved him, and she had to find a way to come to terms with all the rest of it.

Savage stood looking at the array of tools he had lined up in his cabinet over the wooden drawers built along the wall next to the tall wooden cabinet where the jewelry he had for Seychelle was kept. She hadn't even seen the majority of it. He had orders in to have so much more made for her. Now that he had her in his life, he was more than comfortable with his needs. He just had to get her to a place where she was accepting of their lifestyle.

He was a sadist in the bedroom, and he owned what he was. He had exhausted all the avenues open to him to change and knew there was no way for him to be anything but what he was. He needed to see his woman in pain in order to be aroused. He got off on that shit. Putting his handprints or his marks on her gorgeous ass aroused him. But the thought of using his floggers or whips, that was the ultimate for him—that would put steel in his cock like nothing else could. Her tears were his. Her ultimate pleasure was his, and he could give her pleasure like no one else ever could.

She had gone into their relationship fully aware. He had been careful to tell her what he was so there were no surprises on that score. He'd laid it out as plainly as possible, but talking about it wasn't the same as experiencing it. He had been bringing her into his lifestyle faster than he wanted to. He knew that was frightening for her. She responded so beautifully though.

Her body was aroused with clamps. She loved nipple play. He loved it. They hadn't gotten to the more exciting stuff for him, but they were getting there fast. She would both love that and hate it. She was coming to enjoy her spankings a little too much. She wasn't altogether certain she liked the crop that much, but he doubted if she would care for very many of the straps, slappers and tawes he was looking at in his cupboard at the moment.

These were specialized tools, and he chose three tawes, one that would warm her little backside up properly. He would ask her questions and hope she would answer him without lying. She'd never lied to him, but she'd been considering it. The second tawes, also crafted in the rough-hewn center-split leather like the first, was slightly larger and delivered a more punishing strike. She would definitely feel it. The split leather wouldn't feel anywhere near the same as the thicker crop he'd used on her. He'd ask again, and if she still didn't answer him, there was the larger tawes, which she definitely wouldn't enjoy. It was for a severe punishment. A lie. A holdout when there was no reason. He hoped—and doubted—it wouldn't come to that.

Savage would lay it out for her like he always did. She would choose her own consequences. During a punishment she knew there was no calling out "red" for stop. Any other time during sex, she had that right. This was a different circumstance and one she'd agreed to when they first laid down the rules to their relationship.

He'd been somewhat lax about keeping the rules. He'd let them go, didn't keep a guard on her like he should have all the time. It was his fucking fault that his woman was nearly gunned down by a madman. If Seychelle hadn't kept her head and been so resourceful, he wouldn't have gotten there in time. She had essentially gotten herself out of the cottage and was running when the club showed up to deal with Arnold, but it so easily could have gone the other way. All because he'd tried to be someone he wasn't.

He loved her so damn much he would have roped the moon and given it to her if he could have. What he did was let that fucker live the first time he'd turned up stalking Seychelle. Savage knew he should have killed him right then and thrown his body into the ocean or buried him in the forest somewhere deep where he never would have been found. Seychelle's entire ordeal rested squarely on his shoulders because he hadn't done what he was supposed to do—

protect her. He was too busy worrying about her leaving him because he was asking her to accept too damn much in their relationship already.

He was who he really was. She had to know him, not some fucking choirboy he pretended to be. And he damn well wasn't letting her go. She could learn to love all of him, even the not-so-nice parts. She might be afraid of what they did in the bedroom, but she fucking loved it. It was this part, having to answer to him that upset her. She didn't like that his world had to be so controlled. She didn't understand yet just how dangerous he could be if he didn't have everything in place. That meant her—his everything. The center of his universe.

He wasn't taking her bullshit anymore, and she might not realize it, but he was counting every fucking minute she was making him wait. He collected the three leather tawes and closed the cabinet and then crossed to the chair beside the spanking bench. He laid the three tawes out on the table, where she could see them when she came in. They were beautiful examples of Scottish craftsmanship. The leather was perfectly split just right, and each handle fit his palm exactly as he'd instructed.

He knew he had a well of rage in him, and this time it was dark and deep and ugly. He would have to be damn careful, because he wasn't going to punish her for his sins. He was pissed at himself. Not at her. She deserved punishment, and he liked when he was stripping her bare and giving it to her. He'd told her how much he enjoyed it. It aroused him, and he made no secret of it. It aroused her as well, but this time there would be no satisfaction for her at the end of it. He'd asked her several times to tell him what was making her sick, given her every opportunity. His woman had a stubborn streak. Sweet as candy. A fuckin' angel, but did what she wanted when she lifted that little chin of hers at him.

He would have smiled at that thought, but the way she

had looked at him a few times worried him, especially when she'd said she'd had a nightmare. He'd been the one to interrogate that sick fuck Arnold, and he hadn't been polite about it, but then, Savage was known for getting answers when he questioned his prey. He'd never failed the club. He hadn't failed when he was first learning the techniques. He'd studied every poison. Every kind of weapon and where to insert knives to cause the most pain without killing. He studied anatomy, ways to lob off body parts without killing and ways to prolong life. At the club, he had cabinets with all kinds of tools and interesting oils and poisons he'd been taught to use from the time he was a young teen to extract the truth.

He was careful around Seychelle. He was too good at disassociating, far too good at it, and it made him a monster, lost him the humanity Czar, the president of Torpedo Ink, had fought so hard to keep in all of the club members. He had brought them to Sea Haven to give them a chance at life, but they were all so fucked up none of them really fit into society. They didn't understand the rules. They had their own code, the one Czar had given them, and they stuck with that. But Savage . . . He shook his head. He still had a difficult time even with that.

His emotions seemed to come and go. He either felt nothing, or he was as cold as ice, or absolutely enraged. All three of those things were dangerous and would get people killed. Then there was his circle, the people he protected, those he rode with and cared for. His emotions for them were strong, and anyone threatening them should have been killed and buried the moment that threat was found to be real. Like fucking Joseph Arnold. Yeah, he needed to go back to his strict rules, where he knew the people he let into his life were always safe. That meant getting his stubborn, sassy, cute-as-hell, gorgeous, sexy woman under control.

She had that psychic gift of reading his mind when things were too vivid and close. He couldn't go from an intense interrogation that might not raise the blood pressure of a sick fuck like him, but would stick in the corners of his dark soul, and come home to her where an angel like Seychelle could see. Who knew? But it happened. And it might have happened again.

He'd showered multiple times and changed his clothes and burned his interrogation clothes before he'd gone home to Seychelle. He'd had breakfast with another brother, Ice, and his old lady, Soleil, allowing more time to pass and putting other things in his mind. He'd showered again at home before going to bed. He'd taken every precaution, but that didn't mean she hadn't slipped inside his soul.

He sat in the cool leather of the chair, looking at the various views he had from that one spot. The two armchairs were set close, facing the long fireplace built into the wall itself. It was a good twelve feet long and when turned on could flicker low, providing small tongues of orange or red flames, or leaping, rolling red-hot scorching blazes. The curve below the fireplace provided the long bank of handcrafted wooden drawers made by his brothers specifically for his whips and floggers. Fortunately, they were able to fit them into the room with few modifications. The tall jewelry cabinet they'd made for him fit nicely in the corner.

The woodworkers, Master, Player, Maestro and Keys, four of his brothers from Torpedo Ink, also made the rectangular, thinner cabinet housing his straps, slappers and tawes. In all honesty, they made cabinets in all shapes and sizes as they talked music and just messed around together in the shop. One would come up with a design and they'd put it together. If someone wanted it, they could just go get it. Savage had scored several beautiful cabinets that way. He'd needed them and found them at the shop.

Movement caught his eye and his woman emerged from the master bath. Her hair always seemed a little bit wild, as if no matter what she did to try to tame it, there was no way it would fall in line. It was gold and platinum mixed together, streaks of light honey, thick, flowing down her back like a waterfall in waves.

Her eyes were a spectacular blue, like teal, deep and intense, stealing his breath if he looked too long, so that he had the feeling of falling, of drowning, and who the hell gave a fuck if he did, because just look at her. She had a woman's figure. She had tits. Nice round woman's flesh. Nipples he could see, could touch and play with. She had the kind of hips that cradled a man and an ass that invited a man to play. He fucking loved her body. He loved her skin. Smooth and soft, and it marked beautifully for him.

She walked, shoulders straight, back straight, chin up, hips and ass swaying, straight to the spanking bench. She stood, back to him, waiting his orders. She could make his scarred cock stretch like no one could, just at the thought of what he was about to do to that sweet little ass and pussy.

He kept his relaxed position and dropped his hand to the first of the tawes, which was a bit smaller. "This is a tawes, Seychelle. It will warm your ass and get you ready for your punishment. I'll warn you, this is a cut above what you've felt before. It may not look like much, but it delivers. You will feel it."

Her gaze slid to him, and he caught the lift of her eyebrow. His cock jerked hard. She didn't intend to tell him. She was definitely challenging him. He flashed her a grin. He indicated for her to lay over the bench. She did, presenting her ass to him without hesitation. He got up and, using a lazy, silent prowl, came up behind her, put one hand on the small of her back and kicked her left foot out wide.

"You know how to present your ass to me." He bent down and fit a cuff around her ankle to hold her in place.

She frowned and looked over his shoulder. He'd never used any tie she couldn't get out of. He'd always asked her first. They'd talked over everything. He'd told her up front punishments were different. Safe words were off the table. He was solely in charge, and she'd agreed. She might cry foul eventually, but he knew her well enough to know she was stubborn as hell and he would have to do something a lot worse than this to get her to run from him.

He cuffed her left ankle and then did the same with each wrist. He pulled a scrunchie from his pocket, gathered her hair and secured it into a messy knot. Some would escape, but she couldn't hide from him the way he knew she wanted to use her hair to do.

"Now I think we're ready. You look beautiful as always, Seychelle." He curved his palm around the back of her neck gently to give her courage, something he couldn't help doing with her, then ran his finger down her spine as he walked around her again and picked up the tawes.

Already his body was anticipating this. He could feel himself sinking into that place of a sexual rush, a sexual high, and he hadn't even gotten started. It was in his mind, his blood already hot. He rubbed her bottom. Cupped her pussy. Teased her pussy lips. Flicked her clit with tawes, letting her feel the leather.

"You like that, baby?" He patted her pussy with it gently. "We'll see how well you like it, when we're done."

He struck her without warning, using a little muscle, because honestly, this little thing hardly gave much of a sting in his opinion, but she jumped and then settled. He peppered her bottom with the tawes, lighting her up on both cheeks, and then the backs of her thighs. He was right about his woman. Her pussy glistened; her clit was inflamed. Her ass was marked, but she didn't make a sound. After several minutes, he stopped and picked up the second tawes.

"Okay, baby, we're at the main event. What are you being punished for, Seychelle?"

"Because my man loves this shit and wants an excuse to use his fun little toys on me."

He rubbed the marks, his cock swelling to alarming proportions. *Bog*, she was killing him, challenging him like this. He fucking loved it. His hand slipped over the curve of her red bottom, fingers dipping into the heat of her pussy. She was so hot and greedy, her silken sheath tried to suck his fingers deep.

"So needy, baby. You want more, don't you? That is exactly the answer that will buy you more. I'll ask again, why are you being punished?"

"Because my man is being a total asshole right now?"

He patted her ass, smiled and let loose with the medium tawes. Her breath hissed out, and two thin lines that looked like they could welt appeared on her left cheek. Savage rained down more strokes, letting himself enjoy the way her skin bounced, taking the thinner split leather, that terrible bite, and smacked her over and over.

She jerked and moved her bottom, as if trying to get away, but there was nowhere for her to run. He stopped with the vertical stripes and rubbed them with the heel of his hand and then his fingernails. He had spent time on those stripes, taking them from the tops of her buttocks to the sweet curve and then down the backs of her thighs. The tawes was a more moderate punishment, especially if you used it the way he had, careful of his woman, but he still had made sure she felt every stroke he'd laid on her.

"You want to tell me why you're lying over that bench with your gorgeous ass in the air and your pussy on display for me to punish, Seychelle?"

A quiet little sob escaped, and then she sniffed. "You asked me a question and I refused to answer you."

"That's right. Would you like to answer it now?" Deliberately, Savage continued to rub her sore bottom to keep it inflamed, but he gently circled her clit and then strummed it and flicked. When her body shuddered, he bent and used his tongue, stroking caresses and then devouring the liquid spilling from her. He wanted to keep her on edge, mix pleasure and pain until her body didn't know one from the other, until she needed them together to get that explosive rush.

He'd promised to train her, and he used every opportunity, even their punishments. He straightened and tapped her back with the tawes to remind her to answer him immediately. He had to get control back, not necessarily of her. He had to get his control back before he got her, or a member of his club, killed.

"I had a damn nightmare, Savage. I barely remember it. It was all jumbled up. Monsters chasing me in the forest or something silly like that." Seychelle's voice was a barely heard whisper, her tone not matching the defiance of her statement.

Adrenaline mixed with the dark sexual needs rushed through his veins like a freight train. Like a drug he was addicted to. "You are fucking lying to me, Seychelle." He kept his tone velvet soft. Low. In total command of her. "You just fucked up big-time, and I told you what would happen."

He peppered her ass with the tawes, this time putting more muscle into it until she was sobbing, really crying this time. He stalked over to the table, dropped the medium instrument and lifted the large one. He would have to be a little more careful—no—a lot more careful. This one could make a grown man cry. In the right hands it could deliver a blow that would go right through skin and muscle and jar the entire body with a streak of pain so severe it could incapacitate a man and leave him babbling and begging. Savage knew, because when he'd been training, he'd done that very thing multiple times. Of course, he'd been supposed to back then. He'd been thirteen years old and learning how to use all sorts of tools of the trade.

"I cannot believe you fucking lied to me." He bent his head down to snarl the accusation in her ear as he stalked around her, tracking the end of the much longer leather down her spine, causing goose bumps to rise all over her body. Yeah, she was getting it now.

Do you love fiction with a supernatural twist?

Want the chance to hear news about your favourite
authors (and the chance to win free books)?

Christine Feehan
J.R. Ward
Sherrilyn Kenyon
Charlaine Harris
Jayne Ann Krentz and Jayne Castle
P.C. Cast
Maria Lewis
Darynda Jones
Hayley Edwards
Kristen Callihan
Keri Arthur
Amanda Bouchet
Jacquelyn Frank
Larissa Ione

Then visit the *With Love* website and
sign up to our romance newsletter:
www.yourswithlove.co.uk

And follow us on Facebook for book giveaways,
exclusive romance news and more:
www.facebook.com/yourswithlovex

PIATKUS